Riding a Tiger

Riding a Tiger

KHOR ENG LEE

PARTRIDGE
A Penguin Random House Company

To order additional copies of this book, contact
Toll Free 800 101 2657 (Singapore)
Toll Free 1 800 81 7340 (Malaysia)
orders.singapore@partridgepublishing.com

www.partridgepublishing.com/singapore

Contents

1.1 INTRODUCTION

This small book is about the anti-colonial struggle for independence in postwar Singapore.

The decolonisation process in this Crown colony is viewed in relation to the postwar foreign and military policies of an economically weakened Britain which nonetheless was bent on preserving its image of being one of the Great Powers.

Britain dug deep into its severely depleted coffers as it tried in the immediate period after World War II to hold on to its far-flung colonial territories and military bases overseas in the hollow (rather than hallowed) name of Empire. And partly driven by fear of the growing Soviet threat, but impelled more by national pride and ambition, the British Lion developed a modest nuclear capability which however ensured its standing as one of the Big Three in the world – at least until the mid-1960s.

From 1945 when the British returned to the Far East at the end of World War II to late 1971 when they finally packed off their military from their main base (leaving only a residual presence until March 1976) in Singapore, their mighty presence on this small but strategic island was welded to political concerns and strategic interests in the volatile region which became a major battleground in the Cold War following the outbreak of the Korean conflict in mid-1950.

In late April 1956 (a couple of years after the fall of the French fortress Dien Bien Phu in Vietnam) when the Malayan communists were still persisting in their futile armed struggle on the Malayan mainland and their comrades across the Causeway were brewing an urban revolution in Singapore, the Colonial Secretary assured the islanders that "the British Government will not allow Singapore to fall under the domination of Communist rule…" (1) 15.10.2003 0510

In 1961 when the communists came close to capturing power after their open rupture with the ruling People's Action Party (PAP) in late July of that year, Prime Minister Harold Macmillan described Singapore as vital to British interests. The implication was that the British Lion (then a credible nuclear power) would not allow a communist party or any hostile power to take over Singapore with its military bases.

Shortly afterwards, however, Singapore was finally decolonised as part of Malaysia which came into being in mid-September 1963 when Macmillan's forward-looking premiership was drawing to a close.

Macmillan had high regard for both Tunku Abdul Rahman whom he called a remarkable man, and Lee Kuan Yew whom he described as a very remarkable leader.

"Supermac" considered Singapore "vital" to the British role in the regional anti-communist military alliance known as the Southeast Asian Treaty Organisation (SEATO) even when Britain possessed a small but credible nuclear force (certainly one to be reckoned with in the early 1960s) and committed itself to the defence of Europe. (2)

The Singapore base was kept as an important and visible insignia to remind the outside world that Britain remained a great power with a growing nuclear arsenal at home and with a significant military presence east of Suez.

Macmillan proudly recorded in his memoirs that President John Kennedy consulted him throughout the Cuban missile crisis in October-November 1962.

In the early 1960s, Lee Kuan Yew was struggling for political survival after the split of the ruling PAP with the communists in mid-1961. The communists were poised to strike, coming to the climax of their third and most threatening bid for power in postwar Singapore when the anti-colonial struggle was approaching its high point.

Of course, the colonial authorities could intervene and suppress the communist challenge at this critical point as they had the powers to suspend the constitution and to freeze all political activities. Since the British wanted to maintain their military bases (including air and naval facilities and installations), they could not allow the communists to take over the island – whether through constitutional means or not.

The British managed to exercise tight overall control of the situation, however, without resorting to such extreme measures as suspending the constitution or calling out and deploying the military on the ground.

Their ability and readiness to respond to a military or security threat was cavalierly demonstrated by their prompt and effective response to both the revolt in Brunei on December 1962 and the Indonesian campaign (1963-66) to confront and "crush" Malaysia. 15.10.2003 0812

In Singapore, the anti-colonial struggle provided the cover for the more intense competition for political power among the indigenous forces – principally between the Chinese-educated communists who had historically entrenched themselves at the vanguard of the liberation movement, and postwar political parties of English-educated leadership which climbed later into the freedom bandwagon but more amenable to the democratic way of life.

Heroic figures emerged on the scene, some to leave a lasting impact on the future development of Singapore.

As in many other nations, there arose a closely-knit group of founding fathers among whom one was to stand taller than the others.

In Singapore that commanding figure is Lee Kuan Yew – straight and about as tall as any English nobleman, an exceptional intellect, a brilliant speaker, a competent and polished writer, an outstanding political leader, and also described as an administrator *par excellence*. Lee is the leading protagonist in the drama of contemporary Singapore.

Like many a larger-than-life figure, Lee is believed to have a charmed life with a private list of guardian angels and saviours – from ASP Robert Corridon who was reported to have advised his SB boss not to detain the young Lee returning home in 1950 from law studies in Cambridge, to a chummy, pipe-smoking PM Harold Wilson who "saved" Lee in 1965 when "Lee was in danger of being arrested and imprisoned". (3)

Wilson wrote: "The Tunku was becoming more and more incensed with his (Lee's) lively Opposition. Some weeks before the Commonwealth conference (held in London on June 1965) we had received news of an impending crisis (in the wake of the launching of the highly politically charged "Malaysian Malaysia" campaign in Singapore), involving a possible coup against Harry Lee and his colleagues.

"I felt it necessary to go as far as to let the Tunku know that if he were to take action of this kind, it would be unwise for him to show his face at the Commonwealth conference, since a large number of his colleagues – including myself – would feel that such action was totally opposed to all we believed in as a Commonwealth…"

Wilson added: "Many months afterwards, in April 1966, Lee Kuan Yew came to Britain and spent the day with me at Chequers. On that occasion he said quite simply – and he repeated it publicly, in my hearing, at a party conference rally in 1967 – that the action I had taken both before and after the Commonwealth conference in 1965 had 'saved my life'. With all that we were hearing in the summer of 1965 I believe this was not an exaggeration."

Interviewed by John Drysdale in 1980, Wilson said he believed that Lee's "liberty was in jeopardy, his life too". The fear, Wilson added, was that if Lee were detained "there would be an accident one morning and it would be written off as suicide... Easiest thing in the world to organize... British defence had acted as a constraint..." (4)

Interviewed by Drysdale in 1982, Tunku said he could not recollect any warning from Wilson but admitted that he was under considerable pressure to sanction Lee's arrest. And he commented: "There was no point in arresting Kuan Yew because the Chinese would, in my part of the world, have also been in sympathy with him because he was Chinese. I didn't want trouble because of him, just because of Singapore."

Tunku added: "The best thing was for him to go by giving him independence, complete, national independence... I knew that Kuan Yew would be the best man to take over the government of Singapore..." (5) 16.10.2003 0939

Early 1966, shortly after Singapore's separation from Malaysia, Tunku and this writer (then a young scriptwriter) were both viewing a rough cut of a documentary film on the challenge to the Commonwealth posed by rebel Ian Smith's UDI (Unilateral Declaration of Independence) in Rhodesia (Zimbabwe). Only the two of them were in the preview theatre in Filem Negara Malaysia's studios at Petaling Jaya. This official scribe was dumbfounded when the Malaysian Prime Minister told him offhandedly in the dark that he could have detained Lee Kuan Yew.

Almost the same words were later used by Tun Lim Yew Hock, former Chief Minister of Singapore, when he told this writer (then a senior research officer at the Malaysian Foreign Ministry) the same thing around mid-1968 after his return from a stint as Malaysia's High Commissioner in Australia. Both of them were standing shoulder to shoulder at the gents after a long meeting ("morning prayers") in the conference room at Wisma Putra in Kuala Lumpur. Tun Lin then served as the Ministry's Deputy Secretary (Special Duties). 11.12.2014 18:39

In the October 1956 purge of 14 PAP cadres including pro-communist open front leader Lim Chin Siong and the arrests of 60 other troublemakers in the midst of sanguinary student riots in Singapore, Chief Minister Lim Yew Hock could have pulled in Lee Kuan Yew as well. But he didn't.

Lim recollected in his writing: "At one stage when things were getting real hot there was talk of having Lee Kuan Yew detained under the PPSO (Preservation of Public Security Ordinance, a draconian and deterrent law sanctioning detention without trial). I put my foot down…" (6)

If Lim, then known and respected as an anti-communist strongman, hadn't put his foot down, the course of Singapore's history could have changed dramatically.

In the unfolding dramas which culminated in communist defeats on both sides of the Causeway, the anti-revolutionary campaigns yielded political and security paradigms of countering urban revolution (Singapore model) and overcoming armed insurgencies (successful anti-insurgency strategies adopted in Peninsular Malaysia and Sarawak).

These success stories were politically interpreted in the Manichean sense as victories over the forces of "evil". And they succeeded, largely because the masses (including the electorates) opted for law, safety and order and the temporal conditions of day-to-day living in security and tranquility, rather than revolutionary ferment and "dangerous living". (7)

In Chinese folk tales and legends, the sages and the immortals ride comfortably on the back of the fearsome tiger. Old Chinese drawings and paintings have depicted this extraordinary mode of transportation. And the Chinese still believe that riding a tiger marks one as a superior human being. (8)

Lee Kuan Yew said he was riding a tiger. And he rode on it to lead the PAP to its maiden victory in the 1959 general election – the first to be held in Singapore.

But when the PAP leaders decided to merge Singapore with neighbouring Malaya, the political beast shook off its wily rider. And when the two parted company in the middle of 1961, the communists and leftists took away their mass base from the PAP. But they had to leave behind their Trojan horse since they had been using the PAP as their political vehicle in their united open front campaign for capturing political power through constitutional and legal means. Within three hours of the split, however, nearly three-fourths of the branch committees had gone over to the enemy. Except for the hard core of the old guard, the ruling PAP became an almost empty shell – "little more than a skeleton" (to quote Dennis Bloodworth).

While the PAP was struggling for survival, Lee Kuan Yew was fighting for his political life.

Timely merger with Malaya (long envisioned by the PAP founders) and the Borneo territories of Sabah and Sarawak was to serve as a lifeline (if also a political expedient).

While riding the communist tiger to power was crucial to Lee Kuan Yew in the early stage of his political career, battling this political beast of prey became even more dramatic and vital to his survival in the early 1960s.

On the other side, the communists and leftists had earlier struggled for the decolonisation and liberation of Malaya and

Singapore (which had been a single entity before their division in April 1946). Now they came out to oppose merger in their attempt to snatch power from a hard-hit and tottering PAP leadership by preventing the entry of a more powerful force in the form of the strongly anti-communist Alliance government from Kuala Lumpur which had just succeeded in surmounting the 12-year communist insurgency (1948-60) in Malaya. (9)

Operating from his offshore base and sanctuary in the Rhio islands of Indonesia to the south of Singapore, Eu Chooi Yip was the enigmatic mastermind and strategist for the communist campaign in Singapore.

To help the PAP government, the Home Affairs ministry in Kuala Lumpur sent its eminent head of psychological warfare across the Causeway. C.C. Too was one of the world's leading experts in Asian communism, counter-insurgency and psychological warfare. His brief was to assist in the psychological/political campaign for merger as well as to help foil and frustrate the communist plan to seize power in Singapore.

Too considered Eu Chooi Yip, a prewar companion and college mate, to be a superior strategist even when compared with the better-known Chin Peng – the legendary leader of the Communist Party of Malaya since 1947. Under Eu's leadership, the Singapore communists had come so dramatically close to toppling the PAP government through constitutional means.

In Lee Kuan Yew's famous battle for merger, three highly successful campaigns were waged against the communists – the September 1962 referendum which won the popular vote for merger, "Operation Cold Store" conducted in February 1963 to neutralize the communist leadership in Singapore, and the snap general election in September 1963 which gave the ruling PAP a fresh mandate as well as enhanced morale and prestige to continue running the State government.

But the successful merger was short-lived. Because of irreconcilable differences with the Central government in Kuala Lumpur, Singapore was separated from Malaysia on 9 August 1965. And the rest, as they say, is history.

CHAPTER ONE

The Nuclear Lion in London

Britain emerged victorious at the end of World War II, but with a battered economy. Though burdened with a huge trade deficit and handicapped by a declining industrial base, Britain was determined to hold on to its far-flung colonial territories (although it relinquished the vast Indian sub-continent in 1947).

At the same time, it also wanted to keep its military bases and garrisons abroad, of which Singapore (despite the recent destruction of its myth of being an "impregnable fortress" at the hands of the Japanese invaders in mid-February 1942) remained Britain's greatest and most important military base east of Suez.

Moreover, postwar Britain under the Labour government embarked on a new military course to become a nuclear power as well. This development was in line with its ambition to stay on as one of the major powers going into the second half of the 20th century. (1)

Shortly after the sudden break in British-US cooperation in the nuclear field following the American Atomic Energy Act of August 1946, the Attlee-led cabinet in London decided to embark on an independent nuclear weapons programme. And the British had more than a head start, British scientists like John Cockcroft and William Penney having participated in the American Manhattan project (which produced the first two atomic bombs dropped on Hiroshima and Nagasaki in 1945), and having made significant contributions to the A-bomb development including uranium separation and bomb fabrication.

Foreign Minister Ernest Bevin declared in 1946: "We have got to have this thing (a nuclear bomb) whatever it costs… we have got to have a bloody Union Jack on top of it…" (This nationalistic/patriotic line subsequently became the motto of the RAF Bombers Command, which then operated the British airborne nuclear deterrent.)

Lorna Arnold and Andrew Brown have written: "In the aftermath of World War II, the British government embarked on a secret, independent atomic weapons program. Britain saw the bomb not only as a deterrent, but as a means to prevent a U.S. nuclear monopoly and to preserve its own status despite a fading empire…" (2)

British nuclear historian Margaret Gowing has written: "The purse strings (however tight at the time) had been opened and the priorities had been granted because Ministers and officials alike knew that the atomic bomb had revolutionized war…" (3)

The United States of America was the only nuclear power at that time. Then the Soviet Union tested its first atomic device (*Joe 1*) in September 1949, and Britain -- fuelled by its fear of Moscow – followed suit in October 1952.

When Britain deployed a couple of megaton hydrogen bombs in 1961, it burnished its image as one of the Big Three, the nuclear trio. And by 1963, Britain had achieved its modest target of 200 strategic nuclear weapons, although it was not known at the time that the British had less than one-tenth of what the Soviets had in their arsenal.

Unlike the Soviets, the British have wisely opted for what's known as a minimum deterrent. For economic and other reasons, they have abstained from the nuclear arms race while keeping their nuclear credentials and leaving the Soviets to run, to their eventual economic doom, against the much more resourceful Americans.

The development of a nuclear capability coincided with the anti-colonial struggle in postwar Singapore. Soon after Clement Attlee moved into 10 Downing Street following the shock defeat of national war hero Winston Churchill in the July 1945 general election, the Labour government decided to go nuclear.

The same year, the Malayan Communist Party (MCP) decided to capture power in Singapore, through an urban revolution along Leninist lines. But this first bid for power was crushed by the end of 1950.

Another major attempt at urban revolution was launched in 1954. The month of May marked the first clash of Chinese Middle School students with the police in Singapore.

The following month, the Cabinet Defence Policy Committee in London decided to develop a megaton H (hydrogen)-bomb – the so-called "big bang" after the US and the Soviet Union.

In late November 1954, the People's Action Party (PAP) was launched, with its two wings comprising the non-communists (calling themselves democratic socialists) and the communists together with the leftists and pro-communists.

Although Britain carried out its first test of a thermonuclear device in mid-May 1957 as scheduled and two more tests in June, it only succeeded to obtain its first megaton yield in its fourth test on November 1957. They called their one-megaton (1 MT) bomb "Red Snow".

On August 1957, the leftists and pro-communists fought the non-communists to a draw in the contest for seats in the PAP's central executive committee, and Lee Kuan Yew lost control of the party (within three years of its founding), albeit for only a short while (two and a half months).

To put the leftists and pro-communists in their proper place, Chief Minister Lim Yew Hock again resorted to tough action and put five out of the six left-wing CEC members behind bars.

Heavily infiltrated, the PAP was used by the communists in Singapore to serve in their open united front organization while Lee Kuan Yew rode a Red tiger to power with a resounding victory at the first general election held at the end of May 1959. Lee became Singapore's first prime minister.

In 1961, the momentous year which saw the decisive split between the non-communists and the communists/pro-communists in Singapore and the launching of Lee Kuan Yew's historic battle for merger with Malaysia after the controversial meeting of Lim Chin Siong and company with Lord Selkirk, the UK Commissioner, Britain deployed its first two megaton H-bombs.

In 1961 Britain matured as a nuclear power, armed with its first two megaton weapons of mass destruction. Now Macmillan could look into Khrushchev's eyes, without blinking. For Supermac was also carrying a big stick (with the big bang). Kennedy consulted with him in October 1962 when Khrushchev planted nuclear-armed missiles in Cuba close to the American backyard about 200 miles from Florida.

And when Sukarno tried to be wickedly funny a year after the Cuban missile crisis by threatening destruction to Malaya and Singapore, Supermac sent a few nuclear-capable *V*-bombers to Butterworth (north Malaya) and Tengah (Singapore) to show that the newly-formed Malaysia had the strong support of one of the Big Three. Unknown to the outside world, in 1962 Britain started its secret storage of atomic bombs in Singapore for possible use in a war against communist China. 11.11.2014 05:43

ψψψψψ

When Churchill returned to Downing Street after the Conservative victory in the October 1951 general election and began his second term as British premier, he inherited a fission weapon project which was only a few months away from its first A-bomb test (conducted in early October 1952) that won Britain its long-sought entry into the elite nuclear club. 14.02.2015 11:14 11:19

Set by the chiefs of staff at Churchill's behest in mid-1952, the British nuclear policy was spelt out in a white paper on "Global Strategy". At a time of great financial stress, the chiefs argued persuasively that nuclear retaliatory power offered a relatively inexpensive alternative to a deterrent based on a large standing army.

"Once British leaders chose this (nuclear) means to postwar power, they found the logic of massive retaliation even more compelling than U.S. leaders did," David Schwartz wrote. "Britain was less able to afford a standing army and the financial and resource burden of maintaining its global commitments with conventional forces…" (4)

Britain's first atomic bomb was tested in the Monte Bello Islands, off the coast of Australia, on 3 October 1952.

At the end of that year, after the US had exploded its first thermonuclear device (the "super" bomb) in October 1952 at Eniwetok (an atoll in the NW Marshall Islands in the West Pacific Ocean), Churchill decided to go further and build a British H-bomb as well.

Political leaders in London believed that such a highly powerful fusion bomb was required to deter the Soviets (who like their American rivals) were also developing the "big bang" (of over 1 MT, over 50 times the explosive power of the A-bomb that destroyed Hiroshima in 1945).

It was the political demand for more rapid development after 1954 which accelerated the H-bomb project. The target set at the end of 1954 was for Britain to acquire 20 hydrogen bombs by 1960, and to accumulate a significant stockpile over the 1959-1964 period. Churchill told the House of Commons on March 1955 that safety was to be the sturdy child of terror. 18.10.2003 2359

The British took only 28 months compared with 60 for the Soviets and 76 for the Americans, from political decision to demonstration of an experimental device test-dropped from a bomber, according to John Simpson. (5)

He wrote: "This exceptionally rapid progress was the result of the improved level of knowledge about atomic and thermonuclear reactions available to the British weapon designers in 1955 compared with that available to their United States counterparts in 1950; the resources deployed into the project from other government research establishments; and dynamic management and leadership.

"The country's rapidly expanding atomic weapon design knowledge formed an essential basis for the thermonuclear programme…" (6)

William Penny, a leading British theoretical physicist, headed the team which designed and developed the British nuclear and thermonuclear bombs. (7)

By 1957, Britain's first H-bomb was ready for testing, and it was detonated at Christmas Island in the Pacific on 15 May 1957 (within 18 months of the Soviet's first "Big Bang" in late November 1955).

The landmark 1957 Defence White Paper, which was produced under the direction of Harold Macmillan and Duncan Sandys, stressed building up an independent nuclear deterrent. (8)

This was like the Holy Grail to the political and military masters in London. And it was so important to Supermac that he was extremely upset when the news came to him in December 1960 that the US was about to scuttle the development of its Skybolt missile – a delivery system that Washington had promised London for its nuclear warheads.

Having cancelled the development of the Blue Streak long-range ballistic missile, Britain needed an American air-launched cruise missile such as the Skybolt, which could be fitted to the British bombers to extend the operational lifespan of the aging *V*-force beyond the late 1960s. The *V*-bombers (the *Vulcans* and the *Victors*) formed the backbone of the British nuclear deterrent.

Macmillan explained: "My difficulty is that if we cannot reach an agreement on a realistic means of maintaining the British independent deterrent, all the other questions may only justify perfunctory discussion, since an 'agonising appraisal' of all our foreign and defence policy will be required…" (9)

He would explain to President John Kennedy that "if Skybolt broke down, I must have an adequate replacement from the United States, such as Polaris (a ballistic missile carried on a nuclear submarine) – otherwise Britain would have to develop her own system whether submarine or aerial, in spite of the cost." (10)

To drive home his point, Macmillan added that "if the difficulties arising from the development of Skybolt were used, or seemed to be used, as a method of forcing Britain out of an independent nuclear capacity, the results would be very serious indeed. It would be deeply resented both by those of our people who favoured an independent nuclear capability and by those who opposed it. It would offend the sense of national pride and would be resisted by every means in our power." (11)

Macmillan wanted the Polaris urgently – and desperately – as a substitute for the Skybolt. "Certainly Britain with her world-wide commitments must continue, for the present at any rate, to have some independent nuclear force," he so very strongly noted. (12)

According to him, Kennedy "seemed somewhat taken aback." At their Nassau meeting in the Bahamas on December 1962, Kennedy was finally persuaded to make available the Polaris missiles (without nuclear warheads) for installation in a new generation of British submarines of the "Resolution" ("R") class. (13)

To recollect, the Nassau meeting took place less than a month after the end of the Cuban missile crisis (22 October-20 November), during which both leaders kept in close touch across the Atlantic through the teleprinter and telephone (a direct secret line to the White House). Macmillan recorded in his memoirs: "The whole episode was like a battle; and we in Admiralty House (in London) felt as if we were in the battle H.Q." (14)

On one major issue at least, Macmillan and President Charles de Gaulle of France managed to see eye to eye. When they met at Rambouillet in mid-December 1963, they discussed European defence including the role of nuclear weapons.

"Britain already had a considerable nuclear force," Macmillan wrote, "and we were determined to possess this as 'independent' in the sense that its ultimate control would be under a British Government. I felt that this force was important for Britain, just as a similar force would be for France. It was the symbol of independence and showed that we were not just satellites or clients of America. This was one aspect and a vital one. At the same time, we ought to organize our forces jointly with our allies, including the Americans..." (15)

Macmillan wrote on: "De Gaulle said he was glad to hear my opinion about an independent nuclear force. He, too, felt that this was necessary for France. It would not be enormous; but its power would be substantial..." (16)

Out in February 1962, the 1962 Defence White Paper stated that the British nuclear deterrent remained a "significant contribution" to the strategic deterrent capability of the West although it absorbed only about one-tenth of the national defence budget. The official statement stressed that Britain's nuclear deterrent had a retaliatory power capable of inflicting destruction beyond any level which a potential aggressor "would be prepared to tolerate." (17)

The nuclear-armed *V*-force was described as "capable by itself of crippling the industrial power of any aggressor nation." (18)

Commonly known as the Far East Strategic Reserve (FESR), the British Commonwealth Far East Strategic Reserve was established in mid-1953 as a joint military force of British, Australian and New Zealand military to protect Commonwealth interests in Southeast Asia from internal and external communist threats. This tripartite force consisted of a brigade-strength infantry force and a carrier battle group, supported by land- and sea-based fighter and bomber squadrons.

While in Europe the RAF Bomber Command cooperated with the US Strategic Air Command to deter the Soviet Union, Britain regularly deployed the Vulcans and the other V-force bombers such as the Victors to the Far East, particularly Singapore, as part of the British contribution to SEATO operations – to deter Communist China.

In 1959 a fully equipped nuclear weapons storage facility was secretly constructed in Singapore.

In 1960 the RAF Changi formed the RAF Far East Air Force in Singapore. Its first commander Air Marshal Sir

Anthony Selway served from 30 June 1960 to 31 May 1962; the fourth and last commander Air Vice Marshal N.M. Maynard (1 October 1970-31 October 1971) oversaw the British military withdrawal from Singapore until the closure of RAF Changi at the end of October 1971.

At the height of Indonesian confrontation against Malaysia (1963-66), Britain planned to deploy three squadrons of V-bombers and 48 Red Beard tactical nuclear weapons; but this extraordinary show of overwhelming force was then reconsidered as unnecessary and shelved. The Vulcans trained in the region for both conventional and nuclear missions.

From 1963, the Blue Danube (the first operational British nuclear weapon, a plutonium bomb of about 10 to 12 kilotons, of about the same explosive yield as the first American atomic bomb dropped on Hiroshima August 1945) was replaced by the Red Beard (a boosted fission weapon, said to be the most powerful of its kind). Stocks of the new Red Beard were kept in Cyprus (48 of them), and in Singapore (48) which were committed and dedicated to SEATO defence against a communist advance in this part of the world. (19)

The nuclear-armed military base in Singapore was part of British military strategy in East Asia – "to maintain an independent contribution to the nuclear deterrent against China..." (20)

To strengthen its special relationship with Washington as well as to enhance its global image, the leadership in London (both Conservative and Labour) played its self-scripted role in the Cold War, to the extent of pledging its modern nuclear arms to deter both Moscow in Europe and Peking in the East, while waging a vigorous covert propaganda war globally through the Foreign Office's Information Research Department (IRD) from the very early years of the Cold War. (21)

NOTES: CHAPTER ONE: THE NUCLEAR LION IN LONDON

1. In **The Rise and Fall of the Great Powers** (p. 473), Paul Kennedy has written: "When the Labour government entered office in July 1945, one of the first documents it had to read was Keynes' hair-raising memorandum about the 'financial Dunkirk' which the country was facing: its colossal trade gap, its weakened industrial base, its enormous overseas establishments, meant that American aid was desperately needed, to replace the cut-off Lend-Lease..."

   Less than a year before America's entry into World War II triggered by the Japanese attack on Pearl Harbour on 7 December 1941, President Franklin Delano Roosevelt (FDR) proposed to make the United States the "arsenal of democracy" through the Lend-Lease Act which would authorize the President to lend, lease, sell or barter defence articles (i.e. provide military material assistance) under any terms he deemed proper to "the government of any country whose defense the President deems vital to the defense of the United States."

   In **DIPLOMACY** (p. 388), Henry Kissinger has written: "...Secretary of State (Cordell) Hull, normally a passionate Wilsonian and an advocate of collective security rather uncharacteristically justified the Lend-Lease Act on strategic grounds. Without massive American help, he argued, Great Britain would fall (in the war with Hitler's Germany) and control of the Atlantic would pass into hostile hands, jeopardizing the security of the Western Hemisphere."

In **A History of the World in the Twentieth Century** (p. 346), Prof J.A.S. Grenvillle has written: "Without US help, the British economy – geared until mid-1945 to the war effort – was not able to provide the British people even with the standard of living during the war…"

On Britain's postwar policy to join the nuclear club, Kennedy has written (p. 477): "But to the government in London, even when Attlee replaced Churchill, it was inconceivable that the country should not possess those (nuclear) weapons, both as a deterrent and because they 'were a manifestation of the scientific and technological superiority on which Britain's strength, so deficient if measured in sheer numbers of men, must depend' (quoting M. Gowing in **Independence and Deterrence: Britain and Atomic Energy 1945-1952**, vol. 1, p. 184).

"They were seen, in other words, as a relatively cheap way of retaining independent Great Power influence – a calculation which, shortly afterward, appealed equally to the French…"

2. **BULLETIN OF THE ATOMIC SCIENTISTS** September/October 2005, p. 76

3. **Independence and Deterrence**, Volume 2 p. 502

4. David Schwartz, **NATO's Nuclear Dilemmas**, p. 29

5. John Simpson, **The Independent Nuclear State: The United States, Britain and the Military Atom**, p. 104

6. Ibid., p. 104

According to the American nuclear historian Richard Rhodes (**Dark Sun**), Edward Teller's obsession with megaton yields delayed the development of the hydrogen bomb (the Super); otherwise the US could have tested a half-megaton thermonuclear by 1949. By early 21st century, half-megaton is standard for a hydrogen bomb.

The US tested a 10.4 MT hydrogen bomb on 31 October 1952, shortly after the Soviet explosion of *Joe 1* in September 1949.

The Soviets went on to test its first boosted fission bomb of 440 KT yield *Joe 4* on 12 August 1953, and its first multistage thermonuclear of 1.6 MT on 22 November 1955.

7. Adrian Weale, **Eye-Witness HIROSHIMA**, p. 215

8. John Baylis, **Contemporary Strategy,** Vol. II, p. 15

9. Harold Macmillan, **At The End Of The Day 1961-1963**, p. 344

    According to nuclear historian Robert Norris of the Natural Resources Defense Council in Washington, D.C., the UK had 30 nuclear warheads in 1960.

10. Harold Macmillan, **At The End Of The Day 1961-63**, p. 347

    In **NUCLEAR NIGHTMARES** (Penguin Books, 1981, pp. 52-53), Nigel Calder, a well-known British science writer and populariser, has written that the British "had no real stomach for the very expensive business of building advanced missiles; they abandoned their own rocket program and relied on their "special relationship" with the Americans."

In **DIPLOMACY** (p. 601), Henry Kissinger has written: "To extend the life of its aging bomber fleet, Great Britain had decided to buy Skybolt, a long-range American air-launched cruise missile then in the process of being developed. In the fall of 1962, without advance warning, the Kennedy Administration canceled Skybolt, allegedly on technical grounds but in fact to reduce the reliance on airplanes, which were thought to be more vulnerable than missiles, and almost certainly to discourage an autonomous British nuclear capability. A unilateral American decision made without prior consultation with Great Britain doomed the British bomber forces to rapid obsolescence. French warnings against dependence on Washington seemed to be confirmed.

"The next phase of the Skybolt affair, however, demonstrated the benefits of the "special relationship" with America. Macmillan called in some of the chits he had accumulated through his patient fostering of American ties, nor was he any too gentle about it…

"Kennedy and Macmillan met in Nassau, where, on December 21, they agreed to modernize the Anglo-American nuclear partnership. America would compensate Great Britain for the Skybolt by selling it five Polaris submarines and associated missiles, for which Great Britain would develop its own nuclear warheads. To meet America's concern about maintaining central control of nuclear strategy, Great Britain agreed to "assign" these submarines to NATO, except in cases in which "the supreme national interest was at stake." (quoted from the joint communiqué)"

Kissinger has then gone on to comment on the role of the British nuclear arm in NATO: "The integration of British forces into NATO turned out to be largely token. Since Great Britain was free to use the submarines whenever in its "supreme national interest," and since, by definition, the use of nuclear weapons would never be considered except when the supreme national interest **was** at stake, the Nassau Agreement effectively conceded to Great Britain by consultation the same freedom of action France was trying to extort by confrontation. The difference between the British and French attitudes toward their nuclear weapons was that Great Britain was prepared to sacrifice form to substance, whereas de Gaulle, in striving to reassert France's identity, equated form (style) with substance…"

11. Harold Macmillan, **At The End Of The Day 1961-63**, p. 347 19.10.2003 0806

12. Ibid., p. 359

In **SUMARINE** (published by Berkley Books, New York, 1993, pp. 152-153), the best-selling American novelist and military writer Tom Clancy has written: "During this period (of the early and mid-1960s) the British government was trying to find a way of maintaining a credible nuclear deterrent force that would be under *British* control. The force of RAF "V" bombers were quickly losing their ability to penetrate the air defenses of the Soviet Union, and the development of an ICBM (Intercontinental Ballistic Missile) force that would reside on British soil was simply beyond the financial resources of Great Britain. So the British government made the decision to buy the Polaris A3 missile system from the United States and build a force of four SSBNs (strategic ballistic missile submarines, nuclear-powered) to carry them.

"Thus was born the "R" class of SSBNs, the first of which, HMS *Resolution* (S-27), was commissioned in 1967. For over a quarter century the "R" boats have provided the United Kingdom with their nuclear deterrent force, helping keep the peace…"

The *Resolution* class carries sixteen U.S. Polaris A-3 missiles (the first generation of U.S. Navy submarine-launched ballistic missiles), armed with British reentry vehicles carrying British-made nuclear warheads.

While the British Royal Navy has nicknamed its strategic missile submarines "bombers" (probably nostalgically after the obsolescent *V*-bombers which these more modern subs have replaced), the U.S.

Navy's SSBNs have been dubbed "boomers."

13. Harold Macmillan, **At The End Of The Day 1961-63**, p. 347

By the time of Macmillan's meeting with Kennedy in December 1962, Britain had slightly over 200 clear warheads – a quantum jump from 50 in 1961, according to Norris.

14. Ibid., p. 220

In 1962, the earth-shattering year of the Cuban missile crisis, the US had more than 27,000 nuclear warheads, eight times more than the Soviet Union (3,322). Britain had 205.

Relating the nature and outcome of the Cuban missile crisis to the diplomatic tussle in the heart of Europe, Henry Kissinger has commented (**DIPLOMACY**, p. 591): "….Trying to achieve inone stroke the breakthrough which had eluded him for the past three years, Khrushchev placed Soviet intermediate-range missiles into Cuba. Khrushchev had obviously calculated that, if he succeeded in that adventure, his bargaining position in an eventual Berlin negotiation would be overwhelming. For the same reason, Kennedy could not permit such an extension of Soviet strategic power into the Western Hemisphere.

"His bold and skillful handling of the crisis not only forced Khrushchev to withdraw the Soviet missiles but, in the process, stripped his Berlin diplomacy of whatever credibility still remained to it.

"Recognizing that he had run out of expedients, Khrushchev announced in January 1963 that the "success" of the Berlin Wall had made a separate peace treaty with Berlin unnecessary. The Berlin crisis was finally over. It had lasted five years (1958-63)…"

On hindsight, it can be seen that while Khrushchev had miscalculated about the strategic advantage of planting intermediate-range missiles (IRBMs) in the backyard of the US (he had with him the ICBMs which could reach and strike at the American heartland, though not as many as those on the American side), Kennedy himself, with his overwhelming nuclear superiority at the time, had come dangerously close to over-reacting to the virtual threat posed by the Soviet IRBMs in Cuba. The two superpowers had actually brought the world to the edge of nuclear war. After the removal of the Soviet intermediate-range missiles from Cuba, the US removed its own IRBMs in Turkey. 19.10.2003 2329.

15. Harold Macmillan, **At The End Of The Day 1961-1963**, p. 347 Britain had 280 nuclear warheads in 1963, according to Norris.

16. Ibid., p. 348

When Macmillan and de Gaulle met in December 1963, France had no nuclear warheads in stock but acquired four in 1964. France then had 32 in its nascent arsenal in 1965. 20.10.2003 0205

17. **Keesing's Contemporary Archives**

18. Ibid.

Watkinson, Minister of Defence, speaking at the end of the two-day debate on the 1961 Defence White Paper in the House of Commons.

In 1961 Britain had 50 nuclear warheads, the number of which increased to 205 by the end of 1962.

19. **Wikipedia**

20. DO 169/221, p. 50 as quoted in Tan Jing Quee, "Detention in Operation Cold Store: A Study in Imperialism", published in **THE FAJAR GENERATION**, p. 216

21. Lashmar and Oliver, **BRITAIN'S SECRET PROPAGANDA WAR 1948-1977**, pp. 84-87

CHAPTER TWO

A lion's paw in the East:
the Singapore military base

In Singapore a major British naval base was built before World War II, built in the 1930s at great expense (estimated 63 million pounds) to serve as the Headquarters of the Commander-in-Chief in this region. According to Sir Robert Scott (permanent secretary in the British Defence Ministry 1961-63), Singapore's role was essentially strategic as an outpost to protect the approaches to India (then the gem of the British Empire) from the east. (1)

During World War II, however, Britain's so-called "impregnable citadel" fell to the Japanese invaders in February 1942 after only eight days of fighting. The Japanese conqueror General Tomoyuki Yamashita later disclosed: "My attack on Singapore was a bluff – a bluff that worked. I had 30,000 men and was outnumbered more than three to one. I knew if I had to fight long for Singapore I would be beaten…" His audacious plan was to take the island in four days. (2)

When Scott said the strategic importance of the naval base became a myth in the postwar era after India had gained its independence in 1947, he could not foresee Singapore's key role in British military strategy in the region in the emerging Cold War.

In the early period of the Cold War, Singapore became an important air base for the British military in the Far East.

The British Commonwealth Far East Strategic Reserve (FESR) was established in Singapore mid-1953, as a joint force of the British, Australian and New Zealand military to protect Commonwealth interests in Southeast Asia and to counter the growing threat of communism in the region.

Britain routinely deployed its nuclear-capable V-bombers to the Far East, particularly Singapore, in support of its strong commitments to SEATO – to deter Communist China.

In 1959 the British secretly built a fully equipped nuclear weapons storage facility, which subsequently accommodated 48 of Britain's most advanced tactical nuclear weapons known as the Red Beard (about one-fifth of the British nuclear arsenal).

In mid-1960 the RAF Changi formed the RAF Far East Air Force in Singapore, under the command of Air Marshal Sir Anthony Selway.

For the thousands of Commonwealth troops (45,000 of them at the peak) from Britain, Australia, and New Zealand who took part in operations against the Communist guerrillas in Malaya during the First Emergency (1948-60), Singapore served as a key supply depot. (3)

When in May 1958 the colonial authorities agreed to grant a self-governing constitution to Singapore, they recognized the fact that the island had a lesser role in British defence considerations than in the previous years. Its strategic importance was seen to have diminished, according to the Secretary of State for the Colonies Alan Lennox-Boyd. In a 1980 interview with John Drysdale, he said "I think I had reached a point then when almost (all) the colonial obligations (to decolonise under the United Nations charter)) overrode defence considerations, but the fact that defence considerations had diminished made it more easy for the cabinet as a whole to accept (having to grant self-government to Singapore in 1959)." (4) Whatever the colonial secretary may have said, defence considerations continued to override decolonization until Britain finally pivoted its strategic priorities nearer home to become truly Euro-centric.

Only a couple of years earlier, Lennox-Boyd had spoken so very highly of Singapore.

At the abortive conference on the constitutional future of Singapore which broke down on May 1956 after three weeks of negotiation, he described Singapore as occupying a unique position in the world as a very great port, the commercial hub of Southeast Asia, and a bastion in the defence system of the free world.

Following the breakdown of talks in London, the Colonial Office issued a statement which among other things cited "Singapore's great strategic importance in the defences of the free world…" (5)

On 28 August 1957, Defence Minister Duncan Sandys assured the Australian government in Canberra that Britain would maintain substantial land, sea, and air forces in Southeast Asia and the Far East. He also said the British Far East Fleet would continue to be based in Singapore.

On 20 September, Sandys told a press conference in Canberra that Britain would continue to develop and stockpile nuclear weapons for her own and Commonwealth defence. Not known to the outside world then, Britain had only about a score of nuclear warheads in 1957.

He added that Britain continued to regard the three-year-old anti-communist security arrangement for the region SEATO as "a vital factor in the defence of the free world."

Britain would therefore continue to maintain substantial land, sea, and air forces in the SEATO area, including in due course "elements of nuclear power which will greatly enhance the effectiveness of these forces."

He also said that the RAF Canberra bombers, equipped to carry atomic weapons, would be sent to Malaya.

His rather extraordinary statement (probably made more for communicating British intentions to the Communist world) created some concern in Kuala Lumpur where it was interpreted that Malaya might become an "atomic base" whereas the Anglo-Malayan defence treaty (the White Paper on which was published in both London and Kuala Lumpur on 18 Sept) made no provision for any nuclear installation in Malaya.

On 23 September 1957, Sandys said that it had not been decided what atomic weapons would be made available to the British forces in the Far East, or where they would be kept. (6)

After holding merger talks with Tunku Abdul Rahman in Kuala Lumpur late September 1961, Lee Kuan Yew told a press conference in Singapore that if the British refused to budge over the future status of their bases because of their commitments to SEATO, "we can generate heat against them." (7)

On 4 October 1961, Harold Macmillan sent a message to his Australian counterpart Robert Menzies on the progress of the Greater Malaysia plan (to merge Malaya, Singapore and the Borneo territories).

Menzies replied on 18 October: "No doubt the effect of Greater Malaysia on the Commonwealth strategic reserve's participation in SEATO exercises and operations will occupy a large place in your discussions with the Tunku..." (8)

On 22 November 1961, Macmillan and Tunku signed their agreement on Malaysia and the Singapore base. And Macmillan noted in his private writing on the same day: "The Defence part of the agreement is quite satisfactory (which is better than we expected)." (9)

In Macmillan's view, the goodwill and support of the local government and population were "vital" to the maintenance of the British base in Singapore.

Later he wrote in his memoirs: "Although Malaya and the Greater Malaysia Federation, when it came into being, would not be formally associated with SEATO, nevertheless Singapore would continue to offer full access and facilities…" (10) 21.10.2003 0909 959 words

ψψψψψ

Would the colonial authorities in Singapore allow the Communists to take over an island state which fielded Britain's most important nuclear-armed military complex east of Suez? Could the Communists seize power through constitutional means in Singapore? If not, could they "generate heat" (to quote Lee Kuan Yew), incite civil commotion and strife, and challenge law and order to the extent of making the British stay in the colony no longer desirable or tenable?

Issued in late February 1962, nine months after Tunku Abdul Rahman's proposal for the formation of Malaysia, the 1962 Defence White Paper stated that Singapore would remain Britain's main military base in the Far East.

The Singapore base would assist in the defence of the proposed Malaysia, and provide for Commonwealth defence as well as for the preservation of peace in Southeast Asia. This implied that the military facilities on the island could be used to meet British commitment to SEATO.

The 1962 document said: "Our main base will continue to be Singapore with some forces, including our contribution to the Commonwealth Brigade, also stationed in the Federation of Malaya…" (11)

At that time, the British had about 10,000 troops in Singapore and about the same number across the Causeway. Their military presence was to increase dramatically in the mid-1960s, to counter Indonesian confrontation.

With their major naval base at Sembawang, the British also maintained three major air bases in Singapore. They were Tengah where nuclear-capable *V*-bombers were stationed with other strike and fighter aircraft, Changi where long-range transport planes were kept and maintained, and Seletar with its terminal for short-range transport planes.

According to one well-informed source, Singapore accommodated three military airfields at which part of the British nuclear striking force was deployed, a naval base and dockyard capable of serving the largest warships, an army base for 60,000 men, and GHQ (General Headquarters), Far East. (12)

Unknown to the outside world, tactical nuclear weapons were secretly stored in Singapore. According to a British Ministry of Defence (MoD) document declassified in 2000, up to 48 Red Beard nuclear bombs were kept in a highly secured weapons storage facility at Tengah Air Base, between 1962 and 1970. According to Whitehall officials, these nukes were to be used in a war against China or in defence of Britain's regional allies in the SEATO pact. 12.11.2014 08:45

Across the Causeway, the Commonwealth Strategic Reserve was quartered near Malacca at a new base opened in 1960 and financed jointly by the British, Australian and New Zealand Governments (the three Commonwealth signatories to SEATO).

A British jungle training school was sited in Johore while further up to the north was located another major air base at Butterworth – used mainly by the Australian air force. (13) 22.10.2003 0219

While it was true that the Communists, through their influence on, if not control of the opposition Barisan Sosialis (Socialist Front), posed a serious political threat to the ruling PAP government in the early 1960s, there was no way that they could capture power by the use of force (Mao Tse-tung's barrel of the gun).

It was not possible for the revolutionaries to take over Singapore short of seizing the British military installations. They didn't have the means to do that, and, moreover, the British authorities were not going to permit that to happen.

"The left wing had supported David Marshall (a former chief minister and the first in Singapore) at Anson (where a by-election was held on 15 July 1961 less than two months after the Tunku had proposed in Singapore the formation of Malaysia), and Marshall had called for the closing of all British bases on the island. If the left were ever to act on that, the British would quickly bare their canines," wrote Dennis Bloodworth. (14)

The canines of the British bulldog would have been more appropriately invoked in the war years of the early 1940s of Churchill's premiership (1940-45). In the early 1960s of a pro-nuclear Macmillan, an adversary of Britain would probably have to contend with a formidable lion's nuclear paw.

In the early sixties, the military facilities in Singapore remained essential to British commitments to Commonwealth defence and its self-willed participation in SEATO, although Macmillan thought that political and economic strategy would play a greater role than "old-fashioned military methods." (15)

Donald Maclean wrote that the British military presence had a political bearing on Singapore. Of course it had, and it was pivotal to the political destiny of Singapore.

Maclean wrote in 1969 that "the People's Action Party owes its predominance to nearly twenty years of unremitting efforts by the colonial authorities since the war (since the end of World War II) to destroy the powerful Communist movement in Singapore, and that the balance of political forces in the island is to this day affected by the presence of the British bases…" (16)

On the British economic role, he commented: "The extent to which the economies of Malaysia and Singapore are still dominated by British business interests is greater than in another sovereign state in Asia.

"According to official statistics (quoting the Board of Trade Journal, June 10, 1966, data excluding oil companies), in 1964 the earnings of British companies here were 22,400,000 pounds, which is only slightly less than the equivalent figure for the whole of Western Europe (23.5 million pounds) and larger than that for India (21.5 million pounds)…

"Britain also still has a considerable share of the foreign trade of Malaysia and Singapore, though it is diminishing. In 1964 it was 16.6%, compared with 12.1% for Japan and about 6% for the United States and Australia…" (17)

Evidently, the military bases in Singapore served to protect British economic as well as political and security interests in the region. And until London pulled out its military from Singapore (which it finally did at the end of 1971), the British continued to keep their important bases out of harm's way. And for that matter, no local insurgents were at all capable of repeating the feat of the Japanese invaders in World War II. 22.10.2003 1010

Tun Tan Siew Sin, an astute Malaysian political leader but by no means a military expert, told the plain truth in a speech he made in 1966 (shortly after Singapore's separation from Malaysia). He ventured to say in simple layman's language that "it is not easy to stage and, what is far more important, maintain a successful armed revolt against colonial rule in a small island of about 220 square miles. You cannot wage guerrilla warfare effectively under such circumstances. All you can do is engage in some street fighting which, in the military view, could be put down by a couple of infantry battalions in a matter of a mere forty-eight hours." (18)

It may be recalled that the bloody riots in October 1956 were put down by joint police-military operations within four days. Six battalions were quickly withdrawn from the Malayan jungles over 100 miles away and deployed in Singapore within a couple of days.

Among the various measures of the new internal security plan (known as *Operation PHOTO*) prepared only about three months earlier, 29 strategic road blocks were promptly established, covering all roads entering the city. This interceptive measure prevented mobs from building up into a critical mass at the heart of civic life. The largest crowd was estimated to be a manageable 3,000 strong. 22.10.2003 2329

The 1956 riots exacted a toll of 13 fatalities, including only one inflicted by the rioters who were unarmed. No policemen or soldiers were killed although five were hospitalized together with 42 rioters. There were no reports of rioters using firearms. (19)

Recalling that the British got out of Palestine in 1948 and the Suez Canal in 1954 "both times abandoning huge assets and supposedly vital strategic advantages", Richard Clutterbuck wrote that the British were unlikely to quit Singapore even in the face of violence and confrontation by the Communists. And he gave four reasons, including a possibility that "with so much at stake in Malaya and in the port and military base in Singapore, the British would have fought far harder than they had fought in the Middle East, where many of the assets (notably the oil installations) were largely unaffected by the withdrawals." (20)

Of course at the time of writing his book, Clutterbuck could not be privy to Britain's nuclear cache in Singapore. Nevertheless, even if he had known, the British general would rightly have kept mum.

Lee Kuan Yew himself did not think that Singapore could fall easily to the Communists. At a press conference on 1 June 1959, a couple of days after the PAP had swept into power following an overwhelming victory in the first general election in Singapore, he said that he saw no danger of Communist domination in the next five years (a prediction which nearly went awry when he came close to the political precipice in mid-1961).

Moreover, he did not think that the Communists would be "foolish enough to try violence, because four battalions of troops and police on the island could deal with any such situation." (21)

As noted earlier, six battalions working closely with the police succeeded in quelling the 1956 riots within four days. And by 1959, the island's security measures could have been further improved and fine-tuned. (22)

The actual strength of communism was not known although the 1959 estimate by the Special Branch put it at some 300 "hard core" communists with an unknown number of "fringe" sympathizers (probably a few thousand).

It should also be kept in mind that the Communists in Singapore had pursued power – not through armed struggle *a la* Mao (unsuccessfully attempted by their senior comrades across the Causeway) – but through the constitutional and political processes in which they were also represented by their proxies, leftists and pro-communists in the open united front. They had wisely ruled out armed struggle in such a small territory as Singapore which hosted a very strong British military.

David Marshall wrote: "The people of Singapore, living in a confined area which is easily controlled by a few machine-guns at a limited number of crossroads, would never have been able to achieve independence if the British had used bombs and bullets against us."(23)

Although the British military power remained too strong for any local adversary to overcome, it was inconceivable that the colonial authorities would use force to perpetuate their rule and deny independence to the people of Singapore in the 1960s. Of course, they would not have hesitated to use force to protect their military bases.

About a fortnight after the split with the leftists in the PAP, Lee Kuan Yew wrote a letter which was published in the *Straits Times* in early August 1961. He wrote to deny Lim Chin Siong's statement implying that Lee had made threats to his political opponents in earlier days, and that Lee still hoped that the British would nab them for him.

Lee wrote: "I have told him (Lim) many a time that he had better behave himself and get his pro-Communist friends to behave themselves because they were in a conscribed position in which they, in the last resort, would have to deal, not with the Singapore Government, but with the British forces on the island. That is a fact that has not altered…" (24)

Clearly, the most tangible and concrete evidence of the British commitment to the defence of Malaysia and by extension to the safeguarding of their precious economic and military assets in Singapore and across the Causeway was the very strong presence of Commonwealth forces drawn from Britain, Australia and New Zealand to thwart the threat of Indonesian aggression in the early and mid-1960s.

At the peak in 1965-66, this military presence consisted of the stationing of over 50,000 British troops including the Gurkhas. This was as many as the British Army of the Rhine (BAOR) in Germany. Moreover, the British also deployed 50 naval vessels, in the strongest-ever projection of maritime power in Malaysian waters. (25)

NOTES CHAPTER TWO: A lion's paw in the East: the Singapore military base

1. John Drysdale, **Singapore: Struggle for Success**, p. 32

   Scott was Assistant Under-Secretary of State in the British Foreign Office from 1950 to 1953.

   He took over from Malcolm MacDonald as Commissioner-General for the United Kingdom in Southeast Asia from 1955 to 1959. He headed the Imperial Defence College in 1960 and became Permanent Secretary, Ministry of Defence from 1961 to 1963.

2. **Battlefield Guide "The Japanese Conquest of Malaya and Singapore December 1941-February 1942"**, published in Singapore Less than 70 hours before Percival made his surrender to Yamashita on the late Sunday morning of 15 February 1942, Churchill had cabled General Wavell on the afternoon of 12 February to fight "to the bitter end at all costs," reminding the Supreme Commander: ".The honour of the British Empire and of the British Army is at stake…" And based on Churchill's rousing message, Wavell issued the Order of the Day and personally told Percival that the Army was to fight to the end, and with no question of surrender. Frank Owen, **THE FALL OF SINGAPORE**, published as a Classic Penguin, 2001, pp. 183-184.

   Wartime Prime Minister Winston Churchill described the stunningly swift fall of Singapore as "the greatest disaster" in British military history. It was "a grievous and shameful blow to British prestige". Some 123,000 British, Australian, Indian and Malayan troops were under the command of Lt. Gen. Arthur Percival. **THE SUN**, Kuala Lumpur, February 16, 2002

Speaking as the guest of honour on the Australian Broadcasting Commission's network on 24 March 1965, Lee Kuan Yew recalled seeing the Commonwealth troops tramping into captivity: "I saw them tramping along in front of my house in Singapore for three solid days – an endless stream of bewildered men who did not know what had happened, why it had happened, or what they were doing there in Singapore in any case. I was bewildered too. (Lee was 18 then.) We were all unprepared for this. We thought Singapore was an impregnable fortress, and the British Navy was supreme. No one expected the Japanese to march down Southeast Asia and capture us. Nobody had warned us of this. It was a shock…" Alex Josey, **Lee Kuan Yew – The Crucial Years**, p. 255

3. **The Economist Pocket Guide to Defence**, London, 1986, p. 49

4. Drysdale, **Singapore: Struggle for Success**, p. 199

5. **Keesing's Contemporary Archives**

6. Ibid.

The British Defence Minister's statement referring to deployment of "elements of nuclear power" in the SEATO theatre in the Far East was probably propaganda to make the British contribution to the regional anti-communist alliance appear stronger than it actually was. With only 20 nuclear warheads in 1957, Britain could not spare any outside its own home base. By the time of the Cuban missile crisis in late 1962, however, Britain's nuclear arsenal had more than 200 warheads for the first time. And by the time that Sukarno's Indonesia raised the ante in its campaign of confrontation against the newly-established Malaysia in 1964, Britain could count more than 300 nuclear warheads in its precious possession.

7. *Straits Times* October 1, 1961

8. Harold Macmillan, **At The End Of The Day 1961-63**, p. 250

Apart from the United States (whose forceful and assertive Secretary of State John Foster Dulles was the main architect of SEATO), only the three Commonwealth countries of Britain, Australia, and New Zealand took seriously their participation in this seven-nation collective security arrangement to counter Communist aggression and subversion.

Describing its formal obligations as "rather nebulous", Henry Kissinger (**DIPLOMACY**, p. 637) has commented that "SEATO served Dulles' purpose by providing a legal framework for the defense of Indochina."

In **THE ORDEAL OF POWER** (Atheneum, NY, 1963), Emmet John Hughes, an adviser to Eisenhower in the 1952 and 1956 political campaigns as well as a presidential assistant in the White House for one year of the first term, called the alliance a piece of paper "more pretentious than substantial" (p. 163). He even implied that "the political or military value of SEATO was highly questionable" (p. 341).

9. Ibid., p. 251

10. Ibid., p. 251

11. *Straits Times* February 21, 1962

12. Donald Maclean, **British Foreign Policy Since Suez 1956-1968**, London, 1970, p. 244

13. Ibid., p. 244

14. Dennis Bloodworth, **The Tger and the Trojan Horse**, p. 236

Bloodworth wrote this after interviewing Lord Selkirk, UK Commissioner-General for Southeast Asia. Selkirk also chaired the Internal Security Council.

15. Macmillan, p. 250

16. Maclean, p. 243

Speaking at Victoria University on 11 March 1965, Lee Kuan Yew said: "...The only reason why Malaysia emerged from very near chaos, from the early days of the 1950s to the peace and tranquility and progress of the 1960s before confrontation, was because, first, the British had the wisdom to recognise what was irresistible, and therefore not to resist it; and secondly, having decided that freedom movements were irresistible, to try, in so far as they could, to make sure if they could not get anti-communist groups to emerge as the dominant force in a territory they had to abandon, at least that the leadership was non-communist...." Josey, **Lee Kuan Yew – The Crucial Years**, pp. 250-251

According to S. Rajaratnam, the British provided a safety net for the PAP moderates both when they teamed up with the left wing in their anti-colonial struggle in the mid-1950s and also when the moderates were struggling to achieve political power in the late 1950s. He told Bloodworth that the colonial power would keep the communists down "but we had to get into an unassailable position before that safety net was withdrawn." Bloodworth, p. 23

17. Maclean, p. 243

18. J. Victor Morais (ed), **Blueprint For Unity – Selected Speeches of Tun Tan Siew Sin**, Kuala Lumpur, 1972

19. Richard Clutterbuck, **Conflict and Violence in Singapore and Malaysia**, Singapore, 1984

This book by Clutterbuck (Major General retired, British Army), an expert on terrorist movements, gives a detailed account of the 1956 riots in Singapore.

On the failures of the Malayan Communist Party (MCP) in Singapore, Clutterbuck has commented (p. 268): "The aim of the MCP in Singapore up till 1955 was to oust the British colonial government and substitute a Communist one, in conjunction with a similar aim in the Federation of Malaya (across the Causeway).

"During the transition stage to independence (1955-63) when the British were clearly on the way out, their aim became to capture control of the elected Singapore government, either by constitutional or revolutionary means.

"Both of these aims were feasible. The most promising years for the first were 1945-7; for the second, they were 1956-7 (to coincide with Malayan independence) and 1962 (to coincide with the end of British responsibility and of reserve powers of intervention).

"The Party failed in both aims, and achieved little in the way even of erosion of authority; so far from accelerating the British withdrawal and the final attainment of independence, it almost certainly retarded them…"

20. Clutterbbuck, p. 269

21. **Keesing's**

In a broadcast over Radio Singapore on 2 October 1961 shortly after the split with the Communists, Lee Kuan Yew said that "British power is supreme in Singapore. The sovereignty of Singapore is still vested in the British. In the last resort, it is they who have the final say on what happens in Singapore.

"We know, and the Communists also know, that in the last resort the British must take action on their own to protect their military and other interests."

Lee described Singapore in October 1961 as "still a semi-colony, with ultimate power still vested in the British." **Straits Times** October 3, 1961

22. Alan Blades, head of Special Branch at the time of the 1956 riots in Singapore, commented: "It was Lee Kuan Yew's opinion, later on, that it was the sight of tanks and military force, rather than the arrest of the ring-leaders, that caused the trouble to subside and he, and Goh Keng Swee in particular, were all for the earliest show of bayonets etc. when they took over responsibility for internal security after June 1959." Quoted in Clutterbuuck, p. 132

23. David Marshall, **The Struggle for Nationhood 1945-1959**, p. 2

24. **Straits Times** August 4, 1961

25. **The Economist Guide to Defence**, p. 59

A defence analyst and author, Brian Cloughley has written: "...When I served East Of Suez the British fleet based in Singapore had three aircraft carriers, a cruiser, a destroyer squadron, a frigate squadron, about 30 other ships and a social life of some intensity. The total strength of the Royal Navy was about 180 ships..." **ASIA TIMES** Jan 9, 2015 Cloughley, then a lieutenant (later promoted to colonel), saw active service in the period of Indonesia's confrontation against Malaysia (1963-66); while in Borneo he was attached to 42 Commando, Royal Marines. 10.01.2015 07:50

Addressing Victoria University in Wellington, New Zealand, on 11 March 1965, Lee Kuan Yew asserted: "...If in fact Malaysia, if in fact Singapore, and its important geographic position are of no value to the West, or if in fact the Western presence is not desired by the West in Southeast Asia, then nobody will be interested really to expend all this money, to expend all this effort, divert their resources, in defence of freedom (in this part of the world). But it so happens that these things do matter, that whether we perish or we survive does affect the course of events for the big powers…" (referring to British and Commonwealth military presence to counter Indonesian confrontation) Josey, **Lee Kuan Yew – The Crucial Years**, p. 27

CHAPTER THREE

Drawing in the horns:
British military withdrawal
from Singapore

When the British Empire reached its zenith at the end of World War I (1914-18), it covered over a quarter of the global population and a fourth of the earth's land surface. But after a century and a half, the world's superpower started to decline and lost its sway in the fortunes of World War II (1939-45). 13.11.2014 06:06

In postwar Britain the political leaders at Westminster and the top civil servants in Whitehall had to decide on their destination, finding themselves at the crossroads of the old far-flung highway to the British Empire and the short and direct continental route to Europe. Thus in the key Ministries at the Treasury, Foreign and Defence in London, the decision-makers were divided between those who wanted their country to restore national greatness and to remain as a major actor on the world stage, and the others who looked to Europe as the gateway to the future.

Prof. J.A.S. Grenville wrote: "Britain's dire financial plight (after World War II) forced the (Labour) Cabinet to sort out British priorities in the rest of the world. Hugh Dalton, when at the Treasury (1945-7), constantly urged Ernest Bevin at the

Foreign Office to cut back Britain's overseas responsibilities…"
(1) 26.10.2003 0203

But Bevin, the British foreign secretary (1945-51) who carved a name for himself by building bridges to Europe, did not roll back Empire. A financially-strapped Britain could not do much either here or there. Yet it was not easy to bridle national pride (particularly that of a small country, smaller in area than Malaysia, which had ruled over the greatest empire in history). Nor was it simple to adjust quickly to a fast-changing world with the emergence of the United States as the leading economic, military and political power and champion of democracy in the West, and the contending Soviet Union, the Communist superpower-to-be, in the East. And, amidst the shifts in the global geopolitical landscape, there was the rising tide of postwar decolonisation and political emancipation.

Bevin was one of the architects of the Brussels Treaty and the North Atlantic Treaty, both of which brought Britain closer to her European allies. The Brussels Treaty of March 1948 forged a five-nation alliance, including Britain and France, to head off Soviet aggression. Formed in early April 1949, NATO (North Atlantic Treaty Organisation) was to bind the United States, the world's sole superpower at the time, to the collective security of Western Europe in a trans-Atlantic partnership in defence against the growing Soviet menace. 26.10.2003 1932

"Events in Europe proved critical in directing the attention of defense planners away from the idea of Commonwealth defence," John Baylis explained. "The (communist) coup in Czechoslovakia (February 1948) and the Berlin crisis in 1948 finally convinced the Labour government that the Soviet Union was the potential enemy and that the greatest danger to British security lay in Europe.

"This conviction led Bevin to try to 'entangle' the United States in the defense of Europe and reestablish the 'special relationship' between Britain and America that had been built up during the Second World War..." (2)

Bevin's diplomacy led to the formation of NATO. With the US playing the lead role, NATO was America's first peacetime military alliance.

Only about a year earlier, however, Anglo-American relations had been strained by the McMahon Act of 1946 which ended bilateral cooperation in nuclear development (British scientists having worked with their American counterparts in the Manhattan project that produced the world's first nuclear explosives for the atomic bombing of Hiroshima and Nagasaki on August 1945). Subsequently, that nuclear partnership was restored nearly a decade later by the Atomic Act of 1954 (permitting the sharing of data on the external features of nuclear weapons) after Britain had successfully tested her first A-bomb at Monte Bello on 3 October 1952 and thereby joined the highly exclusive club of three nuclear powers.

Despite the strong Euro pull, and despite the increasingly threatening posture of the Soviets who exploded their first nuclear device in September 1949 (less than half a year after NATO's entry on the European scene), Britain, nevertheless, was not drawn totally towards Europe. 27.10.2003 0201

"Neither the Conservatives nor Labour intended to join a united Western Europe, a supra-national Europe. Britain's alliances with her continental neighbours (including historical rivals like France and Germany) were not exclusive: she valued her worldwide Commonwealth ties too highly," commented Grenville. (3)

The Commonwealth (postwar euphemism for old Empire, the obsolescence of which had been pronounced in the United Nations (UN) Declaration on National Independence of March 1943, requiring the colonial powers to liberate their colonies) was Britain's exclusive turf where she was pre-eminent and unchallenged by outsiders. But Britain's ties with the Commonwealth and her "special relationship" with the United States allowed General Charles de Gaulle to question her European identity and to veto her application to join the European Community in January 1963.

Britain was perhaps too psychologically attached as well as financially linked to Empire to pay much heed to the letter and spirit of the Atlantic Charter which President Franklin Roosevelt and Prime Minister Winston Churchill had signed on 14 August 1941, nearly three months before Pearl Harbour and the Japanese invasion of Malaya (and of Singapore about two months later).

Roosevelt interpreted the Atlantic Charter as a commitment to universal decolonisation "to free people all over the world from a backward colonial policy". And he declared the end of the age of imperialism (slightly a year and a half ahead of the UN's clarion call for the liberation of all colonial territories).

The American president should be remembered for his commitment to liberate 1.1 billion "brown people in the East" and help them achieve independence although the political emancipation took place after his death in 1945.

After granting independence to India and Pakistan in 1947, which was in partial fulfillment of the Atlantic Charter, and which provided substantial and timely relief from sub-continental financial, political and other responsibilities, Britain put on hold its schedule for decolonisation for as long as nearly a decade. (4) 31.10.2003 2145

The 1943 UN Declaration on National Independence had, at least on principle, committed the colonial powers to the liberation of their colonies.

But, the considerable colonial assets overruled the calls for colonial liquidation or the political commitment to decolonisation.

Thus Britain banked on exploiting the natural resources of its colonies. Lasmar and Oliver have written: "Although it had imperial possessions stretching around the globe from Hong Kong to the Falkland Islands, Britain was bankrupt and in desperate need of the resources that many of its colonial holdings could provide. Following the Second World War the colonies were exploited by Britain on an unprecedented scale…" (5)

The Suez fiasco in late 1956 brought a sea change to Britain's view of her global role. According to Baylis, the resultant rupture in Anglo-American relations led to "a reappraisal of Britain's role in the world and the gradual movement toward concentrating its political, economic, and military effort on Europe". (6)

Following the humiliating withdrawal of their troops by Britain and France (both described by Nasser as "neither big nor strong") from the Suez Canal, both nations were stripped of their dominant roles in the Middle East. Only two Great Powers remained – the United States and the Soviet Union. The Suez crisis paved the way for the entry of the Soviets into this hot and volatile region where the Americans had to hold and maintain the balance of power.

With the 1957 Defence White Paper, Britain's defence policy went the whole hog on nuclear deterrence with the added stress on defending Europe. Macmillan's mind was fixed on developing an independent nuclear deterrent, but focused on protecting Europe (Great Britain in particular) against a Soviet attack.

At the same time, the Conservative government in London maintained its interest in preserving peace and stability in Southeast Asia (a major source of revenue) and remained strongly committed to SEATO, recently established on the American initiative to help contain militant communism in this turbulent part of the world. Thus the British stated their intention to keep substantial land, sea and air forces in Southeast Asia and the Far East. The British Far East Fleet would continue to be based in Singapore.

In the political field, the engine of decolonisation was re-started in the wake of the Suez fiasco. After Nigeria and Malaya gained their independence in 1957, Cyprus became an independent republic in 1959 after the eruption of violence in 1955.

Following the independence of Sierra Leone and Tanzania in 1961, the freedom train kept rolling on the African continent. Uganda became independent in October 1962, Kenya and Zanzibar in December 1963 shortly after the formation of Malaysia in mid-September that year.

In the British Caribbean, Jamaica and Trinidad became independent on August 1962.

To the considerable credit of Macmillan (whose main concern was cultivating the "special relationship" with the US, leaving the center stage to Washington, to quote Kissinger, "while seeking to shape the drama from behind the curtains"), much the greater part of the decolonisation and dismantling of the obsolescent Empire took place when he was in overall charge as Conservative prime minister (1957-63) in London.

The year 1964 brought independence to Malawi and Zambia. And in 1966, Guyana and Barbados became independent.

Between 1957 and 1967 the "winds of change" came to forty African countries which became independent from Great Britain, Belgium, and France. (7)

Since the late 1950s, Britain had been preparing for her return to the European fold although she had initially in 1958 refrained from joining the proposed Common Market in Western Europe.

On 10 August 1961, Britain applied to join the European Economic Community (EEC), later referred to as the European Community (EC). Earlier on 27 July, Cabinet had agreed to make a formal application to accede to the Treaty of Rome.

Macmillan wrote in his memoirs: "Britain might serve Commonwealth and world interests more efficiently if she were linked with Europe than if she remained isolated, doomed to a diminishing power in a world in which her relative wealth and strength were bound to shrink." (8)

Before making any formal application, Commonwealth governments would be consulted "as confidentially but as fully as possible".

To Robert Menzies, Australian statesman and prime minister (1939-41 and 1949-66) whom he described as "an old and trusted friend", Macmillan wrote a special paper summarizing the past history.

He emphasized: "…The main points were that the E.E.C. was developing into an effective political and economic force, and the Community had acquired a dynamic of its own.

"When we decided at the end of 1955 not to take part in the negotiations for the establishment of the E.E.C. we were influenced by two considerations, in both of which we were to be proved wrong. We thought they would not succeed – or, if they did, that we could work out a satisfactory association. We realized now that it was all-or-nothing and, if we went ahead, it would be in order to discover what 'all' involved…" (8)

When he opened the Commonwealth Prime Ministers' Conference on 10 September 1962, Macmillan reiterated that "we are Europeans, and can play a leading part in Europe."

And he went on to say: "Now it is quite true that in the latter part of the 19th century and the first half of the 20th century (subconsciously referring to the glory years of Empire) we have sometimes tried to ignore the continent of Europe.

But we have never in reality been able to insulate ourselves from developments only 20 miles away. The fact that our people from this small island had spread themselves to other continents and throughout the seven seas made it a tempting delusion that we had ceased to be Europeans..." (9)

Kissinger has written that by the late 1950s, Great Britain could no longer view Europe from a distance, but "only 20 miles away" to quote Macmillan.

"Macmillan was propelled to 10 Downing Street by the Suez debacle, the watershed event in his country's declining global role. Macmillan played his hand with great panache but not without a certain reluctance," Kissinger wrote.

"As a former Chancellor of the Exchequer (his previous job), he knew all too well that Great Britain's economy was on the decline, and that its military role would never match the vast arsenals of the nuclear superpowers (the US and the Soviet Union)..." (10)

Although Macmillan reversed the policy of aloofness from Europe and applied for membership in the European community, Kissinger commented: "Yet, despite the Suez debacle (in which the US intervened to oppose the Anglo-French military invasion and end the crisis), Macmillan's foremost concern remained the cultivation of Great Britain's "special relationship with the United States..." (11)

But, on 20 January 1963, President Charles de Gaulle (with whom Macmillan had powwowed a month and a half earlier at Rambouillet) vetoed Britain's entry into the Common Market.

Britain had to wait for another ten years before making it to Brussels in 1973 (then under the Conservative premiership of Edward Heath, 1970-74), not long after the departure of de Gaulle (1890-1970).

Macmillan recalled: "I was able to be present ten years later at the signing of the Treaty in Brussels, by which Britain and three (*sic*) other powers (the Irish Republic and Denmark) were admitted to membership of the European Community, with the full approbation of the French Government. The wheel had come full circle." (12)

Following the change of government in London and the succession of Harold Wilson on October 1964, the Labour cabinet overhauled both military and foreign policies towards a very strong European orientation.

Baylis commented that the British forces were overstretched by the mid-1960s, "by the attempt to retain an independent global and limited-war capability" without a corresponding increase in necessary funding. This led to the readjustment of strategic thinking in the Wilson government between 1966 and 1968.

Baylis wrote: "Henceforth although Britain was to retain a small capability for limited extra-European operations, the main focus of attention was to be Europe, when it was recognized that both Britain's conventional and nuclear forces must be integrated more effectively into an alliance framework. The key word in British strategy was to be *interdependence* rather than *independence*. Increasingly the total-war theme (*a la* 1957 Defence White Paper) was played down and the emphasis placed on deterring Soviet aggression in Europe by coordinating nuclear and conventional components into an effective general and limited-war alliance strategy." (13)

Baylis also noted: "The independent nature of the deterrent was played down, but the decision was taken to continue with the nuclear force despite the feeling of many in the (Labour) party that it should be abandoned." (14)

With a financial crisis on his hands in 1966, Wilson decided to make major cuts in the budget including defence, and Britain proposed in July 1967 to pack up and withdraw militarily from Singapore.

Wilson told Drysdale (1980) that "also we were trying to get into the Common Market; we were looking at things in a more European and a NATO context. So for all these reasons it was quite clear we were going to draw in our horns." (15)

By the end of October 1971, most of the British troops (over 26,000) had moved out from their bases and barracks in Singapore, leaving behind only a token force for another five years. The Far East Command ceased to exist at the end of October 1971.

The residual British military presence in Singapore was eventually phased out from September 1975 to March 1976 on the watch of Harold Wilson during his second premiership (1974-76).

The total military pull-out from Singapore completed the "Europeanisation" of British defence policy. The Singapore withdrawal was timed in sync with the superannuation of the British airborne nuclear deterrent in 1969 and induction of its seaborne successor with the commissioning of a quartet of "R" strategic nuclear submarines (October 1967-December 1969) – Resolution, Repulse, Renown, and Revenge. 13.11.2014 08:06

Between early 1963 (slightly over a month after the Kennedy-Macmillan meeting at Nassau in the aftermath of the Cuban missile crisis) and late 1965 (within the first year of Wilson's premiership), Singapore had lived through the most eventful and tumultuous period in its history.

In this brief but momentous period, Singapore had merged with Malaysia and thwarted the most serious Communist bid to capture power in 1963, and shortly afterwards gained its independence and sovereignty following its rather unceremonious separation from Malaysia on 9 August 1965.

NOTES CHAPTER THREE: DRAWING IN THE HORNS: MILITARY WITHDRAWAL FROM SINGAPORE

1. J.A.S. Grenville, **A History of the World in the Twentieth Century**, Massachusetts, 1994, p. 352

2. John Baylis, **Contemporary Strategy**, Volume 2, New York, 1987, p. 144

In **DIPLOMACY** (pp. 456-457), Kissinger has written: "...The Marshall Plan (the 1948-52 programme of U.S. economic assistance for reconstruction of Western Europe after World War II) was designed to get Europe on its feet economically. The North Atlantic Treaty Organization (NATO) was to look after its security.

"NATO was the first peacetime military alliance in American history. The immediate impetus for it was the communist coup in Czechoslovakia in February 1948. After the Marshall Plan was announced, Stalin accelerated communist control over Eastern Europe...

"The brutality of the Czech coup reawakened fears that the Soviets might sponsor other, similar takeovers – for example, by fostering a communist *coup d'etat* recognizing a new communist government and using military muscle to prop it up. Thus, in April 1948, several Western European countries formed the Pact of Brussels – a defensive pact designed to repel any forcible attempts to topple democratic governments. However, every analysis of the relative power positions indicated that Western Europe simply did not have sufficient strength to repel a Soviet attack.

"Thus, the North Atlantic Treaty Organization came into being as a way of tying America to the defense of Western Europe. NATO provided an unprecedented departure in American foreign policy: American, along with Canadian, forces joined Western European armies under an international NATO command. The result was a confrontation between two military alliances, and two spheres of influence along the entire length of the dividing line in Central Europe…"

Dr Henry Kissinger served as the US 50th Secretary of State (September 1973-January 77).

3. Grenville, p. 355

The idea of integrating Europe was anathema to de Gaulle who said at a press conference on 29 July 1963 that "France as such would have disappeared" in a "so-called supranational Europe…" He wanted France to lead Europe.

France was one of the original six who had subscribed to the 1958 Treaty of Rome, establishing the Common Market, formally the European Economic Community, shortly before de Gaulle became the first president of the Fifth Republic for over a decade (1959-69), during which he restored political and economic stability to his country.

4. Why did Britain free the vast Indian sub-continent on August 1947?

"In south Asia, India was a special case, imperiled but unconquered by Japan, consciously groomed for independence by an imperial administration anxious to escape from increasingly intractable problems of economic management, famine-fending, and inter-credal unrest," Felipe Fernandez-Armesto, author and history lecturer at Oxford University, has written in **MILLENNIUM: A History of the Last Thousand Years** (published by Simon & Schuster, New York, 1996, p.550).

"The agile solution contrived in 1947 – partition between Hindu-dominated and Muslim states, both of which remained on terms of amity with the retiring power – was applauded by an astonished world, despite inter-communal blood-letting that claimed half a million lives before the borders were stabilized..."

And, why was there a long pause in the process of decolonisation after the political emancipation of India and Pakistan?

In **British Imperialism: Crisis and Deconstruction, 1914-1990** (London, Longman, 1993, p.. 279), historians P.J. Hopkins and A.G. Cain have written: "Far from being abandoned after 1947, the empire was repositioned in Africa, Malaya, and, informally, the Middle East. These regions were sources of vital supplies; they contributed to the hard currency pool through dollar earnings; and they were all directly or indirectly under British control..."

5. Paul Lashmar and James Oliver, **BRITAIN'S SECRET PROPAGANDA WAR** (Gloucestershire, Sutton, 1998, p.84),

Why did the "anti-imperialist" US relent when Britain stopped to decolonise after 1947?

The two English journalists Lashmar and Oliver have commented (pp. 86-87): "While Britain's economic dependence on the empire had increased, colonial exploitation could not be easily squared with support for the United States's new world order, or the Labour Party's commitment to decolonization. However, with the beginning of the Cold War, American attitudes softened towards British colonialism and the British Empire was transformed into 'a bulwark against the Communist menace' (quoting historians Cain and Hopkins, **British Imperialism**).

"Indeed, according to Cain and Hopkins, 'Washington was persuaded, by a mixture of self-induced anxiety and skilful British diplomacy, that a friendly empire spanning the globe would be a useful ally in containing the threat to what was becoming known as the Free World…Liquidation was not on the agenda: the empire was to be given a shot in the arm rather than a shot in the head.'

"Not least to ensure the support of the United States, it became essential that challenges to British colonial rule should be understood within the right framework – that of a substantial Soviet and Communist threat rather than legitimate nationalist demands for an end to colonial rule…" 1.11.2003 1050

6. On the Suez fiasco in late 1956, Lashmar and Oliver have written (p.63): "In July 1956, (Gamel Abdul) Nasser (who became Egyptian president after the overthrow of King Farouk in July 1952) nationalized the Suez Canal Company, much to the fury of the British and the French, who began to threaten the Egyptian government. Nasser remained defiant. Without American support, the British and French hatched a plot. In November 1956 the Israeli Army launched an attack on Egypt as a pretext for the British and French to intervene to 'separate the combatants'. Their forces invaded the canal area. The result was worldwide condemnation and even dissent within the ruling Tory Party. Eventually, (Anthony) Eden resigned and his place (as British premier) was taken by Harold Macmillan. The British withdrew from Egypt in one of the last great fiascos of the empire…"

According to Eisenhower, strong American support for the United Nations ended hostilities in Egypt.

Emmet John Hughes, an adviser to Eisenhower in the 1952 and 1956 political campaigns and a Presidential assistant in the White House for one year of the first term, has observed that "the prologue to this crisis had entailed the chronic deterioration of Anglo-American relations —and the epilogue had consisted of the alarming expansion of Soviet influence throughout the Middle East." (**THE ORDEAL OF POWER**, New York, Atheneum, 1963, p. 340)

However, Kissinger has written that "the Suez crisis had marked America's ascension into world leadership." (**DIPLOMACY**, p. 548)

Britain's part in the Suez crisis increased her dependence on the US (then the sole superpower enjoying a preponderant nuclear superiority until the late 1960s).

Kissinger has written (p. 548): "Turning away from European unity, Great Britain opted for permanent subordination to American policy. Before Suez, Great Britain had already become well aware of its dependence on the United States, though it continued to conduct itself as a Great Power. After Suez, it interpreted the "special relationship" with America as a means of gaining maximum influence over decisions which were essentially made in Washington..."

7. On the momentum of decolonization in Africa generated in the wake of the 1956 Suez crisis and the hasty retreat of the imperialists in the late 1950s and 1960s, Felipe Fernandez-Armesto has written (**MILLENNIUM**, pp. 551-552): "Tunisia, Morocco, and the Sudan – "protected" territories never strictly under European sovereignty – were evacuated in the year of Suez. After that, the skirts of empire were lifted with indecent haste. France seemed unable either to stay or retreat in Algeria, trapped between the resistance of the natives and the fanaticism of the settlers. Realism settled the question in favour of withdrawal.

"All over British Africa, resistance heroes, mothballed in prison or disfavour, were spruced up by establishment valeting. The regalia of chieftaincy – the knob-headed canes, the fly-swatters, the leopard-skin caps – passed, in most cases, to adventitious leaders who came from bushland mission schools or the émigré middle class but rarely from the ranks of traditional rulers. Kwame Nkrumah, who led Ghana during a long transition to independence in 1957, had "PG" for "prison graduate" embroidered on his cap.

"Nineteen-sixty was the *annus mirabilis* of African independence, when fourteen new states – or "nations," as the fashionable jargon inappropriately said – came into being, including a vast swath of continuous territory from the northern Sahara to the River Zaire.

"Most winds of change seemed to blow into Africa from the outside. Democracy in Europe – still patchy and imperfect until after the Second World War – enfranchised constituencies doubtful of or hostile to imperialism, such as the British working class who "did not know the empire exists." American pressure bore down on imperialist clients. A wind from the north blew out of the cold war, as western governments tried tactics of moral hijack in the face of Russian competition, empowering native opposition movements in order to detach them from Soviet influence or control…"

8. Harold Macmillan, **At The End Of The Day 1961-63**, p. 5

To quote Kissinger again (**DIPLOMACY**, pp. 596-597): "Great Britain had rejected the Common Market when it had first been proposed…

"But by the late 1950s, Great Britain could no longer view Europe from a distance, as a place where British forces occasionally intervened to put down a would-be tyrant. Macmillan therefore reversed the policy of aloofness from Europe and applied for membership in the European Community. Yet, despite the Suez debacle, Macmillan's foremost concern remained the cultivation of Great Britain's "special relationship" with the United States.

"Great Britain did not consider itself as an exclusively European power. After all, its dangers had too often originated in Europe while its salvation had come from across the Atlantic Ocean. Macmillan did not accept the Gaullist proposition that European security would be enhanced by dissociation from the United States. When all was said and done, Great Britain was probably at least as ready to fight for Berlin as France, though its motive would have been not so much to vindicate the vague concept of allied occupation rights as to support America in its assessment that the global balance of power was being threatened.

"After Suez, France and Britain drew diametrically opposite conclusions from their humiliation at the hands of America. France accelerated its independence; Great Britain opted for strengthening the partnership with America…"

9. Macmillan, **At The End Of The Day**, p. 15

Established by the 1958 Treaty of Rome, the Western European economic association originally comprised the six nations of Belgium, France, West Germany, Italy, Luxembourg, and the Netherlands.

10. Kissinger, **DIPLOMACY**, p. 596

11. Ibid., p. 596

12. Macmillan, p. 530

13. Why did de Gaulle reject the British application for entry into the European Community?

According to Kissinger, Britain could challenge de Gaulle's perception of French dominance in Western Europe.

Kissinger has commented (**DIPLOMACY**, p. 616): "A disciple of Richelieu, he perceived France's dominant role in the European Community as being threatened by British entry, both because of the weight which Great Britain represented and due to its affinity with the United States."

The 17th century French statesman and cardinal, Richelieu (1585-1642) became the principal minister to King Louis XII and the virtual ruler of France (1624-42) who strengthened his country's role in Europe.

At their meeting on December 1963, Macmillan told de Gaulle that Britain already had "a considerable nuclear force." Britain had 280 nuclear warheads in 1963 (according to Robert Norris, noted American nuclear historian and statistician) when France had none although the French managed to acquire four the following year.

Kissinger has also commented: "Throughout his political life, de Gaulle had resisted the "special relationship" between America and Great Britain precisely because, in his view, it symbolized Great

Britain's status as a Great Power equal to that of the United States while reducing France to a secondary position…"

14. Baylis, pp. 157-158

15. Drysdale, **Singapore: Struggle for Success**, p. 401

CHAPTER FOUR

Act One: The First Communist Revolution In Singapore, 1945-50

With rampant unemployment, overcrowded living conditions, food shortage, widespread poverty, misery and deprivation, postwar Singapore appeared to be in the abject socio-economic state for an urban revolution in the orthodox Leninist mould.

Historian Mary Turnbull wrote that "most Singaporeans were preoccupied with the hardships of everyday living... Secret societies flourished..." (1)

The 1947 survey of the Social Welfare Department showed an appalling state of misery and chronic overcrowding among a population of close to one million in a small island of less than 250 square miles in area. Turnbull wrote: "Most were crowded in the inner city area, where the majority of households lived in one room or cubicle, and a quarter of the unskilled worker families had even less (living space)..." (2)

That year, the Communist strength peaked. The Singapore Communist Party had some three to four hundred members. (3)

When these comrades resurfaced after more than three years in the jungles at the end of World War II, they came back at a time when the Malayan Communist Party (MCP) was at its all-time psychological high. To many Chinese (though not the Malays and the Indians), these guerrilla fighters were freshly minted heroes. For, in the public imagination, had they not fought valiantly against the enemy during the Japanese Occupation (February 1942 to September 1945)?

On their prospects of capturing power, Richard Clutterbuck, a retired British general and a leading expert on terrorism, observed that "the Communists seemed to have a good chance of a quick victory in Singapore in 1945-7. Everything was in their favour at the time of the Japanese surrender. Their prestige was at its peak, and that of the British very low after their humiliation by the Japanese (in February 1942)..." (4)

David Marshall, Singapore's first elected chief minister (1955-56) recalled that popular respect for the MCP reached "a high peak" in 1945, which subsequently declined when they left the path of constitutional struggle in 1948 and took the road of armed struggle across the Causeway. (5)

The MCP (referred to as the CPM after 1963) spearheaded the anti-colonial struggle for self-government and eventual independence, in order to drive out the long-time imperialists, and to communize the country. As the only legal political party after the Second World War, the MCP (then under Loi Tek's leadership) had opted for constitutional struggle in Singapore.

And although the Communists (led by Chin Peng after March 1947) subsequently declared war on the colonial regime after it had crippled the militant labour movement in mid-1948, the terrorist activities of killer squads in the so-called Workers' Protection Corps on this small and circumscribed island paled into insignificance when compared with the armed struggle in the early period of the Communist insurgency on the Malayan mainland. 7.11.2003 0410 0829

Before its ban on July 1948 (a month after the declaration of a state of emergency in Malaya and Singapore), the MCP had a dual but parallel system of organization. The party maintained both open and secret organizations, with its members planted in the open cells of factories, schools and other front organizations, and with highly dedicated cadres operating in the secret cells of various trade unions and schools. The exposed members were generally regarded by their leaders as disposable or expendable in the Communist struggle.

The top party leaders (usually a handful or countable on one hand) were entrenched in the Singapore Town Committee (STC) headquartered at Queen Street in the heart of Chinatown. The STC had its links with the MCP Central Committee which had its HQ at Klyne Street in the heart of Kuala Lumpur's Chinatown in Malaya.

The STC was subordinate to the South Malaya Bureau (SMB) located in the jungle near Kluang in Johore, about 100 km north of Singapore. They communicated through a system of couriers, which of course was subject to disruption or even destruction by the intelligence operations of the Police Special Branch. (6)

In Singapore the Communists resorted to a dual track strategy in their bid to capture power: (1) the united front strategy via Communist-dominated political alliances, and (2) the control and politicization of the labour movement. One to call the political tune, and the other to pull the economic strings of the polity.

The Malayan Democratic Union (MDU), the first postwar indigenous political party formed on December 1945 by English-educated intellectuals of various races to end colonial rule and establish self-government as the first major political goal, became an open front organization for the MCP. But the MDU dissolved itself on 23 June 1948 when the colonial authorities declared "Emergency" (British euphemism for their strong-arm campaign against the Communist Party in Malaya and Singapore)

The left wing of the open MDU was later absorbed into the English-speaking section of the clandestine Anti-British League (ABL) which was created on September 1948 in the early period of the Emergency. The ABL had its cells in the trade unions and Chinese Middle schools. 7.11.2003 0939

Dennis Bloodworth, a veteran journalist with the London *Observer* posted in Singapore since 1956, wrote: "The MDU had maintained liaison with the official Town Office of the CPM, which was in contact with openly declared communist militants among workers and students. But the ABL was controlled by a hidden 'Town Committee' of the Party, which actuated an undercover nerve system of secret cells in trade unions and schools." (7)

This shadow organization was the political powerhouse of the Communist underground, headed by a brilliant but humble Raffles College graduate – Eu Chooi Yip, himself a shadowy figure.

The usual Communist tactics and tricks of the political trade including agitprop (agitation/propaganda) were used to spread the Marxist gospel, subvert existing organizations, agitate the masses, provoke and confront the colonial authorities in public.

The Communist control of the trade unions enabled the open front leaders to wield the powerful strike weapon. They also used their political connections to organize mass rallies and build up public support for their stand on controversial issues.

Labour unrest was initiated as early as October 1945 when 7,000 dockers staged a successful strike for higher wages. This sparked a chain reaction among striking bus workers, hospital employees, firemen and even cabaret girls.

Unemployment was rife, food was scarce and the cost of living kept rising. On December 1945, 6,000 workers demonstrated to protest reduced rice rations and to demand higher wages. The authorities clamped down on all public meetings and processions held without a licence.

Towards the end of January 1946, more than 150,000 workers (about half of the working population) in Singapore joined in a two-day strike over the detention of Soon Kwong, the general secretary of the Selangor MPAJU (Malayan People's Anti-Japanese Union). The men downed tools and all, and people transport ground to a halt. (8)

Denouncing the controversial establishment on 1 April 1946 of the Malayan Union which severed Singapore administratively and politically from the Malayan peninsula, the Communists organized a mass rally of 20,000 (a number which the MCP could readily summon at a snap of its fingers) at Farrer Park (a popular venue) to demand self-government for Malaya as well as equality for all who made it their home. (9) 7.11.2003 2020

In its public statement, the MCP declared: "Our Party is of the opinion that the political framework of Malaya (including Singapore) should be decided in full compliance with the Atlantic Charter (of 1941) and the United Nations Charter (Declaration on National Independence of March 1943)..." (10)

Anticipating that the colonial authorities would resort to the new labour regulations to curb the powerful trade unions and destroy Communist leadership of the labour movement before banning the MCP, Chin Peng said the Central Committee members at their crucial meeting in Singapore on 21 March 1948 unanimously agreed "in principle" of "taking to the jungles" although the timing and strategy of their war path would be decided later. (11)

To break the Communist strong hold on the labour movement, the colonial authorities started registering trade unions under the 1940 Trade Union Ordinance. Subsequently, more drastic legislation to curb Communist manipulation of the trade unions was introduced in mid-1948, only a few days before the declaration of so-called "Emergency" on 19 June in Malaya and four days later in Singapore. And within a fortnight, many officers of de-registered unions had fled to the jungles to take part in the shooting war across the Causeway. (12)

Emergency regulations were imposed, of which the power of detention without trial was to prove the most effective in culling and crippling the Communist leadership in Singapore.

On 23 July 1948 the MCP was declared illegal and banned. By then most of the known Communists had taken to the jungle while many others had been pulled in by the police.

The Communist organization was shattered following the incarceration of leading and senior comrades and virtual destruction of the Town Committee in December1950. Thus ended the first episode (Act One) of the postwar revolution in Singapore at a time when the Communist insurgency peaked on the Malayan mainland.

Clutterbuck recorded in his book: "Their arrest left the MCP in Singapore leaderless through the most critical period of the Malayan Emergency, and it was not until 1954 that it resumed any significant part in the revolution." (13)

By then the back of the armed struggle in Malaya had been broken, and Chin Peng and other Central Committee members of the MCP had moved to their sanctuary in South Thailand.

Comrade Guo, one of those picked up by a Special Branch detective in Singapore's Chinatown on 5 December 1950, said: "The whole Town Committee of the Party was smashed, and we were all rounded up by the British." (14)

But, was the STC really destroyed?

Eu Chooi Yip (who was Comrade Guo's superior) told Goh Keng Swee, his old college mate, that "these (detained) are not the real leaders; the real leaders have not shown themselves." (15)

Goh was to become Singapore's Finance Minister and Deputy Prime Minister. Eu was the Communist mastermind and the underground big boss. The police had never been able to catch him.

According to Bloodworth, Eu was one of the only three cadres of significance on the Town Committee who managed to escape from the police when it was broken up towards the end of 1950. Eu continued to operate from nearby Rhio islands to the south of Singapore. Eu managed to maintain regular contact with the South Malaya Bureau in neighbouring Johore, through a chain of female couriers.

Of the other two senior comrades who evaded the police, one was a young journalist whom Lee Kuan Yew called the "Plen" when both of them held secret meetings in the late 1950s.

The other was Ng Meng Chiang with many aliases including "Comrade D", who was to lead the underground student movement and prepare the young revolutionaries for another big confrontation in the heady mid-1950s. But after four years of mixing socialism and bourgeois social life (including close encounters and liaisons with female comrades), he was later replaced by the "Plen" in the underground. (16).

According to C.C. Too, the psychological warfare expert in Kuala Lumpur, the shadow Town Committee remained intact and operated safely from Rhio. From this offshore sanctuary (Eu's "Yenan") in Indonesian territory, the top strategist for the Communist struggle in Singapore continued to call the shots until the mid-1960s.

To the proletariat or working class in Singapore, the main basic issue was bread and butter (which Lee Kuan Yew was later to equate with local politics).

The ballot box was something new, foreign and unappealing to them. And to put it more precisely in the local context, the gut issue was staple rice, not something as abstract and unknown as hitherto intangible constitutional and political progress which the British colonialists and the local Western-oriented politicians tried to promote on a gradual basis.

In the early 1948 election to the Legislative Council, the first in postwar Singapore, only 23,000 voters registered out of a potential electorate of more than 200,000 (one-fifth of the total population). Although the Chinese represented slightly over 75% of the population, more than half of the candidates (eight out of the 15) were Indians. And for the six elected seats, three of the successful candidates were Indians and only one was a Chinese.

As instructed by the MCP leaders who had decided in late March 1948 to turn to armed struggle, the MDU stayed away from the first elections to the Legislative Council in Singapore held on 20 March 1948. The electoral boycott was said to be a mistake, although it is hard to surmise the impact of an MDU debut.

Why did the Communists fail in Singapore and Malaya?

Although Eu Chooi Yip was known to be brilliant, geography (the terrain of a small island of some 600 sq km with very little forest cover) was fundamentally not to his advantage. Moreover, he waged a political war against a much more powerful and resourceful enemy fully determined to stay put and not yield to any pressure.

The Communist leaders had no game plan to achieve military victory in Malaya. They forgot or ignored one of the basic instructions in the 2,500-year-old Chinese military treatise *The Art of War*: "Careful planning will lead to success and careless planning to defeat. How much more certain is defeat if there is no planning at all!"

The MCP leadership remained chronically divided even after Loi Tek's removal in March 1947 for alleged treacherous dealings with the Japanese military during World War II and with the British intelligence in the early postwar years.

Moreover, intra-party communications had more or less broken down by late 1952 or early 1953. According to Chin Peng, his courier system with his number two Yeung Kuo, Deputy Secretary General who was operating in the heartland from a jungle camp near Kajang in Selangor, had completely broken down.

Even with their strong Chinese base, the Communists lacked overall popular support for the necessary critical mass for victory. The Chinese community was politically bifurcated between the MCP and the KMT (Kuomintang) camps, between the largely downtrodden Chinese-educated and the comparatively better off English-educated, with many ignorantly or knowingly in between or outside of the great divide.

Moreover, the conspicuous lack of vital Malay support had doomed the Communist cause on the Malayan mainland right from the start.

The great 6th century B.C. Chinese military strategist Sun Tzu (600-520 BC) advised: "Do not go to war if you do not have the support of the people."

Although harsh socio-economic conditions in postwar Singapore were conducive to their political struggle, the Communists did not have enough popular support to generate sufficient heat to shake, rattle and rock the colonial authorities. And despite their favourable standing among the Chinese community, by and large they failed to politicize, mobilize and convert the Chinese-educated masses to their revolutionary cause. 12.11.2003 0700 15.11.2014 05:42

ψψψψψ

When the curtain came down on Act One (the first attempt to capture power through constitutional means), the Communists were a spent force in Singapore. Turnbull commented that the MCP had passed its "golden chance" in postwar Singapore. Clutterbuck said that they had missed a good opportunity to bid for power.

Turnbull wrote: "The party defeated its own purposes partly because of its precipitate and blatant bid for power in Singapore in 1945-6 which put the government on its guard and precluded more insidious infiltration, and partly because the years of immediate post-war economic hardship in Malaya coincided with a time when Russia was pre-occupied with her own internal reconstruction..." (17)

The local Communists had only themselves to blame, according to G.G. Thompson, another expert on Communism. He remarked that their own failings brought them to defeat, rather than clever policy on the part of the government.

Although the socio-economic ills in postwar Singapore provided a conducive background for the breeding of a generation of revolutionaries, political consciousness was however lacking among the Chinese masses.

For political apathy prevailed in the postwar scene. While the Chinese majority were more concerned with making ends meet, the businessmen among the community leaders were engaged in making money, with little or no interest in local politics.

Moreover, it should also be noted, that the Communists in China were still fighting for the seat of power in Peking and control of the entire country in an all-out civil war with the Kuomintang forces until their final victory and conquest of the Chinese mainland towards the end of 1949.

Apart from ideological and political support as well as moral, the Communist leaders in both Moscow and Peking were in no position to offer either financial or material assistance to their struggling comrades in Malaya, Singapore and elsewhere in Southeast Asia.

While tackling the problems of postwar reconstruction, Moscow was soon to be involved in imposing its iron will on Eastern Europe starting with the Soviet-sponsored Communist coup in Czechoslovakia on February 1948, as well as being embroiled in contention with the US in the nascent Cold War.

Peking was to intervene militarily in late 1950 in the three-year Korean War (1950-53). By the time the Korean conflict ended on July 1953, military defeat was staring Chin Peng in the face while he was on his "long march" to seek a haven and refuge in Sadao in South Thailand.

But, Eu Chooi Yip was planning to stage another revolution in Singapore about three years after his initial rout towards the end of 1950.

7 pages 2,669 words 12.11.2003 1950 13.11.2003 1827 14.11.2014 06:50

NOTES CHAPTER FOUR: The First Communist Revolution in Singapore 1945-50

1. Turnbull, **A History of Singapore 1819-1975**, p. 232

   In **THE TIGER AND THE TROJAN HORSE** (p. 16), Bloodworth has written on the postwar period: "The war had left Singapore a hungry, crowded, dirty, sick and lawless city in which hardly anything worked except a bribe. The island now had to feed a million souls, including nearly 100,000 squatters, and there was a desperate shortage of clothing and rice and rooms – one official report spoke of cubicle twelve feet square that 'housed and slept sixteen persons' as 'nothing exceptional'.

   The cost of living had quadrupled in six years and some daily needs were sold for ten times as much before.

   "The poisoned atmosphere held promise for the communists, and they quickly began to reconstruct their pre-war General Labour Union. There were no more than 300 Party cadres in Singapore, but it took only a handful of well-placed agitators to bring out the mob on demand..."

2. Turnbull, p. 239

3. Clutterbuck, **Conflict and Violence in Singapore and Malaysia 1945-1983**, p. 59

4. Ibid., p. 45

   After only nine weeks of fighting (8 December 1941 to 15 February 1942), the Japanese invaders completed their military conquest of Malaya and Singapore (after eight days of battle). The invaders had been outnumbered by over three to one by the defenders on the British side in Singapore.

5. Marshall, **The Struggle for Nationhood 1945-1959**, p. 5

6. Clutterbuck, p. 69

7. Bloodworth, p.35

8. Clutterbuck, p.71

On the detention of Soon Kwong, Chin Peng has given his own account, giving it a much more serious significance than other observers (**MY SIDE OF HISTORY**, p. 143):

"If I had to pick a single act that initiated Malaya on the path to inevitable guerrilla warfare, it would have to be the October 12 (1945) arrest of senior Selangor communist, Soon Kwong, by the Royal Air Force police. Soon Kwong had worked with me in Ipoh and I knew him well. From his arrest can be traced a series of incidents that served to drag the colony (Malaya) inexorably towards violent rebellion. Soon Kwong was a widely respected CPM figure with an impressive wartime guerrilla record. The RAF provost involved had moved against him without any approval from, or even reference to, the BMA (British Military Administration).

"Whether or not Soon Kwong was involved, as alleged, in trying to extort a total of $300,000 from a known

Chinese collaborator with the Japanese was really of no consequence....

"As a matter of historical record, I am satisfied Soon Kwong detained Chan (Sau Meng) and extorted money from him as charged. But it is also my view that Chan got away lightly. Had we seized him for his profiteering ways during the (Japanese) occupation we would certainly have eliminated him..."

There's a vituperative description of Soon Kwong, the secret MPAJ chief, in Lim Cheng Leng's book **THE STORY OF A PSY-WARRIOR: TAN SRI DR. C.C. TOO** (pp. 67 69):

The late Too, then a young man of 25, had a meeting with Soon Kwong in the presence of two American OSS officers in Kuala Lumpur shortly before the arrest of the Communist chief. Too described him as "a shallow, conceited, arrogant, egocentric and tyrannical demagogue..."

9. In **MY SIDE OF HISTORY**, Chin Peng has written (p. 181) that the CPM "took strong exception to the Malayan Union idea.

"We attacked, in particular, its citizenship proposals. They were too restrictive to the Chinese. We opposed its provisions for legislative and executive councils..." In a special press statement, the Communist Party declared that the councils "would be entirely under the supervision and control of the British Government and those bodies would not have the slightest tinge of democracy..." 13.11.2003 2156

10. Ibid., p. 161

11. According to Chin Peng, the fateful decision to switch to armed struggle was made by the Central Committee meeting at the Singapore HQ in Queen Street on 21 March 1948, after the MCP leaders had discussed the draft legislation (a stolen copy of which had been passed to a union official, a MCP member, in Kuala Lumpur) which would curb the labour movement and end the Communist control of the trade unions. Anticipating that the colonial authorities would then ban the MCP, the party leaders concluded that they "would have no option but to fight..." (p. 204).

Although Laurence Sharkey, Secretary General of the Communist Party of Australia, had earlier been consulted on how to deal with strikebreakers, Chin Peng has written that Sharkey did not advise them to take up arms. "I should make it clear that at no point during his address to the Central Committee did Sharkey urge us specifically to take up arms against the British," Chin Peng has written (p. 204). "What he said, however, was pivotal in its overall effect."

12. Bloodworth (p.30) has given the more generally accepted version of the start of the revolutionary 'armed struggle' in Malaya: "It could be said to have begun three months before (the declaration of Emergency) in March 1948 when Chin Peng opened a session of the central executive committee of the CPM in Singapore, at which the guest speaker was the Australian Communist Party leader, Lawrence Sharkey. Having first scarified the unblessed memory of Lai Tek for his soft line with the imperialists,

Sharkey preached an end to constitutional dalliance and the onset of bloody insurrection, citing the line laid down by the Soviet theoretician Andrei Zhdanov six months earlier.

"Zhdanov had declared that with the outbreak of the cold war, communist parties must assume the leadership of national liberation movements everywhere in order to mobilize them against their imperialist oppressors and in support of the Soviet Union. It was a call to revolution in the East to destroy the economy of the West; it had been noisily endorsed a month before at a regional conference in Calcutta of the World Federation of Democratic Youth – one of the most active of Soviet marionettes – from which Sharkey had just come, and it put the authentic stamp of the Cominform on the incipient Malayan uprising..."

In May 1943, Stalin disbanded the Comintern, the Communist International, the Communist vanguard vehicle of world revolution.

It was succeeded by the Cominform, the formal grouping of worldwide communist parties, the formation of which was announced in a speech on September 1947 by Andrei Zhdanov, once considered Stalin's closest collaborator. 14.11.2014 07:23

In **British Imperialism: Crisis and Deconstruction, 1914-1990** (p. 280), historians P.J. Cain and A.G. Hopkins have pointed out that in the postwar period a bankrupt Britain resorted to the use of force to maintain its control of resource-rich colonies like

Malaya and Kenya, where "coercion tended to be the first resort of policy. The bogey of Communism was invoked, where it was not already present, and this surfaced in the early stages of the Cold War to legitimize the use of force."

Lashmar and Oliver have written (p. 84) that the job of British propagandists was to spin the anti-guerrilla war in Malaya as a battle against the worldwide Communism. 13-14.11.2003 0106

13. Clutterbuck, p. 71

Chin Peng (pp. 278-279) has written on the Police raids against the MCP's infrastructure in Singapore:

"Communications links with Singapore and my Pahang headquarters were operating effectively at the time (around 1950) and I was getting updated reports of the actions being taken by the colonial authorities against English-educated local intellectuals "Most of the victims of this period of suppression had joined our ranks after the Emergency declaration (June 1948). Some had come to our fold via the Anti-British League. Some, considered reliable by our Singapore underground, had been inducted into Party membership without reference to Headquarters.

"I was puzzled the British were moving against these people. All had been rather open in their public statements and would always have been regarded by us as likely to be exposed. Consequently, there was no possibility of them being moved into sensitive positions within the Party framework.

"I followed carefully the reports I was receiving from our Singapore underground. As the crackdown escalated I issued instructions for all those we categorized as 'open figures' – meaning members who had been publicly exposed – to withdraw to any convenient safe destination. Some left for Indonesia. Others went to China. It was decided that crossing the Causeway into Malaya could not be an option. Fighting there was far too intense and widespread…"

14. Bloodworth, p. 37

15. Ibid., p. 26

Chin Peng (p. 279) has described Eu Chooi Yip (ECY), an economics graduate from Raffles College (thus academically the most highly qualified Communist leader), as a senior Party member and a highly experienced propagandist.

16. Bloodworth, p. 72

Neither the "Plen" (Fang Chuang Pi) nor "Comrade D" (Ng Meng Chiang) has been mentioned in Chin Peng's book. Both Fang (made famous or almost legendary by Lee Kuan Yew) and Ng (almost romanticized by Clutterbuck) were important Communist leaders in Singapore.

17. Turnbull, p. 237

In **MEMOIRS** (pp. 49-50), the former Soviet president Mikhail Gorbachev has written of postwar Russia:: "The country was rising from the ruins after the tragic war… Life was hard for my country. In fact, it was not life, rather a struggle to survive. In wartime people knew that they had to save their motherland. And they believed that after the war and after victory, a decent life would be ahead for us. But nothing much changed after the war, especially during the initial post-war years.

"There was nothing but hard labour again, and the belief that once reconstruction was complete, we would finally be able to lead a normal life. Hope inspired the most laborious, humiliating work, instilling it with a meaning and helping us to endure all hardships…"

The immediate postwar years of 1946-47 also saw the seeding of the Cold War. Moreover, Russia was more concerned with developments nearer home and consolidating its hold on Eastern Europe.

Although Zhadanov, Stalin's right-hand man, could have passed on the so-called Moscow "directive" for armed struggle to the representatives of Asian Communist Parties at their Calcutta meetings on February 1948, Moscow could not provide any financial or material assistance to the Asian comrades.

Chin Peng (p. 247) has written: "…I never sought Russian aid and no Russian, or agent of Moscow, ever approached me personally, or my Party, with offers."

Subsequently, however, Peking provided financial assistance to the CPM for it to resume its armed struggle after its total defeat in the First Emergency (1948-60).

CHAPTER FIVE

Act Two: The Second Communist Revolution In Singapore, 1954-56

The 1954 unemployment rate was higher than at the time of the 1947 social survey, and most working-class families still lived in appalling conditions.

With only about 6% of the population in public housing flats in 1954, the great majority of the people continued to live in miserable hovels and cubicles. And those who dwelt on makeshift bunks in confined cubicles in densely populated Chinatown, Lee Kuan Yew called them "spacemen". He was referring, not to outer space (which made the headlines when on 12 April 1961 Soviet cosmonaut Yury Gagarin became the first man to orbit the earth in his spacecraft Vostok-1). but to terrestrial living space where these people hired by shifts "a little space in the cubicles of Chinatown for their bunks."

When the British colonists returned to Singapore at the end of World War II, they rebuilt their great bastion to protect their national interests in this strategic area of the world. Although the United Nations had called on the colonial powers to liberate their colonies about two and a half years before the end of World War II, and the US and its allies including Britain had agreed in principle to grant national independence, British attachment to Malaya and Singapore was considerably strengthened by financial considerations as they continued to contribute substantially to the coffers in London.

In the event, the colonial authorities dragged their feet in the constitutional/political field. Moreover, they displayed a lack of urgency, sensitivity and effectiveness in addressing the major issues affecting the livelihood and welfare of the Chinese majority – including their rights to citizenship, education and employment. These fundamental human issues were left to fester – and to further alienate the non-English-educated and foreign (China)-born in the seething Chinese community Although automatic registration boosted the electorate from 75,000 in 1954 to 300,000 (most of them Chinese-educated) for the 1955 general election, more than 200,000 remained "aliens" in their country of domicile -- disenfranchised without a citizenship certificate and a registered vote. 17.11.2003 1015

The influential Chinese Chamber of Commerce had started campaigning for citizenship to be extended to these long-term residents who were not British subjects. They had to wait until 1958 for the enfranchisement of over 200,000 alien-born Chinese.

The Rendal commission, which was appointed in 1953 to further the constitutional process towards self-government, denied citizenship rights to about 380,000 Chinese (about one-third of Singapore's population in 1953). Nearly a quarter million (223,000) were of voting age.

The Citizenship Ordinance in 1957 was to beef up the number of Chinese voters by 260,000 – nearly half of the total electorate of 587,787 for the scheduled general election in 1959. (2)

In the tumultuous 1950s, the Chinese community remained obdurately split between the English-educated minority and the Chinese-educated majority. The English-educated were seen to be favoured by the colonial masters with regard to the wherewithal of a decent existence, particularly education, citizenship, and employment opportunities.

Turnbull wrote: "The mass of Chinese blamed their troubles on the colonial regime and resented the privileged position of the English-educated. This was ideal ground for communism and the new generation of militant young student leaders set out to harness the labour movement to their anti-imperialist cause..." (3)

Dr. T.N. Harper, Cambridge historian, wrote: "...Student politics was fuelled by a wider sense of exclusion for the Chinese-educated with a colonial society in which fluency in English was the route to employment and advancement. It was underpinned by resentment of the privileges of the Anglophone Chinese.

"Yet within the Chinese community, graduates of Chinese middle schools were themselves something of an elite. In Singapore in 1954, only seven per cent of manual and low-paid white-collar workers were graduates of middle schools. This relative status, often combined with their participation in the world of work, created an easy bridge from student politics to positions of leadership within the labour movement.

"The student movement honed the organizational and oratorical skills of men such as Lim Chin Siong, and created a platform on which to employ them, especially in the campaign against registration for national service (May 1954)..." (4)

When Lee Kuan Yew first plunged into the political mainstream, he knew he must swim with the Chinese majority or else he would not make it at all.

Bloodworth wrote: "From the outset it was clear to him that his new party (the PAP formed on 23 October 1954) must identify itself with the Chinese Chinese, its leaders walking among them in open-neck shirts, not just staring out at them uncomprehendingly through the windows of shiny limousines..." (5)

But it was important, not only to dress and look like the Chinese proletariat, but also to talk the same language. Thus Lee had to learn to speak Mandarin first and Hokkien dialect. He mastered Malay. There was talk that he also picked up Tamil or a smattering of it. (6)

Across the Causeway, the back of the Communist insurgency was broken by 1954. Even before the turn of the tide in the jungle war, the MCP Central Committee had earlier issued its landmark October 1951 directive to switch the Communist struggle from wanton terrorism (what the Communist leader Mao Tse-tung abjured in guerrilla warfare) to a political offensive among the masses. This was a signal to the comrades in Singapore to return to the political sphere of urban revolution, although it took them a few years to recoup and reorganize after the dislodgement of the Town Committee leadership in 1950.

Following the Communist victory in China in late 1949, the call of the New China became increasingly irresistible to the disaffected Chinese-educated youths in Singapore. Mao Tse-tung, rather than Marx or Lenin, henceforth provided the main inspiration although the fresh Communist bid for power in Singapore continued to rely on Leninist methods of infiltration, subversion, manipulation and control of mass organizations.

With the imminent collapse of its armed struggle on the Malayan mainland, a number of leading cadres of the MCP had by 1954 worked their way back in Singapore to take advantage of a so-called "revolutionary situation". This entailed the resuscitation of the classical Leninist strategy of the open united front in the political arena.

David Marshall, Singapore's first chief minister (April 1955-June 1956), recalled: "The Communists were not interested in our efforts to liberalize trade union laws and work towards self-government. With the possibility of real power for themselves in the offing their aim was to create chaos and capture power through front organizations – riots were to be the means and workers and students the tools in their oft-repeated strategy…" (7) 17.11.2003 2120

The Rendal Constitution came into force in early 1954. As it was seen to be a vehicle for catapulting the English-educated blue-eyed boys of the British in the Progressive Party to the fore in the 1955 general election, the other parties rightly poured scorn on this colonial stratagem to prolong the stay of colonialism. It was also the old dirty trick of divide and rule. Marshall decried it as "a suave political ploy" to perpetuate imperialist rule. (8)

As recorded in the 45th anniversary publication of the PAP (published November 1999): "In Singapore, the desire to strike against empire was felt mainly among the Chinese-educated whose pride swelled at the triumphant revolution in China, and among a small group of English-speaking young men and women (referring to the founding members of the PAP) who did not identify with the lightweight opportunistic parties that were content to continue doing the colonial masters' bidding…"

D. M.K. Rajakumar wrote, with great insight: "… The victory of the Communists in China galvanized Chinese emotions. In the rest of Asia, it was regarded as a victory against Western imperialism, an end to a century of humiliation. Finally, 'China had stood up', said Mao Tse Tung, and his words resonated throughout Asia.

"The Communists in Singapore rode this wave of patriotic pride among young Chinese in Singapore, among young workers and students. More than half of the population of Singapore was under 18 years of age, bulging into a 20 to 30 year old economically active population that was becoming politically conscious.

"As elsewhere in Asia, they wanted the civic rights that were being won by the people of Western nations. They wanted a share of the freedoms that were said to have been earned by the sacrifices made in World War II.

"The conflict in Singapore became brutal once it was seen as part of the fight the British were waging in the global struggle between the West and the Communist states. The internal struggle was between the Chinese educated majority and the small English educated elite, for the control of the destiny of Singapore when the British left…" (9)

15.11.2014 06:46

Three new political parties emerged on the scene. They were the Labour Front which Marshall led to an unexpected victory in the April 1955 election, the People's Action Party (PAP) which took off on a pair of contrary wings (with the English-educated leaders like Lee Kuan Yew and Dr Toh Chin Chye on the right wing and the Chinese-educated prominent pro-communists and leftists like student and union leaders Fong Swee Suan and Lim Chin Siong on the left wing), and the Democratic Party. The last was a conservative party formed by an influential section of the Chinese Chamber of Commerce.

The outcome of the 1955 election was not what the British had wanted, but they were not entirely unhappy about it since no one party gained a dominant position. Marshall could only put up a minority government, having won only 10 out of the 25 elected seats in the Legislative Assembly. He became Singapore's first chief minister and for all his bombast, eloquence, and high legal standing, the colonial authorities granted him but meager respect.

The PAP won three seats. Taking part in this election was not to win, the party said, but to gain a significant number of seats "so as to show up the rottenness of the system (with the new Rendel Constitution) and to build up for the next election." 18.11.2003 1010

April 1955 also marked another milestone event with the holding of the Bandung conference in Indonesia, which came out with its 10-point declaration on world peace and cooperation.

On August 1955, the first general election in Malaya saw the pro-independence Alliance Party rise to power and take centre stage in the future development of the multi-racial and polyglot country.

December 1955 witnessed the staging of the peace talks between the newly elected leaders of Malaya and Singapore with the MCP leadership headed by Chin Peng. After four "very frustrating" sessions (to use Chin Peng's words), neither side got what it wanted.

However, Tunku Abdul Rahman went on to London and got what he wanted – independence for Malaya – and on a platter, as they used to say at that time. But Marshall (the one who spoiled the Baling show in Chin Peng's view) did not get what he wanted (independence for Singapore including full control of internal security) at the first constitutional conference held in London on May 1956, and he resigned as chief minister.

As for Chin Peng, he admitted that the military outlook was gloomy for the MCP; the political justification for taking up arms for the country's independence from the British authorities dissolved historically in the midnight air, to the stirring strains of the new national anthem being played with the raising of the Malayan flag for the first time to mark the end of a century and a half of colonialism in Malaya on 31 August 1957.

To Chin Peng's considerable dismay, independence was accompanied by the disintegration of his guerrilla force in the depths of the Malayan jungles. And by his own admission, the communication lines of the Communist HQ at Sadao in South Thailand to the Communist Command in Southern Malaya "had all been severed."

Nonetheless, the political outlook was more favourable for the Communists across the Causeway. Having wormed their way back into the political mainstream, the highly resilient and resourceful comrades regained the high ground in the anti-colonial struggle in Singapore.

The inauguration of the PAP in late October 1954 had been timely, if also fortuitous, as this spunky new party had opened its main entrance to the Left. "Mr Lee and the other prime movers had a tacit understanding that the new party would admit into its ranks the Communists and left-wing unionists to mount a united front in their fight for independence through merger with Malaya," the PAP has recorded. (10)

Their entry was to develop into an "insidious threat" from within the PAP. "From clandestine *kelong* meetings to smear campaigns and propaganda picnics, the Communists had, within months of the Party's formation, infiltrated the ranks and the Central Executive Committee," the PAP reported. (11)

If the Communist elements worked quietly but corrosively like white ants within the PAP, outside they were openly militant, strident, vociferous and violent. With their recapture of the student and labour movements, they were able to mobilize idealistic and rebellious Chinese-educated students as well as hard-boiled and hardened workers in episodic strikes and riots.

In May 1954, students from two Chinese high schools staged a violent demonstration against national service. As a follow-up, more than 2,500 students from eight Chinese middle schools locked themselves in overnight at the Chung Cheng High School.

In June, about 1,000 boys and girls carried out a three-week camp-in at the Chinese High School to protest the draft.

Bloodworth has written that it was in the wake of the bloody May 13 riot involving clashes between students and policemen that the Chinese-educated open front leaders Lim Chin Siong and Fong Swee Suan came to meet and know the English-educated and Cambridge-trained lawyer Lee Kuan Yew before the formation of the PAP.

Subsequently, the two sides joined up in a united front to battle colonialism, each using the other to capture power, the PAP to seek its political goal through the ballot box and the MCP through revolutionary civil unrest and violence on the streets of Singapore (though not through armed struggle, a futile pursuit which on the Malayan mainland was soon to fold up in dismal failure).

In the Hock Lee bus strikes which began in late April 1955, thousands of students from Chinese middle schools turned out in support of the strikers.

On 5 May Lee Kuan Yew said what's better left unsaid: "If I had to choose between colonialism and communism, I would vote for communism." Not a very wise choice between two evils, it seems.

Bloodworth has written that "exactly one week later, the Hock Lee riot exploded, spattering blood across the streets of the outer city." (12) Four people were killed in a hot and inflammable night of rioting.

Marshall recalled: "Within three months of taking office, it seemed clear to us that communism was gaining rapid ground with our workers and Chinese youth. Urgent measures had to be taken to counter this momentum if democracy were to have a chance – we were dealing with a runaway horse whom we could not stop but had to defect to the right road…" (13)

Was it a horse, as perceived by Marshall? A Trojan horse? Or, was it a tiger? Like Marshall, even the PAP leaders weren't sure when they first came to associate with the political animal on centre stage.

"Horse? Tiger? The truth was that they simply had not understood the nature of the beast," Bloodworth commented. (14)

There were 277 strikes in 1955, almost one every working day, causing a gross loss of nearly one million man-hours in industrial strife – seven times as many as in the previous year. (15)

But, as Turnbull has pointed out, only a third involved claims for better wages and working conditions, while the rest were politically inspired sympathy strikes or demands for the release of imprisoned trade union officials.

Lim Yew Hock, who took over as chief minister when Marshall stepped down on June 1956, resorted to the mailed glove to restore law and order. And to quote Governor Robert Black, Lim "held the ring." (16) 18-19.11.2003 0129

The October 1956 riots followed a protest against the dissolution of the Singapore Chinese Middle School Students' Union (registered on October 1955). These riots took 13 lives, and injured 127, and Lim Yew Hock ordered a purge of the militant leadership.

From September to November 1956, Lim detained 300 communist activists (the great majority of them from the communist united front, CUF) including their leaders Lim Chin Siong and Fong Swee Suan. He also banned nine front organizations including four student and labour unions and five cultural organizations. (17)

Subsequently, Lim Yew Hock was given the political equivalent of a golden handshake; the British gave him what they had not given Marshall – a constitution for Singapore's self-government. And the Colonial Secretary, the same man who had arranged for Lim to be Marshall's successor, indicated to him that his term in office would be up shortly.

Lennox-Boyd had prepared a new script for Singapore's political development. To quote Bloodworth: "For it was already clear that Lim was politically broken-winded after running as a 'British stooge' during the purges of 1956, and the torch must pass to Lee Kuan Yew…" (18)

Lim made history by quashing revolutionary violence on the streets of Singapore in 1956, but he sealed his own political fate (probably as scripted by the Colonial Secretary in London) for not being able to destroy militant communism on the island.

Act Two (the second Communist attempt to stage a revolutionary struggle) was played out before the close of 1956. Why did the Communists fail again?

G.G. Thompson, then in charge of the Singapore Government Information Service, told Clutterbuck that the failure lay with the open front (CUF) leadership, and that Lim Chin Siong failed primarily as a tactician in the revolutionary struggle.

Lim Chin Siong himself later admitted that he had completely misread the mood of the Chinese workers in 1954-56. They were pro-Chinese, rather than pro-Communist, and this rather subtle but critical difference affected the outcome of the revolutionary movement. (19)

With the strong backing of the police and the military, Lim Yew Hock proved his anti-revolutionary mettle and upheld the rule of law and order. But his tough action against the Communists (the great majority of them Chinese-educated Chinese) was to lead to his political downfall.

Down but not out, the militant force of the left was to return soon to the political arena to launch its most serious attempt to capture power in pre-independent Singapore.

Speaking at the State Legislative Assembly on 6 November 1956, even before the dust had time to settle down after the quelling of the riots of 30 October, Lee Kuan Yew sounded rather prophetic (particularly regarding the Communist threat to the PAP leadership): "I think if Members of this House do not grow up and rise up to the revolutionary situation (Communist jargon), then we certainly will perish..." (20)

Clutterbuck commented: "The 1956 riots gave each of the four sides (the British colonialists, Lim Yew Hock's government, Lee Kuan Yew's moderate wing of the PAP, and the Communists) and the public an idea of where each of them stood and how far each was prepared to go. Above all, the success and consequent prestige of the police kept the battle off the streets for the next seven years, enabling Lee Kuan Yew (the British-scripted and duly anointed successor to Lim) to establish his political position and conduct the political struggle with his rivals in the Assembly, in Party Committees and in private meetings, without coercion by mob violence..." (21)

Remarked Sir Robert Black (half in jest): "Much of the violence was in the exchange of argument (Lee's forte) in debates!" (22)

The 1955 election paid put to conservative politics, turned the political course to the left, and persuaded the politicians that they could not succeed without the support of the overwhelming Chinese majority.

Turnbull noted: "The future belonged to politicians of the left who aimed to seize self-government as quickly as possible and to build up mass support against colonial rule…" (23).

Although the first general election was held in Singapore four months earlier than across the Causeway, Malaya managed to leap-frog towards independence after the December 1955 peace talks with the Communist leadership. Malaya became independent at the end of August 1957 while in Singapore the maiden prize of self-government was contested by political parties on the right and the left.

The PAP won the crucial 1959 general election on the strength of Communist support, and Lee Kuan Yew a couple of decades later publicly admitted that he rode "a wild tiger" on the political path to power.

NOTES: CHAPTER FIVE ACT TWO: THE SECOND COMMUNIST REVOLUTION IN SINGAPORE, 1954-56

1. Turnbull, **A History of Singapore 1819-1975,** p.. 250

2. Drysdale, **Singapore: Struggle for Success**, pp. 158, 219

3. Turnbull, p. 250

4. Harper, Lim Chin Siong and the 'Singapore Story', **COMET IN OUR SKY**, pp. 15-16

5. Bloodworth, **The Tiger and the Trojan Horse**, p. 82

6. According to Lee Kuan Yew, he first spoke in Mandarin at a public rally in Singapore's first general election held on April 1955.

    In his own words: "Amongst my documents, I treasure one sheet of paper in simple Chinese, the first and simplest speech I have ever made in Mandarin for general elections in April 1955 at the Bandar Street square.

    "It was before the biggest crowd Singapore had ever seen, around 60,000. With Jek's one sheet of paper, I tried to prove that I was Chinese and Jek (Yeun Thong) kept on writing speeches and pamphlets…" **Straits Times**, March 15, 1982

    An ex-communist (a "prolific ABL scribbler" in Bloodworth's description) and political secretary to Kuan Yew when he became prime minister in 1959, Jek later became a government minister and subsequently Singapore's High Commissioner in London.

7. Marshall, **The Struggle for Nationhood 1945-1959**, p. 8

8. Ibid., p. 7

9. Rajakumar, Lim Chin Siong's Place in Singapore History, **COMET IN OUR SKY**, p. 100

   A medical doctor in Kuala Lumpur, Dr. M. K. Rajakumar was a senior leader of the Labour Party of Malaya.

   To quote him further (pp. 100-101):

   "Hitherto, the Chinese had ignored politics, but now (in the early and mid-1950s), they would not allow a Westernised minority, whom they held in low regard, to take over from the British.

   "However, Singapore Chinese were divided, between the majority who admired the new China under the Communists on one side, and a powerful minority comprising supporters of the defeated Kuomintang who hated the Chinese Communists, on the other side.

   "The supporters of the Kuomintang, and their intelligence services, were to play a silent, efficient role in destroying the Chinese Left in Singapore. In this, they were financed by United States intelligence, who thus intruded into what hitherto was the British sphere..." 15.11.2014 07:02

10. **FOR PEOPLE THROUGH ACTION BY PARTY**, PAP's 45th anniversary publication on November 21, 1999, p. 52

11. Ibid., p. 54

12. Bloodworth, op. cit., p. 124

13. Marshall, op. cit., p. 10

14. Bloodworth, op. cit., p.87

15. Ibid., p. 128

16. In **Conflict and Violence in Singapore and Malaysia 1945-1983**), Clutterbuck has narrated (p. 126) how the October 1956 riots were quickly quelled. At 8.15 a.m. on Oct 26, the Commissioner of Police formally requested for military assistance. By 8.20 a.m. orders had gone out by radio, and by 8.30 a.m. all 29 road blocks at vantage points covering all access roads to the city were established and manned (as according to the new security plan known as "Operation PHOTO", drawn up under newly-appointed Chief Minister Lim Yew Hock in July 1956).

Clutterbuck wrote (p. 129) that by the evening of Oct 26 "the first of the six battalions (led early by the 1st Queens) extracted from the jungle on the mainland had crossed the causeway into Singapore, and the military outnumbered the police on the ground..."

Lee Kuan Yew criticized the Chief Minister whom he took to task, despite the success of the tough security operation, when he spoke in the State Assembly on Nov 1956: "But how can the Hon. The Chief Minister counter the effect of these British troops at barricade points at all bridges? How can he counter the pictures in all the press of Maj. Gen. Tulloch, General Officer Commanding, Singapore Base District, and of Mr Nigel Morris, Commissioner of Police, in charge of the whole operation? The identification in the minds of the people of this government with armed British imperialism is something which will take a long time to live down..." (Quoted in Drysdale, pp. 161-162)

17. Lee Ting Hui, **Armed Communist Movements in Southeast Asia** (Lim Joo-Jock ed.), p. 113

The Special Branch crackdown on the night of 26/27 Oct "scooped up almost the entire open front leadership" and detained 74 union leaders of the Middle Road HQ.

Clutterbuck commented (p. 135): "In the long run these arrests also proved to be of major advantage to Lee Kuan Yew and the moderate wing of the PAP, who were able during the next three years to build up the party to a position of political dominance..."

Clutterbuck added: "If it had not been for the October 1956 riots and these resulting arrests, the story might have been different. So in this respect too the riots proved to be a critical point in the history of Singapore."

18. Bloodworth, p. 153

19. Clutterbuck, p. 137

20. Drysdale, p. 162

21. Clutterbuck, p. 141

22. Drysdale, p. 158

23. Turnbull, p. 258

CHAPTER SIX

Lee on a wild ride, 1954-61

"...The tiger and man are quite alike, in that he is fond of those who feed him and give him succor. He kills only when provoked." – Liang Yang, Imperial zoo-keeper and tiger-trainer, Zhou Dynasty (1100-21BC) (1)

From the time of the launching of the PAP in late November 1954 until its bitter break with the Communist organization in mid-1961, the non-communists and the pro-communists in Singapore's most successful political party (dubbed as left-wing and pro-communist by the colonial authorities) joined hands in the anti-colonial struggle for independence. The inevitable question arises as to who was using whom.

In an insider's account of the genesis of the PAP, Lee Kuan Yew (one of its leading founders) wrote: "We were riding a tiger and we knew it..." (2)

If they really knew they were dealing with a political beast of prey (certainly not a paper tiger), why did they do it?

"Our primary concern was how to muster a mass following (i.e. popular support among the Chinese majority)," Lee wrote.

"How does a group of English-educated nationalists, with no experience of either the hurly-burly of politics or the conspiracies of revolution, graduates of British universities, move a people whose many languages they did not speak, and whose problems and hardships they shared only intellectually?

"The party was to be consciously radical and anti-colonial. We tacitly understood that communists and their fellow travelers would be admitted into the ranks of the party in a united front for the struggle for independence against the British…" (3)

Lee told an Australian correspondent in May 1955: "Any man in Singapore who wants to carry the Chinese-speaking people with him cannot afford to be anti-communist…" (4) The implication being that the majority of them were pro-communist, or viscerally not anti-communist.

Within the PAP, the cooperation between the non-communists (who in the early period called themselves democratic socialists and later labeled themselves as moderates) and the pro-communists (the leftists and the Communists) reached a high in 1955. But heavily infiltrated by the left by 1956, the PAP soon experienced its first crisis when the pro-communists came close to capturing it following an unexpected draw (6-6) with the non-communists in the elections to the executive committee in early August 1957. (5)

The leadership in the non-communist wing, including the PAP chairman Dr Toh Chin Chye and secretary Lee Kuan Yew, resigned and stayed out for over a couple of months.

It was on 13 August 1957 that the pro-communists took control of the Central Executive Committee (CEC) by holding the top posts including chairman and secretary.

Following the government crackdown on 21-22 August detaining 35 people including five out of the six pro-communist members of the CEC, Dr Toh and Lee regained control of the party when they were re-elected as its chairman and secretary-general respectively on 20 October 1957. Two months later, the PAP won 13 seats in the City Council election and the political maverick Ong Eng Guan made history by becoming the first mayor of Singapore and subsequently emerged as a highly controversial figure.

After the non-communist leaders had retained control of the party in late October 1957, the beast of prey became a willing beast of burden. And despite that harrowing tussle on August 1957, Lee Kuan Yew rode it on to the great electoral triumph of mid-1959 – and into the pages of history.

Some observers thought that the Communists took Lee for a ride. Did the tiger take Lee for a ride?

Since the PAP achieved its ultimate political objective of gaining independence for Singapore (ironically through the strange, though not unprecedented, historical process of its brief merger with Malaysia followed by its sudden expulsion) by the mid-1960s after its critical break with the Communists in mid-1961, the records don't show that the tiger took Lee for a ride although it came close to overthrowing its young gutsy and wily rider on at least a couple of crucial occasions.

On the PAP's political liaison with the Communist United Front, Dr Goh Keng Swee told Bloodworth: "It was an act of reckless folly..." (6)

Lee gave the impression that the English-educated political leaders had no choice but to team up with the Communists in order to gain the necessary weight and strength of support of the Chinese majority (very largely Chinese-educated) which would impact significantly on the anti-colonial struggle for national liberation and independence. Basically, it was a pre-eminent political fact of life, that no party could wrest political power without the support of the Chinese majority in Singapore.

But, was the PAP ever used as a cat's paw?

Other observers, Bloodworth notably among them, thought that the PAP was used as a political Trojan horse by the Malayan Communist Party. On their working relationship in the 1950s, Bloodworth wrote that "Lee and his party were the constitutional Trojan horse of the CPM" and "the communist line was to stick with the PAP and subvert it, not split with it and seek other cover." (7)

That was, until the mid-1961 division when the PAP dissidents of the left wing quit the party to oppose merger in the formation of Malaysia and set up the Barisan Sosialis as a new front political party.

And the PAP die-hards, in desperate straits, waged their battle for merger with Malaya to ensure their own survival, as political union with Kuala Lumpur would enable them to outflank and out-stage the Communists in Singapore who had reportedly planned (according to the official propaganda in Kuala Lumpur and Singapore) to use the island as a "Cuba' to subvert the Malayan mainland.

From published records, it was clear that both the PAP and the Communist Party had been using each other to advance their common struggle against colonialism, while engaged in an incestuous struggle for political dominance and power. (8) 29.11. 1825

Turnbull recorded: "The illegal Malayan Communist Party welcomed the possibility of using the English-educated left-wing as a front political party to exploit the new constitution (the Rendel report, published in February 1954, was to usher in a measure of self-government the following year) in preparation for eventual armed struggle. Lee Kuan Yew's group, now fully alive to the force and discontent of the Chinese-educated masses, realized that an alliance with such men, dangerous thought it might be, offered the only path to political success. The future belonged to politicians who could command the allegiance of the Chinese-educated..." (9)

A politically symbiotic relationship existed between these two anti-colonial forces as represented by the two contending factions in the PAP. "Certainly, without the Lim (Chin Siong) faction, the PAP could not have won the mass following it did in the late 50's. Without the Lee (Kuan Yew) faction, the party probably would have been proscribed," wrote Thomas Bellows. (10)

The British probably saw through all this, and they had the final authority over how and when the colony would be politically liberated. In other words, they had the power to decide how and when they would allow which of the locals to take over Singapore from their firm and strong control. And in the interim, the colonial masters would continue to watch very closely the moves of the rival local players on the political stage.

Lim Yew Hock, when he was chief minister, said his government could have banned the PAP in 1956 (instead he detained Communist United Front leaders including Lim Chin Siong in October that year), or in 1957 (when he detained 35 in late August including five pro-communist leaders in the central committee of the PAP).

The strongly anti-communist English daily **Straits Times** (December 6, 1958) commented on the consequence of Lim Yew Hock's tough action of "assuring its (the PAP's) survival by purging it (the PAP) of its extremist elements" in 1956 and 1957 (the milestone agreement on self-government for Singapore having been reached in London early April 1957).

But, riding a political tiger was no joy ride. Moreover, working with the largely Chinese-educated Communists was not easy for the English-educated political leaders in the PAP. There was no end of trouble.

Lee Kuan Yew later admitted (in September 1961) that "often my colleagues and I disagreed with them and intense fights took place, all concealed from the outside world because they were Communists working in one anti-colonial front with us against the common enemy (British colonialism) and it would not do to betray them…" (11)

According to Lee, the pro-communists in the PAP made their first bid to capture the party in 1956 when they tried to change its constitution to allow the branch committees to nominate members to the central executive committee. Four of them were in the redraft sub-committee, including Lim Chin Siong.

But before they could tinker with the party constitution, they were plucked when the SB raids "scooped up almost the entire open front leadership" (to quote Clutterbuck) following the violent rioting in late October 1956. (12)

Clutterbuck commented that the extensive 1956 purge gave "major advantage" to Lee and the other moderates in the PAP to build up the party over the next three years. (13)

In early August 1957, the moderate leaders were shaken when they temporarily lost control of the party after they and the extremists had fought to a draw (as reported earlier) in the crucial election to the central executive committee. "The extremists succeeded in winning half of the seats, the future of the moderates appeared precarious, and Toh (Chin Chye) and Lee (Kuan Yew) stood down from the leadership," Turnbull wrote. (14)

On 13 August 1957 the pro-communist faction took control of the PAP's Central Executive Committee when they filled all the top posts including those of the chairman and secretary vacated by Dr Toh and Lee. 30-11-1.12.2003 0027

About a week later, Lim Yew Hock intervened and wielded the big stick again.

Turnbull wrote: "In face of the widespread communist threat, the Lim Yew Hock government stepped in to arrest thirty-five active communists, including five members of the newly elected PAP central executive committee and eleven PAP branch officials, together with trade union leaders, students and journalists. Lim Yew Hock's object was to purge extremist influence from the student and labour movements, including the Singapore Trade Union Congress which was the basis of his own party's power.

"But the arrests also crippled extremist power in the PAP and gave the moderates the opportunity to regain mastery of their party without incurring unpopularity by taking action themselves against their rivals. This dramatic change of fortune was so propitious for Lee Kuan Yew and his associates that many, including his extremist colleagues, felt that Lee had been privy to the intentions of Lim Yew Hock and the colonial authorities..." (15)

David Marshall said "Lim Yew Hock saved the day and returned the Lee Kuan Yew group to leadership of the party which at that time had a total membership of approximately 4,000..." (16) As pointed out earlier, five out of the six pro-communists in the CEC had been detained under Lim's orders.

"In 1956 and 1957 the PAP was a virtual prisoner of the communists who had strong influence in trade unions, Chinese schools and PAP branches," Government propagandists recorded in **Singapore, An Illustrated History, 1941-1984**, published by the Ministry of Culture in 1984.

Under the heading "Taming The Tiger", the **Straits Times** (September 13, 1957) editorialized that Government arrests saved the PAP from internal Communists.

Lee Kuan Yew, however, complained that the Government had created the wrong impression that the PAP had been dominated by the Communists and thus had to be saved. He also took offence that the PAP had been labeled as a communist front organization simply because of a few Communists in the fold.

Thus he whined, a month after the pro-communist faction had won control of the CEC, and it was more than a month before the moderate and non-communist leadership regained control of the PAP. Dr Toh was re-elected as the party chairman and Lee its secretary-general on 20 October.

Dr Goh Keng Swee recalled: "The Party machine was in a shambles, but it did not take us much time to rebuild the organization, this time with full safeguards against capture." (17) Safety measures included en bloc voting of recommended candidates to the CEC and selection/appointment of cadres by the CEC.

To consolidate their hold on the party, the moderates extended the executive committee's term of office to two years, introduced bloc voting for the CEC, and created a cadre system (comprising 300-400 members appointed by the CEC, to match numerically their Communist counterpart in Singapore). Although the elitist cadre system (a leaf out of the book on Leninist organization) was supposed to make the PAP citadel impregnable, the Communists were subsequently to assault it and induce mass defections of pro-Communist members, sympathizers, supporters and others in mid-1961, leaving only a hard core at the top level to fight for survival. 1.12.2003 1912

British Prime Minister Harold Macmillan came twice to Singapore in early 1958 on his way from London to Canberra and then back. On both occasions, he had meetings with Chief Minister Lim Yew Hock.

At a press conference on 12 February, Macmillan was asked if it was possible that Britain might suspend the new constitution for a self-governing Singapore should an extreme left-wing government come to power. He replied that the British Government had no such intention and would carry out its pledge of self-government for Singapore, in the confident expectation that the people of Singapore would "live up to their great responsibility." (18)

In the first meeting on March 1958 between Lee Kuan Yew and the "Plen" (Fang Chuan Pi), the leader of the Communist underground in Singapore admitted that the July 1957 bid to take over the PAP had been a mistake. He came to extend an olive branch to Lee, and wanted the PAP to contest and win the coming general election with the cooperation of the Communists.

Since Lee wanted him to prove that he was indeed the big boss operating in Singapore, the "Plen" duly arranged for the whirlwind destruction of David Marshall's Workers' Party in the Kallang by-election on 26 July. Lee was then convinced that the Communist underground was "by far the strongest political force in Singapore at that time." (19)

The **Straits Times** (July 28, 1958) commented: "The collapse at Kallang speaks for itself; it has nothing to do with Mr Marshall (whose candidate managed to gather only 304 votes). For the Communists voted PAP on Saturday, and while PAP's present leaders may welcome their victory they must be acutely aware of the problem in store. Mr Lee has spoken of it often enough…"

Lee had four meetings with the "Plen" before the 1959 general election. Lee recalled: "He wanted again and again to find out if we were prepared to let the Communists work together with us in a united anti-colonial front in the PAP…" (20)

Lee gave the impression that the Communist leader was courting him and that the PAP won its 1959 landslide without Communist support.

Although the PAP won 43 of the 51 seats in the Legislative Assembly (84% representation), it had only 53% of the total vote cast. Could the PAP have won so handily without

Communist support? *Four decades later, Lee admitted in late 1999 that "we won on United Front basis, a broad left-wing vote that swept us into power..."* (21) 2.12.2003 1847 3.12 1835

Fong Chong Pik aka the "Plen" wrote: "In my view, to win an election at thetime, the support of the left wing was necessary, because the left-wing had the masses behind it..." (22)

Chin Peng wrote: "Our supporters, sympathizers and fellow travellers went on to provide Lee's grass-roots electoral support. Without them he would never have achieved his stunning 43-seatvictory in the 51 constituencies..." (23)

Bellows wrote: "While the leadership of the PAP continued to be non-communist, the cadre(s) who were recruiting, educating, indoctrinating, disciplining, preparing for the 1959 elections and even, on occasion, engaging in clandestine activities, were the Communist-oriented, Chinese-educated, who continued to co-operate with the non-Communists..." (24)

More than half of the electorate voted for the first time on 30 May 1959. They were the quarter-million alien-born Chinese (the Chinese Chinese) enfranchised with the coming into force of the new citizenship law at the end of 1958.

Turnbull noted that "Lee Kuan Yew's need to retain the support of the Chinese-educated masses and to keep to the left of the Labour Front government had driven him to cultivate an extremist public image, which was at variance with his long-term political thinking..." (25)

Describing Lee as one of the two ablest leaders (the other being Robert Menzies, the long-time Australian prime minister until 1966)) he had met, Richard Nixon commented: "He (Lee) realized that he could only forestall a Communist revolution by appearing to be much more radical than he really was, so he designed a political game plan that could best be described as talking left and walking right..." (26)

Turnbull wrote that the PAP's 1959 election victory "brought immediate internal strains between the moderates, who wanted to woo the Federation (of Malaya) and capitalists in order to boost the economy, and the extremists who wanted to establish a socialist independent state and destroy capitalism and colonialism…" (27)

In his election speeches, Lee had openly announced his coming battle with the left. He said the ultimate contestants would be the PAP and the MCP Chin Peng had thought as much: "In our review of the Singapore election results, the Central Committee rightly predicted that the victorious Lee would one day move against the CPM to consolidate his power. We appraised our cadres accordingly but could do little more…" (28)

The fact that the Communists supported the Lee-led PAP to win the crucial 1959 general election and form the first government in the self-governing State of Singapore, indicated their intention to use the PAP as their political front.

Politically and psychologically as well, it also reflected their confidence in besting the English-educated leadership of the PAP in any future contest for the hearts and minds of the Chinese-educated electorate. 9.12.2003 1818

Asked on election day why the British had given the PAP "a free run of Singapore", Lee answered: "They are playing a long-term game. They know that the PAP is non-Communist. The lesson has been brought home to them that besides the MCP (Malayan Communist Party), the PAP is the only coherent party here. It is the only (indigenous) deterrent force against the Communists..." (29)

On 12 October 1959, the four-month-old PAP Government decided to renew the PPSO (Preservation of Public Security Ordinance) for another five years.

Introduced by David Marshall in 1955 and roundly denounced by the PAP then as a totalitarian law, the PPSO was also amended. Bloodworth commented that Lee and the party reshaped the PPSO "to suit their even more exacting requirements."

The **Straits Times** (October 13, 1959) editorialized: "The MCP remains the real enemy... it knows that it is fighting a Government that is better equipped than any of its predecessors to challenge Communism..."

Described by Lee as "vehemently hostile" to the PAP because of the party's refusal to take an anti-Communist stand before independence, this leading English-language daily now leaned conspicuously towards the new ruling oligarchy.

On 11 May 1961, Lee had his fifth and last meeting (his first and only as Singapore's new prime minister) with the "Plen". The Communist underground leader wanted Lee to press for the abolition of the Internal Security Council (which was provided for under the self-governing constitution to serve as a bulwark against Communism in Singapore, and which Lee considered to be essential for merger with Malaya) at the next round of constitutional talks in London. In return the "Plen" conceded that the British could keep their military base in Singapore. (30)

Lee recalled that they talked about a lot of things during their final nocturnal four-hour session (in a small room lit by a single kerosene lamp, according to Bloodworth, at a newly-built Housing Development Board (HDB) flat in the sleazy district of Whampoa).

"He asked me whether I was likely to get merger soon from the Tengku." Lee recalled.

"I told him that there was no immediate likelihood of it (Tunku was to propose merger on 27 May, a fortnight later) but that I was hoping for common market arrangements with the Federation (of Malaya)."

Lee then said: "Finally, he pressed me to agree to the abolition of the Internal Security Council as the immediate target for the 1963 constitutional talks while deferring the question of independence for Singapore alone or through merger with the Federation."

Lee added that he did not commit himself on this issue. (31) 8.12.2003 1706

Shortly after the sacking in mid-July 1960 of PAP strongman Ong Eng Guan ("The Little Rebel" to the **Straits Times** lead writer) and a few days after the declaration of the end of the Emergency (signifying the complete failure of the Communist insurgency) in Malaya, Lee Kuan Yew came out in early August to warn the public about a resurgence of the Communist underground movement in which the "pro-Communist activists" were rebuilding their strength to fight the Government in "an underground struggle for power".

Lee raised this alarum about a couple of months after his fifth and final meeting with the Communist underground boss.

When taunted by Tun Lim Yew Hock in the Legislative Assembly, Lee gave the assurance that the PAP would fight its own battle against the Communists "at a time of our own choosing."

According to one account, Lee had decided to break with the Communists by the time of the Hong Lim by-election regardless of its outcome. In this by-election held on 29 April 1961, Ong Eng Guan stood as an independent in his old ward and was dramatically returned with 72% of the votes despite (questionable) Communist support for the PAP candidate Jek Yeung Thong, Lee's political secretary and a former student activist in the Communist underground. (32)

Ong's winning margin was astounding; Turnbull and Clutterbuck both thought it was instrumental in persuading Tunku Abdul Rahman to change his mind about merging with Singapore despite the attendant risks. Less than a month after the Hong Lim by-election, Tunku publicly proposed the formation of Malaysia in an address to foreign correspondents in Singapore.

In the final meeting between Lee Kuan Yew and the "Plen" on 11 May (as narrated earlier), the Communist underground leader had asked whether Lee was "likely to get merger soon from the Tunku?" The reply was not likely. (33)

In Tunku's historic address before an assembly of foreign correspondents at the Adelphi Hotel in Singapore on 27 May, the Malayan Prime Minister proposed the formation of Malaysia to bring the neighbouring territories "closer together in political and economic cooperation."

That was a godsend for the PAP which had been contemplating re-union with the Federation of Malaya (both having been severed by the colonial authorities in 1946). When the PAP was formed in late 1954, one of its main political goals was to seek Singapore's independence through merger (re-integration) with the Federation. (34)

On 9 June, Dr Toh Chin Chye, the PAP chairman, announced that the Government would demand complete independence through merger with the Federation.

That, according to Lee, was the PAP's opening shot in the battle for merger and the showdown fight with the Communists. "This was how the fight started," he said. (35)

The political battle lines were drawn at the Anson by-election held on 15 July. The PAP campaigned for support on merger but lost narrowly ("after communists within the Party swung popular support from the PAP" to quote the party scribes).

With the support of the pro-Communist leaders in the PAP and Trade Union Congress, David Marshall beat his PAP opponent by 546 votes and immediately called for "Emperor Lee's resignation."

Lee offered to resign as Prime Minister, but Dr Toh reminded him of the CEC's unanimous choice of Lee as the PM after the 1959 general election.

The Anson by-election saw the open rupture with Lim Chin Siong and other pro-Communist leaders within the PAP. It also marked the point of no return, and started "a new test of strength" with the Communists

Now on Lee's side of the ideological divide, the **Straits Times** (July 19, 1961) commented on "The Decisive Test": "Whether it would not have been wiser to have thrown down the gauntlet before, or during, the Anson campaign, must remain a matter of opinion, but after Anson the Government was left with little choice. Either it girded the loins for battle, or it resigned and committed Singapore to chaos…"

The break with the PAP, according to Bloodworth, had been decided by the left in its all-out opposition to the formation of Malaysia.

Soon after Chin Peng came to Peking in mid-1961 to report the failure of the Communist revolution in Malaya and propose switching to political struggle, he was told to go back to armed struggle.

According to Chin Peng, when Eu Chooi Yip came to see him shortly after his arrival in Peking, the two of them had political discussions with another top-ranking comrade Siao Chang. The three Communist leaders examined the Malaysia plan and plotted to sabotage it, or at least delay its implementation.

In Singapore the pro-Communist leaders within the PAP probably saw the sagging morale of the Lee faction after two successive electoral defeats within less than three months, as providing the psychological moment to move in for the kill against their pro-merger opponents within the party.

The pro-Communists were already strongly positioned within what Bloodworth called, with epic allusions, the Trojan Horse. Now their political objective was not only to deny popular support to the pro-merger wing of the PAP, but also to wrest control of the ruling party.

When they saw the challenge of the pro-merger faction coming their way, they quickly launched their own plan to capture what Lee called the party citadel.

Before doing so, however, they wanted to know whether the British authorities would stand in their way if they acted constitutionally to topple the leadership of the Lee Kuan Yew group ("the original core of leadership" to quote Lee) and take over the ruling party. (Macmillan had fielded a similar question when he came to Singapore about three and a half years back. And the answer this time would be no different. Why should it be?) 8.12.2003 2112 10.12.2003 1947

On the afternoon of July 18, barely three days after the Anson by-election, the hopeful quartet of James Puthucheary, Lim Chin Siong, Sandra Woodhull and Fong Swee Suan sought an urgent interview with Lord Selkirk, the British Commissioner-General for Southeast Asia, in his residence at Eden Hall.

Turnbull wrote of this controversial meeting: "In view of their suspicion that Lee Kuan Yew had long been collaborating with the British, they wished to assure themselves that Britain would not suspend the constitution if the prime minister were voted out of office and they themselves came to power. Not knowing why they wanted to see him, and in accordance with his open-door policy, Lord Selkirk received the four dissident

PAP members and stressed that the constitution was a free one, which they should respect…" (36)

Malaya's top diplomat Ghazali Shafie had met with Lord Selkirk and left half an hour before Lim and colleagues came to Eden Hall. Ghazali recollected: "When I said that the communists might feel encouraged to seize power, Lord Selkirk gave the impression that if the communists themselves were openly to seize power through elections and to govern the country without resorting to violence the British Government would tolerate it and would not lift the Constitution (using its reserve power to suspend the Constitution)…" (37)

Professor Michael Leifer of the London School of Economics and Political Science, after interviewing Lord Selkirk in Singapore on 9 July 1963 (nearly two years after the event), noted in his diary: "Selkirk made reference to his meeting with James Puthucheary and Lim Chin Siong after the Hong Lim by-election. They wanted to know the reaction of the British if they engineered a split within the PAP and formed a government. Selkirk responded by suggesting that if there were no riots or disturbances, etc. the constitution would not be suspended, no matter the background of those involved…" (38)

Drysdale was told by Selkirk: "The essence of what they asked me, was this: 'Was the constitution written for the special benefit of Mr Lee Kian Yew or was it a free constitution?' I said simply this: 'It's a free constitution, stick to it and no rioting, you understand?' That was really the sum of it." (39)

Lee, of course, blew his top when he came to know from his own men about this tea party meeting at Eden Hall, and he got the political message as well. Perhaps it was Selkirk's indirect way of reminding Lee that he too had to bow to the colonial overlord who ruled supreme in Singapore.

Bloodworth, the London **Observer** man on the spot, narrated: "When I took tea with Selkirk at Eden Hall in my turn on 26 July (more than a week after the event), he would say only that he had done no more than spell out the constitution to the leftists and, after all, he could not *not* receive them, could he? They had asked to see him, hadn't they? He hadn't asked to see them. That was all.

"The Prime Minister had started a row with him in order to register his anti-imperialist indignation for general consumption, but instead of putting up his fists for an exhibition match, Selkirk remained obstinately silent, for he was afraid that Lee's outburst might already have alarmed the Tunku and jeopardized merger.

"That was Lee's only real quarrel with him, however. For although the very idea that London and the Tunku would allow extremists to wield power in Singapore was ludicrous, as Selkirk well knew, he had said not a single word to discourage the pro-communists, beyond putting in a rider that there must be no violence…" (40)

Two days after the Eden Hall meeting, Lee brought up this matter in the PAP-dominated Legislative Assembly where he called for a vote of confidence. Speaking for about an hour, he accused the British of plotting and instigating the pro-Communists to attempt the capture of both the PAP government and party.

Less than 48 hours later, however, Lee denied that he had said that the British plotted with the Communists to overthrow the PAP government. "The British never plotted with the Communists," he said. The British lion had taken them for a ride instead. 15.122.2003 2151

"At the meeting, the left sought assurances from Selkirk that should Lee Kuan Yew's government fall, the British would not intervene militarily to maintain control," Cambridge history don Dr Harper wrote. (41)

"It is indicative of Lee's perception of the weakness of his position in mid-1961 that he was immediately suspicious that Selkirk might be willing to ditch him and attempt to work through the left. Lee was to present this as a dark imperialist plot..."

Lee had probably come close to being desperate!

On 27 September 1961, he said in one of his "battle for merger" talks over Radio Singapore: "So the British led Lim and the Communists to believe that they could take power. Once Lim and the Communists believed this they became bold..." (42)

On the third day into the political storm over the controversial tea party meeting at Eden Hall, Lee made merger the main issue of the vote of confidence which was taken at 3.50 on the morning of 21 July at the emergency sitting of the PAP-dominated State Legislative Assembly. When the division came, 27 members voted with the Government, eight (including Lim Yew Hock and David Marshall) against, and 16 abstained including Ong Eng Guan and the 13 PAP dissidents.

Lee challenged the dissidents to vote against the motion and force a new general election. But they abstained because their idea was to capture power from within the ruling party by hopefully knocking out the leadership of the Lee Kuan Yew group, or by winning over more assemblymen to their side to vote out the PAP government and form a successor government themselves.

The 13 dissident PAP backbenchers alleged that the Prime Minister had brought up the motion of confidence in order to destroy intra-party opposition to the leadership. The PAP, they pointed out, had 39 out of the 51 seats in the State Assembly. (43)

Following the motion of confidence on 21 July, three "rebel" political secretaries were dismissed. They were Lim Chin Siong, Fong Swee Suan, and S. Woodhull.

The following day, five parliamentary secretaries including Dr Lee Siew Choh were sacked.

In a joint statement issued at a press conference, the PAP dissidents said that the "discredited leadership" was carrying out a purge and they claimed that district organizing secretaries, assistant district secretaries and party executives of the 51 PAP branches were being removed.

The dissidents said they expected Lee to use the PPSO (Preservation of Public Security Ordinance) against his political opponents.

"Raising the bogey of Communism on the one hand and charging the British with collusion with the Communist Left is a reflection of their recklessness," they stated.

They also described Lee and his group as "exposed and desperate."

They declared, with much apparent confidence: "We have the constitutional means of removing ruthless men in office. The people can rest satisfied that they have the constitutional means of removing these wild men in power." (44) 21.12.2003 1805

The dissidents (members of what Lee Kuan Yew called "an aspiring junta") went ahead on 26 July to form a new party, the Barisan Sosialis (the Socialist Front) as the truly leftist successor to the PAP which had turned politically to the right.

The Barisan Sosialis was launched on 13 August 1961 before "a cheering crowd of 10,000 supporters (an auspicious number to the Chinese) at the Happy World Stadium" (as narrated by Bloodworth). Dr Lee Siew Chor was its chairman, Woodhull vice-chairman, and Lim Chin Siong as the secretary-general.

With the formation of this new party which the "Plen" saw as an alternative to the planned capture of the PAP, it means that the Communists had deserted their Trojan Horse. Hence they had to fight it out with the PAP in the open political arena.

The irrevocable split with the Communists signified that Lee was no longer astride the beast – "a wild tiger" (to quote him). For it had shaken off its wily rider, and was poised to strike.

Lee said the pro-Communists broke from the PAP in July 1961 to fight them in the open. "They were confident they would rout us," he recalled. (45)

And they were in a very strong and advantageous, if not unassailable, position on the ground to be confident. The PAP was "busted" (to quote Goh Keng Swee), but remained standing in a dismal and pathetic state.

Turnbull recorded the heavy toll of the split on the PAP: "The PAP executive's strong parliament majority of 1959 had almost dwindled away (it was down to a majority of one when division was called on the motion of confidence on 21 July morning), but its position outside of the assembly was even more precarious. While the moderates had been in control of the central executive committee since 1957, the communists continued to consolidate their strength at the second level of leadership and at the base of the party structure.

"When the split came in July 1961 most key figures in the party's branches defected to the Barisan, and at the lower level the PAP's organization was almost crippled. Thirty-five branch committees resigned, and nineteen of the twenty-three paid organizing secretaries defected. Large numbers of cadres quitted, and only 20 per cent of the party's former members paid their subscriptions in 1962.

"Many branches were almost destroyed. Eleven had less than twenty-five members each and one had only ten. The PAP lost most of its active party workers and a great mass of supporters, many of whom were not pro-communist but thought the party was doomed and scrambled to leave the apparently sinking ship.

"The Barisan Sosialis started with a great deal of strength at grass-roots level and controlled most of the secondary political associations formerly attached to the PAP. It also had strength outside the party organization among Nanyang University students and graduates and among trade unionists. At the time of the split the Barisan controlled two-thirds of organized labour, and forty-three unions publicly pledged their support for the new party..." (46) 22.12.2003 2245 16.11.2014 09:50

According to Goh Keng Swee, all ground organizations were wrecked. He recalled: "It took less than a week for the CUF (Communist United Front) leaders to achieve this!" (47)

When Toh Chin Chye came to see him at his office in Fullerton Building, Goh was looking at the ceiling wondering what had hit them, and Toh told him that he had just come from Harry's (Lee Kuan Yew's) office where he had seen Harry staring at the ceiling.

(According to a Chinese expression, anyone found looking at a ceiling or a wall (or the sky) reflects a condition of meditative utter helplessness or inexplicable hopelessness.)

Goh told Toh "we are all busted; the party secretaries, the PA (People's Association, a grass roots organization), the organizing secretaries, the Works Brigade (another PAP-run mass organization like the PA). I knew the communists were organizationally much stronger than us. But I did not expect us smashed up like this in just one week..." (48)

Luckily for the PAP, the party chairman (small in size, but brainy, plucky and resilient) refused to go down and was very much in a fighting mood. "The fight has only just begun," Toh thundered. "We should start thinking immediately of our next move – how to rebuild the Party, rally the loyal Party members and how to carry the fight into the enemy camp."

Goh commented: "I will never forget the occasion. What Dr Toh said made sense. I recovered my spirits quickly. This was fortunate as the pro-communists intoxicated by the spectacular successes underrated our ability to fight back and made mistakes which gave us our opening for a counter-attack which eventually succeeded. But, as Dr Toh predicted on that day, it was a long and nasty fight…" (49)

To Lee Kuan Yew, 1961 to 1963 were the years of "dire crisis". But the old guard stood their ground, and they did not blink (to borrow an American expression for Kennedy's response in his eyeball-to-eyeball confrontation with Khrushchev during the 1962 Cuban missile crisis).

"After 25 months of furious and sometimes frenzied propaganda war, from July 1961 to September 1963, they (the Communists) lost," Lee summed it up. (50)

Turnbull recorded: "This dangerous time (following the split with the Communists in mid-1961) proved to be the turning point in the fortunes of Lee Kuan Yew and the PAP. Impelled by the domestic crisis, the Singapore government continued its negotiations for merger with a vigour born of near desperation…" (51)

As Lee would like to say, the PAP finally won the argument.

In fighting for its survival, the PAP skillfully and successfully waged three major campaigns in its battle for merger.

First, it staged the referendum for merger in September 1962 (please see Chapter 9). It followed this up with another concerted political offensive by holding a snap general election in September 1963 (Chapter 11).

In between was a security drive in early February 1963 jointly conducted with the British and Malayan authorities against Communist cadres, pro-Communist political leaders and militant unionists (Chapter 10). This time, the communist/left faction got "all busted" in the prelude to its virtual elimination from the Singapore political scene.

Thus the PAP tore into the enemy, and in doing so, snatched a hard-won but decisive victory from the jaws of defeat.

NOTES: Chapter Six RIDING A TIGER: LEE KUAN YEW ON A WILD RIDE

1. **The Little Book of CHINESE PROVERBS**, compiled by Jonathan Clements, Parragon Book, UK, 2005, p. 24

2. *Straits Times* January 7, 1980

   At their meeting in Lee's Oxley Road residence, the PAP founders "brainstormed the prospects of a new mass-based political party that would be radical and anti-colonial.

   "Mr. Lee and the other prime movers had a tacit understanding that the new party would admit into its ranks the Communists and left-wing unionists to mount a united front in their fight for independence through merger with Malaya..." **FOR PEOPLE THROUGH ACTION BY PARTY**, PAP's 45th anniversary publication November 21, 1999, p. 52

3. *Straits Times* January 7, 1980
4. **Straits Times** May 5, 1955

   At the time of the riots in the mid-1950s, the Communist Party was calling the shots. The ABL paper *Freedom News* (published bilingually in English and Chinese from early post-war years) reported in June 1956 that the MCP was directing the PAP and that Lee was communicating with comrades "at the highest level." Lee was legal adviser to the Middle Road unions, the SCMSSU (Singapore Chinese Middle School Students' Union), and other mass organizations.

In July 1956, the ABL paper described the PAP as the MCP's legal front organization. "The communists were using me purely as a technician," Lee told Bloodworth, "and as a buffer to manipulate the constitutional system" **THE TIGER AND THE TROJAN HORSE**, p. 125

5. Bloodworth has written (pp. 132-34) that the Communists had, within one and a half years of the founding of the PAP on Nov 1954, not only easily penetrated but also captured the PAP. The party branch committees were run by the Chinese-educated, almost to a man, "mostly unemployed and extremely fierce."

   He commented in his acidic idiom: "By 1956 the invaders had gone through the PAP as if it were a mouldering cheese, leaving the isolated and impotent leadership little else but the rind..." According to him, nine of the 13 party branches "had been pocketed by the communists."

   Lim Chin Siong, the leading rat in the open political field, had set the pace for subversion at the Bukit Panjang branch in the rural north of Singapore by pushing through a popular resolution calling on the government to recognize the MCP (what Chin Peng had wanted Tunku Abdul Rahman to agree to at their Baling talks in Dec 1955, also a move which then had the backing of the PAP), and the non-Communists in the executive committee had to play ball.

   When Lee Kuan Yew went to see Goh Keng Swee in London on April 1956, he told Goh that the PAP had been captured by the communists. But they had no choice but to hang on politically and remain "a very junior partner" in the Communist United Front (CUF).

6. Bloodworth reported (pp. 86-87): "Within the PAP, the Middle Road group and the moderate faction were both feeling for holds. Each needed the other in order to gain access to an alien world – one English-speaking, the other Chinese-speaking; each wanted the other to be part of its own united front against colonialism; each tacitly conceded that they must combine to drive out the British before they turned on each other. But both sides knew that day must come..."

7. Ibid., p. 138

8. Until the late 1950s, the Communists continued to cultivate the PAP which they described in a 1957 document as "comparatively the most resolute force of anti-colonialism" (quoted in Bellows, **The Singapore Party System**, p. 39)

   In fact, the "Plen", the Communist underground boss, maintained his clandestine dialogue with Lee Kuan Yew until May 1961 – a fortnight before Tunku's proposal for merger with Singapore through the formation of Malaysia.

9. Turnbull, **A History of Singapore 1819-1975**, p. 253

10. Thomas J. Bellows, **The Singapore Party System**, p. 31

   Speaking in the Singapore Legislative Assembly on 6 Nov 1956, Lee Kuan Yew said: "...I am not convinced myself that communism is an evil force. In fact, I agree with about 75 per cent of what they want to do. But it is that 25 per cent of how they do it that I object and oppose…" (Quoted in Drysdale, **Singapore: Struggle for Success**, p. 163) 25.12.2003 1800 2.2.2004 1107

11. The British authorities could have banned the PAP after the Hock Lee riots in May 1955. "We were five foolish men and we walked right into it," Goh Keng Swee told Bloodworth (p. 112). Though he did not name them, the five probably were Lee, Goh, Toh Chin Chye, S. Rajaratnam, and K.M. Byrne.

Bloodworth (p. 129) has written: "Lee had warned the left that once the colonial power suspected they were trying to take over the PAP they would all be in jeopardy, and neither faction wanted to provoke the irritable British into banning it…"

12. Quoted in Clutterbuck, **Conflict and Violence in Singapore and Malaysia 1945-1983**, p.105 13. Clutterbuck, p. 135

13. Sir Robert Black, who was governor at the time when Lim Yew Hock launched "Operation Liberation" in late October 1956, told Drysdale (p. 157) that Lim took the decision to quell the riot "and as a result, there were detentions but law and order were restored, parliamentary government continued, and the advantage went to the PAP. It was bound to be…"

Lim did not hesitate to take tough action and although outsiders like the Americans and Australians applauded him for holding the ring, Lee did not desist from criticizing and abusing him for resorting to a "purgatory" instead of using argument and persuasion (a legalistic approach favoured by Lee and his forte). Lim was committed to restoring peace and security, and stated plainly in the State Assembly that he was "not anxious to remain in office." He did not, but Black paid tribute to his courage which was a victory "for the future of Singapore." This is a point that historians should note since Lim's bold (if not unexpectedly audacious) leadership in a stormy situation has been generally underrated.

14. Turnbull, p. 266

15. Turnbull, p.266 2.2.2004 1159

As told by the party scribes in the PAP's 45th anniversary publication in 1999 (p. 54):

"…From clandestine *kelong* meetings to smear campaigns and propaganda picnics, the Communists had, within months of the Party's formation, infiltrated the ranks and the Central Executive Committee.

"They made a bid to capture the CEC in its 1957 party conference, when six of the 12 elected into the central decision making body were Communist United Front members.

"To force a purge the non-Communist leadership led by Mr Lee refused to take office, despite nine days of intense lobbying.

"The pro-Communists had to assume leadership of the Party stripped of the respectable cover of the non-Communists.

"Meanwhile, the Labor Front government reacted to the Communists' moves to capture the unions by arresting 37 pro-Communists trade unionists, five of whom were the PAP CEC members.

"The Party's non-Communists then swung into frenzied action, setting up an Emergency Council. The council held a special party conference on September 20, 1957 and for the first time since its founding, the CEC had no pro-Communists."

To prevent the Party from being taken over again by the pro-Communists, the Emergency Council introduced the bloc vote system for the CEC and also switched to the cadre system (appointing cadres selected from among tested and loyal members). Moreover, the Party also embarked on a re-registration exercise to weed out the pro-Communists and their sympathizers.

These prophylactic measures, however, failed to prevent a near-fatal attack by the pro-Communist faction in mid-1961.

To return to the record of the official scribes:

"A permanent parting of the ways, however, came only in mid-1961 when their leaders were expelled after their repeated and increasingly undisguised attempts to wrest control of the Party. They included 13 assemblymen who later formed the Barisan Sosialis, bringing on board with them defectors, including 35 of the 51 branches, all of whose members abandoned the PAP…"

In other words, the "wild tiger" which Lee had mounted over the past half a dozen years or so, left a tottering PAP to its fate.

It's been one hell of a ride," famous Spanish singer Gloria Estefan sings in *Famous*, one of the songs she has written for her new English-language album *Unwrapped* (**THE SUN** October 18, 2003). 2.2.2004 1315

16. Marshall, **The Struggle for Nationhood 1945-1959**,p. 13 . Pang Cheng Lian wrote her 1971 book **SINGAPORE'S PEOPLE'S ACTION PARTY** (pp. 4-5):

"In the Sessional Paper Cmd. No. 33 of 1957, the Government explained that the thirty-five (trade unionists) had been detained because of their communist subversive activities which had become more frequent and blatant. It cited communist documents to prove that the MCP intended to penetrate the PAP, and it seemed to imply that the purge was intended to save the latter from capture by the communist group.

"The PAP, on the other hand, alleged that the purge was meant to forestall an attempt by these trade unionists to capture control of the TUC (Trade Union Congress which had been organized by Lim Yew Hock of the Labour Front).

"In the Legislative Assembly on 12 September 1957, Lee Kuan Yew denied that the communists had obtained domination of the PAP. In fact he would only refer to the communists as a "dissident faction in the PAP who tried to oppose and reverse the policy of the last Central Executive Committee (elected at the second Party conference in July 1956) of the PAP".

"His later writings however, indicate that he was aware of the communists' attempts to capture the Party.

"The purge, therefore, must have served as a welcome respite to the moderates who resumed control of the Party."

Pang added: "After this failure to capture control of the Party, and especially after the Government's arrests, the pro-communists' strength was reduced considerably..." Though not, it may be further added retrospectively, for long.

Although Lim Yew Hock claimed that his government had saved the PAP, Lee Kuan Yew described Lim's crackdown (with or without the privy knowledge and tacit consent of the colonial authorities) on the subversives as an emergency operation to save his own skin in the TUC and the Labour Front. Lim's strong-armed tactic did not save him (as he had anticipated) but led subsequently to his virtual political destruction (an outcome which perhaps he had not expected) in the 1959 general election in which only four of the 39 candidates of his new coalition, the Singapore People's Alliance, won, and all the 32 Liberal-Socialists bit the dust. However, Lee rode the political tiger to a rousing triumph; the PAP captured 43 out of the 51 seats, and polled over 53% of the total votes cast.

According to Pang (pp. 59-60), the PAP had no record of membership figures until 1958 when there was a re-registration campaign. And according to her study,

PAP members numbered less than 2,000 in 1958 (in a population of around 1.5 million).

According to the Party's 1999 publication on its 45th anniversary (p. 56), the PAP had over 15,000 members, including a few thousand cadres, in the Vision 1999 year (the year of Singapore becoming a developed nation with a population of about three million).

17. Goh's letter published in the **Straits Times** on August 14, 1961, in reply to Woodhull's statement on the July 18 meeting with Lord Selkirk.

18. **Keesing's Contemporary Archives**

19. Bloodworth, pp. 177-178

Drysdale, pp. 201-202

20. **Straits Times** September 23, 1961

21. PAP's 45th anniversary publication on November 1999, p. 104

22. Fong Chong Pik, **The Memoirs of a Malayan Communist Revolutionary**, p. 139

23. Chin Peng, **MY SIDE OF HISTORY**, p. 409

24. Bellows, p. 30

Pang (p. 8) has cited two main factors for the PAP's overwhelming success at the 1959 polls. One was the split of right-wing votes. The other was the great mass of voluntary workers who more than made up for the Party's lack of a proper electoral machine in 1959, referring to "the countless voluntary helpers (mostly members of the left-wing trade unions and Chinese middle-schools' students) who worked tirelessly for the Party."

In **MY SIDE OF HISTORY** (p. 409), Chin Peng, the CPM leader, has written: "…From our Sadao headquarters we naturally observed the run-up to the Singapore polls in May, 1959, with considerable interest. We had concurred with our Town Committee on the island (which, historically, had always functioned with a high level of autonomy, according to him, and he has also admitted that throughout the 1948-60 Emergency he had been unable to exert any reasonable degree of control over the CPM's operation in Singapore) that the CPM should solidly throw its support behind lawyer Lee Kuan Yew and his People's Action Party (PAP).

"A leading PAP election agent who worked closely with Lee was our man. He was a card-carrying member and reported regularly to his Town Committee. I am sure Lee didn't realize the electoral agent was a hard-core communist at the time. He certainly knew the man had close and useful communist contacts. I always felt that Lee's attitude towards our underground activist in his camp was purely pragmatic.

"The young PAP leader would use him as much as he could and use his 'contacts with the devil'. We regarded the arrangement in very much the same light.

"I cannot, with any degree of accuracy, place a figure on the numbers of people we controlled among the

Singapore voting public in 1959. But I can certainly say that most of the island's workers sympathized with the left-wing trade unions and members of these unions well appreciated they were under the control of the CPM. The pro-government unions then functioned in name only. Our supporters, sympathizers and fellow travelers went on to provide Lee's grass-roots electoral support. Without them he would never have achieved his stunning 43-seat victory in the 51 constituencies up for decision at the May 30 polls…" 2.2.2004 2045

25. Turnbull, p. 271

26. Richard Nixon, **LEADERS** (1983), p. 326

27. Turnbull, p. 276

28. Chin Peng, p. 409 has written: "In our review of the Singapore election results, the Central Committee rightly predicted that the victorious Lee would one day move against the CPM to consolidate his power. We appraised our cadres accordingly but could do little more…."

29. **Straits Times** May 30, 1959

30. Bloodworth, p. 224

31. **Straits Times** September 26, 1961

32. Lee Ting Hui, essay on the communist open united front in Singapore published in **Armed Communist Movements in South-East Asia,** edited. by Lim Joo-Jock, p. 118. Lee Ting Hui has written:

"Early in 1960, a split occurred within the ranks of the non-communists (within the PAP). Lee Kuan Yew's leadership was challenged by Ong Eng Guan, who had been Mayor of the City Council and had built up extensive mass support for the party through the administration of that authority. Ong was expelled from both party and government (27 June 1960), but in April 1961, won a by-election in his constituency against a candidate from Lee's group, Hong Lim.

"In his tussle with Lee, Ong appealed for the support of Lim Chin Siong and his followers. The communists chose to support Lee rather than Ong. However, in exchange, they wanted Lee to make the British abolish the Internal Security Council or to grant Singapore independence, both of which would present better opportunities for them to carry out their activities. Lee resisted the pressure…"

On hindsight, it would appear that Communist support for the PAP was questionable. In any case, it did not prevent Ong from pulling off a crushing victory over the PAP at Hong Lim. Both the Hong Lim and Kallang by-elections were two electoral battles that the PAP historians would prefer to leave out from their party records.

33. Bloodworth, p. p. 225

34. Merger was to swerve as a political lifeline to Lee's PAP in its darkest hour of crisis. And before that, the merger issue provided the Lee group with a pretext (if they needed one) to sever ties with the pro-Communists in the party and to battle them into oblivion.

35. *Straits Time* September 28, 1961

36. Turnbull, p. 278

According to Lee Ting Hui (pp. 118-119). Lim Chin Siong's group met twice with the British to sound them out whether Dr Lee Siew Choh (who became chairman of the Barisan Sosialis) would be acceptable to them and whether Dr Lee's group could take over the government from the Lee Kuan Yew group. The pro-Communists even tried to force Lee Kuan Yew to step down as prime minister.

37. Ghazali Shafie, **MEMOIR on the formation of Malaysia**, p. 65

38. Drysdale, p. 277 2.2.2004 2039

39. Drysdale, p. 277

40. Bloodworth, p. 230

Bloodworth (p. 263) has reported that Lim Hong Bee, the London-based editor of the Communist newsletter *Malayan Monitor*, derided those "who ran a revolution in accordance with 'colonialist legality'."

A Queen's Scholar and law student at Cambridge, Lim was a founding member and first secretary of the Malayan Democratic Union. Chin Peng (p. 352) has written that Lim was only "a Party sympathizer, never a Party member."

41. **COMET IN OUR SKY**, p. 35

At the time of the Commonwealth Parliamentary Association (CPA) of Asia meeting in Singapore on 17-18 July 1961, Ghazali Shafie came for a two-day visit to meet with Singapore leaders (including Lee

Kuan Yew, Goh Keng Swee and S.Rajaratnam) as well as with Lord Selkrik.

"From my discussions in Singapore for two days, I had the impression that although Lee Kuan Yew was not in a state of panic, he was extremely worried over the situation in Singapore. At the same time he thought he was on a good wicket since the communists had made merger the main issue, placing the communists in rather a bad light except to some of the chauvinistic Chinese elements," Ghazali recalled (**MEMOIR**, p. 63).

"There seemed to be some justification in the deduction of the PAP leadership regarding the double game played by the British as seen in the conversation I had with Selkirk. The communists would certainly not move forward if they knew that the British would not have them as the legal government (should they manage to openly seize power through the general elections without resorting to force or violence).

"There was also something in the belief that the British would encourage the communists to quarrel with PAP so that the PAP, instead of the British or the Internal Security Council, would take the measures of detaining the communists. If these were true then there was a miscalculation on the part of the British authority…" 16.11.2014 07:37

42. *Straits Times* September 28, 1961

43. **Straits Times** July 22, 1961

44. **Sunday Times** July 23, 1961

45. **Straits Times** January 7, 1980

46. Turnbull, p. 279

47. Lee Kuan Yew's speech at the first valedictory dinner of the PAP, published in the **Straits Times** March 15, 1982

48. Ibid.

49. Ibid.

50. **Straits Times** January 7, 1980

51. Turnbull, p. 279

CHAPTER SEVEN

The Communist Mastermind In Singapore

The mastermind and strategist of the Communist underground in Singapore, the nondescript-looking but scholarly Eu Chooi Yip operated with the stealth of a cat and the elusive skill of a ninja master. Though not a shadowy figure, he was known mainly to his many college mates and office colleagues, and well respected by them. Neither was he a public figure. Of course, the Police Special Branch kept a file on him with an old photograph of him (and perhaps several copies of the same). But he managed to keep himself beyond the reach of the authorities.

In the published works on local communism, Eu first surfaced in John Drysdale's 1984 book on Singapore's recent history. But this fairly weighty tome contains hardly half a dozen brief mentions of this little-known communist leader although it carries a photograph (the first for public consumption) of Eu looking quite serious and somewhat glum. (1)

Drysdale has described Eu as a Marxist, the same description given by the late C.C. Too, the top Malaysian expert on Asian communism and master of psychological warfare, and an old friend of Eu in pre-war Kuala Lumpur of the late 1930s.

Referring to Eu's letter in the **Straits Times** (June 22, 1948), Drysdale reported that Eu, "a young pro-Communist of high intelligence and a leading member of the (Malayan) Democratic Union", had written that his party deplored both "the recent killings upcountry" (the communist slayings of White planters and miners in Perak that had triggered the declaration of Emergency in Malaya on 19 June and in Singapore on 23 June 1948) and the brutal police action in which eight workers had been "beaten to death by constables armed with riot sticks". As secretary of the anti-British MDU, he also repeated the clarion call for political freedom. (2)

On June 23 the following day, Philip Hoalim (chairman) and Eu (secretary) signed a statement dissolving the Malayan Democratic Union (formed 21 December 1945 to oppose colonialism to the end); the MDU had become an open front organization of the Malayan Communist Party (MCP). The two MDU leaders expressed the "absolute futility" of continuing its anti-colonial struggle through constitutional means in the politically circumscribed environment of the newly-imposed Emergency regulations.

On June 23, a state of Emergency was declared by the colonial authorities in Singapore four days after its promulgation in Malaya which marked the official start of a 12-year counter-insurgent campaign in the peninsula. The MCP was banned a month later on 23 July.

Drysdale wrote that the MDU's dissolution ended "the first Communist attempt in Singapore to carry out an urban revolution through a united front." Eu fled to one of the nearby islands in Indonesia. (3)

With greater access to official documents and personal interviews with the protagonists and others over a period of three decades (1956-85), Dennis Bloodworth had more to say about Eu in his 1986 insightful account of the political struggle in postwar Singapore. According to the veteran journalist (chief Far East correspondent of the London **Observer** for a quarter century and resident in Singapore since 1956), he had "exceptional access to original source material." (4)

From Bloodworth's sparse but bold lines, a clearer picture of Eu emerged. Of the man Devan Nair (a former communist and union leader who subsequently became president of the Republic of Singapore) once described as "a profound scholar, head and shoulders above the rest". (5) Nair himself was well-read and he also wrote well with an excellent command of the English language (mainly self-taught).

When the police were arresting all known communist cadres in Singapore "after the end of the first act in 1948" (to quote Bloodworth), Eu impishly told an unsuspecting Goh Keng Swee (his close pre-war college mate at Raffles) that "these are not the real leaders; the real leaders have not shown themselves."(5)

Eu did not tell his good friend that he was one of them. The MCP leader Chin Peng described "ECY" as a senior communist leader.

Bloodworth wrote: "Impishly, because it was Eu Chooi Yip, the thin, humble, unassuming, tubercular, witty, learned, *decent* secretary of the MDU, with his racking cough and his little tin of sputum, who would emerge as the powerful undercover communist boss of the island during the turbulent nineteenfifties." (6) 4.2.2004 2229

Eu was a pal and fellow student of Goh Keng Swee who studied economics at the Raffles College in Singapore before the outbreak of World War II. To Goh, Eu was witty and learned, and "a decent man". (7)

Both friends were brilliant scholars. (Their friendship withstood the test of time in the heat of political trials with Eu heading the communist revolution in Singapore and Goh teaming up with the PAP stalwarts like Lee Kuan Yew, S. Rajaratnam and Toh Chin Chye in their pursuit of independence and prosperity for Singapore. Goh went on to become a nation-builder par excellence.)

Eu was also a good next-room neighbour of S. Rajaratnam (another scholar) at 15 Chancery Lane. He was respected and admired by the then young, diffident Ceylon (now known as Sri Lanka) Tamil in the late 1940s (who subsequently became Singapore's Minister of Culture and then the Republic's longest-serving and most distinguished Foreign Minister).

Bloodworth narrated: "It was a relief to turn to the diminutive, quiet-spoken Eu Chooi Yip, who had the room next to the Rajaratnams, for this unobtrusive, round-faced young Chinese journalist with the cheap, ill-fitting glasses and the sensitive mouth seemed to earn the respect of everyone with whom he came into contact.

"Eu was bilingual in English and Chinese, wrote both with a quick, sure and incisive pen, and had worked in turn on the right-wing English-language **Straits Times** and the left-wing Chinese-language **Nam Chiao Jit Poh**..." (8) 5,2.2004 1527

Eu was the top Communist propagandist, fluent and effective bilingually in Enlish and Mandarin. And Raja, who later became a leader writer, was himself a prolific reader and a very good writer.

There was no doubt that Eu was very highly regarded "'He had a brilliant mind,' Rajaratnam recalls with admiration. 'But he was a sick man. He used to cough away in the middle of the night...'

To further quote Bloodworth: "He was content to earn a bare living, eating whatever was put in front of him, refusing to ride in a rickshaw on principle, a humble man whose thin, protesting frame was nevertheless actuated by an unyielding conviction, the stuff that medieval saints were made of. But no saint..." (9)

As the communist boss in Singapore, Eu had a chain of female couriers to provide two-way communication with the MCP leaders of the Johore-based South Malaya Bureau in Kluang across the Causeway.

He managed the legal MDU in the late1940s as well as the underground Anti-British League (formed in September 1948). 18.2.2004 1809

Eu escaped from the so-called "destruction" of the MCP's Town Committee (the local communist leadership) in Queen Street early December 1950. He then quietly slipped away in early 1951 when the others like his close colleagues Devan Nair, Sharma, Samad Ismail and James Puthecheary were nabbed by the Special Branch.

Bloodworth reported: "From being the master mole within the MDU, and then running the English-speaking ABL, he now sank from view to live a fugitive existence during which he not only contrived to put out **Freedom News** under increasingly perilous conditions, but controlled a disoriented scatter of undercover Party units on whom the Town Committee had died. He had direct lines to the communist chiefs in Malaya, however, and he was to retain them after another small boat took him to the nearby Rhio Islands in 1953, also according to plan..." (10)

At that time, there was a $5,000 reward out for Eu, as compared with only $2,000 for Fong Chuan Pik (also spelt as Fang Chuang Pi) – "a promising young Chinese on the editorial committee of **Freedom News** who was later to become the Plen (Lee Kuan Yew's top-level communist interlocutor in the late 1950s), the underground master of the CPM in Singapore..." (11)

When C.C. Too, head of Psychological Warfare in Kuala Lumpur, went to Singapore in early June 1962 (at a time when the PAP leadership was locked politically in mortal combat with the communists), he was taken to the SB Headquarters at Thompson Road and allowed to look through the files on political subversion and dossiers of communist leaders and leading suspects who had yet to surface, i.e. expose their presence on the ground. There was a file on Eu Chooi Yip, who happened to be an old friend of Too's.

According to Too, they had met from time to time in prewar Kuala Lumpur. Too remembered Eu as a Raffles College economics graduate. Too himself was at Raffles, one or two years junior to him.

According to Too, Eu came from a poor family, was soft-spoken, and a most capable organizer. He was a senior Government labour officer in Selangor, living at the Government quarters in Jalan Inai within the uptown precinct of the present Golden Triangle in Kuala Lumpur.

Owner of a second-hand Morris 8, Eu used to take Too for joy rides in the countryside out of Kuala Lumpur. Too also recalled that he had a "driving lesson" in Eu's car. Later, the psywar head was the first in Malaysia to own a magnificent red Jaguar E-type sports coupe (fitted with extra exhausts).

On the eve of World War II, however, Eu simply disappeared from view. And they never met each other again.

While Too strategised and managed the propaganda war against the communists on the mainland until his retirement in 1983, Eu directed the communist struggle in Singapore.

When Too came to Singapore in mid-1962, he found that the communists were poised to pounce on the tottering PAP and to seize power from Lee KuanYew. He was convinced that the Town Committee had remained intact all this while, and that Eu had been in charge of the shadow organization – beyond the ken of the intelligence and internal security operatives.

At the first meeting (a three-hour encounter) with Lee Kuan Yew in City Hall, Too looked straight at the Prime Minister and told him that the communists were virtually ready to take over power in Singapore. The PAP leadership was cut off from the masses and the communists were telling the people that merger was a sham.

As fate would have it, Too came to Singapore to avail himself of his considerable expertise in anti-communist psywar – but this time to help outwit a formidable adversary who had once been a close personal friend.

As described by Too, Eu was pint-sized, sickly-looking but with slightly pinkish cheek bones, a chain smoker on a cheap brand which probably made him cough a lot and so suspected of having TB.

Too himself was short but stout. Though not one to suffer fools and highly parsimonious in giving praise, he too thought very highly of Eu. He had a higher opinion of Eu than of Eu's big boss – Chin Peng, the legendary overlord of the communist movement in Malaya/Malaysia.

In the professional opinion and assessment of C.C. Too who had waged a highly successful propaganda war against Chin Peng and his political mafia since the early 1950s, the godfather of the communist underground in Singapore was a more brilliant communist leader and strategist. (12)

"The most prominent and senior communist leader we allowed to return to Singapore from China was Eu Chooi Yip," Lee Kuan Yew (Singapore's first prime minister 1959-90) wrote in his memoirs. (13)

"Eu Chooi Yip was the director superior in the MCP of Fang Chuang Pi, the leader of the communists in Singapore whom I had met in the 1950s and named the Plen, short for "plenipotentiary", of the communists…" (14)

Academically, Eu was probably the most highly qualified communist leader in Southeast Asia. But, he was not academic.

Eu Chooi Yip (1918-95) was a truly tested revolutionary, one of the unsung heroes and immortals of the communist revolution in Asia.

According to Rajaratnam, Eu was "completely dedicated to his communist cause…" (15)

Following a fairly long stay in Communist China, Eu expressed (in Mandarin) his admiration for the Chinese Communist Party (CCP) – the party responsible for China's political emancipation after a "century of humiliation" (1850-1950) and its subsequent modernization and rapid progress. (16)

NOTES: CHAPTER SEVEN: THE COMMUNIST MASTERMIND IN SINGAPORE

1. John Drysdale, **Singapore: Struggle for Success**

2. Ibid., p. 30 27.2.2004 1839

> In Foreword of **The Fajar Generation** (pp. x-xi), Lim Kean Chye, described as the doyen of the Malayan
>
> Democratic Union (MDU), has written: "...The appointment of Eu Chooi Yip as general secretary pulled in more graduates. This humble man, then ill with tuberculosis who had resigned from the plum job of assistant commissioner of labour, was popular in college (Raffles College in Singapore), a fact demonstrated by many graduates visiting the office of the MDU, then located above the Liberty Cabaret (in the heart of Singapore city)..." 08.10.2013 22:21

3. Drysdale, p. 30

4. Dennis Bloodworth, **The Tiger and the Trojan Horse**, p. xi

5. Ibid., p. 26

6. Ibid., p. 26

> In his memoirs **MY SIDE OF HISTORY** (p. 279), Chin Peng has described Eu Chooi Yip (whom he and other leading comrades called ECY) as "a senior Party member who had secretly run **Freedom News**, our Singapore underground newspaper. An economics graduate from Raffles College, he had been more openly associated with the Tan Kah Kee

owned **Nan Chiau Jit Pao**, a pro-CPC (Communist Party of China) publication... A highly experienced propagandist, Eu was one of very few comrades leaving Singapore then (1951) who would remain fully active in exile. He established himself in the Rhiau Islands and then continued clandestine Party activities..."

According to Chin Peng (p. 437), the senior Singapore communist leader and he met shortly after Chin Peng's arrival in Peking on June 1961. The two of them and Siao Chang met to discuss the progress of the communist struggle in Malaya/Singapore. They decided to sabotage the Malaysia plan or "at least we might substantially delay its implementation."

A Politburo member, Siao Chang left Peking in 1963 and arrived (after a long delay in Bangkok) to assume control of the CPM at its HQ in South Thailand.

7. Bloodworth, p. 22

8. Ibid. p21

9. Ibid. p. 21

10. Ibid. p. 38

11. Ibid. p. 38

In **The Memoirs of a Malayan Communist Revolutionary**, Fong Chong Pik wrote (p. 139) that his responsibility in the 1950s as a cadre was in propaganda and publications. Since the closure of **Freedom News**, he had been "waiting for employment" for a long time until his appointment by Eu Chooi Yip (then in Djakarta) to head the communist underground in Singapore in the late 1950s and early 1960s.

12. A more detailed account of C.C. Too's personal knowledge of Eu Chooi Yip and his 1962 political mission in Singapore can be found in Lim Cheng Leng's biography on the late Too: **THE STORY OF A PSY-WARRIOR: TAN SRI DR. C.C. TOO**, Chapter 15.

13. Lee Kuan Yew, **From Third World To First**, published 2000, p.138

14. Ibid., p. 138

According to Fong Chong Pik (p. 123), he had probably been recommended and nominated by his old comrade Eu to lead the communist underground in Singapore: "In fact, in temperament, Old Eu (an old friend) and I were very different. Simply put, he was a scholar always in search of proof, while I a sportsman preoccupied with winning... But with respect to personal relationships, most of the time, I looked up to him, while he took care of me..."

Fong summed it up (p. 124): "...Our mutual understanding and confidence allowed two persons of different characters to become happy working partners and intimate and united comrades in arms."

15. Irene Ng, **The Singapore Lion: A Biography of S. Rajaratnam**, published 2010, p. 97

Raja would later describe Chooi Yip as "very intelligent, very dedicated" and "one of the few who, unlike the poseurs, believed in the philosophy of communism with unyielding conviction…"

16. **uas.gov.sg** interviewed by Lim How Seng, National Archives of Singapore, Oral History 25 September 1992

CHAPTER EIGHT

Psywarrior From Kuala Lumpur

The head of psychological warfare (1956-83) in the Ministry of Home Affairs in Kuala Lumpur, C.C. Too was widely acknowledged as one of the world's experts in counter-insurgency and psywar against the communists. When he was sent in mid-1962 by the Ministry as a consultant to the PAP Government at the request of Prime Minister Lee Kuan Yew, he was probably recommended to Lee by the MI5 (Military Intelligence, section five), Britain's internal security agency in charge of counterintelligence and anti-subversion activities. Or MI6, the British foreign intelligence service. Or both the MI5 and the MI6 in Singapore. (1)

According to Too, he stayed in Singapore for about three months as a guest of the government but remained incognito to help Lee and the PAP Government wage a propaganda campaign against the Communist United Front (CUF) then spearheaded by the newly-formed Barisan Sosialis.

The CUF was commanded by the "Plen" in his secret hideout, but directed by Eu Chooi Yip from his offshore base on a nearby island in Indonesia to the south of Singapore. On the ground were the tiger generals and street fighters, with Lim Chin Siong at the forefront. 6.3.2004 1725 18.11.2014 09:03

As Too had put it, Lee was in a critical situation following the defection of the pro-communist faction within the PAP to form the Barisan Sosialis (BS) to take away the mass base from the ruling party to the CUF opposition in late July 1961. Too said the PAP "was left dangling in mid-air" while the BS was positioning itself to deliver the final knockout (KO) punch. Too had come to Singapore less than a year after Lord Selkirk's meeting with Lim Chin Siong and Company who had wanted to find out whether the colonial authorities would stand in the way to prevent another political group from taking over power from the PAP government. (2)

According to Too, it was the communists who had turned to the English-educated professionals like Lee Kuan Yew ostentatiously to lead and front their political struggle, i.e. to make use of them to serve their revolutionary cause and to further their anti-colonial struggle along constitutional lines. That was the only way to confront and challenge the colonial authorities, as authorized by them, short of taking up arms.

Lee Kuan Yew was invited to be their leader. The English-educated elite like Lee with their command of the colonial master's language had charisma, but were unable to speak and write Chinese. Moreover, they had little knowledge of the way of life and the aspirations of the Chinese majority in Singapore. In short, they had no rice-roots support.

"…Although he neither wrote nor spoke Chinese, Lee was already the legal adviser to a number of left-wing trade unions and organisations. The thing that stood out most was that Lee himself and the active elements among the Chinese middle school students who constituted the core of the mass movement had established a very close relationship…

"How could they not respect and actively support an elite lawyer from the English-speaking world who spoke for them, defended them, and helped them hold up their heads high?...

"The left-wing accepted him; we the cadres (over 50 of them) of the Communist Party gave him our approval. In this way, it was formally decided that the PAP and Lee Kuan Yew would be the object of our united front cooperation in the left-wing anti-colonial struggle," so wrote Fong Chong Pik (alias the "Plen") in his **Memoirs**. (3)

Although Fong nominally headed the CPM's underground organization, he admitted: "Of course, Lim Chin Siong was the left-wing's most important person. After the appearance of the "Plen" (to take charge of the Communist Party in Singapore early 1958 following Eu Chooi Yip's departure to Jakarta), he (Lim) remained the most important left-wing person (the first to stand on the frontline), one with even greater influence and authority (on the ground)..." (4)

The Chinese-educated communist cadres could get down to the ground and mobilize the masses. Thus, once Lim Chin Siong and gang left to form the Barisan Sosialis, they took away the mass base with them as well as some 70% of the PAP branches. Lee Kuan Yew's mantle of leadership in the populist open front organisation was transferred to another Lee – Lee Siew Choh, chairman of the Barisan Sosialis. A former PAP parliamentary secretary, Siew Choh had been sacked with four others on 22 July 1961. 10.3.2004 1755 14.12.2013 07:52

In Singapore, the Chinese electorate was divided between the Chinese-educated (who formed the large majority) and the English-educated. According to an analysis of electoral results, there's a hard-core of some 20 to 30 per cent in permanent opposition to the government side.

According to Too, the PAP had also alienated the civil service with their wage cut or freeze soon after coming to power in 1959. (To make up for this early transgression, however, wages were restored before the September 1962 referendum on merger.) The civil servants had voted for the PAP in the 1959 general election.

Too concluded that the PAP had antagonized practically the whole population of Singapore. Needless to say, this assessment was a sweeping and dramatic generalization – one calculated to arouse the ire of an irascible young and arrogant Lee.

Nevertheless, Too admitted that Lee Kuan Yew was a hard-headed leader, and he added that Lee had requested him to help "save the situation". Too noted: "There was no doubt that whatever his faults (including his arrogance and unpopularity at that time), Mr Lee was not lacking in the courage to face facts squarely…" Moreover, Lee listened to, and acted on, good counsel.

But when Too remarked that Lee had opted for merger as "the last straw", he was again not quite right. He was wrong both metaphorically and factually, since Lee had desired and sought merger with next-door Malaya for his "whole adult life" (to quote Lee). Merger had also featured as a major objective of the PAP platform in the 1959 general election which this party had swept and won a very strong mandate.

However, merger in the broader form of Tunku Abdul Rahman's May 1961 proposal (to establish Malaysia through the integration of the Federation of Malaya, Singapore, and the neighbouring territories of Borneo) was a strategic move to thwart the communist threat in Singapore. And, timely merger saved Lee and the PAP politically.

9.4.2004 1645

Too had a three-hour meeting with Prime Minister Lee Kuan Yew in City Hall the day after his arrival in Singapore on early June 1962. And on Lee's insistence, Too said he typed overnight a 35-page proposal including an analysis of the political and security situation in Singapore and a blueprint to win over the population for merger as well as to "save" the situation.

Too's blueprint contained two key points: (1) to get the necessary public support, in a referendum, for merger, and (2) to neutralize the communist leadership in Singapore through a full-blooded operation against the principal subversives (as officially classified).

During his (typically) blunt session with Lee, he noticed that George Bogaars, head of the Singapore Special Branch, had been sweating profusely in the air-conditioned office while the local expert from Kuala Lumpur must have conjured up a more dire and daunting Communist threat than depicted in the SB's so-called White Paper, calling for a crackdown on the Communist leadership in the United Front.

Too said his mission was "to prevent a Communist takeover of the island" (of Singapore). This he did, according to him, "by providing Lee with a master plan which enabled his tottering PAP Government to win its referendum for merger with the Federation of Malaya, thus ensuring the political survival of Mr. Lee himself and his PAP Government, and at the same time making it possible for the formation of Malaysia..." (5)

He added in explanation: "At that time, this (proposed formation of Malaysia) was entirely out of the question without the inclusion of a Singapore which had to retain a comparatively stable and non-Communist government." A stable and non-communist state was politically de rigueur, and, of course, it was the Tunku's condition for agreeing to take in Singapore after much reluctance to do so.

Security, particularly eradication of the communist threat in Singapore, was the main factor in the rationale for the anti-communist purge carried out on February 1963, less than eight months before the establishment of Malaysia. (6)

Too described his blueprint as "simplicity itself". It would tell the people in Singapore to choose between a communist government and a PAP government within the new Malaysian framework. The same message would be addressed to the influential Chinese Chamber of Commerce to get its blue ribbon support for merger. (7)

A top-down approach was suggested with the Prime Minister making his pitch to the electorate and appealing to the community leaders in the Chinese Chamber of Commerce (CCC), who in their turn must work on the guilds and associations, and so on down to the rice-roots level of the Chinese-educated masses.

The business leaders would be offered an economic carrot, through merger Malaysia would create a bigger market for their goods and services. (The PAP already had this in mind when in 1958 it proposed the concept of a common market with the envisioned (re-) union of Malaya and Singapore.)

The people of Singapore would be told to choose between a totalitarian regime (a la Mao in Peking) with very tight control over their lives, and political independence (the end of British colonialism) and brighter prospects through merger (in the proposed formation of Malaysia).

The message to the masses boiled down to: communist rule with all its constraints, or merger for peace, security and prosperity. 10.4..2004 1650 14.12.2013 08:12

Although the Chinese in Singapore were generally very proud of the success of the communist revolution in China, their relatives and friends there had written letters to them with harrowing accounts of widespread abject poverty and famine in the wake of the disastrous Great Leap Forward campaign (1958-61).

In China 1960-62 has gone down in history as the "three hard years", and the great famine in 1960-61 took away some 20 million lives or more. Moreover, this human catastrophe coincided with the ideological/political split in 1960 between China and the Soviet Union – the two giants in the Communist world.

As advised by C.C. Too, Lee's main target was to be the Chinese leadership in the field of commerce and industry. The leaders in the Chinese Chamber of Commerce could be persuaded if they were told to choose between a communist government and a continuation of PAP rule with Singapore forming an important component of the proposed Malaysia, which would provide them with both political stability and enhanced economic well-being.

Historically, the PAP had been very interested in the attractive economics of scale in a common market with Malaya, which would enable Singapore to make an economic breakthrough. The envisaged market formed the Party's economic rationale for merger with the Federation. Tunku himself envisioned Singapore serving as a "New York" and Kuala Lumpur as "Washington" for the peninsular mainland. (8)

The various Chinese guild and associations came under the Chinese Chamber of Commerce. And traditionally, the captains of commerce and industry were community leaders. Furthermore, they were also very big and important employers. It was up to Lee Kuan Yew to use his authority and rhetoric to win them over to his side.

And, offered a choice between a red Singapore as a hostage to fortune and a secure and prosperous Malaysia including an economically dynamic and thriving Singapore, it was not hard to tell which the hard-nosed business and mercantile leaders would plump for.

As it turned out, the communists and leftists also tried to garner the support of the CCC but instead of using sweet and reasonable persuasion (as recommended by C.C. Too), the "Plen" tried to intimidate the millionaires into opposing merger. And this ill-conceived threat boomeranged against them.

Even before the split with the pro-communists in the PAP, it had hardly been a secret that the authorities would crack down hard on the communist cadres and pro-communist/leftist leaders in the political arena. And C.C. Too also said that part of his Singapore mission was to help prepare the publicity campaign for the mass arrest of subversive elements on the island. According to him, this move was essential for Lee's political survival. Too's job was to assist in preparing for the propaganda war (in which he had vast expertise) – to portray the communists as working against the interests of the people of Singapore. (9)

In fact, Lee had initiated his own political/propaganda campaign with his dozen radio talks in his memorable "Battle for Merger" series on air, from mid-September to the second week of October 1961. Well done, Harry!

As advised by C.C. Too, Tunku insisted that the security operation be carried out **before merger**, and certainly not after. (10)

Since the radicals got wind of such a big swipe several years earlier, "Operation Cold Store" did not come as a surprise at all (although the colonial authorities cooked up a politically expedient pretext or so-called rationale for its execution). But its timing (the unknown element) was important. And although the Singapore Special Branch head remarked that it was to "put them away for a little while", "Operation Cold Store" put Lee's most formidable political foes permanently out in the cold. It's goodbye, for good, as they say.

Notes Chapter Eight: Psywarrior from Kuala Lumpur

1. Curriculum vitae of Too Chee Chew, better known as C.C Too, self-compiled in 1984

    Gen. Richard Clutterbuck described Too as "a brilliant young Chinese graduate of Raffles College" when appointed in February 1951 as a Chinese Assistant in the Psychological Warfare Section at the height of the Malayan Emergency I (1948-60).

    According to Too, he pursued a three-year diploma course in Pure Science (chemistry, physics and maths) at the Raffles College (1939-41). But his studies ended with the Japanese bombing of Singapore on 8 December 1941. However, in 1947 he was awarded a War Diploma in Science – equivalent to B.Sc.

    Too entered Raffles College the year his good friend Eu Chooi Yip, the postwar Communist mastermind, graduated with Honours in Economics.

    Before the historic powwow with the top communist leader Chin Peng at Baling on December 1955, senior British and local officials held a "dress rehearsal" (or dry run) in which Too played the part of Chin Peng (when they had first met briefly about a decade earlier, Comrade Chin Peng had presented a small bottle of brilliantine to Too "during those days I still had a fair amount of hair on my head"). At this simulation exercise, Too "predicted the major moves made by the Communist Party of Malaya" (to quote him).

Too was present as an observer at Baling where Chin Peng "looked quietly nervous about his own safety" (this meeting, it should be noted, was not held on neutral ground). He found Chin Peng's performance a great disappointment, without giving a reason.

What has Chin Peng got to say about it?

"We were being brow beaten to give up. Capitulate and be chastised – this was the message at Baling," Chin Peng has written in **MY SIDE OF HISTORY** (p. 514).

"I had desired peace but it was fundamental that my men and women were not roundly humiliated…"

Nearly three and a half decades later (after another futile round of armed conflict, Emegency II 1968-78) did they manage to get what Chin Peng described as "peace with dignity" in the December 1989 pact signed by both the Malaysian and Thai governments and the Communist Party of Malaya.

That 1989 peace accord which ended four decades of communist armed struggle in Peninsular Malaysia (the longest insurgency in history), rankled and riled C.C. Too to no end.

"C.C. Too's constant advice to the government was to obtain no less than surrender terms from the CPM, and to seek its complete destruction," Lim Cheng Leng, another senior Malaysian psychological warrior, has written in his biography of C.C. Too, **THE STORY OF A PSY-WARRIOR** (Preface, p. 5).

The late Tan Sri Dr C.C. Too's grandfather Too Nam was once a Chinese tutor to Dr Sun Yat Sen, founder of the Kuomintang Party in 1911, and a leading fellow revolutionary in the founding of the Republic of China in 1911. Too Nam later came to Malaya, where he stayed in Kuala Lumpur until his death in 1939.

C.C. could probably have imbibed the KMT spirit and culture from young.

2. Too wrote in **Far Eastern Economic Review** 14 December 1989:

"Singapore's People's Action Party (PAP) was deeply penetrated, with its grassroot cadres almost completely in communist hands, while the few non-communist top leaders, such as party secretary-general Lee Kuan Yew, were dangling in mid-air, not knowing what to do…"

In his book **OUSTED!** Patrick Keith, a veteran journalist and confidant of the Malayan Prime Minister, has recorded (p. 20): "…It seemed to the Tunku that there was a real danger communism could take hold on the island and soon capture power (in the early 1960s). In the Tunku's opinion, Lee had tried to be a little too clever at one stage, believing he could make use of the communists to fight the British (politically) and then discard them when the struggle for freedom had been won.

"Other men like him, had mounted the communist tiger but finished up in its stomach, and Lee, in the Malayan leader's view, was already half-way down its throat…"

3. Fong Chong Pik, **The Memoirs of a Malayan Communist Revolutionary**, pp. 125-126

    In one of his "Battle for Merger" talks over Radio Singapore in September-October 1961, Lee Kuan Yew explained that the English-educated revolutionaries co-operated with the communists within the PAP to get rid of the British colonialists. He also said that the English-educated had "bridged the gap to the Chinese-educated world – a world teeming with vitality, dynamism and revolution, a world in which the Communists had been working for over the last thirty years with considerable success…"

    As quoted in Clutterbuck, **Conflict and Violence in Singapore and Malaysia 1945-1983**, p. 105

4. Fong Chong Pik, p. 170

5. In a recap, Too later wrote in **Far Eastern Economic Review** 14 December 1989, p. 26:

    "The political future of the PAP depended on the outcome of the referendum. Likewise, the realization of the proposed Federation of Malaysia would not be possible if the PAP should be defeated in its referendum and if Singapore should lose its non-communist PAP government. The British would hardly have left the island to the communists or to anarchy…"

    Please also refer to Chiang Siew Lee's report in **New Sunday Times** December 3, 1989

6. At the emergency meeting of the Internal Security Council (ISC) on 14 December 1962 called by the Malayan Home Minister, Dr Ismail said merger would

not proceed unless the communists were arrested. Lee Kuan Yew agreed.

The British position was that the Brunei revolt (8 December 1962) provided the perfect opportunity for joint action. The three parties then agreed on taking joint responsibility and issuing a joint public statement on their preemptive operation ("Operation Cold Store" of 2 Feb 1963).

Info from CO 1030/1160 T, no. 582, 14 December 1962, as quoted by Tan Jing Quee, "Merger and the Decimation of the Left Wing in Singapore", published in **THE FAJAR GENERATION**, SIRD, Petaling Jaya, 2010, p. 284

7. After a visit to Singapore in mid-1961, John Strachey (Labour Secretary of State for War in the Atlee Cabinet) commented that the PAP was facing increasing difficulties. He wrote in **New Statesman** (August 18, 1961): "Public men in Singapore will have to declare themselves in favour of some such federal scheme or accept the leadership of the Chinese Government and its powerful agency in Singapore, the illegal, but formidable Communist Party…"

8. In the late 1950s and early 1960s, Singapore's most critical problem (publicly submerged in the political hubbub and turbulence) was her economy. Dr Goh Keng Swee, who became Finance Minister in 1959, "aimed to throw off the degradation of poverty by rapid economic growth. The key to this was large-scale industrialization which would mop up unemployment and finance social measures, of which the most crying need was to

rehouse the population decently…" (to quote Turnbull, **A History of Singapore 1819-1975**, p. 275).

As recommended in the 1955 World Bank report on economic development, Goh planned to promote industrialization in the context of a common market with mainland Malaya.

Historian Mary Turnbull has also recorded the acrimonious pre-merger haggling over finance, taxation, and trade; the financial arrangement concluded in July 1963 was favourable to Singapore, including a provision for a common market.

"Singapore had secured financial advantages at the expense of losing a great deal of goodwill in Kuala Lumpur, and the wounds inflicted on the relationship failed to heal," Turnbull wrote her highly perceptive comments (pp. 286-287).

"Despite the clash of economic and financial interests, it appeared in September 1963 that the two territories' immediate political interests coincided, because both governments wanted to hold in check the extreme left wing in Singapore.

"Paradoxically, it was political conflict which embittered the relations of the two partners and within two years brought the brief unhappy marriage to (a) stormy divorce…"

9. An old friend and colleague of C.C. Too in the field of counter-insurgency, **Lim Cheng Leng** has written and published the first authorized biography on the great psychological warrior, who passed away in April 1992.

Entitled **THE STORY OF A PSY-WARRIOR: TAN SRI Dr. C.C. Too**, this groundbreaking book on Malayan/Malaysian psychological warfare techniques, contains a detailed full-chapter account of Too's special mission to Singapore in mid-1962, on the cusp of history.

10. As recorded in Lim's bio on Too (p. 201): "...Too's advice to the Tengku was emphatically to carry out the mass arrest before merger and the formation of Malaysia; otherwise it would be better not to proceed with the proposed merger..."

In a letter to the British High Commissioner in Kuala Lumpur which the Tunku wrote on 6 January 1963, the Malayan prime minister repeated the decisive point that the Malayan government would not accept Singapore into Malaysia unless the arrests were made before merger.

Released for public information: British High Commissioner, Kuala Lumpur, to UK Commissioner in Singapore, CO 1030/1576, no. 19, 6 January 1963

Chapter 8): Psywarrior from Kuala Lumpur

1. Curriculum vitae of Too Chee Chew, better known as C.C. Too, self-compiled in 1984

   Clutterbuck (**Conflict and Violence in Singapore and Malaysia 1945-1983**, p. 193) has described Too as "a brilliant young Chinese graduate of Raffles College" when appointed in February 1951 as Chinese Assistant in the Psychological Warfare Section at the height of the Malayan Emergency, the anti-communist insurgent war.

According to Too, he pursued a three-year diploma course in Pure Science (chemistry, physics and maths) at the Raffles College (1939-41) in Singapore. But his studies ended with the Japanese bombing of Singapore on 8 December 1941. However, in 1947 he was awarded a War Diploma in Science – equivalent to a general degree B. Sc.

Too was particularly proud of his early postwar liaison work (September 1945-April 1946) which he had volunteered, while looking for a full-time job as a 25-year-old, with the British Military Administration (BMA) and a small American detachment from the OSS (Office of Strategic Services, a US intelligence agency formed with British assistance during World War II to support the American military, a predecessor of the Central Intelligence Agency or the CIA). At the same time, Too was mixing gingerly with the local communist leaders in Kuala Lumpur. One of them, a CPM Central Committee member, had been a 1934 classmate in the Confucian Middle School in Kuala Lumpur where Too himself had completed junior middle in Chinese education (then the highest level) before moving on to the Methodist Boys' School and then emerging as the top student in the 1938 Cambridge School Certificate Examinations in Kuala Lumpur.

Too described the cocky communist leaders with whom he had associated, as "a gang of half-educated, swollen-headed, power-mad adolescent demagogues trying to take over the country" in the wake of the Japanese surrender at the end of World War II following the atomic bombings of Hiroshima and Nagasaki early August 1945.

He added: "Nevertheless they were extremely aggressive and daring in their activities, and the real threat they posed was not to be taken lightly". 06.04.2014 20:45

According to Too, he was instrumental in the defection of a key executive in the "most vital front organization the Malayan People's Anti-Japanese Union (MPAJU) which had been set up by them parallel to their Malayan People's Anti-Japanese Army (MPAJA) during Japanese occupation". Although he did not say so, the high-level defection of Comrade Chan Tai Chee was a personal triumph for Too in his own undeclared war against communism.

It led to the arrest and trial of the "fabulous and mystical underground chief" (also described as "the most feared and hated person in Kuala Lumpur at that time"). Too described him as "a short and slightly built, cocky young Chinese" about as short and as old as Too himself but at least 10-15 years younger than the turncoat key executive.

For the record, Soon Kwong, Selangor MPAJU general secretary, was arrested on October 1946, convicted for extortion, and banished to China.

Too recorded that the "fabulous MPAJU chief" was arrested and tried in open court for extortion as an ordinary criminal. His conviction and removal from the communist struggle completed the collapse of the MPAJU from which it never recovered. It also triggered a chain reaction in which the other communist front organisations came down like falling dominos. And at the top level, it subsequently created disenchantment and dissension in the Central Committee itself. All in all, an ominous prologue to the 12-year-long communist insurgency which the colonial authorities declared as "Emergency" (1948-60) in Malaya on 19 June 1948. The Emergency was declared a few days later in Singapore on 23 June.

Back to Too, who reported: "The top leaders were driven with their backs against the wall. There was no escape. In sheer desperation they resorted to drastic and even dangerous measures to save themselves and the party from imminent and total destruction.

"The whole development took place in roughly six months, during which I somehow managed to accomplish much more than what I had originally set out to do (without spelling it out). I watched the rapidly changing scene with fascination and awe, amazed at my own temerity and happy at the thought that my efforts were not made in vain. The rare opportunity was given only to the very few, and I was deeply grateful for it." (Too was only 26 years and a half old at that time.) And, he said, simply and curtly: "I did not like them at all." For a graphic account of Too's role in Comrade Chan Tai Chee's defection and MPAJU chief Soon Kwong's dramatic fall-on fall and political demise, please refer to Lim Cheng Leng, **THE STORY OF A PSY-WARRIOR**, pp. 67-70.

The Baling peace talks on December 1955 marked the definite but dilatory decline in the communist insurgency which was to lead to the declaration of the official end of the Emergency on 31 July 1960. Malaya became an independent and sovereign country on 31 August 1957.

Before the historic powwow with the top communist leader Chin Peng at Baling on December 1955, senior British and local officials held a "dress rehearsal" or dry run in which Too played the part of the communist chief (when they had first met briefly about a decade earlier in Kuala Lumpur, Comrade Chin Peng had presented a small bottle of brilliantine to Too "during those days I still had a fair amount of hair on my head"). At this simulation exercise, Too "predicted the major moves made by the Communist Party of Malaya" (to quote him).

Too was present as an observer at Baling where Chin Peng "looked quietly nervous and worried about his own safety" (this meeting, it should be noted, was not held on neutral ground). He found Chin Peng's performance a great disappointment.

What has Chin Peng got to say about it?

In **MY SIDE OF HISTORY** (p. 512), he has written: "… There was nothing in Baling that inspired a frank and honest exchange of ideas required in the resolution of conflict. Apart from the fact that the British were clearly calling the shots, there was also the absence of genuine motivation.

"The Tunku used the occasion as a propaganda boost to enhance his political image and strengthen his bargaining position (for political independence, national freedom and sovereignty) with London…"

In **MY SIDE OF HISTORY**, Chin Peng has written (p. 514) on the failure of the 1955 peace talks: "…We were being brow beaten to give up. Capitulate and be chastised – this was the message at Baling…

"I had desired peace but it was fundamental that my men and women were not roundly humiliated…"

In mid-1968 the Communist Party of Malaya launched a new offensive to mark the start of Emergency II (1968-89), another protracted campaign to capture power, on a longer time frame but at a lower level of intensity with a focus on the urban struggle. The second round of armed struggle ended with the signing of the peace agreement in Haadyai on 2 December 1989.

Nearly three and a half decades after Baling peace talks, did the communists manage to get what Chin Peng has described as "peace with dignity".

Chin Peng has commented (ibid., p. 514): "The 1989 peace accords were reached because the Malaysian government, the Thai government and the Communist Party of Malaya all genuinely wanted a resolution to hostilities. All parties looked to a bigger picture, to a future offering peace and prosperity. So the CPM got a reasonable solution to its struggle – peace with dignity. We failed to win the revolution but neither did we suffer the ignominy of surrender. It is the kind of peace for my people I can accept and with which I can live with some satisfaction…"

C.C. Too was not happy about the Haadyai resolution of the communist armed struggle. It should be noted, however, that less than a year after the Baling fiasco in late1955, Too was appointed the head of Psychological Warfare Section until his retirement at the end of January 1983.

For a concise analytical study of the communist armed struggle in Malaya/Malaysia, the first attempt of its kind, please refer to Lim Cheng Leng and Khor Eng Lee, **WAGING AN UNWINNABLE WAR: The Communist Insurgency in Malaysia (1948-1989)**.

1 (a) Apart from MI5 (Military Intelligence/State Security), C.C. Too's role in the secret mission to Singapore June 1962 could have been suggested by someone high up or influential in the MI6 (Military Intelligence/Espionage) or even the anti-communist Information Research Department, set up early 1948 within the British Foreign Office to counter Soviet

propaganda and launch an anti-communist campaign in the context of the nascent Cold War.

According to Paul Lashmar and James Oliver in their 1998 book **BRITAIN'S SECRET PROPAGANDA WAR 1948-1977** (p. 28), the IRD had from the start, close links with the Secret Intelligence Service (SIS, also known as MI6).

The IRD opened its regional office for Southeast Asia in Singapore in 1949, the year of the Communist victory in mainland China.

Lashmar and Oliver have reported (ibid., p. 41): "IRD became an important part of the organization built up by the British at Phoenix Park in Singapore to counter Communist insurgency in the area (South-East Asia). J.B. Smith, a CIA liaison officer at Phoenix Park in the early 1950s, reported that IRD was running a joint operation with MI6, represented at that time by Maurice Oldfield assisted by Fergie Dempster. Oldfield was later to become director of the Secret Service…" 1,514 words 06-07.04.2014 00:34

2. Too wrote in **Far Eastern Economic Review**, 14 December 1989:

   "Singapore's People's Action Party (PAP) was deeply penetrated, with its grassroot cadres almost completely in communist hands, while the few non-communist top leaders, such as party secretary-general Lee Kuan Yew, were dangling in mid-air, not knowing what to do…"

3. In his "Battle for merger talks" over Radio Singapore in September-October 1961, Lee Kuan Yew explained that the English-educated revolutionaries co-operated with the communists within the PAP to get rid of the British colonialists. He also said that

the English-educated had "bridged the gap to the Chinese-educaated world – a world teeming with vitality, dynamism and revolution, a world in which the Communists had been working for over the last thirty years with considerable success…" As quoted in Clutterbuck, p. 105

The young left-wing activists and leaders like Lim Chin Siong and Fong Swee Suan had courted their English-speaking legal advisor and champion in the person of Lee Kuan Yew, who was then debuting as the new political superstar in Singapore.

As narrated by Fong Chong Pik (aka the "Plen") in his **Memoirs** (pp. 125-126): "…Although he neither wrote nor spoke Chinese, Lee (Kuan Yew) was already the legal adviser to a number of left-wing trade unions and organizations. The thing that stood out most was that Lee himself and the active elements among the Chinese middle school students who constituted the core of the mass movement had established a very close relationship… How could they not respect and actively support an elite lawyer from the English-speaking world who spoke for them, defended them, and helped them hold up their heads?…

"The left-wing accepted him; we the cadres (over 50 of them) of the Communist Party gave him our approval. In this way, it was formally decided that the PAP and Lee Kuan Yew would be the object of our united front cooperation in the left-wing anti-colonial struggle…"

Although the "Plen" nominally headed the communist underground, Fong admitted in **Memoirs** (p. 170): "Of course, **Lim Chin Siong** was the left-wing's most important person. After the appearance of the "Plen" (to take charge of the Communist Party in Singapore early 1958 following Eu Chooi Yip's departure to Jakarta), he (Lim) remained the most important left-wing person (the first to stand on the frontline), one with even greater influence and authority (on the ground)…" 18.09.2014 12:27

4. After a visit to Singapore in mid-1961, John Strachey (former Labour Secretary of State for War in the Attlee Cabinet 1945-51) commented that the PAP was facing increasing difficulties.

    Strachey wrote in the **New Statesman** (August 18, 1961): "Public men in Singapore will have to declare themselves in favour of some such federal scheme (as the formation of Malaysia proposed by Malayan Prime Minister Tunku Abdul Rahman on 27 May 1961) or accept the leadership of the Chinese Government (in Peking) and its powerful agency in Singapore, the illegal, but formidable Communist Party…"

About a month after C.C. Too's first meeting with Prime Minister Lee Kuan Yew in the City Hall, Britain and Malaya quietly concluded and signed in late July 1962 an agreement on the formation of Malaysia. The British Government had planned to merge (re-unite) Malaya and Singapore which had separated since the short-lived establishment of Malayan Union on 1 April 1946.

Lord Landsdowne, the colonial minister of state who chaired the Inter-Governmental Committee responsible for the detailed constitutional arrangements for Malaysia, had early made it clear that the British Government (HMG) could not accept forming Malaysia without Singapore. As officially recorded: "We would find it virtually impossible to resist the inevitable demand for independence in Singapore, and independence would mean a Communist Singapore. The Federation (of Malaya) has understood this when they had taken the initiative (with Tunku's proposal made in Singapore on 27 May 1961) towards merger and the formation of Malaysia..." --- CO 1030/1462, 11 May 1963, as quoted by Poh Soo Kiat, **THE FAJAR GENERATION**, p. 195

5. C.C. Too's CV Chiang Siew Lee's report in **New Sunday Times**, December3, 1989

(a) Under the circumstances, Selkirk was reluctant to go along with the Tunku's intention to lock up the Communist leaders in Singapore although the UK Commissioner was aware that merger might be prejudiced without these arrests. Selkirk wrote that Tunku had thoroughly frightened Lee by suggesting that the Federation would abandon the Malaysia plan. Selkirk also wrote that Lee would be "quite clearly attracted by the prospect of wiping out his main political opposition before the next Singapore election" (scheduled for 1963).

--- Selkirk to R. Maudling, Colonial Secretary, On Internal Security Position in Singapore, before meeting with Lee Kuan Yew in London, as recorded in CO 1030/998, 28 April 1962, and quoted by Tan Jing Quee, "Merger and the Decimation of the Left Wing in Singapore", **THE FAJAR GENERATION**, p. 283

(b) In a recap, Too later wrote: "The political future of the PAP depended on the outcome of the referendum (conducted on 1 September 1962 following PAP defeats in two by-elections in 1961 at Hong Lim in late April and Anson in mid-July). Likewise, the realization of the proposed Federation of Malaysia would not be possible if the PAP should be defeated in its referendum and if Singapore should lose its non-communist PAP government. The British would hardly have left the island to the communists or to anarchy…"

--- **Far Eastern Economic Review**, 14 December 1989, p. 26

6. It may be recalled that the Chinese Chamber of Commerce had opposed the separation of Singapore following the creation of the Malayan Union on April 1945.

Although the CCC fared dismally in the 1955 general election, it retained its economic clout among the Chinese community in Singapore.

In the late 1950s and early 1960s, Singapore's most critical problem (publicly submerged in the political hubbub and turbulence) was its economy in the doldrums. Dr Goh Keng Swee, who became Finance Minister in 1959, "aimed to throw off the degradation of poverty by rapid economic growth. The key to this was large-scale industrialization which would mop up unemployment and finance social measures, of which the most crying need was to rehouse the population decently" (to quote historian Mary Turnbull, **A History of Singapore 1819-1975**, p. 275).

As recommended in the 1955 World Bank report on economic development, Goh planned to promote industrialization in the context of a common market to be formed with mainland Malaya across the Causeway.

7. In the general election held on 21 September 1963, within a week of the birth of Malaysia on 16 September, Lee's PAP was returned to power in nearly three-quarters of the 51 constituencies though winning less than half of the total votes cast (47 per cent). With renewed confidence, Lee looked forward to turning Singapore into the "New York" of Malaysia, the industrial base of "an affluent and just society". He announced that his government's first task was to harmonise with Kuala Lumpur, as bilateral relationship was already strained even before actual merger.

(a) Turnbull recorded (ibid., pp. 286-287): "The months before the final Malaysia agreement was drawn up (finally concluded on July 1963) had been a time of acrimonious haggling over finance, taxation, and trade, and for a time it appeared that negotiations had reached an impasse because Singapore was trying to drive too hard a bargain.

"The terms hammered out in July 1963 were financially favourable to Singapore and included provision for a common market, which Singapore sought more eagerly than Kuala Lumpur. Both Malaya and Singapore were industrializing and ultimately wanted the expanded domestic market which economic union would bring. But their immediate economic interests conflicted. Singapore was unwilling to abandon her free port status, while the Federation did not want to open her tariff walls to the competition of Singapore industry with its initial benefit of tax-free raw materials.

"Singapore succeeded in getting a provision written into the Malaysia agreement for a progressive common market to be introduced over the next twelve years, causing the least possible upset to her entrepot trade.

"Singapore had secured financial advantages at the expense of losing a great deal of goodwill in Kuala Lumpur, and the wounds inflicted on the relationship failed to heal. Despite the clash of economic and financial interests, it appeared in September 1963 that the two territories' immediate political interests coincided, because both governments wanted to hold in check the extreme left wing in Singapore.

"Paradoxically, it was political conflict which embittered the relations of the two partners and within two years brought the brief unhappy marriage to (a) stormy divorce…"

8. When the Barisan Sosialis tried to intimidate the Chinese Chamber of Commerce which had advised its members to vote for the form of merger favoured and espoused by the PAP Government (known as Alternative A), the CCC bought space in all Chinese and English dailies for two consecutive days towards the end of August 1962 announcing its full support for "Alternative A". Refer Drysdale, **Singapore: Struggle for Success**, p. 310

9. An old friend and colleague of C.C. Too in the field of counter-insurgency, Lim Cheng Leng has written and

published the first authorized biography on the late Tan Sr (Dr) C.C. Too who passed away on April 1992.

Entitled **THE STORY OF A PSY-WARRIOR: TAN SRI DR. C.C. TOO**, this groundbreaking book (published in 2000) contains a detailed account (Chapter 15) on Too's special mission to Singapore in mid-1962.

(a) During the flight with the Tunku from Kuala Lumpur to Alor Star and back on the morning of 12 February 1962, Ghazali Shafie recalled that the Prime Minister shared his thoughts on the security situation in Singapore. In his book **MEMOIR** on the Formation of Malaysia (p. 191), Ghazali has written:

"He (Tunku) said he had a strong feeling that the *Barisan Sosialis* and the communists and those opposed to the Malaysia Concept would now mount their best efforts and even actively plot to make as much trouble on the eve of the merger or just before the realization of Malaysia.

"He admitted that he had no information but he had a clear hunch or intuition which he felt strongly. He envisioned strikes, arson and willful damaging of government property everywhere. There would be terrorist intimidations and shooting of policemen. He saw the scenario that in order to bring about peace and order, some emergency measures and force would have to be used. This, according to the Tunku, would mean that the hands of the government would be soiled with blood. Such a situation must be avoided to preserve the good record of the government…

"The Tunku then instructed me to inform Dr. Ismail (Dato Dr Ismail bin Dato Abdul Rahman), the minister responsible for Internal Security, that he should consider establishing a strong liaison in intelligence with the Singapore Special Branch. The Tunku was anxious to substantiate his hunch. He also wanted to know (about four months before C.C. Too's first meeting with Lee Kuan Yew in the City Hall of Singapore) how much Lee Kuan Yew knew about the situation (the communist threat in Singapore) and whether he had facts and figures to support his surmises. With regard to the Singapore *Barisan Sosialis* he had been toying with the idea of having a heart to heart talk with its leaders at an appropriate time.

"According to the Tunku, the British authorities in Singapore should start cleaning up operations to remove the communists. It would be impossible for the British to deny any knowledge of communist activities. Unless the British were prepared to clean up Singapore before merger it would be difficult for the merger to take place…"

Ghaz then talked to Deputy PM Razak, Dr Ismail and Lee about the Tunku's anxieties. In the course of his work early 1962 with the Cobbold Commission to ascertain the views of the people in North Borneo (now Sabah) and Sarawak, Ghazali transited and stopped over at Singapore where he had a number of informal meetings with Lee Kuan Yew. On one occasion, they spoke about cleaning up Singapore politically. Ghazali has written (p. 196):

"…Lee Kuan Yew said the Tunku should allow him to conduct the affairs of Singapore in his own way since he knew the communists. Lee Kuan Yew was working on a plan to lead public opinion to such a point that when action was taken against the communist leaders, nobody would sympathise with them. If action was taken without any preparation those subversive elements would be regarded as martyrs which must be avoided…"

According to Ghaz (p. 249), British Prime Minister Harold MacMillan sent a note to the Tunku on 28 July 1962 suggesting that they declare their intention to conclude a formal agreement for the transfer of sovereignty on 31 August 1963, with safeguards for the special interests of North Borneo and Sarawak. The guidelines on defence agreements "had already been agreed to."

Ghaz, who had the benefit of a quick glance with his keen eyes through MacMillan's suggested plan, has put on record (p. 250): "The two Prime Ministers also agreed but not for public knowledge that if Singapore Government fell to the communist elements or that its collapse to the communists was imminent, then Malaysia should be formed as quickly as possible..."

Ghaz has followed with a personal note (p. 250): "The Tunku said to me confidentially and confidently that he would do everything in his power to assist Lee Kuan Yew in order to obviate a situation which might trigger all kinds of undesirable eventualities..." 28.07.2014 13:11

10. C.C. Too was dispatched to Singapore early June 1962 to help Lee Kuan Yew make up his mind about merger and the necessary action against the communist threat.

(a) According to Too, he had advised both the Prime Minister Tunku Abdul Rahman and his deputy Tuan Abdul Razak Hussein that action must be taken against the communist leadership in Singapore **before** merger.

As recorded in Lim Cheng Leng's biography of Too (**THE STORY OF A PSY-WARRIOR**, p. 201): "... Too's advice to the Tunku was emphatically to carry out the mass arrest before merger and the formation of Malaysia; otherwise it would be better not to proceed with the proposed merger..."

(b) At the emergency meeting of the Internal Security Council on 14 December 1962 called by Dr Ismail, the Malayan minister said merger would not proceed unless the communists were arrested. Lee Kuan Yew agreed. The British position was that the Brunei revolt (8 December 1962) provided the perfect opportunity for joint action. The three parties then agreed on taking joint responsibility and issuing a joint public statement on their preemptive operation.

--- CO 1030/1160 T no. 582, 14 December 1962, as quoted by Tan Jing Quee, "Merger and the Decimation of the Left Wing in Singapore", **THE FAJAR GENERATION**, p. 284

10 (c) In a letter to the British High Commissioner in Kuala Lumpur on 6 January 1963, the Tunku repeated that the Malayan government would not accept Singapore into Malaysia unless the arrests were made before merger.

--- British High Commissioner, Kuala Lumpur, to UK Commissioner in Singapore, CO 1030/1576, no. 19, 6 January 1963

CHAPTER NINE

Fusion Politics in
the making of Malaysia

On April 1946 the British colonial masters in the postwar Labour government of Clement Attlee (prime minister 1945-51) separated Singapore from mainland Malaya across the Johore Causeway (a 1.2km-long road and rail link built in 1924). But less than a couple of decades later, they were to merge both territories within a new and larger geopolitical framework. A new nation called "Malaysia" was established on 16 September 1963 – out of the union of newly-independent Malaya, self-governing Singapore, and the colonies of Sabah and Sarawak in Borneo.

The British had first taken out the small but strategic island of Singapore and then put it back like a piece in a political jigsaw puzzle.

Of course, Singapore's separation in 1946 and then its reunion with Malaya in 1963 was child's play compared with the geopolitical delineation of the Indian subcontinent in 1947 to complete its decolonization and usher in the political liberation of India (officially colonized since 1858) and newly-created Pakistan.

Did this rejigging of Singapore with Malaya and the two Borneo colonies make sense? All this was done in the name of decolonization, but why in this rather offbeat manner?

Historically, the idea of separating Singapore came from civil servants in the Colonial Office in wartime London. Then under Winston Churchill's premiership (1940-45), they were planning in the early 1940s for the postwar constitutional reconstruction of British colonial territories in Southeast Asia. Although Churchill and his close friend United States President Franklin Roosevelt had earlier signed the so-called "Atlantic Charter" on August 1941 to initiate the decolonization process in the postwar era, the dissolution of Empire did not feature in the planning of the more zealous officers in the head office of British colonialism.

During Attlee's premiership (1945-51) in the mid- and late-1940s, the Labour Party's self-declared commitment to decolonization was turned on its head by economic and ideological forces – the natural resources of the colonies and the anti-Soviet communism of Foreign Secretary Ernest Bevin (1945-51) hoping "to repel Communism", strongly aided by the 1947 "Truman Doctrine" of the 33rd US president Harry S. (1945-53) to counter Communist aggression across the globe.

"…Washington was persuaded, by a mixture of self-induced anxiety and skillful British diplomacy, that a friendly empire spanning the globe would be a useful ally in containing the threat to what was becoming known as the Free World," historians J.P. Cain and A.G. Hopkins wrote. (1)

"Liquidation was not on the agenda: the empire was to be given a shot in the arm rather than a shot in the head…"

With the beginning of the Cold War, Cain and Hopkins noted that "American attitudes softened towards British colonialism and the British Empire was transformed into a 'bulwark against the Communist menace…'"

At the Foreign Office in London, diehard colonialists honed their plan to establish a "Malayan Union" out of the former four Federated and five Unfederated Malay States on the Malayan peninsula together with the old Straits Settlements of Penang and Malacca. But Singapore was left out, to form a separate British crown colony with the even much smaller islands of the Cocos (Keeling) and Christmas Island far down south in the Indian Ocean.

Close to the end of World War II, there was also a military plan (which was being finalized in Rangoon mid-August 1945, shortly after the end of the great war in Europe) to recapture Singapore by early 1946 and then to use the island as the main operational base for the Allied forces to liberate Japanese-occupied Malaya, Burma and the Netherlands East Indies (now known as Indonesia).

The atomic bombings of Hiroshima and Nagasaki on August 1945 ended the war in the Pacific. The Allied counter-offensive plan "Operation Tide-race" was called off after Japan surrendered in mid-August, within a week of the nuking of Nagasaki on 9 August.

25.09.2014 20:32

Soon after their return to Malaya in September 1945, the British colonialists tried to push through their Malayan Union plan, which was doomed from the start in April 1946 and shipwrecked shortly afterwards in the surging tide of strong Malay resistance. Although the Malayan Union was then dismantled to make way for the succeeding Federation of Malaya in February 1948, Singapore remained cut off from the political mainstream on the other side of the Johore Causeway.

The colonial separatists at Whitehall had argued that "Singapore should be kept separate as a free port, an imperial defence base, and also because of the Malay States' long-standing fear of Singapore's domination" (to quote historian Mary Turnbull). (2)

It was also politically expedient to keep Singapore out at the time. More crucially, the inclusion of Singapore Chinese would have extended the wafer-thin Chinese majority in Malaya's multiracial composition then.

Turnbull wrote that Sidney Caine, then economic adviser to the Colonial Office and later Vice-Chancellor of the University of Malaya (in Singapore), advised against foisting a ready-made plan (evolved in secrecy) on the local people. By then the prewar myth of British "invincibility" had been demolished by Japanese rifles, tanks and Zero fighter planes, and political consciousness stirred into life among the educated locals in the aftermath of war.

There was also a dissenting voice, though forlorn, among a small group of Londoners who had prewar experience in Malaya. Turnbull noted: "They all agreed on the need for radical changes but the majority favoured a federation rather than a unitary state and advocated the inclusion of Singapore." (3)

At that time, merger was sought by a clutch of well-to-do Malayan Chinese seeking refuge in India. In November 1943, Tan Cheng Lock (who subsequently founded the Malayan Chinese Association, the first postwar Chinese political party in Malaya) wrote as president of Overseas Chinese Association, a long memorandum to the Colonial Office.

Turnbull recorded that Tan had written "appealing for a union or federation of the Straits Settlements with the Malay states, and for equal rights and representation for all who made Malaya their home. He emphasized the long connexion of the Straits Chinese with Malaya and pointed to the service of China-born volunteers in the final defence of Singapore (in early 1942) as evidence of their potential loyalty as citizens." (4)

Apart from including Singapore as one of the Straits Settlements, Tan's proposal did not differ much from the Malayan Union plan. But the gentlemen in London nicely shelved his early memo, which was diplomatically consigned to oblivion.

Turnbull wrote: "The Colonial Office approved of the moderate tone of the memorandum but were not swayed by his arguments. They thanked Tan Cheng Lock, referred vaguely to closer liaison in the future, then filed the booklet away and forgot it." (5)

The colonials had already made up their minds and mapped out Singapore's postwar role as the bastion of British imperialism in the Far East!

The irony of history is that all the prominent political parties that surfaced in the rising currents of anti-colonialism in postwar Singapore supported and sought merger with the Federation of Malaya. And why not? The destiny of a separate Singapore, small and exclusive, did not register in their minds.

Formed in December 1945, the Malayan Democratic Union was set up in Singapore to fight colonialism to the end and to seek self-government for a united Malaya and Singapore within the Commonwealth. The brainchild of a couple of radical Cambridge-educated lawyers and a handful of communist leaders, the MDU later became a united front cover for the communists, but subsequently dissolved itself following the declaration of the Emergency (the anti-communist campaign) in mid-1948. 17.10.2014 16:07

Launched on August 1947, the Progressive Party wanted self-government in Singapore before merging with the Malayan Federation as a fully independent country. Led by English-educated intellectuals, this pro-British party did not set a timeline for freedom and seemed to favour a slow waltz to its first political goal.

Founded September 1948 on the model of Britain's ruling Labour Party, the Singapore Labour Party sought self-government by 1954, and then full independence through merger with the Federation.

These political objectives were inherited by its reincarnation in the Labour Front which emerged in 1954 – the year the People's Action Party (PAP) entered the political scene to seek independence through merger with Malaya. David Marshall led the Labour Front to its astonishing victory in the April 1955 general election held for the first time in the colony of Singapore.

Marshall met with Tunku Abdul Rahman soon after the Malayan prince became Chief Minister of Malaya after a sweeping win in Malaya's first general election on August 1955.

But merger did not feature in Tunku's political agenda in 1955. He wanted to push on towards complete independence for Malaya, having sounded his call for Merdeka in 1951. "Singapore is a strategic island of defence for Britain," he said, "and independence for the Federation will be delayed if we seek to coordinate ourselves with plans of Singapore's Labour Front government..." (6)

Tunku's line of vision accorded with the British military policy to hold on to the bases in Singapore, as the Cold War developed in the wake of the Korean War (1950-53), the 1953 Berlin uprising, and the virtual collapse of the French military in Indochina following the fall of Dien Bien Phu on 7 May 1954. In early September 1954, five Western countries (the USA, France, UK, Australia and New Zealand) teamed up with three Asian countries (Pakistan, the Philippines and Thailand) to form an anti-communist military alliance known as the Southeast Asian Treaty Organisation (SEATO).

According to Richard Clutterbuck who was based in Kuala Lumpur for two years (1956-58) to help in the counter-insurgency as a top soldier working at the Police Headquarters, it was not the time to tango politically with Singapore with its Chinese majority and its host of socioeconomic problems. He recalled "a widespread feeling amongst British and Malayan officials that Singapore was a cesspit of Communism and must be kept out of the Federation at all costs..." (7)

Before long, however, Tunku changed his mind and thought that merger was OK. When, and why did he relent?

He had won political independence for Malaya at the end of August 1957. His victory in the anti-communist war was sealed with the official declaration of the end of the Malayan Emergency on the last day of July 1960. By then he was probably confident enough to meet head-on the challenge posed by a risky political merger with Singapore. And both pressure and support emanated from the British game plan of synchronizing its regional defence role and the due process of decolonization.

Although the anti-communist feeling was strong and contagious particularly at the top level and Kuala Lumpur continued publicly with its "hands off" policy towards Singapore, there was a significant breakthrough when the new constitutional agreement (which was signed in London on 28 May 1958) proposed joint responsibility for Singapore's internal security.

A seat with a casting vote was given to a Malayan Minister in a seven-member Internal Security Council (ISC), with three Singaporeans and three British members. Malaya's single vote could prove crucial as a 'swing' factor in a tie breaker.

The UK Commissioner of Singapore was to chair the ISC. Britain was to remain fully in charge of defence and external affairs in the new State of self-ruling Singapore.

While David Marshall who had sought earlier sought domestic control over internal security and then demanded independence for Singapore, resigned as chief minister in protest against the new constitution, Lee Kuan Yew came to its defence.

Clutterbuck commented: "Lee defended the Constitution on the grounds that Singapore, as an important British military base in a predominantly Chinese island, was most unlikely to be granted independence from Britain as a separate state, so that the overriding object of the Singapore people must be a merger with the Federation; and that this would never come about unless the Federation had the means to ensure that the MCP (Malayan Communist Party) was not being allowed to establish a base in Singapore..." (8)

The Constitutional Agreement provided for self-government in the new State of Singapore after its first general election in 1959.

In early 1958 Fong Chong Pik (the "Plen" to Lee Kuan Yew) returned to Singapore after a short stay in Jakarta, Indonesia where he had been briefed and instructed by Singapore MCP leader Eu Chooi Yip to head the communist underground and to strengthen the anti-colonial united front struggle in Singapore. Between March 1958 and June 1959, Fong had four secret meetings with Lee Kuan Yew who became Singapore's first prime minister after the general election at the end of May 1959. In their fifth and final meeting on 11 May 1961, Lee was urged to insist on the abolition of the ISC.

The early period of the PAP rule was marked by fierce intra-party strife, featuring the charismatic maverick Ong Eng Guan, Minister for National Development, in open defiance against the ruling elite led by Prime Minister Lee Kuan Yew.

Ong's cavalier resignation from the State Legislative Assembly led to the Hong Lim by-election on 29 April 1961 which he won with consummate elan. Though the "Plen" dismissed him as "small fry", Dennis Bloodworth of the London **Observer** wrote: "The PAP had lost in spite of communist support, and Ong had won without it." Ong had won with a thumping majority of nearly 5,000 in a constituency of 12,000 voters. 24.10.2014 07:55

Ong retained his old ward despite communist support (generally assumed but questionable in the event) for his PAP rival (the PAP interpreted it as political sabotage by "communists within the Party"). Ong triumphed by exploiting his immense popularity (despite personal scandals), Chinese chauvinism and reportedly even anti-communism. He then demanded immediate and unconditional independence from Britain.

While other analysts gave more weight to the Anson by-election in mid-July 1961 (which David Marshall won by 546 votes with communist support which triggered first the call for Kuan Yew's resignation, and then leftwing defection from the PAP), Turnbull thought that Hong Lim was crucial in bringing a sea change in Tunku's political thinking.

She commented: "This (Hong Lim) by-election was crucial. It threatened to topple the government (though she did not say why and how, the PAP's glaring defeat appeared ominous to the ruling party), but the very danger of the ruling group (the threat to the moderate leadership) in the PAP led to its salvation.

"Hitherto Tunku Abdul Rahman had aimed to keep the Federation clear from the turbulent politics of Singapore.

"Now, in view of the possible overthrow of the Singapore government and the rise of more extreme left-wing leaders (those associated with Lim Chin Siong, and not Ong Eng Guan), the Malayan leader feared that Singapore might achieve independence in 1963 as a communist state, potentially a 'second Cuba' and a danger to Malaya's security.

"Despite the immense difficulties of establishing a successful merger, the Malayan prime minister came to the reluctant conclusion that the dangers of a hostile, independent, communist-controlled Singapore were even more frightening..." (9)

Tunku made his proposal for the formation of Malaysia in a speech before foreign correspondents in Singapore on 27 May – about one month after the Hong Lim by-election, but more than a month and a half before the PAP's second electoral defeat in the Anson by-election which triggered the traumatic fission within the ruling party.

The withdrawal of communist support in the double whammy in mid-1961 shook the PAP leadership to the core.

Did the British change Tunku's mind? No, according to Lord Selkirk, Commissioner-General to Southeast Asia. "No one suggested it to him. It would be absolutely untrue to say that I, or someone else, gave him the idea..." (10)

But, but Bloodworth told a different story in his report on the controversial meeting between Lord Selkirk and the pro-communist quartet of Lim Chin Siong and Company three days after the Anson rumble in mid-July 1961: "The British had contrived the issue by talking the Tunku into merger, while hinting to the militant left that they could dodge that nemesis (a Kuala Lumpur-backed merger) by ditching the moderates and taking power themselves..." (11)

Mohamed Noordin Sopiee also recounted the influence of the British prime minister.

According to his father Mohamed Sopiee who was then based in London as Malayan Information Attache with ministerial rank, Harold Macmillan used two main arguments to make Tunku decide to form Malaysia – based on British concern for Singapore – when they met at the Commonwealth Prime Ministers' Conference on February 1961. That was three months before Tunku's proposal on forming Malaysia which he announced to the world in his 27 May speech to foreign correspondents in Singapore.

One argument hung on the doubt about Malaya's ability to cope with an independent, communist Singapore at its very doorstep. The other related to the problem of British intervention in Singapore. Noordin wrote: "The British could not hold on much longer. To control Singapore's internal security and thus protect the Federation (of Malaya), it was necessary that the island be brought under Kuala Lumpur..." (12)

In retrospect, that argument based on British military presence and Singapore's internal security turned out to be perfectly specious. The might of the British military remained in Singapore until late 1971 when the bulk of it pulled out by October 1971. Its residual presence was subsequently phased out from September 1975 to March 1976.

Moreover, by 1961 the British military had already initiated their secret plan to store nuclear weapons in Singapore for SEATO defence in a full-blown conflict with Communist China.

Singapore's internal security was further boosted by the Gurkhas who would be able to hold the militant threat (should it manifest) at bay.

According to Noordin's reading of the Singapore situation, security considerations were probably uppermost in the Tunku's mind. There was fear that Singapore would fall to the militants of the extreme left and become an ideological base and centre (like Castro's Cuba) to subvert the mainland. There was also fear that an independent Singapore would swerve to a hostile camp with the communists "right at our very doorstep..."

(As a matter of fact, the communists had been entrenched at the neighbouring Thai border since Chin Peng and his armed guerrillas moved north from Pahang in the heart of the Malayan mainland to their sanctuary in south Thailand in 1953. The communists returned to armed struggle in mid-1968 following Chairman Mao's fighting statement in support of the Afro-American struggle in the US after the assassination of Martin Luther King on 4 April 1968. It was interpreted as Mao's clarion call for "people's war" across the globe.)

Furthermore, there was also concern that a communist Singapore could lead to local embroilment in the Cold War. Of course, the British had been involved in it from the very start, their seminal role in the Cold War subsequently magnified by their ever-staunch commitment to SEATO since1954 and the nuclearization of the British military in Singapore in the early 1960s.

Tunku considered the formation of Malaysia as a means of containing communism and preventing its spread from Singapore.

Noordin noted that Whitehall was also persuaded that the anti-communist government in Kuala Lumpur "would probably be in a better position to contain communism in Singapore and Sarawak than a colonial power". And he added this salient point: "The security of the Singapore base, a policy objective of paramount importance at the time, would also be assured in a period when Singapore's radical left was strongly clamouring for its removal." (13)

In other words, it was politically persuasive and valid for a local government, rather than a colonial power, to accommodate the formidable British military presence in the heartland of Southeast Asia. The radical left could only raise a hue and cry for its dismantlement, but it was inconceivable that the local communists and leftists could do anything physical to the British military.

So, after all, did the Colonial Office in London plant the idea of merger? According to Tunku, he had been talked into it. He was reported to have said on 11 June 1965 (just about a couple of months before Singapore's separation): "I wish I had not listened to all that persuasive talk before…" (14)

Tunku later wrote in the **Star** newspaper (April 14 1975): "I can reveal now that I only accepted Singapore because of Britain's unequivocal stand, which was that unless we could take Singapore in they would not relinquish their hold on the island colony, as they were too deeply immersed in Singapore's welfare in respect of defence, trade and its economy. So it is evident I had no choice…" (15)

Imperial interests, military underpinning of the Cold War, and economic investments in the region bound the British overlord to the political fate of Singapore.

ΩΩΩ

The "Malaysia" concept was actually old hat. Originally when Edward Gent, head of the Eastern Department in the Colonial Office in London, first penned his proposal in 1942 for the Malayan Union (during Churchill's wartime premiership, 1940-45), it was to incorporate the Straits Settlements (including Singapore) and eventually Sarawak, North Borneo (Sabah) and Brunei as well. (The newly-knighted Gent became Governor of the Malayan Union when it was inaugurated on 1 April 1946 to replace the postwar British Military Administration (BMA), then became High Commissioner of the Federation of Malaya when formed on 1 February 1948 to supersede the highly unpopular and ill-conceived Malayan Union.)

Although Gent's proposal subsequently dropped Singapore and the Borneo territories, the Colonial Office noted that this exclusion did not "preclude or prejudice in any way the fusion of the two administrations (in Kuala Lumpur and Singapore) in a wider union at any time, should they both agree that such a course were desirable…" (16)

David Marshall, who became Singapore's first chief minister on 2 April 1955, tried to revive the "Malaysia" proposal when he went to London in December 1955 to prepare for the constitutional talks to be held in April 1956.

He recalled: "At December 1955 meeting I made an official request to Lennox Boyd (Colonial Secretary) that the British Government should use its good offices with the Governments of the Federation of Malaya and the States of Sarawak, Brunei and North Borneo (Sabah) to urge consideration of a federation of all these territories and Singapore. I received from the Secretary of State for the Colonies a coldly angry reply to the effect that these were matters for the people of the territories concerned in which H.M. Government would not consider it appropriate to intervene…" (17)

The intended impression was that territorial/political fusion would be through self-determination, not through colonial fiat. Whatever, it was a humiliating rebuff.

At the constitutional talks in London on April 1956, Lennox Boyd did not mince his words when he told Marshall that Singapore could not survive if granted independence. "We do not intend," he said, "that Singapore should become an outpost of Communist China and, in fact, a colony of Peking…"

Marshall's political overtures were also rejected by the Tunku. The first time when the two chief ministers met in Singapore on August 1955; the second time when Marshall came to Kuala Lumpur after his London trip of December

1955, coming with his proposal for a confederation of two equal states; and when he came with his deputy Lim Yew Hock to see Tunku again in Kuala Lumpur. But Tunku remained adamant in his "Merdeka" mission to attain independence for Malaya; merger with Singapore didn't register.

After Marshall-resignation as chief minister in mid-1956, his successor Lim Yew Hock remained faithful to the vision of a re-union with Singapore's immediate neighbor. At the opening of the second session of the Legislative Assembly on August 1956, the Governor of Singapore said that bilateral links would be further strengthened to ultimately bridge the gap and bring about "the fusion of the two territories in a single united nation…"

Up to mid-1960 or even later, Tunku was known to be against merger. An editorial in the **Straits Times** (June 3, 1960) pointed out that Tunku rejected merger.

But, why then did Tunku propose to include Singapore in his watershed May 1961 public statement on the creation of Malaysia?

Turnbull wrote that the communist threat in Singapore changed his mind. Noordin also submitted in his doctoral thesis that the communist scare "contributed greatly to the Tunku's initiative on Malaysia…" (18)

Why, why did the communists oppose merger?

Turnbull had this explanation: "The left wing dreaded the prospect of Singapore coming under the control of the anti-communist government in Kuala Lumpur and instead wanted independence for a separate Singapore, in which (with control of internal security in local hands), they were confident they would have the upper hand…" (19)

She added: "The communists would have liked to see Singapore part of a republican Malaya but not of a conservative federation including the Borneo territories, which was designed by Tunku Abdul Rahman to prevent a communist takeover in Singapore, not to facilitate it…" (20)

Tunku remained staunchly anti-communist, on the same ideological/political wavelength as the leaders in London and Washington and thus entangled, knowingly or not, in their Cold War. His successful campaign against the communist guerillas was help up as a model of counter-insurgency to many other countries plagued by revolutionary militants.

25.10.2014 08:03

19.11. 2014 06:09 08:55 09:00

In Singapore, however, the communists were gaining confidence that victory was within sight. But their political goal could come to naught in the event of merger as the authorities in Kuala Lumpur would not hesitate to put them behind bars. Noordin Sopiee pointed out that the communists and pro-communists also feared for their personal security. (21)

The opponents of merger, particularly the PAP dissidents, thought that the PAP leadership would be toppled if they managed to sabotage and wreck the merger plan. Noordin Sopiee wrote: "If merger was frustrated, there was a strong probability that the PAP would be thrown out of office at the next election. Power would then fall into their hands. This was an important consideration to the PAP dissidents, especially to those whose defections arose out of the desire to abandon what was seen as a sinking ship and to hitch their wagons to a rising star…" (22)

Thinking that Lee Kuan Yew pursued merger mainly to make use of the Malaysian government "to suppress the left-wing and consolidate his rule in Singapore", the "Plen" planned to slow down the process of merger. (23)

The top CPM leaders including Chin and Eu Chooi Yip planned to sabotage or "substantially delay its implementation". (24)

While the Tunku's "Malaysia" proposal came as a political time bomb to the communists and leftists in Singapore, it sounded like a stirring bugle call to the PAP leaders to do battle.

A day after the bitter break with the PAP dissidents and the motion of confidence in the State Legislative Assembly on 21 July 1961, Lee Kuan Yew told a press conference that the British had taken the communists for a ride (referring to Lord Selkirk's meeting with Lim Chin Siong and colleagues). Lee stated that Singapore's economic and economic problems could be solved by a common market and merger with the Federation.

If there was no way out for Singapore, there would be chaos. "I am not threatening chaos," Lee stressed. "I am predicting it…" (25)

An independent Singapore, he warned, would be disastrous. For one thing, it must be established by violence, and it would also mean a communist Singapore. But he did not say why. (26)

Through a brilliantly conceived and masterfully delivered series of 12 radio talks broadcast from 13 September to 9 October 1961, Lee Kuan Yew launched his momentous battle for merger – his propaganda war against the communists, leftists and pro-communists.

The basic thrust of his political argument(which probably won him the vital support of the great majority, if not the entire lot, of English-educated Singaporeans) was that the communists were using their proxies to cloud and confuse the merger issue and lead the people up the garden path.

Calling it "a battle for the minds of the people", Lee said: "We must convince you, the people, that what we propose – independence through merger with the Federation – is in your best interest…"

He added that "we have to convince the Chinese-speaking not only that Lim (Chin Siong) and his friends are Communists, working under instructions from the Communist underground but also that what they are doing is not good for all of us in Singapore…" (27)

The renowned counter-insurgency expert Clutterbuck commented: "The struggle for control of the PAP was at the time far from over and Lee's courage in laying it bare played a big part in his winning the referendum for merger and the subsequent general election in 1963…" (28)

The referendum itself was also expediently designed game plan which submitted three pro-merger alternatives for the electorate to vote on. The voters had no way of rejecting merger except through or spoilt votes.

The PAP leaders carried their plan through, with considerable aplomb and persuasive skills in their propaganda campaign – albeit aided by their official command of the mass media.

But while Lee courted the leaders of the Chinese business community, the communists tried to intimidate the Chinese Chamber of Commerce which reacted strongly by advertising its full support for merger in all the Chinese and English newspapers for two consecutive days on the eve of the referendum.

The "Plen" issued orders to cast blank votes, a move which was duly supported by Lim Chin Siong. Then, a couple of days before polling, Lim further confounded the Chinese-educated by proposing "super merger" with Indonesia (which was to announce its confrontation policy against Malaya/Malaysia in late January 1963).

In effect, the Barisan Sosialis messed up its anti-merger campaign and bungled its important debut in the political arena, and at a crucial and critical point in Singapore's history.

Even so, the outcome remained uncertain up to the polling day.

Turnbull commented: "The campaign leading up to the Singapore referendum held in (1) September 1962 was as heated as an election, since the government's survival depended on the issue. Seventy-one per cent of the electorate voted in favour of the government's proposals, but 25 per cent showed their disapproval by returning blank or spoiled votes..." (29)

Most of the blank votes were cast in the hostile rural constituencies. Bloodworth commented that those blank votes for the communists "emphasized their formidable power over the masses, making it almost appear as if they had deliberately thrown away the game..." (30)

Despite compulsory voting by law, about 10 per cent of the registered voters did not turn up.

According to Lee Kuan Yew, some 40% of Singapore Chinese voted against merger. That probably included more than half of the Chinese-educated (Chinese Chinese) and alien-born. All in all, Lee estimated that the left had 30% of the votes cast in the September 1962 referendum. (31)

Lee greeted his hard-won victory with tears of joy when the result was announced at eleven that memorable evening of 1 September (Friday, in the year of the bull in the Chinese almanac). (32)

The PAP won its first crucial campaign against the communists and pro-communists since their split in July 1961. Dr Goh Keng Swee said the PAP had fought back from "a position of total collapse". (33)

The PAP's successful run in the referendum marked its first major victory in its battle for merger.

NOTES Chapter 9 Fusion Politics and the making of Malaysia

1. Hopkins and Cain, **British Imperialism: Crisis and Deconstruction, 1914-1990** (London, Longman, 1993), pp. 266-267

Churchill was against independence for India. Trying to restore the British Empire then in decline, he once declared, "I will not preside over a dismemberment…" Roy Jenkins, **Churchill: A Biography** (2001).

"Throughout the British Empire's declining years the great threat to its survival was widely thought to be the international Communist movement," Brian Lapping observed in his book **The End of Empire** (London, Paladin, 1989, p. 209).

"British newspapers like the *Daily Express* and the *Daily Telegraph* continued to declare, year in year out, that the Empire was under siege by Communists…"

The communist rebellion against British rule in Malaya (1948-60) and the anti-colonial struggle in Singapore (1945-63), however, showed that the end of colonialism and concomitant retreat from Empire were inevitable, if not overdue.

"Given the economic plight in which Britain found itself at the end of the Second World War, it was no coincidence that the areas of the empire with the greatest economic value were those where Britain's determination to maintain control was most obvious," British journalists Paul Lashmar and James Oliver (also a historian) have written in **BRITAIN'S SECRET PROPAGANDA WAR 1948-1977**

(Gloucestershire, Sutton, 1998, p. 84).

According to Cain and Hopkins, two such areas were Malaya and Kenya where "coercion tended to be the first resort of policy." They wrote (**British Imperialism**, p. 280): "The bogey of Communism was invoked, where it was not already present, and this surfaced in the early stages of the Cold War to legitimize the use of force…"

To go back to Lashmar and Oliver (**BRITAIN'S SECRET PROPAGANDA WAR**, p. 85): "The Malayan Emergency (1948-60) was Britain's longest colonial conflict after the Second World War. At its core was the vast wealth provided to Britain from Malaya's natural resources, especially rubber plantations – mainly run by British owners…" 923 words 25.09.2014 21:07

2. Turnbull, **A History of Singapore 1819-1975**, p. 220

On 24 March 1965, Singapore's Prime Minister Lee Kuan Yew addressed the Institute of International Affairs in Melbourne, Australia: "…They (the British) tried in many diverse ways to keep a foothold in the region (after World War II), and one of the biggest mistakes they made, not with malice, was to divide Singapore from Malaya and allow the development to go on in the two territories, one more or less Malay, in which Malays were predominant, and the other with Chinese predominance. For eighteen years it went on – 1945 to 1963 – until the two territories were brought together again. And the problems we are facing today (in early 1965) are problems which need never have arisen if that artificial political division had never taken place…"

Above as quoted in Alex Josey: **Lee Kuan Yew – The Crucial Years**, pp. 257-258

3. Turnbull, **A History of Singapore 1819-1975**, p. 221

4. Ibid., p. 221

    The Malayan Chinese Association (MCA) was founded on 27 February 1949, and Tan Cheng Lock became its first president for nine years until 27 March 1958.

5. Ibid., p. 221

6. Report in the London **Observer**, August 7, 1955; quoted in Drysdale, **Singapore: Struggle for Success**, p. 128

7. Clutterbuck, **Conflict and Violence in Singapore and Malaysia 1945-1983**, p. 367

8. Ibid., p. 145

9. Turnbull, **A History of Singapore**, pp. 277-278

    Quoting S. Rajaratnam's account in **PAP's 10th Anniversary Celebration Souvenir**, Pang Cheng Lian wrote in **SINGAPORE'S PEOPLE ACTION PARTY** (pp. 10-11) that "the PAP leaders contemplated resigning from the (State Legislative) Assembly after the Hong Lim defeat, but the pro-communists were against it because they feared that the PAP might be replaced by an anti-communist government which would seek to suppress them brutally. The rumours of a PAP's resignation did not frighten the extreme left-wing forces only. In fact it is believed by some that they were meant to force the Malayan Government to take a more positive stand towards merger..."

Pang commented: "By threatening to resign the PAP was actually confronting the federal Government (in Kuala Lumpur) with two alternatives – either to accept merger thus enabling the moderate left-wing PAP to remain as the Government, or to do nothing and thereby allowing Singapore to shift to the extreme left. The PAP was convinced that unless it secured merger, it would lose out to the extreme left..."

10. Tunku Abdul Rahman, **Star**, March 2, 1975

   Article reprinted in Tunku's book **LOOKING BACK**, p. 128

   The lordship's somewhat glib remark was a turn of diplomatese.

11. Bloodworth, **The Tiger and the Trojan Horse**, p. 238

12. Mohamad Noordin Sopiee, **From Malayan Union To Singapore Separation**, p. 138

   In **MEMOIR on the Formation of Malaysia**, Tan Sri Ghazali Shafie (then the head of the Foreign Ministry in Kuala Lumpur) has written (pp. 35-36): "What had moved the Tunku, the UMNO, the Alliance Party and the Malayan Government to make his May'61 statement in Singapore proposing a plan for Singapore, British Borneo territories and states of the Federation of Malaya was their anxiety that the People's Action Party (PAP), the party which was heavily loaded with communist elements, had won the 1959 general elections. There was, in the view of the Malayan leadership, the real possibility for the communists taking control of the PAP and therefore Singapore.

"The idea of a merger had always been there but the Tunku had chosen to hasten it slowly. With the dangerous situation in Singapore in the face of a constitutional review (on the granting of independence to Singapore) and the development (communist success) in Laos, the Malaysia Plan became relevant although British and Singapore leaders thought that a merger of Singapore with the Federation of Malaya would resolve that problem.

"However, Malayan leadership at that time would not accept just a merger of Singapore with Malaya but a Malaysia Plan would have the support of the people in Malaya with certain conditions. The solution of security for Malaysia was not hinged mainly on Singapore, but in the wider context of Southeast Asia. Nevertheless, Singapore then was a key factor." 30.10.2014 04:44

In **ONE MAN'S VIEW OF THE World** (2013), Lee Kuan Yew has written (pp. 159-160):

"Those from my generation (born in the early 1920s) had always believed that Singapore and Malaya were one. The British kept us as a separate colony after the war (WW2) and we fought for merger.

"The leaders of Malaya did not want us initially because the large number of Chinese in Singapore would have upset the overall racial mix.

"Eventually the British persuaded Tunku Abdul Rahman, Malaysia's first prime minister, that with the leftists gaining strength in our Chinese schools, the danger of Singapore going communist was simply too grave. He finally agreed to take us in along with Sabah and Sarawak, which had lower proportions of Chinese, to balance us…" 30.10.2014 04:59

13. Noordin Sopiee, **From Malayan Union to Singapore Separation**, p. 147

14. **Straits Times** June 12, 1965

15. Reprinted in **LOOKING BACK**, p. 128

16. Quoted in Drysdale, **Singapore: Struggle for Success**, p.

17. Marshall, **The Struggle for Nationhood 1945-1959**, p.12

18. Noordin Sopiee, p. 163

Although the Red bogey was invoked to support and rationalize the security crackdown ("Operation Cold Store") in February 1963, Tunku told Drysdale (p. 258) in a 1982 interview that the so-called communist scare (a potential "Cuba" in Singapore) did not affect his decision to accept merger with Singapore. But Tunku admitted (p. 372) that he accepted merger because he had no option (without saying why) but "if things don't go well, we can always break away…"

19. Turnbull, p. 278

20. Ibid., p. 280

21. Noordin Sopiee, p. 158

22. Ibid., p. 158 A rising star, according to Noordin Sopiee. A comet, as embodied by Lim Chin Siong, the foremost leader in the leftwing united front, according to Dr Rajakumar in **COMET IN OUR SKY**.

23. Fong Chong Pik, **The Memoirs of a Malayan Communist Revolutionary**, p. 160

24. Chin Peng, **MY SIDE OF HISTORY**, p. 437

25. **Straits Times** July 23, 1961

26. Years later, Lee Kuan Yew said that apart from merger, independence was an option for Singapore. "An independent Singapore, which at the time (early1960s) would be facing the Chinese Middle School students' drive to extend their. They may well have won…" As recorded in **ONE MAN'S VIEW OF THE WORLD**, p. 167

27. **Straits Times** October 3, 1961

28. Clutterbuck, p. 348

On the Battle for Merger exhibition held at the National Library on 11 October 2014, Prime Minister Lee Hsien Loong posted on Facebook:

"The radio talks were a crucial moved in winning the hearts and minds of the people. It led to Singapore joining Malaysia, then separation and today's independent Singapore. Had Mr Lee and the non-communist side lost, our history would have been totally different…"

29. Turnbull, p. 280

30. Bloodworth, p.263

31. **Straits Times** January 7, 1980, in Lee's article on the PAP history

32. "In many ways it was a personal triumph for Lee (Kuan Yew). No man struggled harder for the creation of Malaysia," Alex Josey wrote in **Lee Kuan Yew – The Crucial Years** (p.9).

"Lee Kuan Yew wept when the result of the referendum was announced on 1 September," Josey then commented(p. 161). "He had been working at high pressure for weeks. Malaysia was his political ambition. He admitted that in a sense the referendum had been a calculated risk. The communists hadput up a fierce fight, but they had in the end been rejected by the people and Lee's tears were of relief and joy…"

The leading article in the **Straits Times** (September 3, 1962) waxed eloquent on the PAP's magnificent victory which it described as a "victory for common sense and a shock defeat for the Barisan Sosialis and their allies…"

The **ST** leader cited the strong support of the Singapore People's Alliance and Singapore UMNO for merger.

Although there remained much doubt about PAP strength, the daily commented: "It is especially reassuring that the pro-Communist elements have been so soundly defeated, a victory owed no little part to leaders of the Chinese commercial community and to trade unionists who have Malaysia's true interests at heart..."

A.P. Raja, a political pioneer from early postwar years and Alliance Party state assemblyman, spoke in the house on July 1963 (a couple of months before the 21 September 1963 general election): "We in the Alliance provided him (Prime Minister Lee Kuan Yew) the elbow room during the referendum time to perform adequately... So never let the PAP government forget that Malaysia was not a party affair. It was a joint effort by the people of Singapore who believed in Malaysia..." **Straits Times** July 31, 1963

While more than half of the electorate were Chinese-educated, 20 per cent were English-educated and another 20 per cent Malay-educated with the rest mainly Indian-educated, according to Lee Kuan Yew when he addressed a PAP rally at Fullerton Square on March 1961. **Straits Times** March 31, 1961

33. Bloodworth, p. 262

CHAPTER TEN

Towards Merger in the making of Malaysia

The "Malaysia" concept was actually old hat. Originally when Edward Gent, head of the Eastern Department in the Colonial Office in London, first penned his proposal in 1942 (during Churchill's wartime premiership, 1940-45) for the Malayan Union, it was to incorporate the Straits Settlements (including Singapore) and eventually Sarawak, North Borneo (Sabah) and Brunei as well.

Although Gent's proposal subsequently dropped Singapore and the Borneo territories, the Colonial Office noted that this exclusion did not "preclude or prejudice in any way the fusion of the two administrations (in Kuala Lumpur and Singapore) in a wider union at any time, should they both agree that such a course were desirable." (1)

As noted earlier in Chapter 9, the local seeds of fusion politics, particularly merger with Malaya, were sown soon after the end of World War II on the Singapore side of the Causeway.

David Marshall, the legendary criminal lawyer who became Singapore's first chief minister on 2 April 1955, told how he tried to revive the "Malaysia" proposal when he went to London in December 1955 to prepare for the constitutional talks to be held in April the following year. He said: "At December 1955 meeting I made an official request to Lennox Boyd (Colonial Secretary) that the British Government should use its good offices with the Governments of the Federation of Malaya and the States of Sarawak, Brunei and North Borneo to urge consideration of a federation of all these territories and Singapore. I received from the Secretary of State for the Colonies a coldly angry reply to the effect that these were matters for the people of the territories concerned in which H.M. Government would not consider it appropriate to intervene…" (2)

Across the Causeway, Tunku Abdul Rahman became Malaya's first chief minister of the Alliance government in Kuala Lumpur on 31 August 1955.

When Tunku came to Singapore for the first formal meeting between the two chief ministers, Marshall sounded him out on the merger issue but Tunku's response was negative. After London, Marshall went to Kuala Lumpur to see Tunku who rejected his proposal for a confederation which would put the Federation and Singapore on an equal footing. Tunku wanted independence for Malaya within a couple of years, and he got it after his electoral triumph in the first federal elections in July 1955 followed by his political/psychological drubbing of the CPM leader Chin Peng in their late December 1955 "peace talks" at Baling.

On 3 March 1956 Marshall went with Lim Yew Hock to see Tunku again in Kuala Lumpur. But, Tunku remained adamant on his "Merdeka" mission before merger.

At the constitutional talks in London late April 1956, Lennox-Boyd did not mince his words when he bluntly told Marshall that Singapore could not survive if granted independence. "We do not intend," he said (with a strong hint of imperial arrogance), "that Singapore should become an outpost of Communist China and, in fact, a colony of Peking."

Britain, it may be recalled, played its self-imposed role to the hilt in the anti-communist military alliance of SEATO, formed in September 1954. And when Britain developed its nuclear deterrent, it secretly kept a small but significant stock of its nuclear bombs in Singapore from early 1960s, for use in a war against China.

During Tunku's premiership, the communist threat was also entrenched in the political psyche of the Alliance government in Kuala Lumpur.

After Marshall's resignation as chief minister in June 1956, his successor Lim Yew Hock remained faithful to the vision of a re-union with Singapore's immediate neighbor. At the opening of the second session of the Legislative Assembly on August 1956, the Governor of Singapore said that bilateral links would be further strengthened to ultimately bridge the gap and bring about "the fusion of the two territories in a single united nation."

Up to mid-1960 or even later, Tunku was known to be against merger. An editorial in the **Straits Times** (June 3, 1960) pointed out that Tunku rejected merger.

Why then did Tunku propose to include Singapore in his 27 May 1961 proposal for the creation of Malaysia?

Turnbull wrote that the communist threat in Singapore changed his mind. Noordin also submitted in his doctoral thesis that the communist scare "contributed greatly to the Tunku's initiative on Malaysia…" (3)

Barely ten months earlier, at the end of July 1960, the Kuala Lumpur had officially declared the end of the Emergency (colonial neologism or whatever for the Communist insurgency) in Malaya.

Merger should have been a non-issue to the communist ideologue since the CPM from its very inception operated on the basis of the political and territorial integrity of Malaya and Singapore. In terms of party organization, the Singapore Town Committee had nominally been subordinate to the South Malaya Bureau in Kluang, Johor, although the STC had operated mostly autonomously since the ouster of the CPM leader Loi Tek @ Cheong Hong, Chin Peng's old boss, in March 1947. But yet, why did the CPM oppose merger?

In the run-up to the Anson by-election in mid-July 1961, the "Plen" told a senior cadre and former Chinese High School colleague "Ah Q" (Bloodworth's nom de guerre) that the split with the right had reached the point of no return "the day the PAP announced support for Greater Malaysia". (4)

Why, why did the communists oppose merger?

Turnbull had this explanation: "The left wing dreaded the prospect of Singapore coming under the control of the ant-communist government in Kuala Lumpur and instead wanted independence for a separate Singapore, in which (with control of internal security in local hands) they were confident they would have the upper hand..." (5)

The historian added: "The communists would have liked to see Singapore part of a republican Malaya but not of a conservative federation including the Borneo territories, which was designed by Tunku Abdul Rahman to prevent a communist takeover in Singapore, not to facilitate it..." (6)

As noted earlier, Tunku remained staunchly anti-communist. His successful campaign against the communist guerrillas was held up as a model of counter-insurgency to many countries plagued by revolutionary insurgents.

In Singapore, however, the communists were gaining confidence that victory was within sight. But their political goal could come to nought in the event of merger as the authorities in Kuala Lumpur would not hesitate to put them behind bars. Noordin pointed out that the communists and pro-communists also feared for their personal security. (7)

The communists had anticipated a purge. In a joint operation with British and Malayan authorities, the Singapore Special Branch carried out a large-scale and decisive crackdown in early February 1963, seven and a half months before merger. And the detention of communist cadres and pro-communist leaders was one of the conditions for merger. It was de rigueur for Tunku. (8)

The opponents of merger, particularly the PAP dissidents, thought that the PAP leadership would be toppled if they managed to sabotage and wreck the merger plan. Noordin wrote: "If merger was frustrated, there was a strong probability that the PAP would be thrown out of office at the next election. Power would then fall into their hands. This was an important consideration to the PAP dissidents, especially to those whose defections arose out of the desire to abandon what was seen as a sinking ship and to hitch their wagons to a rising star..." (9)

A more direct bid for power would be by capturing the party leadership or by gaining control of the legislative assembly through which to call off merger. As exposed by Lee Kuan Yew in one of his radio talks early October 1961 while he was desperately campaigning for merger, the communists first planned to capture power by getting 26 Assemblymen on their side, and then to direct this simple majority in the house against the PAP government. Failing all this, their alternative plan (the third option) was to turn on the heat to force the government out. (10)

When the political split within the PAP came about in July 1961, the peninsular communists (still nursing, and smarting from their wounds of defeat) knew that their contention for power had touched rock bottom. Chin Peng was in Peking to report the failure of their armed struggle. However, since their prospects appeared brighter (or Redder) in Singapore where they could smell victory in the air, it made sense for them to perpetuate the existing political divide and to shun merger.

Fong Chong Pik, whom Lee Kuan Yew referred to as the "Plen", wrote in his Memoirs that merger was pursued by Lee Kuan Yew and "mainly aimed at making use of the Malaysian government to suppress the left-wing and consolidate his rule in Singapore…" So the communist underground leader thought of "slowing down the process of merger" to counter Lee's "haste in pushing through the merger…" (11)

Meeting in Peking mid-1961, Chin Peng, Eu Chooi Yip and Siao Chang, three of the very top CPM leaders, planned to sabotage merger or "substantially delay its implementation…"

As narrated by Chin Peng: "We took the position that Singapore should be kept a separate entity from Malaysia, despite the fact that, right from the start of our struggle, we had envisaged unity between the island and its peninsular neighbor.

"We interpreted Lee Kuan Yew's keenness for the Malaysia concept as due in part to his perception of the advantages it provided him in moving against the CPM. We were convinced Lee was planning to manoeuvre behind the Tunku and, though manipulation, smash us not only in Singapore but throughout Malaya.

"Our interpretation was wrong. Ultimately it was the Tunku who determined the timetable for Lee's move against the CPM…" (12) 26.10.2014 07:18

ΩΩΩΩΩΩΩΩΩΩΩΩΩΩ

Why did the PAP leadership try its very utmost in 1961 to push through merger with the Federation of Malaya?

Since its inception in late 1954, the party's founding fathers had its compass on the course of fusion with Malaya. Moreover, Tunku's proposal for a "greater Malaysia" in May 1961 was timely since its support by the moderates within the PAP completed their rupture with the pro-communists within the party. And the split of its left wing in July that year accelerated the PAP's drive towards the long-envisioned merger.

Tunku himself observed that Lee Kuan Yew became "keener than ever". (13)

And, to quote Lee Kuan Yew: "...My calculation was that we had to rejoin them in order to have a united whole. Singapore and Malaya were one historically..." (14)

Nothing wrong, nothing insightful, in such rationalization made in retrospect.

Turnbull noted that the Singapore government pursued merger "with a vigour born of near-desperation". She wrote: "The PAP leaders sought merger as a matter of urgency not only to achieve political independence but also to guarantee Singapore's economic survival..." (15)

Goh Keng Swee told a public rally in March 1959 that a PAP government would make its immediate task to forge a common market with the Federation, as the basis for further industrialization.

Goh was on the same wavelength as Dr Albert Winsemius, a Dutch economic expert in the United Nations Bureau of Technical Assistance who led a UN industrial survey team to advise on Singapore's industrialization in late 1960. Dr Winsemius concluded that Singapore needed a common market with the Federation to support the proposed industries on the island.

Winsemius also proposed to the Prime Minister of Singapore as the first item on the agenda for action: "Number one: to get rid of the Communists; how you get rid of them does not interest me as an economist, but get them out of the government, get them out of the unions, get them off the streets. How you do it, is your job…" (16)

Important as those economic considerations were, the windfall from a timely merger was more crucially and substantially political in content. According to Lee Kuan Yew, the "Malaysia" concept had been discussed at ministerial level since January (before Tunku's public proposal towards the end of May 1961).

Clutterbuck commented that Lee "realized that some form of merger was essential to his political survival…" (17)

Bloodworth wrote: "Lee courted the feudalistic Tunku, bent on a marriage of convenience that he saw as salvation and the Party (CPM) saw as nemesis…" (18)

Moreover, political fusion would empower the authorities to outflank the communists on the island and position them within range of the "strongly anti-communist" regime in Kuala Lumpur. (19)

While Tunku's "Malaysia" proposal burst like an exploding time bomb to the CPM, it sounded like a stirring bugle call to the PAP to do battle.

A day after the historic break with the PAP dissidents and the motion of confidence in the State Legislative Assembly on 21 July 1961, Lee Kuan Yew told a press conference that the British had taken the communists for a ride (referring to Lord Selkirk's meeting on 18 July 1961 with a handful of dissident leaders headed by Lim Chin Siong). Lee stated that economic and political problems could be solved with a common market and merger with the Federation.

If there was no way out for Singapore, there would be chaos. "I am not threatening chaos," he stressed. "I am predicting it." (20)

He said there must be merger, with or without the Borneo territories, and the sooner the better.

An independent Singapore, he said, would be disastrous. For one thing, it must be established by violence, and it would also mean a communist Singapore. But he did not why or how.

The communist threat had probably been magnified for propaganda and political/strategic expediency. Kuan Yew and the others knew that the colonial masters held the big club (of advanced conventional weapons) although they had no inkling at all of the nuclear cache in their island. And, they knew as well that British imperial power was supreme in Singapore and Southeast Asia at large.

Lee Kuan Yew launched his battle for merger, through a brilliantly conceived and masterfully delivered series of 12 radio talks broadcast from 13 September to 9 October 1961. It was his propaganda war against the communists and pro-communists.

The basic thrust of his political argument (which probably won him the vital support of the great majority, if not the entire lot, of English-educated Singaporeans) was that the communists were using their proxies to cloud and confuse the merger issue and lead the people up the garden path.

Calling it "a battle for the minds of the people", Lee said: "We must convince you, the people, that what we propose – independence through merger with the Federation – is in your best interest."

He then added that "we have to convince the Chinese-speaking not only that Lim (Chin Siong) and his friends are Communists, working under instructions from the Communist underground but also that what they are doing is not good for all of us in Singapore..." (21)

Tunku went along with Lee, going by his reported statements. For example, Tunku was reportedly alarmed by the threat (as articulated by Lee) that an independent Singapore would go communist. We must do all we can, Tunku said, to save the situation. (22) 27.10.2014 08:37

Clutterbuck gave full marks to Lee for disclosing all the relevant facts to the public in his radio talks. The renowned counter-insurgency expert commented: "The struggle for control of the PAP was at the time far from over and Lee's courage in laying it bare played a big part in his winning the referendum for merger and the subsequent general election in 1963." (23)

The referendum itself was an expediently designed game plan which submitted three pro-merger alternatives for the electorate to vote on. The voters had no way of rejecting merger except through blank or spoiled votes. The PAP leaders carried their plan through, with considerable aplomb and persuasive skills – albeit much aided by their official command of the mass media. (24)

However, two straw polls conducted jointly by the left-wing clubs in the two local universities indicated a massive political disaster for the ruling PAP. In the July poll held at the Tanjong Pagar constituency of Lee Kuan Yew, nearly 90% of voters said "no" to merger when given a straight choice. And in the second poll conducted in Goh Keng Swee's constituency of Kreta Ayer in the heart of Chinatown, 97% cast blank votes. These twin massive negatives for the top two PAP leaders must have hyper-inflated the confidence of the opposition.

So while Lee prudently courted the influential leaders of the Chinese business community, the communists tried to intimidate the Chinese Chamber of Commerce which reacted by advertising its full support for merger in all the Chinese and English newspapers for two consecutive days on the eve of the referendum.

In the run-up to the referendum, however, the PAP lost its working majority in the State Assembly when its sole assemblywoman defected to the Barisan Sosialis. In a statement issued on 3 July 1962, the Prime Minister indicated sense of regret that a long-time PAP stalwart Madam Ho Puay Choo left, having "under pressure, lost her nerve at this late stage".

They had gone through the worst in July last year, he said. He then added: "Until the Opposition outvotes us, we are constitutionally the Government."

In his brief fighting statement, Prime Minister Lee Kuan Yew reiterated the PAP's business and primary duty "to govern and to see the country's destiny in a Federation of Malaysia secured" through merger.

Ho's departure on 3 July 1962 left behind a hung state assembly. Lee's political position looked precarious.

"There is absolutely no doubt that if Lee falls before Malaysia is established, Barisan Sosialis will take his place and all hope of achieving Malaysia will be lost since Barisan itself is unalterably hostile to it and Tunku, for his part, would not pursue it with a Barisan Government in power in Singapore," Sir Donald MacGillivray, British High Commissioner in Kuala Lumpur, reported to the Foreign Office in London on 4 July 1962. (25)

On August 21, the PAP suffered the loss of another leader when the Minister of Labour Ahmad bin Ibrahim passed away at the age of 35. However, the by-election for the vacant seat of Sembawang was suspended – "since the seat would almost certainly have fallen to the Barisan," Turnbull commented. (26)

Only a week earlier, however, the PAP had got a timely shot in the arm when Tunku agreed to Lee's proposal for a common citizenship in Malaysia. When Lee disclosed this good news on 14 August 1962, he also announced that the referendum would be held on 1 September.

Was merger already in the bag? Lee told Bloodworth: "The referendum was settled that night (14 August). The communist argument had been demolished." (27) That, of course, was Lee's gut feeling, to assure himself more than others.

"Lee was to use the issue of merger to engineer a break with the pro-communists within the PAP, and flush them out into an open fight with him and his democratic-socialist colleagues," Edwin Lee narrated. (28)

"Once this happened, the Plen retaliated with all he had at his command. It was to be the greatest battle ever waged for the future of Singapore…"

On the opposition side, the newly-launched Barisan Sosialis made its maiden run in the referendum race. But it ploughed into the choppy political waters, without a clear sense of direction.

The communists tried to arouse anti-merger feelings among the alien-born Chinese who were only recently enfranchised, but formed the bulk of the faithful to the Barisan.

The "Plen", the boss of the communist underground, was reported to have issued orders to cast blank votes. And Lim Chin Siong was reported to have toed the Red line. (29)

To further confound the Chinese-educated electorate, Lim also reportedly proposed "super merger" with Indonesia, a couple of days before polling.

In effect, the Barisan Sosialis messed up its anti-merger campaign and bungled its important debut in the open political arena – and this at a crucial and critical point in Singapore's history. Moreover, the media had also probably distorted or mangled its case.

Even so, the outcome of the referendum remained uncertain up to the polling day. Turnbull wrote: "The campaign leading up to the Singapore referendum held in September 1962 was as heated as an election, since the government's survival depended on the issue. Seventy-one per cent of the electorate voted in favour of the government's proposal (Alternative A), but 25 percent showed their disapproval by returning blank or spoiled votes…" (30)

Most of the blank votes were cast in the hostile rural constituencies. Bloodworth commented that these blank votes for the communists "emphasized their formidable power over the masses, making it almost appear as if they had deliberately thrown away the game." And he quickly added: "It would not be for the last time." (31)

Despite compulsory voting by law, about 10% of the registered voters did not turn up.

According to Lee Kuan Yew, some 40% of Singapore Chinese voted against merger. That probably included more than half of the Chinese-educated (the Chinese Chinese) and alien-born. All in all, Lee estimated that the left had 30% of the votes cast in the September 1962 referendum.

Lee greeted his hard-won victory with tears of joy when the result was announced at eleven that memorable evening. (32)

The PAP won its first crucial campaign for survival against the communists since their split on July 1961. Goh Keng Swee said the PAP had fought back from "a position of total collapse". (33) 29.10.2014 07:52 30.10.2014 09:05 09:15

Notes Chapter 10: Merger in the making of Malaysia

1. Quoted in Drysdale, **Singapore: Struggle for Success**, p. 7

2. Marshall, **The Struggle for Nationhood 1945-1959**, p. 12

3. Noordin, **From Malayan Union To Singapore Separation**, p. 163

   Although the Red bogey was invoked to support as well as rationalize the security crackdown ("Operation Cold Store") in February 1963, Tunku told Drysdale (p. 258) in a 1982 interview that the so-called communist scare (a potential "Cuba" across the Causeway) did not affect his decision to accept merger because he had no option (without saying why) but "if things don't go well, we can always break away."

4. Bloodworth, **The Tiger and the Trojan Horse**, p. 229

   In **SINGAPORE'S PEOPLE'S ACTION PARTY**, Pang Cheng Lian wrote (p. 13): "...The break occurred largely because the pro-communists found themselves facing the alternatives of either accepting the idea of obtaining Singapore's independence through merger, or of leaving the Party. Being unwilling to accept the former they had to withdraw from the united front..."

5. Turnbull, **A History of Singapore 1819-1975**, p. 278

6. Ibid., p. 280

7. Noordin, p. 158

8. Alan Blades, a former Singapore Police Special Branch head, told Clutterbuck (**Conflict and Violence in Singapore and Malaysia1945-1983**, p. 369) that the detention of Lim Chin Siong and associates before merger was a Kuala Lumpur condition – "a condition which suited Lee Kuan Yew as long as he could lay it at the door of the federation."

   Because of racial implications, Tunku was particularly meticulous in avoiding culpability for any drastic action that could be misconstrued as a Kuala Lumpur initiative, thus the tripartite involvement of Kuala Lumpur and Singapore SB operatives with British intelligence in the conduct of "Operation Cold Store" early February 1963, seven and a half months before merger and Malaysia. Please also refer Chapter 11.

9. Noordin, p. 158

10. **Straits Times**, October 6, 1961

11. Fong Chong Pik, **The Memoirs of a Malayan Communist Revolutionary**, p. 160

12. Chin Peng, **MY SIDE OF HISTORY**, p. 437 1,957 words 5 pages 26.10.2014 07:23

13. Tunku Abdul Rahman, **Star**, March 2, 1975 reprinted in **LOOKING BACK**, p. 85

14. Lee Kuan Yew, **ONE MAN'S VIEW OF THE WORLD**, 2013, p. 168

15. Turnbull, pp. 275, 279

16. Extract of 1961 report by Prof Winsemius in Drysdale, **Singapore: Struggle for Success**, p. 252

17. Richard Clutterbuck, **Conflict and Violence in Singapore and Malaysia 1945-1983**, p. 156

18. Bloodworth, **The Tiger and the Trojan Horse**, p. 198

19. Noordin, **From Malayan Union To Singapore Separation**, p. 158

20. **Straits Times**, July 23, 1961

21. **Straits Times**, October 3, 1961

22. **Straits Times**, October 28, 1961

23. Clutterbuck, p. 348

24. According to Ghazali Shafie (**MEMOIR**, p. 131), Tunku told Lee Kuan Yew on the afternoon of 23 October 1961 in their meeting at the Residency in Kuala Lumpur that he could not agree to a complete merger as one of the alternatives in the proposed referendum: "Lee Kuan Yew said if it was generally known that a complete merger would not be acceptable to the Federation Government then the communists would work their best to get everybody to support the formula for complete merger which in effect would amount to a vote not favouring merger…"

At the meeting, Razak (Tunku's deputy) expressed his objection to an alternative to merger in the referendum. In his opinion, any such alternative would encourage and tempt the people to vote alternative.

Subsequently when Ghazali met with Lee Kuan Yew in his office at the City Hall in Singapore on the afternoon of 26 October 1961, Lee told him that both the Chinese chauvinists and the English-educated workers would reject a complete merger.

Two types of merger came to their minds: complete merger and reserved merger of the Northern Ireland Type (with the right to opt out of it).

25. As quoted by Professor Michael Leigh, A country born of a shaky idea **NEW STRAITS TIMES** September 11, 2014

26. Turnbull, p. 281

27. Bloodworth, p. 260

28. Edwin Lee, **Singapore: The Unexpected Nation**, published by Institute of South East Asian Studies (ISEAS) 2008, p. 177

29. In his **Memoirs** Fong Chong Pik, the "Plen", did not shed light on the communist opposition to merger except reiterating why he "did not agree to the merger" (p. 161) because of worries that a racial conflict would result in the event that the left-wing "fought back" its political suppression by the Malaysian government.

30. Turnbull, p. 280

Alex Josey commented in his book **Lee Kuan Yew –The Crucial Years** (p. 9): "…In many ways it (referendum) was a personal triumph for Lee. No man struggled harder for the creation of Malaysia…"

An official report noted that the contest for votes had "all the verve and vitality of a general election campaign". **Singapore Year Book, 1965**, Government Printer, Singapore, p. 60

31. Bloodworth, p. 263

32. A. Josey wrote in **Lee Kuan Yew –The Crucial Years** (p. 161): "Lee Kuan Yew wept when the result of the referendum was announced on 1 September. He had been working at high pressure for weeks. Malaysia was his political ambition. He admitted that in a sense the referendum had been a calculated risk. The communists had put up a fierce fight, but they had in the end been rejected by the people and Lee's tears were of relief and joy..."

The leading article in the **Straits Times** (September 3, 1962) waxed eloquent on the PAP's magnificent victory which it described as a "victory for common sense and a shock defeat for the Barisan Sosialis and their allies."

The **ST** leader cited the strong support of the Singapore People's Alliance and Singapore UMNO for merger.

Although there remained much doubt about the PAP strength, the daily commented: "It is especially reassuring that the procommunist elements have been so soundly defeated, a victory owed in no little part to leaders of the Chinese commercial community and to trade unionists who have Malaysia's true interests at heart."

A.P. Raja, a political pioneer from early postwar years and Alliance Party state assemblyman, spoke in the house on July 1963: "We in the Alliance provided him (Prime Minister Lee Kuan Yew) the elbow room during the referendum time to perform adequately... So never let the PAP government forget that Malaysia was not a party affair. It was a joint effort by the people of Singapore who believed in Malaysia…"

Straits Times July 31, 1963

While more than half of the electorate were Chinese-educated, 20% were English-educated and 20% Malay-educated with the rest mainly Indian-educated, according to Lee Kuan Yew speaking at a PAP rally in Fullerton Square on March 1961. **Straits Times** March 31, 1961

33. Bloodworth, p. 262

(a) In **The Memoirs of a Malayan Communist Revolutionary**, Fong Chong Pik @ the "Plen" has written (p. 155): "I have to admit that when I was still in Singapore in the early 1960s (before his departure for Indonesia early 1963 on the eve of "Operation Cold Store"), the suddenness with which the "merger" issue was brought up, and the absolute certainty of its implementation, took me by complete surprise. When I realized the implications, it was too late for me to do anything…

"I could not understand Mr Lee's impatience to implement the "merger" plan, and his absolutist stance on the matter of choice… Mr Lee had already decided to implement the British-designed "merger"… He had already determined that "merger" was his road towards supreme authority. He had become fanatical, and was not only incapable of listening to any contrary opinion, but also firm in his endeavor to shut it out…"

(b) Objecting to the terms as spelt out in the White Paper on Merger, the Barisan Sosialis, the left-wing protagonist, demanded common citizenship for all Singaporeans, with free movement for work and residence as well as proportionate parliamentary representation. The principal leftwing party also demanded the holding of a general election for a clear mandate on the question of merger. Please refer to Tan Jing Quee: "Lim Chin Siong – A Political Life" in **COMET IN OUR SKY**, pp. 85-86

CHAPTER ELEVEN

Belling the cat:
Defusing the third communist
revolution in Singapore, 1961-63

The postwar history of Singapore has shown that the proscription of the Communist Party has not prevented its revolutionary cadres from operating in the open and pursuing their political objectives through constitutional means.

The communists attempted in the immediate postwar years, and again in the mid-1950s, to make revolution and capture power. But they failed both times.

However, with their penetration of the PAP which swept to power in Singapore's first general elections in mid-1959, the communists and the leftists were to mount their strongest bid for supremacy in the open political arena despite the intra-party strife and the traumatic split between the two contrary wings of the PAP in late July 1961.

In the split which almost destroyed the ruling party and in the ensuing bitter struggle for power, Lee Kuan Yew and the other leaders of the old guard had to hang on and fight for dear political life.

About the same time in mid-1961, Chin Peng had arrived in Peking to report the failure of the armed struggle (1948-60) in Malaya. He had wanted to change course, but was told to carry on the war. The MCP then announced through Radio Peking that the armed struggle should never be abandoned. Its instruction was according to Mao's maxim of "permanent revolution".

The communist threat loomed large in the region. Despite the success of the counter-insurgency campaign in Malaya, the authorities remained religiously on their guard.

Formed when Singapore became a self-governing colony in 1959 (and within a year of the official end of the Emergency in Malaya), the Internal Security Council (ISC) pooled the intelligence, surveillance, and security resources of the British, Malayan and Singapore authorities. The communist leadership was the prime target of this three-in-one security watchdog – with the eyes of Argus.

It was therefore understandable that the communists, through their powerful underground chief Fong Chong Pik @ the "Plen", and through their most prominent open front leader Lim Chin Siong, sought and demanded the dissolution of the ISC in their bid for political power.

The ISC was a juggernaut, "able to stop the communists from capturing Singapore and converting it into a 'Cuba'" (to quote Bloodworth).

Under the ISC which was first convened in late August 1959 and chaired by the British Commissioner Lord Selkirk (a former First Lord of the Admiralty), Britain retained the last-resort and ultimate power to suspend the constitution and resume direct rule in the self-governing colony of Singapore. (Britain's economic and strategic interests must prevail.)

"Over the next two years, the Internal Security Council became the centre of complex political wrangling between Singapore, Kuala Lumpur and the British," Cambridge historian Dr. T. N. Harper has noted. (1)

The ISC members played a waiting game. Within the council, each one looked to the other/s to take action.

Neither the British authorities (including the UK Commissioner at the top) nor the PAP government in 1961 and 1962 wanted to bell the big cat. According to the Malayan psychological warfare expert C. C. Too, they wanted Kuala Lumpur to do it – but only **after merger** and the formation of Malaysia.

Bloodworth reported: "Whereas the Federation government wanted Lee Kuan Yew to take the initiative (and the blame) for arresting the ringleaders before Malaysia was formed, Singapore wanted to wait until merger was a reality, when the burden could be shifted to Kuala Lumpur – 'We were quite happy, to put it cynically, to let the dirty work be done by the Tunku,' as Goh Keng Swee was to comment with dry candour…" (2)

But why should KL do it when the communist threat emanated from across the Causeway? Would there not be a racial fallout should an UMNO-dominated government be seen to be cracking the whip?

For that matter, the British themselves remained cautious, sensitive and sensible. They did not want to be seen as the ringmaster before bringing down the curtain on their colonial stage after nearly a century and a half of imperial rule.

Five days after the defeat of the PAP in the Anson by-election and two days after Lord Selkirk's meeting with four of the leaders of the pro-communist faction of the PAP in late July 1961, Lee Kuan Yew told the state assembly that the UK Commission had been fraternizing with them. He said after the British had led them into believing that a non-

Communist government was no longer necessary and that a pro-Communist government was possible, "obviously these men were going to try and capture the PAP and the government…" (3)

And the ruse, according to Lee, was that the British probably hoped that "under attack and threat of capture, the PAP would fight back and finally suppress the Communists, something they have so far failed in persuading the PAP to do…"

Why was Lee Kuan Yew so reluctant to use the big stick? Why didn't he want to appear tough like his predecessor Tun Lim Yew Hock?

The simple answer is that Lee did not want to go down into history the way that Lim did. Since Lee had been assiduously courting the Chinese electorate since 1955, he could not afford to act tough – even if he had wanted to. Especially when he was involved in mortal combat with the communists for "the hearts and minds of the people" (a famous phrase from Lt General Sir Gerald Templer – "a supreme egoist" in the opinion of his arch rival Chin Peng). And the communists were operating – like fish in water – among the Chinese masses on the ground. 30.10.2014 08:43

"You did it in a different way," Lee told Governor William Goode in 1959. "When you found Communist cells, you picked off the tops of the daisies, but they grew up all the stronger. My way is different. I am going to win the minds of the people and that will take it out from the roots and that's the way to win…" (4)

At the height of the crisis following the split with the communists and pro-communists in mid-1961, Lee moved a vote of confidence in the house two days after Lord Selkirk's meeting with Lim Chin Siong and company. Lee again rejected taking a leaf from Tun Lim's law-n-order book – a short-cut through a purge or purgatory. He stuck to political argument "to win this battle in men's minds…"

Lee wound up the debate in the Legislative Assembly with these words expressing confidence while carrying a threat to the PAP dissidents and opponents of merger: "I say this is an argument which we can win, because I think if they oppose merger they will be making a mistake second only to the starting of the Emergency in 1948..." (5)

The authorities in Kuala Lumpur were well-versed in both psywar and tough action (wielding the big stick and guns a la the persuasion of power – psychological and military) against militant communists operating in the cities and in the jungles. They wanted Lee to do more than talk. Lee's propaganda battle (the referendum for merger) was important to nail the Communist lie, as he rightly argued, as well as to expose their opposition to merger.

But both the Malayan and British authorities who had successfully campaigned against the enemy on the Malayan mainland, realized that some tough action had to be taken to blunt the communist spearhead in Singapore. And it was time to lop off, and uproot the daisies in the field.

Even the communists foresaw another big swipe against them. According to Chin Peng, they had expected it for almost four years, and the crackdown came following "strong pressure on Lee from both the Tunku and the British..." (6)

Bloodworth narrated: "After the Tunku had foreshadowed Malaysia in May 1961, orders had gone out for the underground cadres to withdraw to safety, and they had begun to slip across the water to Indonesia; only those in the open were to stay behind in Singapore. This meant that the best were to go, leaving the expendable second-best to fight a forlorn rearguard action to stave off merger – and their own fate..." (7)

Bloodworth wrote that the Plen had explained to Lim Hock Koon, one of his senior aides, that the "British imperialists and the reactionaries" were determined to push through their merger plan, after which the PAP expected the Tunku to wipe out the leftists in Singapore for them. On this second point, the Plen who himself took to his heels, turned out to be as wrong as Dr Goh of the PAP.

The timing of the purge was crucial, argued C. C. Too, the Malayan master of psychological warfare ; and it had to be **before merger**. (8)

S. Woodhull, vice-chairman of the newly-formed Barisan Sosialis, told another story when he spoke to a branch union meeting of motor workshop employees on 12 August 1961. His version hung on possible British intervention.

"Immediately after the Anson by-election (held 15 July 1961), Dr Goh Keng Swee told Mr. James Puthucheary (a committee member in the Barisan) that if we thought the British would sit back and see the left destroy the PAP then we must be wishful thinkers," Woodhull said.

"The PAP crisis had come to a head. British intervention, according to Dr. Goh, was imminent. Since Dr. Goh is a member of the Internal Security Council we had to take him seriously.

"Mr. Lee Kuan Yew and his colleagues warned that if we opposed them in public they would fold up and let the British finish us off.

"This was a stock threat which Mr. Lee and his men have been making since they came into office (in mid-1959).

"It was their smug assumption that the British would not tolerate a government of any left-wing force other than the PAP leadership.

"It was therefore, our responsibility to find out for ourselves the attitude of the U.K. Commission…" (9)

Thus the controversial tea party meeting with Lord Selkirk on 18 July 1961. It was a meeting quickly arranged by James Puthucheary who turned up with three other leading PAP dissidents including Lim Chin Siong, Woodhull himself, and Fong Swee Suan.

Having read the Sunday paper report on Woodhull's speech at the union meeting the day before, Dr Goh quickly shot back a rebuttal which appeared in the **Straits Times** on Monday 14 August 1961. He denied that he had tipped off James Puthucheary that "a big swipe of the pro-Communists was in the offing (one year five and a half months before "Operation Cold Store" on 2 February 1963)…" Goh stated that it was too laughable that a Minister of State "would betray an official secret of the gravest security import."

In a long statement, Goh repeated what Lee Kuan Yew had said earlier about the "great anti-colonialists" (Lim Chin Siong and colleagues including Woodhull, Puthucheary and Fong Swee Suan) seeking assurances about their safety from "the great colonialist, Lord Selkirk."

Goh stated: "Mr Lim Chin Siong was led to believe that a government elected by pro-Communist organizational support was acceptable to the British Government provided the military bases were undisturbed." (10)

Goh added: "At the same time, the U.K. Commissioner was repeatedly rebuking us for our reluctance to use our constitutional powers to sweep the Communists into Changi Jail. And here there was no misunderstanding as to whom we were talking about. They were Mr. Lim Chin Siong and his colleagues…"

And Goh went on to reiterate Lee's argument that the British were encouraging Mr Lim to mount an open fight, in the hope that the PAP Government would be panicked into using their special powers to lock up Lim and Company.

The British side had its own version: both Lord Selkirk and his deputy in Singapore, Philip Moore, were reported to have resisted calls for arrests of political opponents. For economic, political and strategic reasons, the British authorities resisted any extensive clampdown. (11)

But, who was to bell the cat? And when?

The answer (such as it appeared to the cohort of authorities) came out of the blue, in the wake of an abortive revolt against the sultanate in Brunei on 8 December 1962. According to Australian history lecturer Greg Poulgrain, he was told that the Brunei rebellion was launched by the British Special Branch. (12)

Whatever, this outbreak of violence in Brunei "triggered" the big swipe in Singapore after a time-lapse of six weeks: "Operation Cold Store" was carried out in the early morning hours of 2 February 1963 by the SB officers after attending a party.

Alan Blades, former SB head in Singapore, told Clutterbuck that the Brunei revolt persuaded "the U.K. Government, almost overnight, that it must abandon a position which it had taken up over a Kuala Lumpur condition for Merger – that Lim Chin Siong and the rest of his associates should again be put in detention before Merger became effective in August 1963 – a condition which suited Lee Kuan Yew so long as he could lay it clearly at the door of the Federation…" (13)

Singapore-based British veteran journalist Dennis Bloodworth commented: "The Brunei revolt shook the Tunku out of his inertia, and gave him an argument for insisting that the purge could not wait for merger; it provided an excuse for drastic action, and therefore left Lee to call boldly for quick arrests; and it jolted the British out of a charitable inclination to give the left wing more rope to hang themselves…" (14)

In a telegram sent on 12 December 1962, Duncan Sandys, having received the British Prime Minister's personal approval to take prompt action, advised Selkirk in Singapore to proceed with the mass arrests.

"I am sure that the insurrection in Brunei (8 December 1962) provides the best possible background against which to take this action. I consider therefore that we should move at once, before the atmosphere of emergency evaporates as it quickly will when active fighting in Brunei ceases," the Colonial Secretary advised the UK Commissioner-General for Southeast Asia.

"We must of course identify ourselves with the decision. But the public announcement must make it clear that the Malayan and Singapore Governments share equally with us in the decision," the message concluded. (15)

Bloodworth described "Operation Cold Store" conducted in the early morning of 2 February 1963 as "possibly the most stylish <u>razzie</u> in police history". Special Branch officers dressed in tuxedos carried out their "dirty work" (to quote Dr Goh) after attending a black-tie do at the police officers' mess. About 500 police were deployed, according to Bloodworth.

George Bogaars, the Singapore SB director who was present at the first meeting between C.C. Too, the psychological warrior from Kuala Lumpur, and Prime Minister Lee Kuan Yew at the City Hall in June 1962, directed the operation which was jointly conducted with the Police Field Force. Dressed in dinner jackets, the SB officers launched "Cold Store" at three a.m., according to Drysdale's account. (16)

Issued on 2 February 1963, only a few hours after the operation, the official statement said that the Internal Security Council had met in Kuala Lumpur the day before "to consider the internal security situation in Singapore in the context of the threat to the territories of the proposed Federation of Malaysia following the outbreak of violence in Brunei."

Chaired by Lord Selkirk on 1 February 1963, the ISC decided to act at once (as directed by the Colonial Secretary on 12 December 1962). "All members of the Council agreed that

242

action must be taken to safeguard the defence and security of Singapore and of the territories of the proposed Federation of Malaysia," the official text said.

"This action must be taken immediately and cannot be left until after August 31, 1963 (the scheduled date of merger)."

Returning from the ISC meeting in Kuala Lumpur, Dr Goh Keng Swee told reporters in Singapore that the mass arrests were to safeguard the security of the proposed Malaysian federation. (17)

The Communist threat should be dealt with now and not after merger, Goh said. And that was the Tunku's position from the start.

On 3 February 1963, a long statement was issued in Kuala Lumpur giving the background of the Communist conspiracy in Singapore. (18)

The statement pointed out that the communists in Singapore, taking their directions from the CPM Central Committee, had adopted the United Front strategy since 1955.

Although the communists had heavily infiltrated the PAP, they "never succeeded in exploiting it as a subservient and effective instrument of the United Front."

After both Malaya and Singapore agreed to a merger as proposed by Tunku under the Malaysia plan, the communists made "a last desperate attempt" to capture the PAP government and party.

Their strategy, Kuala Lumpur stated, was to develop a safe base in Singapore and use it as "a beach-head from which to mount a continuous political offensive against the Federation."

The official text pointed out that some leaders of Barisan Sosialis had openly stated that they wanted Singapore to become the "Cuba of Malaysia". (19)

Eventually when the Federation was "sufficiently softened up", they hoped to move to "the second stage of the revolution". That would be armed struggle. 4,556 words 01.11.2014 08:400

Returning to Singapore on 3 February 1963, Lee Kuan Yew told a press conference that concerted action by the Communists in Singapore and in places outside the State would have endangered the security of Malaysia. He said he was confident that their capacity to do anything now had been "considerably diminished". (20)

But, he added, if left alone, without outside factors, the Singapore Government would never have contemplated such sweeping action.

"I think it is fair to say that for the Singapore Government, it would have been easier to leave this action over till after Aug. 31 (the scheduled date for merger to coincide with the sixth anniversary of Merdeka in Malaya), but as I have said on several previous occasions, on issues of national importance like merger and Malaysia, defence and the stability of Malaya and Malaysia, we will work with the Federation."

Lee then went on to stress that the operation ("Cold Store") had not been made to help him or his Government.

In "Operation Cold Store" 111 persons were picked up in Singapore and across the Causeway. The Barisan Sosialis lost 24 cadres, the unions lost 21 of their militant leaders, the left-wing rural associations seven activists, and the old boys' associations another five.

Lee described those arrested as the "expendables" in the communist united front. Seasoned but overexposed "tiger generals" like Lim Chin Siong and Fong Swee Suan were put behind bars. Lee said communist tactics had always taken into consideration the regular sacrificing of such people.

Lee also said 18 "top-ranking" communists had escaped the big sweep. The real leaders like the Plen and town committee members (the "brains trust" of the party) remained at large, probably in and around Singapore.

The Special Branch in Kuala Lumpur had earlier detained 50 people including Ahmad Boestamam and eight other leaders of the Socialist Front. That was in mid-December 1962 – about a week after the start of the abortive Brunei revolt, and nine days after Indonesia's declaration of its confrontation against emerging Malaysia.

According to Lee Kuan Yew, the action against front leaders in Kuala Lumpur and Kuching rang the alarm bell and Lim Chin Siong "gave a directive to all cadres never to sleep in the same place regularly…" Thus 18 big fish managed to escape the dragnet. Though not Lim himself – significantly the most important leader in the political opposition.

Historian Turnbull wrote: "The detainees included Lim Chin Siong and half of the Barisan's central executive committee, and the arrests provoked riots of protest, which in turn led to further arrests, mainly of second-echelon Barisan leaders.

"Once again the PAP party executive's rivals had been removed at a dangerous time in circumstances in which the Singapore government could lay the responsibility at the doors of others, this time the British and Malayans.

"The arrests were a severe blow to the Barisan.

"Tension in Singapore over the impending merger lessened, and Lee Kuan Yew gained considerable personal success in negotiating the final terms of the union which were very favourable to Singapore…" (21)

Chin Peng noted: "Operation Cold Store shattered our underground network throughout the island. Those who escaped the police net went into hiding. Many fled to Indonesia…" (22)

Lawyer Tan Jing Quee has written: "The two main pillars of the left wing movement in Singapore, the Barisan Sosialis and SATU (the Singapore Association of Trade Unions), were decapitated…

"The mass arrests marked a watershed in the political history of Singapore. The traumas and terrors of 'Operation Coldstore' would leave permanent scars and a profound dampening effect on political discourse for decades…" (23)

Greg Poulgrain concluded: "…'Coldstore' ended all opposition – initially preserving UK interests but ultimately at the cost of democracy…" (24)

A. Mahadeva, a former journalist and detainee of "Coldstore", concluded that Lim Chin Siong, a loyal friend to many people, "will long be remembered as a staunch anti-colonial fighter." (25)

"Of course, Lim Chin Siong was the left-wing's most important person. After the appearance of the "Plen", he remained the most important left-wing person, one with even greater influence and authority," Fong Chong Pik @ the "Plen" recorded in his book **Memoirs.**

"Lim Chin Siong was a heroic person who, in the most difficult times, could unite, mobilize and provide leadership to all forces to struggle for a common cause (Singapore's independence)…" (26)

Dr M. K. Rajakumar, a former acting chairman of the Labour Party of Malaya (LPM), described Lim as a "charismatic freedom fighter" and concluded his assessment of Lim's leadership ("like a meteor, bringing hope and excitement to a people coming out of the intellectual darkness of the colonial era"): "Singapore's history begins when he is given his proper place in its annals." (27)

Notes Chapter 11: To bell the cat

1. T.N. Harper, Lim Chin Siong and 'the Singapore Story', **COMET IN OUR SKY**, p. 31

2. Dennis Bloodworth, **The Tiger and the Trojan Horse**, p. 275

    Lee Kuan Yew told the State Assembly on 20 July 1961, a few days after the PAP's loss in the Anson by-election: "…For two years the British Government has tried to manipulate the PAP into a position where we will become the successor to Lim Yew Hock's policy, where the communist party will be attacked not by British imperialism, which is the supreme power in Singapore, but by us, the locally elected Government with limited powers…" As quoted by Alex Josey, **Lee Kuan Yew – The Crucial Years**, p. 140

3. **Straits Times** July 21, 1961

    On Lord Selkirk's controversial meeting with Lim Chin Siong, James Puthucheary, Sandra Woodhull, and Fong Swee Suan – four of the leading figures in the pro-communist faction of the PAP, please refer to Chapter Six of Bloodworth's narrative **The Tiger and the Trojan Horse**.

4. Quoted in John Drysdale, **Singapore: Struggle for Success**, p. 224

    Yes; Lee would certainly try to win over the minds of the people – through argument and persuasion, himself legally trained and a highly accomplished speaker. But when the political scenario changed so threateningly to his own position of power by mid-1961, and when he "saw the looming crisis in apocalyptic terms" (to quote Cambridge history don, Dr. T. N. Harper, **COMET IN OUR SKY**, p. 33), Lee continued to press the Internal Security Council to make mass arrests of the political opposition in Singapore.

The United Kingdom High Commission had on various occasions to restrain his bids for large-scale incarceration. For instance, on 5 October 1962, Lord Selkirk wrote to Duncan Sandys to advise that Lee "is probably very much attracted to the idea of destroying his political opponents. It should be remembered that there is behind all this a very personal aspect…"

But, the supreme *kiasu* (no-lose) exponent wanted others like the Tunku in Kuala Lumpur or the colonial masters in Singapore and London to do the dirty job for the PAP government.

5. Quoted in Drysdale, p. 280

Speaking at a forum organized by the University of Singapore Students' Union on 21 June 1962, a year after the great thrashing at the Hong Lim by-election, Lee said if the PAP had been hostages to political office, the Government could have crushed the "united front" and held on for another five years. Although he did not say how, he then went on to stress that he was not going to solve the political problem, as many had urged, by locking up the opposition.

In answer to Tun Lim Yew Hock's argument, at a radio forum held on the same day, that if the the

Barisan Sosialis were communists then it was the government's duty to put them away, Lee said he would use the referendum to nail the Communist lie on merger. To put them away before nailing their lie in the propaganda battle (the referendum being part of it), would make them political martyrs "the way Tun did the last time" (referring to "Operation Liberation" on October 1956). Please refer to Drysdale, p. 301.

6. Chin Peng, **MY SIDE OF HISTORY**, p. 439

7. Bloodworth, **The Tiger and the Trojan Horse**, p. 265

    According to Fong Chong Pik @ the "Plen", the Singapore MCP withdrew more than 50 cadres from the island from late 1961 to 1963-64. "Those cadres who were believed to have exposed themselves and whose safety was therefore threatened were taken out on a priority basis," Fong recorded in his book **The Memoirs of a Malayan Communist Revolutionary**, p. 172. "As a result, practically the entire effective strength of the organization was withdrawn. We successfully preserved the cadres, but our struggle in Singapore began to wane and eventually faded..."

8. C. C. Too persuaded both the Tunku and his deputy Datuk Abdul Razak to insist on arresting the subversives in Singapore **prior to**, not after, the formation of Malaysia.

    "If the proposed new Malaysian Government were to carry out the mass arrests of Singaporeans – predominantly ethnic Chinese – it would result in accusations of an ethnic Malay-dominated government persecuting the Chinese after swallowing up

Singapore," Too wrote later (**Far Eastern Economic Review**, 14 December 1989, p. 27), in explaining his call for timely action against communist leaders and other subversive elements on the island.

According to his argument, a crackdown by Kuala Lumpur after the establishment of Malaysia "would exacerbate racial conflict not only in Singapore but on the peninsula (across the Causeway) as well…"

9. **Sunday Times** August13, 1961

10. **Straits Times** August 14, 1961

11. On 27 July 1962 Selkirk advised the Commonwealth Secretary Duncan Sandys that he believed that both Tunku and Lee Kuan Yew "wish to arrest the effective political opposition and blame us for doing so…"

In the top-level meeting at Chequers in London on 28 July 1962, it was reported that the Tunku was not happy about forming Malaysia "were it not for the Communist danger." The report added: "In his view, Singapore was bound to go Communist unless something was done soon."

Australian historian Dr Harper has written that in that meeting at Chequers, the official country residence of the British prime minister in Buckinghamshire, "the British were prepared to offer the arrests as a lubricant to a final agreement on Malaysia." (**COMET IN OUR SKY**, p. 40)

It was the Tunku's essential pre-condition for merger with Singapore. But, a pretext had to be found for a large-scale incarceration of political foes. The left-wing leaders knew that many of them would be detained. But when?

12. Greg Poulgrain, a history lecturer at Griffiths University in Brisbane, Queensland, Australia, clarified the SB role in the Brunei rebellion after interviewing Roy Henry, former head of the Sarawak-Brunei Special Branch. In the expose in his article on LIM CHIN SIONG IN BRITAIN'S SOUTHEAST ASIAN DE-COLONISATION (**COMET IN OUR SKY**, pp. 114-124), Poulgrain has written (p. 115):

"...Libraries of historical texts all testify incorrectly that (Sheikh A.M.) Azahari was to blame (as the most prominent Brunei politician involved in the rebellion), when it was Roy Henry and his operatives who had penetrated the inner-circle of advisers in Azahari's Brunei People's Party..."

As recorded in **Keesing's Contemporary Archives**, a large-scale revolt broke out on 8 December 1962

in the British-protected Sultanate of Brunei. The R.A.F. Transport Command quickly flew in strong reinforcements from Singapore and Malaya to Brunei and adjacent territories. During the first three days of the uprising, the units flown to British Borneo included the 1st Battalion 2nd Gurkha Rifles, the 1st Battalion Queen's Own Highlanders, the 42nd Royal Marine Commando, the 1st Green Jackets, an armoured car squadron of the Queen's Irish Hussars, and units of the R.A.F. Regiment.

At the same time, a strong British naval force was sent from Singapore to British Borneo waters – comprising the 23,000-ton Commando carriers H.M.S. Albion and H.M.S. Bulwark, the 10,000-ton cruiser H.M.S. Tiger, the 2,200-ton destroyer H.M.S. Cavalier, and minesweepers, tank landing craft, and auxiliary vessels.

Lieut-Gen. Sir Nigel Poett, C-in-C, Far East Land Forces, estimated the rebel strength at about 2,000.

On 17 December 1962, Lord Selkirk, UK Commissioner-General for Southeast Asia, announced in Labuan (35 miles away from Brunei) the collapse of the Brunei rebellion.

13. Richard Clutterbuck, **Conflict and Violence in Singapore and Malaysia 1945-1983**, p. 369

Having referred the matter to Prime Minister Harold Macmillan who urged restraint, the Colonial Secretary Duncan Sandys approved the political purge as demanded by the Tunku. Sandys gave the green light on 12 December 1962 in the midst of the Brunei revolt although "Cold Store" was carried out on 2 February 1963, six weeks after. The official rationale in a long statement of 3 February 1963 probably appeared credible only to its spin doctors in Kuala Lumpur and Singapore.

14. Bloodworth, **The Tiger and the Trojan Horse**, pp. 275-276

15. CO 1030/1160, No. 546 in the Public Record Office, London.

As quoted by Poh Soo Kai in his article "Detention in Operation Cold Store: A Study in Imperialism", **FAJAR GENERATION**, p. 188

16. Drysdale, **Singapore: Struggle for Success**, p. 319

17. **Sunday Times** February 3, 1963

18. **Straits Times** February 4, 1963

19. How credible was the imminent threat posed in the so-called "Cuba" theory?

Since the communists had been operating throughout the length and breadth of the peninsula during Emergency I (1948-60), and since mid-1953 had been running their show from their base and deep jungle sanctuary (their "Yenan") at Sadao on the Betong salient in southern Thailand, it is questionable whether they needed to set up another base in such a constricted urban environment in Singapore with its complex of British military bases.

It is of interest to note, however, that the "Cuba" theory itself had earlier been espoused by none other than Lee Kuan Yew himself.

Speaking to foreign correspondents in Singapore on April 1962 (only the first part of text was published in **Straits Times** April 20, 1962), Lee narrated when, and explained why he parted with the pro-communists in the PAP who "believed a Cuban Castro type of Singapore was possible" and who hoped to "mount a Cuban type of revolutionary fervor and ferment in Singapore" to help "in leavening up" the situation across the Causeway where a 12-year communist insurgency had just been subdued. Castro used armed force to wage and win his revolutionary struggle. Could any militant use force to advantage in Singapore in the presence of the overwhelming British military might?

It should also be noted that in Peninsular Malaysia, the communists launched another armed struggle (the Emergency II) in mid-1968 – less than two years after the end of Indonesian confrontation and about three years after the separation of Singapore.

And, in Sarawak where the British also arrested known members of the Clandestine Communist Organization (CCO) while crushing the Brunei revolt in December 1962, about 1,000 young Chinese fled across the border into Kalimantan where they were promptly trained by the Indonesians. They subsequently returned to their homeland to take part in guerrilla action after Indonesian troops had started their confrontation in early 1963.

Although the communist guerrillas were defeated on the mainland by 1960, the communist threat was moving towards its apogee in Singapore. But the nearby Rhio islands to the south, rather than Singapore, served as the offshore sanctuary for elite cadres and communist fighters some of whom subsequently returned as the "south swallows" to join Indonesian paratroopers who landed in Pontian (about 50 miles to the north of Singapore) in mid-August 1964, and later to take part in the revived armed struggle on the peninsula in the mid-1970s.

The second communist insurgency, referred to as Emergency II, was actively waged on the ground for nearly a decade, starting from mid-1968. The protracted but futile armed campaign for power was finally concluded with the signing of the peace agreement on 2 December 1989 at the Lee Garden Hotel in Haadyai, south Thailand.

Addressing foreign correspondents in Singapore April 1962, Lee Kuan Yew spoke of the split with the communists in mid-1961 and told why he opted for independence through merger with the anti-communist Federation of Malaya. "And I missed what might have been an interesting experience in leading a Fidel Castro revolution in Southeast Asia," he quipped. Or he tried to, with not much sense of realism.

With home-grown revolutionaries in neighbouring countries like Indonesia, Thailand, Burma, Cambodia, Laos,

Indochina, and the Philippines, no Fidel Castro was needed in this turbulent part of the troubled world. Nor was there any need for any latter-day revolutionary from Singapore to export revolution to this storm-tossed region, cratered with cesspits of communism.

It was said to be a 1948 Moscow directive that ignited the first post-WW2 rash of armed revolts across Southeast Asia, and then in mid-1968 it was Mao's call for "a sustained and vigorous offensive" that revived revolutionary violence and communist insurgencies in this region.

20. **StraitsTimes** February 4, 1963

21. Mary Turnbull, **A History of Singapore 1819-1975**, p. 281

On "Operation Cold Store" conducted jointly by Malayan and Singapore police, Chin Peng wrote in his narrative **MY SIDE OF HISTORY** (p.439): "The Singapore crackdown we had been expecting for almost four years had, in fact, only materialised after strong pressure on Lee from both the Tunku and the British. Our deliberations with ECY (Eu Chooi Yip, the senior Singapore communist leader) two years earlier had correctly forecast the event, but had failed to visualize putting into place any form of effective counter measures. My plea to 'prepare for the worst' had been to no avail…"

According to Chin Peng, the two of them and Siao Chang, another senior CPM leader, had met in Peking in mid-1961 to discuss a plan to disperse all exposed underground activists remaining in Singapore, and how best to preserve intact what was left of the communist underground on the island.

Chin Peng recalled (p.437): "Two years earlier the CPM Central Committee had warned that Lee Kuan Yew, having secured such a resounding electoral victory (with strong communist support) in May, 1959, was likely to move heavily against the Party's island-wide infrastructure…"

In his 1959 election speeches, Lee had boldly and openly announced his coming battle with the left, and he said the ultimate contestants would be the PAP and the MCP.

Shortly after the sacking of PAP strongman and rebel Ong Eng Guan in mid-July 1960, Lee warned about the resurgence of the communist underground in its struggle for power.

22. Chin Peng, **MY SIDE OF HISTORY**, p. 439

23. **COMET IN OUR SKY Lim Chin Siong in History**, pp.87, 88

24. Ibid., p. 12325. Ibid., p. 157

26. Fong Chong Pik, **The Memoirs of a Malayan Communist Revolutionary**, pp. 170, 176

CHAPTER TWELVE

The denouement:
Fission politics in the separation
of Singapore, 1962-65

Lee Kuan Yew's campaign for a "snap" general election constituted the third and final phase of his all-out battle for merger. This was a one-man show, which he quietly launched in November 1962, two months after his triumph in the referendum on merger.

It was at a radio forum in late September 1961 that Dr Goh Keng Swee argued for holding a referendum, and Dr Lee Siew Chor of the Barisan Sosialis agreed that public opinion should first be sought through a referendum. This forum was held to answer the question whether the issue of merger "should be decided by a referendum now or a general election later." (1)

There were probably, obvious reasons why the PAP opted first for a single-issue referendum which would limit the scope of public discourse, and anyway the electorate had to vote on three pro-merger alternatives instead of a simple "yes" or "no" to merger. Such an expedient way to elicit public opinion on a first-time issue was less risky for the ruling party. While the PAP would have to wager its political life on the scales of a general election, less was at stake in a referendum – uncertain as was its outcome.

Of course, a defeat would not only entail a loss of face with extensive collateral psychological damage so soon after the intra-party split with the communists and leftists, but would also probably trigger a groundswell of popular feeling for a general election to settle the issue once and for all. In which case, a referendum would still provide a kind of buffer, affording precious time for the ruling party to shore up its position.

After scoring a politically resounding as well as a psychologically reassuring victory in the September 1962 referendum, Lee Kuan Yew got down to the ground again – but this time on a solo trek to visit all the constituencies in Singapore. With the next general election in mind, he set out to consolidate the PAP's gains on the battlefield.

With merger more or less in the bag, Lee would skillfully (if also craftily) time the next major electoral victory to consummate his hard-won political quest.

This third campaign for merger had two main political objectives. One was further vindication for his merger stand. The other was a fresh mandate to lead a new Singapore under the Malaysian sun.

Lee started his ten-month political odyssey by barnstorming "enemy territory" in rural strongholds which had cast the most blank votes in the 1962 referendum.

Bloodworth wrote of this minor epic: "Lee worked like a man possessed. He would set out as the offices and factories closed in the late afternoon, and make twenty or even thirty speeches in English, Hokkien and Malay in what remained of the day and beyond – pouring sweat, changing his shirt five times en route, returning home after midnight. By July 1963 he was spending three days, and then five days a week on this relentless roundabout, for the campaign – a one-man election campaign conducted in the thinnest of disguises – was drawing towards the climax of the coming hustings…" (2)

The **Straits Times** (September 5, 1963) editorialized that the PAP government "will campaign, as the Prime Minister personally has done for weeks, as the victor over communism and the organizer (as far as Singapore is concerned) of Malaysia… Up to twelve months ago the PAP would have courted practically certain disaster had they accepted the challenge of election… The PAP now appears to have regained much of its popularity, although the Barisan Sosialis clearly can claim a large following. But Malaysia is a powerful fistful of cards, and Mr Lee can be expected to play them skillfully.

"He has two other advantages. Some of the infighters who would damage the PAP most are out of harm's way – detained, it must be noted, for subversive and not political activities – while the voter who would like a change will not find it easy to spot, in all the ranks of the opposition, anything which looks like an alternative government."

The new sovereign nation of Malaysia came into being on 16 September 1963. Five days later, the PAP won a fresh mandate in the "snap" general election.

Historian Turnbull wrote: "…Once union with Malaya was achieved, the basis for co-operation with the Alliance assemblymen disappeared. Hitherto the government had relied on their support to ward off left-wing attacks, but now it needed a fresh mandate to renew its power.

"Three major parties contested the September 1963 election: the PAP, the Barisan Sosialis and a new Singapore Alliance, which consisted of the remnants of Lim Yew Hock's Singapore People's Alliance, together with the Singapore branches of the UMNO, Malayan Chinese Association and Malayan Indian Congress.

"The result of the contest hung in doubt. While the PAP had lost much of the mass support it commanded in 1959, it had made a vigorous attempt to revive its organization and recruit new members, particularly among the Malay and Indian communities. The PAP's position was much stronger than it had been in its darkest hours two years before. Many of its leading opponents were in jail, but there were also more positive reasons for the party's improved fortunes. It had achieved its main political goal in successfully negotiating merger with the Federation and winning independence from colonial rule within the time limit promised in 1959. As the ruling party it held the initiative. For a long time the government had intended to hold an election immediately Malaysia came into being and planned its strategy accordingly…" (3)

The **Straits Times** (September 5, 1963) had earlier described the timing of this snap election as "adroit". A masterstroke of political timing, it betrayed much cunning (fed by uncertainty about the electoral outcome) – coming a year after the successful referendum, seven and a half months after "Operation Cold Store" with its toxic political fallout – and its nine-day electioneering campaign was waged for the greater part during Lee's brief interlude of discretionary authority following his "UDI" (unilateral declaration of independence) on 31 August 1963 (the original target date for merger and Malaysia).

Bloodworth wrote that "Lee called a snap election, giving the minimum legal notice (five days), cutting the campaign to the minimum legal length (nine days) and timing it so that canvassing would be interrupted by the celebration of Singapore's entry into Malaysia on 16 September, just half way through the hustings. This meant that if by chance the Barisan won the election, they would find themselves already trapped inside an anti-communist Federation run by Kuala

Lumpur – 'There was the nagging doubt that things could still go wrong,' Lee explained.

"The Barisan were left with only a few days in which to fill out nomination papers, to run off posters and pamphlets (assuming they could find a printer), and to hire halls and organize rallies (assuming they could obtain the necessary police permits). Then, on the eve of polling day, Goh Keng Swee warned a mass meeting called by the PAP that if the people put the Barisan into power Kuala Lumpur would put Malaysian troops into Singapore and take over the island. And there was no time for the Barisan to reply…" (4)

Lee Kuan Yew said: "We planned to start off the general elections in Singapore before merger, before the Malaysian central government had time to take over and exercise enough power over the police to have any significant influence on the conduct of the elections. Polling Day, Sept 21 was after merger.

"Many people feared we would lose to the Barisan Sosialis. They made detention of their open-front leaders and our alleged "sell-out to Malaysia" the burning issues of the elections.

"Barisan election rallies drew large crowds; their speakers were wildly cheered. Posters carrying the photographs of the leading detainees – Lim Chin Siong, Fong Swee Suan and others – were part of their appeal to the voters.

"The huge crowds at Barisan rallies proved the communists were good at organizing big crowds to intimidate neutral onlookers. They were meant to demoralize and rout our supporters. They failed…" (5)

Although the PAP won a strong majority with 37 seats (72.5% representation in the new legislative assembly), the ruling party carried less than half of the electorate.

This was Lee's analysis: "As it turned out, out of the 53 percent votes the PAP won in 1959, 32.91 per cent (over 60% of the total votes for the PAP in 1959) went to the Barisan

Sosialis in the September 1963 elections; they were a mix of pro-communist and pro-left chauvinist votes.

"Partly by our design, but more through the intimidating show of almost overwhelming strength by the communist united front, our chances of survival were enhanced. Many people feared the communists would win; the conflict became so stark that the choice for people was clear-cut.

"Making up for this loss of 32.91 per cent to the Barisan Sosialis, 26 per cent of total voters, nearly all those who in 1959 supported either the Singapore People's Alliance, the Liberal Socialists or the United People's Party, swung over to the PAP to make up the 46.5 per cent the PAP won..."

The PAP owed its 1963 victory largely to its new so called "right" votes, accounting for over 55% of the total votes cast for the ruling party. Electoral support for the PAP had gone down from 53% in 1959 to 46.5%, a majority of less than half of the electorate.

Lee's own takings went down to only 50% from 75% in 1959 and a near-stratospheric high of 78% in 1955. Lee described the defining 1963 general election as the toughest for the PAP, for all his gruelling 10-month groundwork. (6)

Although the Barisan Sosialis attained only 13 seats (25.5% representation in the new house), it collected 33% of the total votes cast in the 1963 general election (about 3% more than in the 1962 referendum, according to Lee's reckoning).

Lee stated that these 33% were swung away from the PAP to the Barisan Sosialis in 1963. This shift took away a huge chunk (over 60%) of the votes cast for the PAP in the 1959 general election which swept the party into power for the first time. In short, the PAP could/would not have come to power in 1959 without communist support.

The 1963 general election saw the exit of two former chief ministers – Tun Lim Yew Hock who did not contest, and David Marshall who lost his deposit.

Ong Eng Guan took Hong Lim again, the only seat won by his party the United People's Party, which fielded candidates in 46 constituencies. He resigned from his seat in June 1965. Then, like the other two political heavyweights before him, Ong too faded out from the scene.

The right wing collapsed when the Singapore Alliance failed to capture any seat; it polled a total of 49,000 votes (8% of the total) in 46 constituencies. The right wing had won 40% in 1959.

The fall of the Alliance was to further undermine the already stressed and strained relationship between Kuala Lumpur and Singapore. (7)

On the fate of the communist/leftist struggle for political power in Singapore, Bloodworth commented: "…The fragile dream that the left wing might one day capture Malaysia by constitutional means had been finally shattered by that most callous of statements in simple figures known as the (electoral) bottom line…" (8)

The communists and their loyal supporters pursued power through the ballot box in Singapore because they had strong popular support, in spite of which they fell short. Apart from mass support, the political battleground and terrain was not at all to their advantage. Prevailing conditions and circumstances constrained and conspired against their grand design. The Fates did not favour the communists and leftists.

The "Plen", the communist underground boss, has rightly concluded "that on the tiny island of Singapore where the colonial government had exercised tight control over a long period, the mobilized and organized masses alone fighting the combined forces of the island's reactionary rulers, the hostile government of the Federation, and the British colonial power could never stand a chance of winning (acquiring political power)..." (9) 07.11.2014 09:43

ΩΩΩΩΩΩΩΩΩ

About 100 days to Malaysia Day, Lee Kuan Yew said: "Merger is inevitable, either by free will or force... The future of Singapore and Malaya is intertwined. There is no other way for us and no other way for them..." (10)

Lee waged a 26-month battle for merger – from the split with the communists in July 1961 to Malaysia Day on 16 September 1963.

It took less time to undo merger – within 24 months, from the September 1963 general election when the seeds of political fission were sown across the land to the separation of Singapore on 9 August 1965.

Separation was necessary, if not inevitable, to avoid a disastrous head-on collision and conflict. It had to be by free will or force, and both sides chose to part peacefully, albeit acrimoniously. Tunku told Lee Kuan Yew there was no other way.

Announcing Singapore's separation on TV, a visibly-shaken Lee Kuan Yew said: "...For me it is a moment of anguish. All my life, my whole adult life, I have believed in merger and unity of the two territories..."

Many years later, Tunku presented a copy of his autobiography to Lee Kuan Yew, signed with these words for history to judge: "To the man who worked hard to help form Malaysia, but who worked even harder to break away." (11)

Lee said two momentous decisions taken by the PAP led to separation – one to enter the peninsular political scene, and the other to forge a united opposition front and promote

"Malaysian Malaysia" politics. Both party decisions, he pointed out, were taken during his absence.

But it's hardly credible that the party's supremo and the state's prime minister as well had not at all been consulted or even informed. Unless his own inner circle (Old Guard) associates had inconceivably played such games behind his back.

According to Lee, he was away in early 1964 on an African tour on Tunku's behalf. He said: "When I came back I found that the CEC (Central Executive Council) had decided to fight the Malaysian federal elections. I was not enthusiastic. There was a gentleman's understanding between the Tunku and me that we should stay out of each other's backyard. This was known to the CEC.

"But the Tunku had allowed Peninsula Umno and MCA-MIC Alliance leaders to intervene in the Singapore general elections in September 1963.

"So the CEC considered all bets off. Although I was not personally enamoured of the proposal, I abided by the decision. We fought, we lost.

"We had made serious, solemn promises to the people of Singapore about what Malaysia was about..." (12)

Tensions built up, Lee said. On 9 May 1965, when he was away attending the Socialist Youth Conference in Bombay, the CEC, with Dr Toh Chin Chye leading and Rajaratnam supporting, forged the Malaysian Solidarity Convention (MSC) which brought togetherfive opposition parties from Sabah, Sarawak and Peninsular Malaysia. Lee said he returned to find this a fait accompli, with a rally fixed for the Sunday morning of 6 June 1965 at the National Theatre.

But he did not say whether as the PAP secretary-general and Prime Minister he had at any time been consulted, or if he had been kept in the dark about such fateful decisions.

He went along with them, nevertheless, and played a leading role in both the PAP's clamorous and dismal debut on the mainland and in the emotion-charged and divisive "Malaysian Malaysia" campaign.

The PAP contested in only nine urban constituencies in the April 1964 general election in Peninsular Malaysia. Calling it a "token" participation, Toh said its purpose was "to cooperate with Umno and the central government of Malaysia to help Malaysia succeed." (13)

Thousands (including this humble author) turned up at the opening rally at the Suleiman Court near the heart of Kuala Lumpur where Lee himself kicked off the highly spirited PAP campaign on the evening of 22 March 1964. His was a new vibrant voice in the political heartland of Malaysia.

The PAP rallies in Kuala Lumpur, Seremban and Malacca drew large and spell-bound crowds, many having come out of sheer curiosity.

In the event, the PAP succeeded only in Bangsar (Kuala Lumpur) which it won by a narrow margin in a triangular competition with the MCA and the Socialist Front.

The PAP took quite a hammering in two Chinese-dominated constituencies – Tanjong (Penang) and Kluang Utara (Johor).

But, the MCA had good innings. In eight contests against the PAP and the Socialist Front, the MCA emerged victorious in six constituencies. (14)

Turnbull commented: "Singapore's premature rush into federal politics was fatal to the unity of Malaysia. Tunku Abdul Rahman and Tun Abdul Razak, Malaysia's deputy prime minister, considered Lee Kuan Yew had broken a pledge to stay clear of federal politics and not mobilize the peninsular Chinese. This drove the UMNO/MCA partners closer together, created suspicions about the personal ambitions of

Singapore leaders, particularly of Lee Kuan Yew, and set the relationship between Singapore and the central government on a downhill track, along which it continued to slide with increasing momentum…" (15)

In Singapore, the People's Alliance was renamed the Malaysian Alliance Party of Singapura. Opening its convention on 17 April 1965, Tunku said that Lee Kuan Yew had in mind a share in the running of Malaysia. "This was considered as unacceptable since the Alliance is strong enough to run the country on its own," he argued, and rejected power-sharing with the PAP. (16)

Ten days after Tunku's "NO to PAP" speech in Singapore, Dr Toh Chin Chye announced on 27 April 1965 the formation of the Malaysian Solidarity Convention (MSC) – a united opposition front. And it was to launch the highly-divisive but short-lived "Malaysian Malaysia" campaign.

Earlier, in early March 1965, Lee Kuan Yew told reporters at the airport before leaving for a month-long tour of Australia and New Zealand: "The immediate issue, from our point of view, is whether this is going to be a Malaysian nation, and all those who believe that Malaysia should become a Malaysian nation should come together…" (17)

Re-invigorated after his visit Down South, Lee delivered a fighting speech on May Day at the Jalan Besar Stadium, saying that Singapore "need never be cowed nor submissive". He said Malaysia's problems could be solved either arbitrarily or democratically and constitutionally. And he warned: "Once arbitrary methods are used then the consequences both internally and internationally will be such as to bring ruin on all in Malaysia…" (18)

On 9 May 1965, the Malaysian Solidarity Convention met in Singapore and a mass rally at the National Theatre signaled the start of its campaign for a "Malaysian Malaysia".

But this battle cry was too disconcertedly discordant to the Malay ears on the mainland. And in the eyes of the ultras and others, the PAP-led campaign was seen to be an open challenge to the Umno leadership and Malay political dominance in Malaysia.

Tun Razak himself viewed the "Malaysian Malaysia" campaign as being directed against Umno and the Malays. (19)

A week after the MSC meeting in Singapore, the Umno general assembly unanimously passed a resolution demanding Lee Kuan Yew's arrest and detention. (20)

Returning from Laos on 21 May 1965, Lee told a large crowd at the airport: "If we must have trouble, let us have it now instead of waiting for another five or ten years. If we find Malaysia cannot work now, then we can make alternative arrangements…" (21)

Addressing a union meeting of traction company employees on 23 May 1965, Lee said: "If Malaysia does not belong to you and me, why should we fight for it? We must make some other arrangements. These are fundamental issues on which we cannot give way…" (22)

Did Lee Kuan Yew imply that the PAP Government should find a way out?

Did it also imply pulling out of Malaysia?

If so, when did the PAP decide that they should seek their own separate destiny, that they should go their own way?

5,491 words 08.11.2014 07:29

A close reading of the various developments in tumultuous 1964 and the rush of events towards the cliffhanger in mid-1965 would suggest that the PAP had probably decided to steer its own course, either towards the very end of 1964 or by early 1965.

Following its highly controversial entry into peninsular politics in the April 164 general election in Peninsular Malaysia, the PAP went on to mount its "Malaysian Malaysia" campaign to force the issue.

Speaking in Singapore on October 1964, not long after the two rounds of racial violence on the island in late July and early September, Tan Siew Sin, Finance Minister and MCA president, helped to spread publicly a "wild rumour" which he said he had heard in Singapore and questioned its validity.

It was that Singapore could secede from Malaysia if it wished to do so. Tan described it as "completely erroneous" and he said: "There is no provision in the Constitution for any state to secede from the Federation (of Malaysia)…" (23)

Speaking in Singapore on 9 December 1964, Tunku himself suggested a breakaway as the only solution if Singapore politicians continued to disagree with him (as the Malaysian prime minister). But he warned that it would be a calamity for Singapore and Malaysia.

In early 1965 Dr Goh Keng Swee, then Singapore Minister for Finance, came to realize "that the economics of Singapore within Malaysia as part of a common market was not working out, and pragmatically decided that separation was the best option." (24)

Subsequently, the inauguration in Singapore on 9 May 1965 of the Malaysian Solidarity Convention (MSC) marked the historic point of no return.

When Lee Kuan Yew submitted his amendment to the motion of thanks to the King for the opening of the new session of parliament on 25 May 1965, Lee said he had wanted the motion to express regret that the Royal Address had not reassured the nation that Malaysia would become a Malaysian Malaysia. (25)

When he flew back to Singapore one weekend while Parliament was still in session, Lee said in a public speech: "The agreement in the constitution must lead to a Malaysian Malaysia, and if they want to stop it they must use unconstitutional methods to stop it."

He then said: "So, I say, if they want to do that – do it now!

"It will be easier for us to make other arrangements.

"If that is what they want, we have got other ideas of looking after ourselves.

"Those states which want a Malaysian Malaysia can get together..." (26)

Within Singapore, the PAP's political position was virtually unassailable by 1964. "Operation Cold Store" of early February 1963 had more or less crushed the communist underground organization. The September 1963 general election had given the PAP a very strong mandate with over a two-thirds majority in the legislative assembly. And its subsequent trouncing of the left in a straight fight at the Hong Lim by-election in July 1965 was to confirm its ascendancy over the communists and leftists.

Within a fortnight of the Hong Lim by-election, Tunku was finally persuaded that separation was the solution for Malaysia and the way out for Singapore.

Bloodworth thus commented: "The PAP victory told the Tunku two things: there was no dislodging Lee Kuan Yew, and so there was no danger of a communist takeover in Singapore. The obnoxious island therefore could and should be cut adrift..." (27)

The year 1964 (the fire-dominant year of the dragon in the Chinese almanac) turned out to be highly restive and quite sanguinary for Singapore.

In mid-1964, large-scale riots broke out again – nine years after the Hock Lee episode. And this time, communal violence reared its ugly visage in an unexpected return long after the Hertogh riots of 1950.

On 21 July 1964, racial rioting erupted in Singapore and went on for five days, taking 22 lives and injuring 454 people.

This sudden outbreak of racial violence must have shocked the PAP Government with its avowed commitment to non-communalism. Lee Kuan Yew said Tunku would "be appraised of the full picture because he must make the decision whether Malaysia as proclaimed is to endure and flourish, or split asunder..." (28)

On 17 August 1964, a strongly armed Indonesian force of about 90-100 paratroopers landed on the swampy coastland in the Pontian district of Johore, about 50 miles north-west of Singapore.

In early September, rioting exploded again in Singapore and continued for another five days and nights. Some 10,000 police and troops were called into action. Clutterbuck described the two five-day episodes of riots as "the worst and most prolonged in Singapore's post-war history." The double whammy claimed 34 lives, as compared with 18 in the 1950 Hertogh racial riots. (29)

On 20 September 1964 Tunku flew to Singapore and told the leaders of the Singapore Alliance: "This trouble in Singapore was manufactured by Sukarno and I have proof of it. Unfortunately, some politicians in Singapore have not been free from blame. They have created an atmosphere which could be of help to Sukarno in his plan to wreck our society." And to "crush" newly-established Malaysia, to quote the cocky, combative and impassioned Indonesian president. (30)

With the communist fading into the background, Indonesian confrontation now care to the fore hand in hand with communalism – with Indonesian agents plotting and instigating communal rioting in Singapore, and Indonesian paratroopers landing north of the Causeway to threaten peace and security.

Indonesian saboteurs exploded a number of bombs in Singapore between September 1963 and May 1965, and gunboats seized many Singapore fishing craft.

Moreover, Indonesian confrontation affected the island's entrepot trade. "Singaporeans began to resent the strains and irritations which merger in Malaysia involved, "Turnbull noted. (31)

Although 1964 was stormy for Singapore, a silver lining appeared towards the end of the year. Following the Labour victory in the October 1964 general election in the UK, Harold Wilson moved into 10 Downing Street in London. Wilson's timely entry was reassuring to fellow socialists in the PAP sanctum of power.

Drysdale recorded that "it had been fortunate for Lee Kuan Yew that Harold Wilson and his Labour Party had come to power in (late) 1964 and Wilson had given his personal support to Lee at a critical moment in Singapore's relations with the central government of Malaysia…" (32)

With British military installations and British troops boosted (by the threat of Indonesian confrontation) and deployed on both sides of the Johore Causeway, Wilson could be counted to help enforce the peace if necessary – apart from resisting Indonesian confrontation. (33)

The security of the small British nuclear arsenal in Singapore also factored strongly in the algorithm of British military strategy in the region.

Lee Kuan Yew recalled: "We stood our ground (in the face of venomous attacks from Malay communalists). We avoided being provocative or aggressive, we did not yield. But we were realistic; faced with a probable blow-up, we accepted separation…" (34)

According to Lee's analysis, the couple of momentous decisions by the PAP to venture into peninsular politics in early 1964 and then to spearhead the "Malaysian Malaysia" crusade inmid-1965 led to the critical third – the separation of Singapore on August 1965.

But, the third, and final decision was the Tunku's. When, and why did he make it?

7,068 words 09.11.2014 06:57 07:00

About three weeks after the early September 1964 racial riots, Tunku came to Singapore and when he spoke to the leaders of the Singapore Alliance, he clearly hinted that Lee Kuan Yew, the man he helped to save from possible political extinction, was now challenging his leadership and aspiring to oust and replace him. Patrick Keith wrote: "What a stab in the back!" (35)

When new taxes were introduced in November 1964 to raise spending on defence against Indonesian confrontation, there was a public hue and cry across the Causeway.

"The Singaporeans mounted a massive campaign against the new taxes. They used them to try to discredit the central government and divide the people," Keith wrote. "The Tunku found it intolerable…" (36)

When Tunku came to Singapore on 9 December 1964, he warned that if its politicians continued to disagree with him the only solution would be for Singapore to break away from Malaysia. He also warned that separation would be a mutual calamity.

A very good writer himself noted for his clear, direct and simple style of writing, Tunku has written that the initial impetus to the separation move came with Lee's motion in the Dewan Rakyat seeking an amendment to the King's Speech on 31 May1965. Tunku wrote: "He brought up many issues which disturbed the equilibrium of even the most tolerant Members of the House... Nothing said or done after that speech of his could improve relationships between Mr. Lee and some of our Party (Umno) members, who grew very bitter about him, and became much too restless..." (37)

To Tunku, that speech of Lee's was the proverbial straw that broke the camel's back!

Tunku also narrated how instead of continuing to take part in the Commonwealth Prime Ministers' Conference which started in mid-June 1965, he landed late June in a London clinic on Harley Street to seek treatment for a nerve-racking attack of shingles.

He recalled very clearly: "Every movement caused grinding pain, but my mind was alive and active; so as I lay there, I was thinking of Mr. Lee Kuan Yew. And what I thought did not drive the pain away, but made it worse.

"The more pain I suffered, the more I directed my growing anger at him pitying Singapore for all its self-imposed problems. Whichever way my restless mind turned, I could not help but come to one conclusion – and that was to cut Singapore adrift from the rest of Malaysia..." (38)

According to one account of a senior journalist and confidant of the Tunku, the Tunku made a lot of calculations on a hospital bed in London. He "weighed the pros and cons of having Singapore in Malaysia" which ran into several foolscap pages. And he concluded that Malaysia and Singapore "should part" for their mutual well-being and security. (39)

On 1 July 1965, Tunku wrote what was in his mind in a letter to Tun Razak and asked him to talk over it with Lee Kuan Yew.

After meeting with Lee for nearly two hours, Razak replied to Tunku on 22 July reporting that Lee would probably continue his "crusade against a feudal Malay-dominated Alliance Party..."

(Towards the end of May 1965, Lee had said, referring to Mahathir's speech in Parliament, Singapore had never agreed to Malay rule. (40) Razak himself had been antagonized, and probably riled up, by Lee's adversarial and defiant stand.)

Razak also relayed to Tunku, Dr Goh Keng Swee's suggestion that "to separate Singapore from the Central Government" was "the only way to stop a head-long collision" between Kuala Lumpur and Singapore.

As suggested by Razak, Goh then consulted Lee Kuan Yew and senior PAP leaders Lim Kim San and E. W. Barker; they all agreed that separation would be "the best way to avoid collision and trouble..." (41)

Tunku's historic decision jelled soon after that. (42)

Nearly a decade after the separation of Singapore on 9 August 1965, Tunku wrote in the **Star** (April 14, 1975): "...The psychological battle (Lee's argument) had gone on much too long, and had gone too far. Any attempt to repair the breach would, so to speak, tear the fibre to shreds.

"When facing this dilemma, I found that only two choices lay before me. One, to take positive action against Mr. Lee Kuan Yew; and, two, break with Singapore and save the nation from a bloodbath.

"So I chose the second course. The UMNO "ultras" did not like it at all. They wanted me to take Mr. Lee Kuan Yew to task, suspend the Singapore Constitution, and administer the State until such time as the crisis had calmed down..." (43)

Tunku wrote that the Umno "ultras" charged him with being soft, "but it was not a question of my taking on Lee Kuan Yew in single combat, like knights of old, or of letting our forces fight it with Singapore soldiers..."

Tunku stressed: "What was of immediate concern to me was to prevent any possible outbreak of violence that would cause the loss of innocent lives in both territories. Nothing is worse than civil war…"

Turnbull wrote: "Tunku Abdul Rahman and Abdul Razak decided they must either depose the Singapore government or eject Singapore from Malaysia. To remove the PAP government by force was not practicable, and in any event such a move would have been resisted by the British and Australians, who still held a crucial place in defence and security. The expulsion of Singapore seemed the only solution…" (44)

Tunku recalled: "But Lee Kuan Yew was keen. He knew what he would get when he joined Malaysia. The least he would get was independence for Singapore." (45) 10.11.2014 08:06

Notes Chapter 11 The denouement: Fission politics in the separation of Singapore

1. **Straits Times** September 22, 1961

2. Dennis Bloodworth, **The Tiger and the Trojan Horse**, p. 280

3. Mary Turnbull, **A History of Singapore 1819-1975**, p.

    The Legislative Assembly was dissolved on 3 September 1963. Lee announced nomination of candidates to be on 12 Sept and polling day for the general election on 21 Sept 1963.

    In **Lee Kuan Yew—The Crucial Years**, Alex Josey wrote (p. 6): "For two years the Right votes of Lim Yew Hock kept Lee Kuan Yew in power. Yet in the end it was Lee himself who decided the date of the general elections. Seldom in parliamentary history could there have been a more masterly performance. With supreme confidence, having helped to bring about merger and Malaysia as dreamed of more than a decade before, Lee Kuan Yew went to the people seeking approval to continue his work…"

    A. Josey didn't mention Lee's double debt of gratitude to Lim Yew Hock: (1) for having spared him but not Lee's top adversaries in the PAP in the SB crackdown of late October 1956, and (2) Lim's support for the PAP government in the state assembly following the July 1961 split between the ruling party and its communist/left-wing.

4. Bloodworth, p. 282

Speaking in the Legislative Assembly on 5 March 1957, Lee argued why Tunku should put aside his fear about merging with Singapore, and recalled that "on one occasion the Tunku said that, if necessary, he would send troops to occupy Singapore..."

Lee then asked: "Sir, would it not be better to have us as part of the federation under the control of the Federation without having the necessity to send troops to invade and conquer?"

As quoted in Drysdale, **Singapore: Struggle for Success,** p. 167

5. **Straits Times** January 7, 1980, carrying Lee's account of the history of the PAP on its 25th anniversary.

6. **Straits Times** January 7, 1980

"When people talk of a ferocious tiger, the listeners are frightened. But none is so frightened as the man who has suffered tiger attacks in the past," said Cheng Yi of Northern Song Dynasty (5th-6th century AD), reminding us of the psychological impact of personal experience in a mortal struggle with a formidable foe. Quote from **The Little Book of CHINESE PROVERBS**, compiled by Jonathan Clements, Parragon, UK, 2005, p. 123.

Interviewed in the PAP's 45th anniversary publication on November 1999, Lee Kuan Yew (Secretary-General 1954-1992) described the September 1963 General Elections pitting the ruling party against the opposition Barisan Sosialis as the toughest.

Lee said: "Well, I think 1963 because '59 we won on United Front basis, a broad left-wing vote that swept us into power. Non-communists, communists, fellow travelers all voted for us. Then '61 the communists broke away, and formed Barisan, and they fought us for two years, backed by all their unions and all their organisations.

"So '63, after two years of bitter fighting, we went into elections not knowing how the realignment will take place, because the left-wing and the chauvinist vote, Chinese chauvinist vote, the pro-communist and the pro-Chinese vote will go to Barisan and Ong Eng Guan's party.

"So, we had to carry as much of the middle ground and of the right as we could. And the right-wing was still fielding candidates. So if we did not hold sufficiently part of the left-wing vote, capture the middle ground and win part of the right-wing, we would have lost.

"And we could not know until the results how it was going to go. The communists were quite confident they would win. They had big rallies, they were very good at them. They gathered their supporters, made an impression. I think they were very disappointed.

"There was really a realignment of political loyalties in '63. That was the critical year where (when) people knew exactly where we stood. They knew after four years, since '59 what we meant by a socialist, non-communist, democratic society because before that the party was wrapped up with the communists.

"And from then onwards we just widened both on the left and on the right but never moving from the centre. I think that's a critical factor…"

In her book **SINGAPORE'S PEOPLE'S ACTION PARTY**, Pang Cheng Lian described the 1963 general election as "the most crucial and difficult one in the PAP's history". She explained (p. 17):

"This was because at this election the Party had to fight against the very forces which had largely accounted for its overwhelming success (and its capture of power) in the 1959 elections, namely the communists and their sympathisers. Many of the PAP leaders readily admit that success was never a certainty in 1963.

"The results of the elections are an indication of how close the fight was. Although the PAP won thirty-seven seats with 46.6 per cent of the votes, it had a majority of only 13.6 per cent over the Barisan (33%) in terms of total votes cast…"

7. While the PAP triumphed in the watershed 1963 general election, the total defeat of the Singapore Alliance aggravated the growing distrust and ill will on both sides of the Causeway.

Writing in **NEW STRAITS TIMES** (October 25, 1999) on Singapore's separation in 1965, Tan Sri Ghazali Shafie, a former senior Malaysian minister(and the Foreign Ministry's permanent secretary in Kuala Lumpur at that time) recollected:

"…In fact the relationship between the leaderships of both the Alliance and the PAP (had) not been smooth since Malaysia was established. Lee had not held any reserve on his criticism of the Tunku for changing (delaying) the Malaysia formation date from Aug 31, 1963 to September (16, 1963). What made the Alliance leadership even more angry was the complete annihilation of the Singapore Umno-Alliance at the September 1963 elections in favour of PAP…"

Subsequently, the PAP's controversial and divisive debut in peninsular politics to challenge the MCA in the April 1964 general election and then its launching of the confrontational "Malaysian Malaysia" campaign in mid-1965 led to the final political fission and Singapore separation on the morning of 9 August 1965.

8. Bloodworth, p. 284

9. Fong Chong Pik, **The Memoirs of a Malayan Communist Revolutionary**, p. 171

10. **Straits Times** May 4, 1963

11. Quoted in Drysdale, **Singapore: Struggle for Success**, p. 394

Fred Emery of the London **Times** interviewed Lee Kuan Yew on 12 August 1965, three days after Singapore's separation. Lee said that in Kuala Lumpur one of the versions of the trouble was that he wanted to be Prime Minister of Malaysia, and was therefore a man of overweening ambition who wanted to oust the Tunku and take over.

Emery asked: "Didn't you want to be Prime Minister of Malaysia one day?" Lee replied: "One day, perhaps, but not for a very long time. We want to bring the races and the States together. It takes time, for the thing to happen. And we were quite prepared to help them in a secondary capacity. But they didn't want it…" (As quoted in A. Josey, **Lee Kuan Yew – The Crucial Years**, p. 287

12. **Straits Times** March 15, 1982

Pang Cheng Lian was told by one CEC member that the PAP had all along meant to participate in the Malayan elections. In **SINGAPORE'S PEOPLE'S ACTION PARTY**, she wrote (p. 18): "Apparently Lee Kuan Yew had come to some sort of an understanding with the Tengku that his Party would not take part in the Federal elections. However, the rest of the CEC were against this and he was over-ruled. If this is true, it is one of the rare instances when the Secretary-General of the PAP has been known to be over-ruled…"

As recollected by Ghazali Safie, writing in **NEW STRAITS TIMES** October 25, 1999):

"…I waited for the return of Lee from the African tour (early 1964). The country was agog with election fever. I went to the Singapore Guest House next to the Royal Golf Course (in Kuala Lumpur) to wait for him. He arrived by car in the evening via Malacca. I at once confronted him on the fielding of the PAP candidates.

"Holding a glass of beer, he immediately said that it was the work of Dr. Toh Chin Chye (then PAP chairman and Deputy Prime Minister of Singapore). I did not exactly say "bullshit", but I expressed my disgust at the reply since I knew then that nothing in the PAP could happen without Lee's consent…"

13. **Straits Times** March 2, 1964

Dr Toh's "token" was most probably a euphemism for a political test run, to test the blue waters for a major campaign in the next general election.

Deputy Prime Minister Tun Razak was brusque in reacting to the PAP's trial run in mainland elections.

"There is a new party," he said, as reported in **Straits Times** March 24, 1964. "We don't know the sincerity of the party and its leaders. We doubt their sincerity towards the Malays, their interests and their welfare…"

Patrick Keith, in his account of Singapore's expulsion from Malaysia **OUSTED!**, reported (p. 51) on the grave misgivings of the Tunku in early 1964 with Sukarno threatening national survival and the PAP stridently challenging the Alliance leadership in Kuala Lumpur: "…The Tunku was convinced that the Malays in the mainland would never trust Lee. They had already judged his character and his intentions. They regarded him as the spearhead of a dangerous Chinese attack on their special position, and they resented his entry into the Malaysian election…"

14. **Straits Times** April 27, 1964
15. Turnbull, **A History of Singapore 1819-1975**, pp. 289-290

16. **Straits Times** April 18, 1965

17. **Straits Times** March 6, 1965

Lee was to play his confrontational role to the hilt with his make-or-break address in the august house. Speaking on the fateful motion of thanks to the Yang di-Pertuan Agong for his speech from the throne, Lee stated in Parliament on 27 May 1965: "...either a Malaysian Malaysia or nothing... we cannot agree to anything but a Malaysian Malaysia... we are prepared to play in accordance with the rules for five, ten or fifteen years, but ideas we represent must come true..."

As quoted in A. Josey, **Lee Kuan Yew—The Crucial Years**, p. 265

18. **Straits Times** May 2, 1965

19. Writing in **NEW STRAITS TIMES** (October 25, 1999), Ghazali Shafie recalled: "...In May 1965, Lee formed the Malaysian Solidarity Committee (read Convention) which had "Malaysian Malaysia" as a platform on matters which had been explained **ad nauseum** to him that the timing was inappropriate and if adopted, would definitely be taken by the Malays and other Bumiputeras as being against them. Umno was up in arms against the Tunku and Tun (Dr) Ismail (then Home Affairs Minister) for being soft on Lee..."

Though the "Malaysian Malaysia" slogan appeared perfectly innocuous at first blush, many of its strongest opponents found it to be politically spiked (toxic).

Felix Abisheganaden, a former senior NST journalist and a confidant of the Tunku, wrote in **NEW STRAITS TIMES** (October 25, 1999): "...Things got worse when in May 1965, the PAP formed the

Malaysian Solidarity Convention (MSC) together with four opposition parties in Peninsular Malaysia and Sarawak. The idea: To establish a multi-racial Malaysian Malaysia.

"While the MSC claimed to be non-communal, the 'equality' it sought implied the phasing out of Malay privileges. And this inflamed racial passions.

"Lee was the target of Umno leaders. They interpreted the Convention as a means of pitting Singapore, Sarawak and Sabah against Kuala Lumpur.

"They suspected Lee of plotting to seze power himself and his open attacks on the Federal Government appeared to confirm this suspicion..."

As recorded by former British Labour Prime Minister Harold Wilson (1964-70 and 1974-76) in **A Personal Record – The Labour Government 1964-1970** (p. 130): "...Harry Lee decided to go into Opposition in the ultimate hope of leading a Federation-wide Opposition large enough eventually to become the Government of the greater area.

"The Tunku was becoming more and more incensed with his lively Opposition..."

In **ONE MAN'S VIEW of the WORLD**, Lee Kuan Yew has written (p. 160): "...As the convention gathered strength, the Tunku got upset and we were told that Singapore had to leave Malaysia or there would be bloodshed..."

Lee's political brinkmanship brought both sides close to an eyeball to eyeball confrontation. Neither side blinked. And then Tunku made the decisive move "to cut out Singapore from Malaysia" (to quote Tunku, **Star** April 7, 1979).

In Tunku's view, this timely surgery was to save the rest of Malaysia from political "gangrene".

20. **Straits Times** May 16, 1965

21. Quoted in Drysdale, **Singapore: Struggle for Success**, p. 382

22. **Straits Times** May 24, 1965

23. Patrick Keith, **OUSTED!** pp. 153-154

24. **Worldscientific.com**

25. Patrick Keith, p. 131

26. Ibid., p. 73

27. Bloodworth, **The Tiger and the Trojan Horse**, p. 289

28. **Straits Times** August 1, 1964

29. Richard Clutterbuck, **Conflict and Violence in Singapore and Malaysia 1945-1983**, p. 321

30. Patrick Keith, p. 109

31. Mary Turnbull, **A History of Singapore 1819-1975**, p. 290

32. Drysdale, **Singapore: Struggle for Success**, p. 409

33. In **A Personal Record – The Labour Government 1964-1970** Harold Wilson wrote (p. 131) how he intervened to "save" Harry Lee only a few days after

Singapore's separation. Wilson was holidaying in Scilly, an uninhabited island, when news came to him of the bitter break.

He wrote down: "There had been angry scenes between the Tunku and Lee. This had led to Singapore being virtually expelled from the Federation (of Malaysia) and told to set up on its own account. Lee was in a desperate state, bursting into tears in front of the television cameras and regretting the break-up. Nevertheless, he determined to make a go of the newly-independent Singapore."

Wilson recalled that there was great anxiety at Whitehall, and he decided to fly across to the mainland to RNAS (Royal Naval Air Station) Culdrose for meetings with Cledwyn Hughes, Minister of State, Commonwealth Office (in the absence of the Secretary of State), the Secretary of State for Defence and their advisers.

Wilson recorded: "We took the necessary decisions and made the dispositions that had to be made, sending very strong messages to both leaders (Tunku and Lee) to avoid any action that could lead to an outbreak of hostilities, or, indeed, of internal subversion. We authorized talks to take place to review the Anglo-Malaysian defence agreement, on a basis fair to all the parties concerned..."

In **LOOKING BACK** (p. 128), Tunku said he wrote on August 17, 1965 to reassure Wilson: "Now the Central Government and the Government of Singapore have reconciled themselves and have settled

down to normal business…" Tunku then apologized
for not advising Wilson beforehand of the move to set
up Singapore as a separate country.

34. **Straits Times** January 7, 1980

35. Patrick Keith, p. 64

36. Ibid., p. 64

37. Tunku, **Star** 7 April 1979, reprinted in **LOOKING
BACK**, p. 120

38. Ibid., p. 122
Tunku told Felix Abisheganadan (**Straits Times**
August 10, 1965) that he had reached his decision on
Singapore's separation on 29 June 1965 to avert "racial
bloodshed".

In **Lee Kuan Yew—The Crucial Years**, A. Josey
wrote (p. 284): "Malaysia's Prime Minister, better
versed in world affairs than all his colleagues,
knew what the world Press would have said about
Malaysian leaders had Lee's government been toppled
by an outrageous detention order against Lee and
Lee's Cabinet. The Tunku saved the day. He did all
he could. Mr Rajaratnam, independent Singapore's
Foreign Minister, described the separation at that
final stage as an act of statesmanship. Bloodshed was
averted…"

On Singapore's separation, Ghazali Shafie commented
in **NEW STRAITS TIMES** October 25, 1999:

"…Singapore was brought in to resolve the communist
problems and since the problem (posed by the threat

of a communist takeover in Singapore) was over and PAP looked stronger than ever (after its decisive victory in the September 1963 general election) to stand on its own, the Tunku took the opportunity to rid Malaysia of Singapore. He could not see any further advantage of keeping Singapore in Malaysia."

Ghazali disclosed that was his thought when he called on the Malaysian King to relay the Tunku's decision on that fateful morning of 9 August 1965. He then added: "I believe most sincerely that a major racial conflagration had been averted and May 13, 1969 (racial violence in Peninsular Malaysia) could have been worse and more difficult to mend…"

The PAP, in its 4th anniversary publication in 1999, told its side of the story in ten words (p. 55): "…after 22 unhappy months, Singapore was ousted from the Federation."

39. **Sunday Times** August 15, 1965

Separation, as an option, did not originate in Tunku's mind when he was for the first time, according to him, stretched out on a hospital bed in a clinic at Harley Street in London.

In a December 1964 dinner speech at the King Edward VII Hall of the University of Singapore, Tunku said he anticipated trouble if the PAP chose to make politics its main springboard in Malaysia.

He warned: "If the politicians of various colours and tinges and flashes in Singapore disagree with me, the only solution is a breakaway, but what a calamity that would be for Singapore and Malaysia!"

Report in **Straits Times** December10, 1964

Although that strong hint of separation became a harsh reality eight months later for Singapore, Tunku's negative pronouncement on its outcome was unexpectedly, and fortunately, off the mark.

Separation has turned out to be a great blessing in disguise for both Singapore and Malaysia.

40. Patrick Keith, **OUSTED!** p. 132

41. Tunku, **LOOKING BACK**, p. 123

On 22 July 1965 Dr Goh had a meeting with Razak and Dr Ismail.

In an oral history interview with Melanie Chew in 1996, Dr Goh said: "I persuaded him (Razak) that the only way out was for Singapore to secede, completely."

Reading from a state secret file which he called Albatross, Goh added: "It should be done quickly, and before we get more involved in the Solidarity Convention."

Then, he further added: "You want to get Singapore out, and it must be done very quickly. And very quietly, and presented as a fait accompli."

Turning back to Melanie, Dr Goh then said: "It must be kept from the British. The British had their own policy. They wanted us to be inside Malaysia. And they would have never agreed to Singapore leaving Malaysia…"

MC: How did Tun Razak and Dr Ismail react?

Dr Goh: Oh, they themselves were in agreement with the idea. In fact, they had themselves come to the conclusion that Singapore must get out. The question was, "how to get Singapore out?"

MC: So the secession of Singapore was well planned by you and Razak! It was not foisted on Singapore!

Dr Goh: No, it was not.

Above extract from **GOH KENG SWEE: A Public Career Remembered** co-published by World Scientific Publishing, Singapore, and S. Rajaratnam School of International Studies, 2012

42. According to Patrick Keith, a long-time associate and confidant of the Malaysian leader and premier, it was on 25 July 1965 that the Tunku "wrote to Razak again, this time asking him to go ahead with the legal and constitutional preparations for the removal of Singapore from the federation…" **OUSTED!** p. 181

43. Reprinted in **LOOKING BACK**, p. 127

44. Turnbull, **A History of Singapore 1819-1975**, p. 293

In an interview published in **The Asia Magazine** on 5 February 1967, Tunku said that Singapore's separation did not come as a surprise to Lee Kuan Yew: "He (Lee) knew almost a year before that. When he made many requests and demands I told him things could not go on like this. I pointed out to him that the only way out was for Singapore to be independent. In fact I did mention earlier to Mr Goh Keng Swee who was acting as Mr Lee's agent, that separation was the only alternative. We had all these discussions either on the golf course or here in my drawing-room. So in the end, the final decision did not come as a surprise to the Prime Minister of Singapore. He was ready and willing to accept separation." Quoted in A. Josey, **Lee Kuan Yew – The Crucial Years**, pp. 85-86

45. Drysdale, **Singapore: Struggle for Success**, p. 258

In **MEMOIR** Ghazali Shafie recalled Tunku's 'soft spot' for Lee Kuan Yew, and he wrote (p. 212): "… the Tunku had a special feeling for Lee Kuan Yew whom he wanted eventually to be the leader of the Chinese in Malaysia. He had even hinted this to Lee Kuan Yew…"

PREFACE: On the cusp of history

This small book provides a brief historical analysis of the first two tumultuous decades in postwar Singapore (1945-65), focusing on the anti-colonial struggle for independence. The communists and leftists were at the vanguard of this struggle for freedom from more than a century of British colonial rule.

As the Malayan Communist Party (MCP/CPM) was the oldest and most experienced political organization in the country, the communist cadres commanded the high ground in the anti-colonial movement. They had easy access to the Chinese masses (the demographic/ethnic majority), and they could exploit from time to time the postwar legacy of widespread poverty, rampant unemployment, food and housing shortages, and other social ills. They therefore pursued political power through constitutional means on the tiny island of Singapore, while their comrades on the Malayan mainland waged a protracted but futile armed insurgency just across the Johore Causeway.

"The armed struggle in the peninsula was meeting with major setbacks (by the mid-1950s)," recalled Fong Chong Pik (dubbed the "Plen" by Lee Kuan Yew). "Looking at it nationally, Singapore was isolated and politically on its own…" (1)

But, for all their popular support, the communists in Singapore needed the English-educated intellectuals to front their political campaign while the latter in their political venture needed communist support to reach the

Chinese-educated mass/proletariat. Thus from the mid-1950s, the communists/leftists and the newly-formed People's Action Party (PAP) worked together to end more than a century of British colonialism.

Lee Kuan Yew said he was riding a tiger, and he rode on it to power with a thumping victory in Singapore's first general election at the end of May 1959.

But shortly afterwards the two wings of the PAP split, and their open rupture led to a showdown which culminated in a crushing defeat for the communists and leftists on this strategically-located island in the heart of Southeast Asia.

"My friends and I formed a united front with the communists. From the start we knew that there would have to be a parting of the ways and a time for reckoning," Lee Kuan Yew wrote. (2) "When it came, the fight was bitter, and we were fortunate not to have been defeated…"

When the political split occurred in July 1961, however, the communists and leftists took away their mass base from the PAP, and the PAP dissidents formed the opposition Barisan Sosialis to topple the ruling party. Moreover, mass defections left the PAP on the verge of collapse. The PAP Government came under siege by the communists and leftists, now confident of a quick kill.

Timely merger with neighbouring Malaya (which the PAP had sought from its inception in late October 1954) provided the political lifeline to Lee Kuan Yew and the old guard in what was generally seen to be a "sinking ship". Until then reluctant to take in Singapore but stirred by the looming spectre of communist domination across the Causeway, and no doubt moved by subtle but unrelenting British persuasion and pressure, the Malayan Prime Minister Tunku Abdul Rahman now changed his mind. Even so, he made it an essential condition that merger would take place only with a Singapore free from communist dominance and politically stable.

At the height of the crisis, Kuala Lumpur despatched its top expert in psychological warfare to help "save the situation" across the Causeway. Thus **C.C. Too** had his first meeting with Prime Minister Lee Kuan Yew the day after his arrival in early June 1962. Too remained as a guest of the PAP Government for about three months, and helped to prepare for the coming propaganda war against the communists. His brief was to help win popular support for merger, and to thwart the goal of the communist leadership to capture power in Singapore (what he had done so successfully, since 1951, against Chin Peng and the political Mafia in the MCP).

While leafing through the Special Branch files on internal subversion and dossiers on communist leaders in Singapore, Too found out that that the communist campaign was directed by **Eu Chooi Yip** who was the communist mastermind in Singapore, but who was also a prewar friend and fellow collegian at the Raffles College in Singapore.

Lee Kuan Yew brilliantly waged his battle for merger and he bested the communists and leftists on the political field. But merger with the Federation did not last and the bitter break came. After the PAP's dismal debut in peninsular politics in the April 1964 general election, the Party leaders must have decided to force the issue shortly before they launched their "Malaysian Malaysia" campaign in mid-1965 to openly and audaciously challenge the leadership of the Umno-dominated Alliance Government in Kuala Lumpur.

The fast-deteriorating bilateral relationship was then pushed to a razor's edge.

The out-of-the-blue separation (totally unexpected though apparently inevitable) of Singapore on the morning of 9

August 1965 led to its complete independence, nationhood and sovereignty – the consummation of its sacred political quest.

The communists and leftists in postwar Singapore conducted three revolutionary campaigns to capture power and although they failed to do so, they had come dramatically close to their political goal on all three occasions. The communist challenge of 1961-63 was a very close call for Lee Kuan Yew and the PAP Government.

But, but, would the colonial authorities ever have allowed the communists to take over the running of Singapore where the British military, with its cache of nuclear weapons, maintained its most important and valuable base in the Far East?

One of only three countries armed with nuclear weapons in the early 1960s (before France acquired its few nukes in 1964 and China joined the nuclear club in mid-October 1964), Britain was one of the Big 3 in the whole world, fully and stubbornly determined to exercise its influence despite its diminished global role post-Suez 1956, in the turbulence of the Cold War.

While dedicated to the defence of Europe, Britain remained strongly committed to its self-styled SEATO role in this much-troubled region, and Singapore was central to its military posture and strategy in a region seen to be endemically vulnerable to communist insurgents, militants, revolutionaries and subversives.

The underlying argument of this short historical survey is that there was no way the communists and leftists could take over Singapore.

The communist underground leader himself has said so. The "Plen" admitted that pitted against the combined forces of the PAP leadership, the hostile (staunchly anti-communist) government of Tunku Abdul Rahman in Kuala Lumpur, and the British colonial power, the left wing "could never stand a chance of winning..." (3)

A few days after the PAP's loss in the Anson by-election in mid-July 1961 (David Marshall won with communist support), Lee Kuan Yew addressed the State Assembly where and when he described British imperialism as "the supreme power in Singapore..."

Perhaps part of the British genius was to allow the indigenous forces more-or-less free play to work out their political destiny. But the locals had to play the game according to the colonial rules (including the draconian Emergency Regulations). And overriding British interests must still prevail as long as they held the reins of power.

Although a communist victory in a general election could not be ruled out, an insurgent takeover of the strategic island state was simply incogitable in the presence of such a strong British nuclear-armed military in Singapore, with thousands of its combat-ready troops strategically stationed on both sides of the Johore Causeway.

Did the colonial masters write their script on decolonization? Of course, they did. But the local forces of self-determination were not entirely within their control. That's the gist of this political survey.

Singapore 16
Chronology

6 August 1945	**Atomic bombing of Hiroshima**
9 August 1945	**Nuking of Nagasaki**
15 August 1945	**Japan surrenders, ending World War II**
7 September 1945	British Military Administration in postwar Malaya and Singapore
23 December 1945	Malayan Democratic Union (MDU) launched in Singapore
22 January 1946	White Paper on Malayan Union
late January 1946	150,000 workers on strike in Singapore
1 April 1946	Malayan Union formed, and Singapore becomes a separate Crown colony
5 March 1947	Chin Peng becomes Secretary-General of Malayan Communist Party (MCP) to replace Lai Teck purged in his absence August 1947 Progressive Party (PP) formed in Singapore
15 August 1947	**Independence for India and Pakistan in the decolonization of the Indian subcontinen**
1 February 1948	Federation of Malaya established in place of the highly controversial and unpopular Malayan Union
February 1948	**Conference of Southeast Asian Youth in Calcutta**

March 1948	**Brussels Treaty forges a five-nation alliance against Soviet threat** May 1948 Labour law amended to cripple the communist-controlled leadership of the trade union movement in Malaya and Singapore
19 June 1948	Emergency declared in the colonial anti-insurgency in Malaya
23 June 1948	Emergency declared in Singapore MDU self-dissolved
23 July 1948	Malayan Communist Party(MCP) banned
September 1948	Singapore Labour Party formed
September 1948	Anti-British League (ABL) formed in Singapore
April 1949	**NATO formed as a multinational umbrella for collective security in Western Europe to counter Soviet aggression in the newly-emerging Cold War between the East and West**
1 October 1949	**Mao Tse-tung proclaims the People's Republic of China in Peking following the communist victory over the Kuomintang forces in their civil war**
December 1950	Special Branch cracks down on the Singapore Town Committee leadership of the MCP
3 October 1952	**Britain tests its first A-bomb to register its arrival as the world's third nuclear-armed military power**

31 October 1952	**US tests its (the world's) first hydrogen bomb (H-bomb), the 'Super'**
July 1953	Rendel Commission appointed in Singapore to conduct its constitutional review in the context of decolonization of the island state 01.12.2014 08:23 **Chronology**
February 1954	Rendel report published
13 May 1954	Chinese Middle School students' first clash with the police in Singapore
8 September 1954	**SEATO, an anti-communist military alliance formed by the US, France, UK, Australia and New Zealand with the three Asian countries of Pakistan, the Philippines and Thailand**
23 October 1954	People's Action Party (PAP) formed
21 November 1954	PAP launched in Singapore, with Dr Toh Chin Chye elected as chairman and Lee Kuan Yew as its secretary
2 April 1955	David Marshall becomes Singapore's first Chief Minister with Labour Front winning 10 out of 25 seats in the Legislative Assemnly.

	Contesting four seats in a token display of protest against the Rendel Constitution which the PAP sees as framed to extend colonialism and to delay Singapore's independence, the party wins in three wards: Lee Kuan Yew in Tanjong Pagar, Goh Chew Chua in Punggol-Tampines, and Lim Chin Siong in Bukit Timah.
12 May 1955	Hock Lee riots in Singapore
August 1955	First general election in Malaya
22 November 1955	**Soviets test their first H-bomb (Soviet 'Super')**
28 December 1955	Baling peace talks between Chief Minister of Malaya Tunku Abdul Rahman and Singapore's Chief Minister David Marshall with the MCP leader Chin Peng 543 words 01.12.2014 09:36
23 April – 15	May First constitutional conference in London with David Marshall at the 1956 head of the First All-Party Constitutional Mission from Singapore, including Lee Kuan Yew and Lim Chin Siong of the PAP
June 1956	Lim Yew Hock becomes Chief Minister following Marshall's resignation.
8 July 1956	PAP executive committee election
25 October	1956 Chinese student riots in Singapore to protest against dissolution of Singapore Chinese Middle School Students' Union ; 13 people killed.

	Preservation of Public Security Ordinance (PPSO) amended and passed.
30 October 1956	"Operation Liberation" detains Communist United Front and pro-communist leaders including Lim Chin Siong, Fong Swee Suan and Devan Nair.
Late Oct-Nov 56	**Suez crisis – British military intervention with French forces in the Suez conflict. The failure of this joint expedition to occupy the Suez Canal early November marks the end of their historic roles in the Middle East.**
5 February 1957	**Defence White Paper in London spells out British policy on the nuclear deterrent and development of the megaton H-bomb.**
11 March	– Second All-Party Constitutional Mission to London, led by Lim Yew Hock
11 April 1957	with Lee Yuan Yew as a member of the Singapore delegation.
11 April 1957	Agreement on self-government for the colony.
15 May 1957	**Britain tests its first H-bomb at Christmas Island in the Pacific.**

13 August 1957	The pro-communist faction of the PAP gains control of the Central Executive Committee by holding key posts including those of Party Chairman and Secretary.
22 August 1957	35 arrested in a big SB operation, including five of the six newly elected PAP CEC members and 11 PAP branch officials, trade union leaders, students and journalists.
31 August 1957	Independence for Malaya with Tunku Abdul Rahman as Prime Minister.
20 October 1957	Re-election of Dr Toh Chin Chye as the PAP Chairman and Lee Kuan Yew as Secretary-General.
21 December 1957	PAP wins 13 seats in the City Council Election, and Ong Eng Guan becomes the first mayor of Singapore. 06.12.2014 15:49
February 1958	British Prime Minister Harold Macmillan meets with Chief Minister Lim Yew Hock during stopover in Singapore.
March 1958	First of four clandestine meetings between PAP Secretary-General Lee Kuan Yew and communist underground leader Fang Chuan Pi aka the "Plen".
12 May 1958	Third All-Party Constitutional Mission to London.

28 May 1958	Constitutional Agreement signed in London for self-government in the State of Singapore after the general election to be held in 1959.
26 July 1958	PAP wins Kallang by-election with strong communist support.
30 May 1959	PAP wins Singapore's first general election, obtaining 43 seats and 53.4% of the votes on its political platform of independence for Singapore through merger with a "democratic, socialist but non-communist Malaya". PAP wins with communist support.
	Singapore People's Alliance wins 4 seats, UMNO 3, and an independent 1 seat.
	Lee Kuan Yew becomes the first Prime Minister of Singapore.
28 August 1959	The newly-formed Internal Security Council (ISC) meets for the first time.
12 October 1959	PAP Government renews and reinforces the PPSO (Preservation of Public Security Ordinance).
13 February 1960	**France tests its first fission (plutonium) device**
27 June 1960	PAP expels three dissident senior members Ong Eng Guan, S V Lingam and Ng Teng Kian who then form the United People's Party.
31 July 1960	Official end of Emergency I (1948-60) declared and celebrated in Kuala Lumpur.

January 1961	Chin Peng's departure from Sadao HQ to Peking to submit his "progress report" on the Malayan Revolution to Chairman Mao Tse-tung.
29 April 1961	PAP defeated in Hong Lim by-election, won by Ong Eng Guan in a landslide victory (with 72% of votes).
11 May 1961	Lee Kuan Yew tells the "Plen" in their fifth and final meeting that merger with Malaya is "unlikely".
27 May 1961	Tunku Abdul Rahman proposes the formation of Malaysia in a luncheon speech delivered at the Adelphi Hotel in Singapore.
9 June 1961	PAP Chairman Dr Toh Chin Chye announces that Singapore Government will seek independence through merger with the Federation of Malaya.
15 July 1961	PAP defeated in Anson by-election, with David Marshall winning by 546 votes and calling for "Emperor Lee's resignation".
	PAP Chairman Dr Toh replies to Lee Kuan Yew's offer to resign as Prime Minister on the same day, affirming the unanimous choice of Lee as the PM by the Central Executive Committee (CEC).

18 July 1961	The controversial Eden Hall Tea Party meeting of Lord Selkirk with the quartet of dissident PAP leaders Lim Chin Siong, James Puthucheary, Sandra Woodhull, and Fong Swee Suan.
21 July 1961	PAP wins motion of confidence in the Legislative Assembly. PAP expels 13 leading dissidents and assemblymen, including Lim Chin Siong, Fong Swee Suan, S Woodhull and Dr Lee Siew Choh.
30 July 1961	The expelled PAP leaders form a new political party, Barisan Sosialis (Socialist Front) with Dr Lee as Chairman, Woodhull as Vice-Chairman, Lim Chin Siong as Secretary, etc.
10 August 1961	**Britain applies to join the EEC.**
13 August 1961	Dr Lee launches the Barisan Sosialis, telling a cheering crowd of over 10,000 supporters at the Happy World Stadium that the party has been registered, as the successor to the PAP "for deviating to the right…"
13 September 1961	Lee Kuan Yew starts his series of radio talks on merger to launch his "battle for merger" campaign in Singapore.
22 November 1961	**Macmillan and Tunku Abdul Rahman sign an agreement in London "about Greater Malaysia and the Singapore Base".**

20 February 1962	**Defence White Paper issued in London stresses Britain's nuclear deterrent and states that Singapore (with its British naval base in East Asia since 1922) will remain Britain's main military base in the Far East.**
June 1962	C.C. Too's secret mission to Singapore
1 September 1962	PAP wins the referendum on merger, with 73.8% of the voters supporting the proposal to merge Singapore with the Federation of Malaya.
22 Oct-20	Nov'62 **Cuban missile crisis, with the two nuclear superpowers on the brink of war (World War III) on Saturday afternoon of 27 October (29th day of the ninth lunar month in the year of the Fire Tiger)**
November 1962	Lee Kuan Yew starts a 10-month tour of all 51 constituencies in a solo pre-
September 1963	election campaign across the length and breadth of Singapore.
December 1962	**Nassau meeting between Harold Macmillan and President John Kennedy, US agrees to provide Polaris missiles (less nuclear warheads) for new British strategic nuclear-armed submarines which will replace the ageing airborne nuclear deterrent.**
8 December 1962	Brunei revolt
20 January 1963	Indonesia's Foreign Minister Dr Subandrio announces confrontation policy against Malaya/Malaysia.

20 January 1963	**President Charles de Gaulle vetoes Britain's entry into the European Common Market**
2 February 1963	"Operation Cold Store" launched against the communist, leftist and pro-communists leaders in Singapore before merger and Malaysia.
8 July 1963	London agreement on Malaysia.
31 August 1963	Lee Kuan Yew's UDI (unilateral declaration of independence) in Singapore
16 September 1963	Malaysia formed, with Singapore as a component State in political conjunction with the Federation of Malaya and Borneo States of Sabah and Sarawak.
21 September 1963	PAP wins "snap" general election with 37 seats and 46.6% of the votes cast in Singapore. Barisan Nasional wins 13 seats, United People's Party one seat. Singapore UMNO loses all three Malay-dominated constituencies to PAP.
25 April 1964	PAP's fateful debut in peninsular politics with its "token" participation in the general election in Peninsular Malaysia. Only one parliamentary seat (Bangsar) for nine PAP candidates in the dismal fray.
21 July 1964	Communal riots in Singapore on Prophet Mohamed's birthday.

17 August 1964	Landing of Indonesian paratroopers at Pontian to the north of Singapore.
2 September 1964	Another round of racial violence in Singapore.
16 October 1964	**China tests its first A-bomb.**
October 1964	**Harold Wilson becomes British Prime Minister after Labour's victory in the UK general election.**
17 April 1965	Tunku Abdul Rahman says "no" to PAP at the opening of the convention of Malaysian Alliance Party of Singapura in Singapore.
27 April 1965	PAP Chairman Dr Toh Chin Chye announces formation of the Malaysian Solidarity Convention (MSC)
9 May 1965	Inaugural MSC meeting and mass rally in Singapore to launch "Malaysian Malaysia" campaign.
15 May 1965	UMNO general assembly in Kuala Lumpur passes a resolution calling for Lee Kuan Yew's arrest and detention.
10 July 1965	Hong Lim by-election, won by PAP candidate Lee Khoon Choy against UMNO-backed Barisan candidate Ong Chang Sam.
25 July 1965	Tunku's final decision on the separation of Singapore from Malaysia.
9 August 1965	Separation of Singapore to become and an independent nation, sovereign city-state and republic.

Following the bulk withdrawal of the British military by end of October 1971, its residual force in Singapore was finally phased out from September 1975 to March 1976 – in tandem with the retirement of the British airborne nuclear deterrent and induction of its sea/submarine-based successor.

FOREWORD

This book provides a brief historical analysis of the first two tumultuous decades in Singapore after the end of World War II in mid-August 1945, focusing on the anti-colonial struggle for independence in the early stages of the postwar decolonization era. The communist and leftist leaders were at the vanguard of the national struggle for freedom from British colonialism and imperialism.

As the Malayan Communist Party (MCP/CPM) was the oldest and most experienced political organization in the country, the communist cadres commanded the high ground early in the anti-colonial movement. They had easy and ready access to the Chinese masses, they talked the same language, and they could exploit from time to time the postwar legacy of widespread and even abject poverty, rampant unemployment, food and housing shortages, and other socioeconomic ills.

They therefore pursued political power through constitutional means, while their comrades on the peninsular mainland across the Johore Causeway had to abandon their political struggle in mid-1948 and went on to wage a protracted but futile armed insurgency against the colonial authorities. To quote Fong Chong Pik aka the "Plen",the communist underground leader in Singapore in the late 1950s and early 60s: "…Looking at it nationally, Singapore (MCP/CPM)was isolated and politically on its own…" (1)

For the political struggle in Singapore, however, the largely Chinese-educated communists and leftists needed the more charismatic English-educated intellectuals to front their constitutional campaign while the latter in their political ventures needed communist support to reach the Chinese-educated proletariat. Thus from the mid-1950s, the communists and the newly-formed People's Action Party (PAP) worked together to end more than a century of British colonialism.

Lee Kuan Yew said he was riding a tiger, and he rode on it to power with a thumping victory in Singapore's first general election at the end of May 1959.

But shortly afterwards the two wings of the PAP split, and their open rupture led to a showdown which culminated in a crushing defeat of the communists and pro-communist leftists on this strategically- located island with its British nuclear-armed military base.

Lee has written in the second volume of his memoirs: "My friends and I formed a united front with the communists. From the start we knew that there would have to be a parting of the ways and a time for reckoning. When it came, the fight was bitter, and we were fortunate not to have been defeated…" (2)

When the split occurred in July 1961, the communists and leftists took away their mass base from the PAP and the dissident PAP leaders formed the formidable opposition Barisan Sosialis (Socialist Front) to topple the ruling (but then-tottering) party. Mass defections left the PAP on the verge of collapse. The PAP Government came under siege by their former comrades who were now confident of a quick kill. 502 words 08.12.2014 13:13

Timely merger with neighbouring and strongly anti-communist Malaya (which the PAP had sought from its own inception in late October 1954) provided the political lifeline to Lee Kuan Yew and the Old Guard in what was generally seen to be a "sinking ship". Until then reluctant to take in Singapore with its large Chinese majority, Tunku Abdul Rahman now changed his mind, motivated as he was by the looming spectre of communist domination across the Causeway, and moved as well by subtle but strong British persuasion and pressure.

Even so, Tunku made a condition that merger would take place only with a Singapore free from communist dominance and politically stable.

At the height of the crisis, Kuala Lumpur despatched its top expert in psychological warfare to help "save the situation" in Singapore. Thus C. C. Too had his first meeting with Prime Minister Lee Kuan Yew the day after his arrival in early June 1962. Too remained as a guest of the PAP Government for about three months, and helped to prepare for the coming propaganda war against the communists. His brief was to help him popular support for merger, and to thwart the goal of the communist leadership to capture power in Singapore (what he had done so successful, since 1951, against Chin Peng and the political Mafia in the MCP/CPM).

While leafing through the Special Branch files on internal subversion and dossiers on communist leaders in Singapore, Too found out that that the communist campaign was directed by Eu Chooi Yip who was the real communist mastermind in Singapore, but who was also a prewar friend and college mate of his. Too thought very highly of Eu. And to the highly-knowledgeable Too, Eu was a more brilliant communist leader and strategist than the legendary Chin Peng, the first and only local overlord of the MCP as its secretary-general from the time of the ousting of Vietnam-born Lai Teck early 1947. (3)

Lee Kuan Yew brilliantly waged his battle for merger and won. But merger with the Federation did not last and the bitter break came. After the PAP's disastrous debut in peninsular politics in the April 1964 general election, the Party leaders must have decided to force the issue when they launched their "Malaysian Malaysia" to challenge the UMNO leadership of the Alliance Government, and drove the fast-deteriorating Kuala Lumpur-Singapore relationship to a razor's edge. They had to separate, to avoid possible large-scale Violence. And the separation of Singapore on 9 August 1965 led to its complete independence – the consummation of its political quest.

Of the three attempts to capture power in postwar Singapore, which eventually failed despite having come close to success, the communist challenge of 1961-63 was a very close call for Lee Kuan Yew and the PAP Government.

But, but, would the colonial authorities ever have allowed the communists to take over the running of Singapore where the British military maintained its most important and valuable base in the Far East, and secretly stored a cache of atomic bombs for possible use in a war against Communist China?

The underlying argument of this short historical survey is that there was no way that the communists could take over Singapore.

The communist underground leader, the "Plen" to Lee Kuan Yew, ruled out a communist victory in Singapore. In his memoirs, Fong Chong Pik admitted that pitted against the combined forces of the PAP leadership, the hostile government of Kuala Lumpur, and the British colonial power ("the supreme power in Singapore" as Lee himself told the State Legislative Assembly in mid-July 1961), the left wing "could never stand a chance of winning…" (4)

Perhaps part of the British long-ingrained cunning or colonially-cultivated genius was to allow the indigenous forces, particularly those favoured and supported by Whitehall imperialism, more-or-less free play to work out their own destiny. But the locals had to play according to the rules. And overriding British interests (economic and military/strategic) must still prevail as long as they held the reins of power.

Although a communist victory in a general election could not be ruled out, an insurgent or militant takeover of this small island state was simply incogitable, in the presence of such a strong nuclear-armed British military in Singapore.

Notes: Foreword

1. Fong Chong Pik, **The Memoirs of a Malayan Communist Revolutionary**, 2008, p. 141

2. Lee Kuan Yew, **From Third World To First**, 2000, pp. 11-12

3. Lim Cheng Leng, **THE STORY OF A PSY-WARRIOR: TAN SRI DR. C. C. TOO.** A close friend of CC, Lim has given a detailed account of Too's secret mission in Singapore in this first-ever biography, authorized and supported by the late Too's brothers and family.

4. Fong Chong Pik, **The Memoirs**, p. 171

Who's Who

Tunku Abdul Rahman President of UMNO and Prime Minister of Malaya (1957-63) and Malaysia (1963-70).

Tun Abdul Razak A long-time deputy to Tunku, Razak became Malaysia's second PM when his distinguished predecessor stepped down in 1970 shortly after the racial riots of May 1969 in Kuala Lumpur.

Sir Robert Black Governor of Singapore, who paid tribute to Chief Minister Lim Yew Hock's courage in taking tough action against rioters in the mid-1950s as a victory "for the future of Singapore..."

K. M. Byrne Permanent Secretary to the Ministry of Commerce and Industry when Lim Yew Hock was Chief Minister, Byrne resigned in September 1958 to take part in the 1959 general election as a co-opted member of the PAP's Central Executive Committee, was appointed Minister for Labour and Law following the PAP's electoral victory in May 1959, in which he had contested and won in the state constituency of Crawford.

Chin Peng A guerrilla leader in the Anti-Japanese Army in Perak and deputy to party leader Lai Teck, 22-year-old Chin Peng took over leadership of the Malayan Communist Party (MCP/CPM) after the Central Committee had met in Kuala Lumpur early March 1947 and openly attacked Lai Teck for treachery and absconding with party funds.

Eu Chooi Yip A pre-war graduate of Raffles College and colleague of Goh Keng Swee, Eu succeeded the first secretary of the Malayan Democratic Union (formed

December 1945) when Lim Hong Bee returned to law studies in London. Eu also served as leader of the English-speaking clandestine Anti-British League (formed September 1948). A humble and self-effacing scholar, highly respected by friends and others, but little (if at all) known to even the people of Singapore, he was a top-class bilingual propagandist and writer, and served as the real mastermind of the Singapore Town Committee and the main strategist of the communist movement in Singapore. Strongly anti-colonialism, staunchly pro-communism. A dedicated senior CPM leader, Eu expressed his admiration for the Chinese Communist Party (CCP).

Fong Swee Suan A member of the Singapore Students' Anti-British League in 1951 and a union leader (general secretary of the Singapore Bus Workers Union), Fong was a founding member of the PAP and appointed a political secretary following the party's victory in the 1959 general election. Like his close comrade Lim Chin Siong, Fong was detained three times. He became a committee member of the Barisan Sosialis in 1961.

Dr Goh Keng Swee Director of Social and Economic Research Division in the Chief Minister's office, Goh resigned in September 1958, was co-opted into the PAP's Central Executive Committee and then appointed Singapore's first Finance Minister after the May 1959 general election for the first Legislative Assembly under the Rendel Constitution, having himself won the state constituency of Kreta Ayer. One of the three Singapore members in the Internal Security Council, together with Prime Minister Lee Kuan Yew and Minister for Home Affairs Ong Pang Boon.

Sir William Goode Chief Secretary to the Singapore Government 1953-57, Governor of Singapore 1957-59, and the first Yang d-Pertuan Negara for six months when Singapore became a self-governing Colony in June 1959.

Khaw Kai Boh According to John Drysdale, Khaw had attempted as a senior Special Branch officer to arrest Lee Kuan Yew. He was known to have been a powerful critic of the PAP leadership and policies. Was given special treatment by the British authorities to retire on favourable terms before the PAP came to power in June 1959, he crossed the Causeway and resided in Kuala Lumpur where he joined the MCA and subsequently became Minister of Local Government and Housing.

Lai Teck Joined the Malayan Communist Party (MCP) in 1934, became Secretary General in 1939 and emerged as a legendary figure until he quietly disappeared and left Malaya in early 1947 shortly before his purge. He went to Bangkok where he was assassinated, according to Chin Peng.

Lee Kuan Yew Founding member and Secretary-General of the PAP (1954-92), first Prime Minister of Singapore(1959-90). A dynamic leader and eloquent speaker, one of the pre-eminent founders of independent Singapore. 11.12.2014 20:22

Dr Lee Siew Choh Parliamentary Secretary to the Ministry for Home Affairs, expelled from the PAP in July 1961, Lee and other leftwing leaders formed the Barisan Sosialis (Socialist Front) to become its Chairman with Lim Chin Siong as Secretary-General and Fong Swee Suan as one of the 13 committee members.

Allan Lennox-Boyd British Secretary of State for the Colonies who in the April/May 1956 constitutional talks in London shot down David Marshall's demand that Singapore government take over sole responsibility for internal security. While the Colonial Secretary paid tribute to the Chief Minister's fight against Communism, he said Singapore would not be allowed to become an outpost of Communist China "where perhaps for a while the essential defence bases might be tolerated because they helped to keep down unemployment, but which would assuredly be crippled in times of emergency by strikes or sabotage." Marshall resigned after the failure of the constitutional negotiations in London.

Lim Chin Siong A pre-eminent union leader and founder member who led the leftwing faction of the PAP, elected with Lee Kuan Yew and Goh Chew Chua in the 22 April 1955 elections for the first Singapore Legislative Assembly under the Rendel Constitution.

Described by Lee as "the most important Open Front leader of the MCP. Introducing him to David Marshall in 1955, Lee said: "He (Lim) will be our next Prime Minister" (meaning, Singapore's first PM)…"

Fong Chong Pik aka the "Plen" wrote: "The bitter experience of Lim Chin Siong during his entire life was a graphic reflection of the living reality of the struggle against colonialism for independence by the people of Singapore.

"The three words "Lim Chin Siong" stand mightily, forming a brilliant light in the fire of anti-colonial struggle by the people of Singapore. He symbolized the fighting spirit of the people..."

On Lim Chin Siong's place in Singapore history, Dr M.K. Rajakumar, last acting chairman of the Labour Party of Malaya (LPM), has written: "His passage from student activist, to workers' leader, to charismatic freedom fighter, and the years of his young life spent in political prisons, is the stuff of revolutionary legend. Singapore's history begins when he is given his proper place in its annals."

Lim Kim San Appointed Minister for National Development and Chairman of Housing and Development Board (HDB) following the expulsion of PAP maverick and rebel Ong Eng Guan in July 1960, stood and won in Cairnhill in the 21 September 1963 general election and retained his Cabinet post as Minister for National Development, then became Finance Minister in independent Singapore after its separation from Malaysia on August 1965.

Lim Yew Hock Successor to David Marshall as Chief Minister when the latter resigned in May 1956, Lim served for three years in that high capacity during a tumultuous period in Singapore's history until the PAP won the May 1959 general election and Lee Kuan Yew became the first Prime Minister of a self-governing Colony.

Harold Macmillan British statesman and Conservative Prime Minister (1957-63), he presided over the signing of the Malaysia Agreement in London on 8 July 1963. The decolonization process gained momentum and accelerated during his premiership.

David Marshall Charismatic leader of the Labour Front, Marshall became Singapore's first Chief Minister after the

April 1955 election. He resigned from his post in May 1956, left the Labour Front in April 1957 to form the Workers' Party, narrowly won the Anson by-election in mid-July 1961 but lost in the September 1963 general election and exited from the political scene. 14.12.2014 00:55

Ng Meng Chiang alias Wong Meng Kiong alias "Comrade D" (to Dennis Bloodworth).

Underground boss of the MCP in Singapore from 1954 to 1958 when the "Plen" took over from him.

Ong Eng Guan A leading member of the PAP, Ong became the first and only Mayor of Singapore following the capture by the party of 14 out of 15seats in the City Council elections in December 1957.

Elected as the PAP Treasurer at the end of May 1959, a day after the general election in which he had won the largest majority. Appointed Minister for National Development.

Expelled from the PAP in July 1960 after challenging the party leadership, Ong formed United People's Party (UPP) with two other Assemblymen. He resigned from his Hong Lim constituency in December 1960 but recaptured it in the April 1961 by-election with an overwhelming majority. Ong was the only UPP candidate to win in September 1963 general election. He resigned from the Singapore Legislative Assembly on 16 June 1965. Following David Marshall and Lim Yew Hock, Ong stepped down into history.

Plen (Plenipotentiary of the MCP, as designated by Lee Kuan Yew). Personally known as Fang Chuang Pi (Pik) alias Fong Chong Pek. Properly named himself as **Fong**

Chong Pik. Had four secret meetings with Lee Kuan Yew between March 1958 and June 1959.

At their fifth and final meeting on 11 May 1961, he urged PM Lee to insist on the abolition of the Internal Security Council (ISC) in the constitutional talks to be held in London in 1963. Lee revealed his identity in mid-October 1963. Although Fong headed the MCP Town Committee in Singapore until 1962 when he left for Indonesia, he did not rank very high in the Communist Party hierarchy. But a good writer and propagandist.

James Puthucheary A union leader and prominent member of the leftwing faction in the PAP, he joined the expelled PAP dissidents to form the Barisan Sosialis on August 1961 in which he was a committee member.

S. Rajaratnam He joined the Central Executive Committee after the PAP's resounding victory and was appointed Minister for Culture in Lee's first Cabinet. Also a member of Lee's 'inner cabinet' with Dr Toh Chin Chye, Dr Goh Keng Swee and Ong Pang Boon.

Appointed Minister for Foreign Affairs and Culture when Singapore became independent and separated from Malaysia in August 1965.

Duncan Sandys British Commonwealth Secretary, he took part in the negotiations for the Malaysia Agreement and witnessed its signing on 8 July 1963 at the Malborough House in London.

Lord Selkirk The Earl of Selkirk came to Singapore in January 1960 to assume the post of United Kingdom Commissioner of Singapore and Commissioner-General for Southeast Asia. Also acted as Chairman of the Internal Security Council (ISC).

Tun Tan Siew Sin President of the Malayan (Malaysian) Chinese Association (MCA) and Finance Minister of Malaya/Malaysia.

Too Chee Chew Better known as C. C. Too. Head of psychological warfare (1956-83) in the Ministry of Home Affairs in Kuala Lumpur. One of the world's leading experts in counter-insurgency and psywar, he was sent in mid-1962 by the Malayan government as a consultant to the PAP government to assist in the propaganda campaign against the communists in Singapore and "to prevent a Communist takeover" (to quote CC).

Dr Toh Chin Chye Founding chairman of the PAP, Toh became Deputy Prime Minister in the 1959 Cabinet.

Harold Wilson British Labour statesman and Prime Minister (1964-70, 1974-76). His timely ascent to power in late 1964 provided a political boost to the PAP leadership involved in a tussle with Kuala Lumpur. Wilson "Europeanised" British foreign and military policies, initiated British military withdrawal from Singapore in the mid-1960s and saw to its final conclusion in March 1976.

Sandra Woodhull A prominent union leader, he was appointed one of the seven political secretaries in the PAP Government after its resounding success in the May 1959 general election. He left with the other expelled leftwing dissident leaders to form the Barisan Sosialis and became its vice-chairman in mid-August 1961. 4 pages

Bibliography

(A)   Books

Tunku Abdul Rahman Putra Al-Haj. **LOOKING BACK**. Kuala Lumpur: Pustaka Antara, 1977.

Baylis, John, ed. **Contemporary Strategy**. Volume II. New York: Holmes & Mier, 1987.

Bellows, Thomas J., "The Singapore Party System". Essay in **Problems in Political Development**. Edited by Peng-Chuan Chong. California: McCutchan Publishing, 1970.

Bloodworth, Dennis. **The Tiger and the Trojan Horse**. Singapore: Times Books International, 1986.

Chin Peng. **MY SIDE OF HISTORY**, as told to Ian Ward and Norma Miraflor. Singapore: Media Masters, September 2003.

Clutterbuck, Richard. **Conflict and Violence in Singapore and Malaysia 1945-1983**.

Singapore: Graham Brash, 1984.

Drysdale, John. **Singapore: Struggle for Success**. Singapore: Times Books International, 1984.

Fong Chong Pik. **The Memoirs of a Malayan Communist Revolutionary**. Petaling Jaya, Selangor: Strategic Information and Research Development Centre (SIRD), 2008.

Ghazali Shafie. **MEMOIR on the formation of Malaysia**. Bangi, Selangor: Penerbit Universiti Kebangsaan Malaysia, 2004 (second printing).

Goh Keng Swee. **The Economics of Modernisation.** Singapore: Asia Pacific Press, 1972.

Grenville, J.A.S. **A History of the World in the Twentieth Century**. Massachusetts: Harvard University Press, 1994.

Josey, Alex. **Lee Kuan Yew—The Crucial Years**. Singapore: Times Books Inteernational, 1994.

Kaldor, Mary et al eds. **Democratic Socialism and the cost of defence**. London: Croom Helm, 1979.

Keith, Patrick. **OUSTED!** Singapore: Media Masters, July 2005.

Kennedy, Paul. **The Rise and Fall of the Great Powers**. London: Fontana Press, 1989.

Lee Kuan Yew. **The Battle For Merger**. Singapore: Government Printing Office, 1961.

Lee Kuan Yew. **From Third World To First.** Singapore: The Straits Times Press, 2000.

Lee Kuan Yew. **ONE MAN'S VIEW OF THE WORLD**. Singapore: The Straits Times Press, 2013.

Lee Ting Hui, "The communist open united front in Singapore, 1954-66". Essay in **Armed Communist Movements in South-East Asia**. Edited by Lim Joo-Jock. Hampshire, England: Grover Publishing, 1984.

Lim Cheng Leng. **THE STORY OF A PSY-WARRIOR: TAN SRI DR. C.C. TOO.** Published by Lim Cheng Leng, Batu Caves, Selangor, 2000.

Lim Yew Hock. **Reflections**. Kuala Lumpur: Pustaka Antara, 1986.

Maclean, Donald. **British Foreign Policy Since Suez 1956-1968**. London: Hodder and Sloughton, 1970.

Macmillan, Harold. **Pointing the Way 1959-61**. London: Macmillan, 1977.

Macmillan, Harold. **At The End Of The Day 1961-1963**. London: Macmillan, 1977.

Marshall, David. **The Struugle for Nationhood 1945-1959**. Singapore: University Education Press, 1971.

Singapore 18: Biliography Morais, J. Victor, ed. **Blueprint For Unity – Selected Speeches of Tun Tan Siew Sin**.

Kuala Lumpur: MCA Headquarters, 1972.

Moss, Norman. **Men Who Play God**. Penguin, 1970.

Nixon, Richard. **LEADERS**. New York: Warner Books, 1983.

Mohamed Noordin Sopiee. **From Malayan Union To Singapore Separation**. Kuala Lumpur: Penerbit Universiti Malaya, 1976.

Pang Cheng Lian. **SINGAPORE'S PEOPLE'S ACTION PARTY**. Singapore: Oxford University Press, 1971.

Rhodes, Richard. **The Making of the Atomic Bomb**. London: Simon and Schuster, 1986.

Rhodes, Richard. **Dark Sun**. London: Simon and Schuster, 1995.

Schwartz, David N. **NATO's Nuclear Dilemmas**. Washington, D.C.: The Brookings Institution, 1983.

Simpson, John. **The Independent Nuclear State: The United States, Britain and the Military Atom**. London: Macmillan Press, 1986.

Tan Jing Quee and Jomo K.S. eds. **COMET IN OUR SKY: Lim Chin Siong in History**.

Petaling Jaya, Selangor: INSAN, 2001.

Turnbull, C. M. **A History of Singapore 1819-1975**. Oxford University Press, 1977.

Weale, Adrian. **Eye-Witness HIROSHIMA**. London: Robinian, 1995.

Wilson, Harold. **A Personal Record – The Labour Government 1964-1970**. USA: Little Brown, 1971.

(B)   **Reference Books**
The Economist Pocket Guide to Defence. London, 1986.
SIPRI Yearbook 1990. Oxford University Press, 1990.

(C)   **Newspapers and Periodicals**
Bulletin of the Atomic Scientists
Far Eastern Economic Review
Keesing's Contemporary Archives
Star (Kuala Lumpur)
Straits Times (Singapore)
Sunday Times (Singapore)

DEDICATION

I humbly dedicate this small book

to the five most meaningful persons in my life:

my late mother **Tan Gaik See**

my late father **Khor Peng Kim**

my late godmother, affectionately known and

remembered as **Tungshua Shim** ("China Aunty")

my dear departed wife **CHAN KOW LOAI**

aka YAN YIT SEONG

and my wife's loving sister, my caring and

generous sister-in-law **YAN HUN KEUN**.

May **Amitabha Buddha** always protect and bless them

in the Infinite Light of His Great Compassion and

Omniscience.

NAMOAMITABHA BUDDHA